Susanna Gregory was a pol an academic career. She h sultant during seventeen fie has taught comparative anatomy and biological anthropology.

She is the creator of the Matthew Bartholomew series of mysteries set in medieval Cambridge and the Thomas Chaloner adventures in Restoration London, and now lives in Wales with her husband, who is also a writer.

Praise for Susanna Gregory

'A lively and intelligent tale set vividly in turbulent medieval England'   *Publishers Weekly* on *An Unholy Alliance*

'A good, serious and satisfying read'
                    Irish Times on *A Masterly Murder*

'Excellent . . . the historical research is first rate. All in all, great entertainment for cold winter days'
                    Eurocrime on *To Kill or Cure*

'Once again Susanna Gregory has combined historical accuracy, amusing characterisation and a corking good plot to present a section of British history that is often overlooked: the emergence from the Dark Ages to Renaissance in the field of education and medicine'
                    Historical Novel Society on *A Poisonous Plot*

'Carefully researched, imaginative and evocative . . . this is a gritty but humorous period mystery'
                    Good Book Guide on *The Cheapside Corpse*

'Gregory never fails to impress with her immaculate research, creating an exciting and vivid historical, social and political backdrop and embellishing her stories with authentic detail and thrilling atmosphere'
                    Lancashire Evening Post on *T   angler*

Also by Susanna Gregory

The Matthew Bartholomew series

The Thomas Chaloner series

SUSANNA GREGORY

THE HAND OF JUSTICE

THE TENTH CHRONICLE OF
MATTHEW BARTHOLOMEW

sphere

SPHERE

First published in Great Britain in 2004 by Little, Brown
First published in paperback in 2005 by Time Warner Books
This edition reissued in 2018 by Sphere

3 5 7 9 10 8 6 4 2

A CIP catalogue record for this book is available from the British Library.

ISBN 978-0-7515-6944-5

Typeset in New Baskerville by Palimpsest Book Production Limited,
Falkirk, Stirlingshire
Printed and bound in Great Britain by Clays Ltd, Elcograf S.p.A.

Papers used by Sphere are from well-managed forests
and other responsible sources.

MIX
Paper from
responsible sources
FSC® C104740
www.fsc.org

Sphere
An imprint of
Little, Brown Book Group
Carmelite House
50 Victoria Embankment
London EC4Y 0DZ

An Hachette UK Company
www.hachette.co.uk

www.littlebrown.co.uk

For Pam Davis

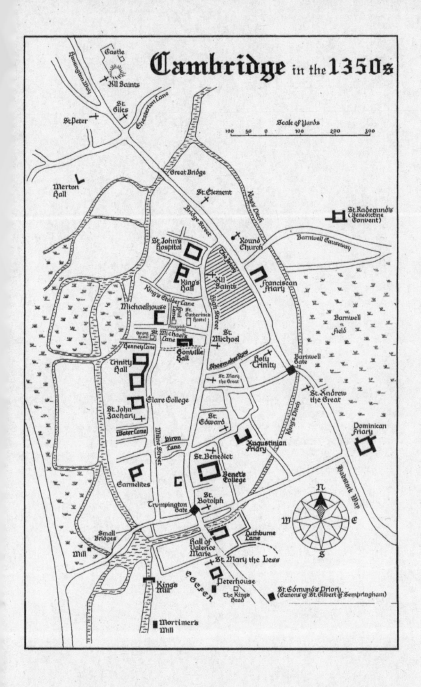

Cambridge in the 1350s

Castle
All Saints
St. Giles
St. Peter
Chesterton Lane
Huntingdon Way

Scale of Yards
100 50 0 100 200 300

Great Bridge
Merton Hall
St. Element
King's Ditch
St. Radegund's (Benedictine Convent)
Bridge Street
St. John's Hospital
Round Church
Barnwell Causeway
King's Hall
XII Saints
Franciscan Friary
King's Childer Lane
Michaelhouse
St. Catherine's Hostel
High Street
Barnwell Field
Fyszwick Hostel
St. Michael's Lane
Penny Lane
Gonville Hall
St. Michael
Trinity Hall
Shoemaker Row
Holy Trinity
Barnwell Gate
Clare College
St. Mary the Great
St. Andrew the Great
St. John Zachary
Water Lane
Milne Street
St. Edward
Augustinian Friary
Dominican Friary
Hiron Lane
St. Benedict
Bene't College
Carmelites
St. Botolph
Trumpington Gate
King's Ditch
Peasant's Way
N
W E
S
Small Bridges
Mill
Luthburne Lane
Hall of Valence Marie
St. Mary the Less
King's Mill
Peterhouse
The King's Head
St. Edmund's Priory (Canons of St. Gilbert of Sempringham)
Mortimer's Mill

PROLOGUE

The bones were stored in a sumptuous wooden casket, which was studded with semiprecious stones and inlaid with gold. With great care, Father William of Michaelhouse opened the lid and took out the satin-clad parcel that lay inside. He even removed his gloves for the task, as a sign of his respect – no small sacrifice in the frigid winter weather, when the cold bit deep and hard, even inside a fine building like the Church of St Mary the Great. He laid the bundle on the table and, with infinite reverence, began to lift away the folds of cloth to reveal the object inside. His lips moved as he worked, offering silent prayers to the relic that was said to be imbued with such great power. He stood back when he had finished, so the man who had paid handsomely for the privilege could appreciate its full glory.

'Is that it?' asked Thomas Deschalers the grocer, acutely disappointed. 'It looks . . . ordinary. And a bit dirty, if the truth be known.'

'It is the Hand of Valence Marie,' pronounced William grandly. He was a grimy person himself, and did not care that the object in his keeping failed to meet the merchant's more exacting standards. 'Named for the College near which it was found. And *I* have been entrusted by no less a person than the University's Chancellor himself to be its guardian. The Hand is sacred, and therefore it is only right that it should be in the care of a Franciscan friar. Me.'

1

'I see,' said Deschalers noncommittally, declining to enter a debate about which of the many religious Orders in Cambridge should be entrusted with the task of looking after what was becoming an increasingly popular relic – among townspeople and University scholars alike. He stared down at the collection of bones that lay exposed in front of him.

They comprised what had once been a living human hand. The bleached finger bones were held together by sinews, giving them the appearance of a claw rather than something that had once been warm with life. On the little finger was a blue-green ring, which Deschalers's skilled eye told him was not valuable, although it was pretty enough. He moved to one side, and examined the rough striations that criss-crossed the wrist, where a saw had been used to remove it from the rest of the body.

The grocer laid his own hand next to it. His palm was soft and his fingers free from the calluses of manual labour: wealthy merchants did not toil with sacks and casks when they had plenty of apprentices at their beck and call. Then he looked at the skeletal claw. By comparison, it was huge – and Deschalers was above average size himself.

'Are you sure this belongs to the martyr?' he asked doubtfully, wondering whether he had wasted a gold quarter-noble on the private viewing. 'I do not recall him owning limbs as massive as this.'

William was immediately defensive – and a little furtive. 'Who else's would it be?'

'When it was first discovered, there were rumours that it was hacked from the corpse of a simpleton,' said Deschalers, watching him carefully. 'Not the martyr. The tale was all over the town, and I am not sure what to think.'

'Brother Michael and Doctor Bartholomew – both Fellows of my own College – were responsible for circulating those particular claims,' replied William, tight-lipped with disapproval. 'But you can see they were wrong. Of course the Hand is holy: why else would it be housed in such a splendid box and shrouded in the finest satin money can buy?'

Deschalers regarded him warily, not sure whether the friar was attempting to be droll: even his newest apprentice knew that a tavern's most handsome jug did not necessarily contain its best wine. But then he saw William's face, which was lit with savage, unshakeable fanaticism, and realised the friar was quite serious. Deschalers knew it would be a waste of time to point out that there were objects all over the country languishing in satin and surrounded by jewels, purporting to be something they were not.

'There was some suggestion that the martyr arranged for this "relic" to be discovered himself, while he was alive and still in possession of both his hands,' he went on cautiously.

'Details,' said William evasively. 'The Hand is sacred, no matter who it came from.'

'How can that be?' asked Deschalers uncertainly. 'It either belongs to the martyr or it does not – which therefore means it is either holy or it is not.'

'It *is* sacred, but it did not belong to the martyr,' admitted William. He lowered his voice conspiratorially, and leaned close to Deschalers, treating the grocer to a waft of breath that indicated he had recently eaten onions. 'It belonged to another saint, but not many folk know about this.'

'Which one?' asked Deschalers, beginning to think he had indeed wasted his quarter-noble. He shivered, and wished he had not ventured out on such an inane escapade when the weather was so bitter. He wanted to be home, huddled next to a fire, and with a goblet of hot spiced ale at his side.

'A man named Peterkin Starre,' declared William with some triumph. He raised an admonishing finger when Deschalers released a derisive snort of laughter. 'You knew him as a simpleton giant. He drooled like a baby and took delight in childish matters. But he was more than that. God is mysterious, and chooses unusual vessels for His divine purposes.'

'Very unusual,' agreed Deschalers dryly. 'Are you telling me Peterkin Starre was a saint, and that the bones sawed from his poor corpse are imbued with heavenly power?' He wondered whether William would return his money willingly, or whether he would have to approach the Chancellor about the matter. He hated the thought of being cheated.

'I am,' said William firmly. 'That is the thing with saints: you do not know they are holy until they die and start to produce miracles. Look at Thomas à Becket, who was just a quarrelsome archbishop until he was struck down by four knights in his own cathedral. Now the spot where he died attracts pilgrims from all across the civilised world.'

'You consider Peterkin Starre akin to St Thomas of Canterbury?' asked Deschalers, startled.

'I do,' replied William with such conviction that Deschalers felt his disbelieving sneer begin to slip. 'But do not take my word for it: ask those whose prayers to the Hand have been heard and answered. They will tell you it *is* holy, and that it does not matter whose body it came from.'

'I see,' said Deschalers, regarding the bones doubtfully, and not sure what to think.

William was becoming impatient. Other people were waiting to view the relic, and he did not want to waste his time arguing about its validity with sceptical merchants – especially when so many folk were prepared to make generous donations just to be in the same room with it. He knew Deschalers was ill – he could see the lines of pain etched into the grocer's face, and the sallow skin with its sickly yellow sheen – but there was a limit to his tolerance, even for those who would soon be meeting their Maker and would need the intercessions of the saints. Deschalers's life had not been blameless, and William thought he was wise to prime Higher Beings to be ready to speak on his behalf. But he wished the man would hurry up about it.

'Do you want to pray or not?' he asked, a little sharply. 'If you do not believe in the Hand's sacred powers, then I should put it away and save it for those who do.'

'No,' said Deschalers, reaching out to stop him from replacing the bones in the reliquary. 'I was just curious, that is all. Perhaps you could let me have a few moments alone? My prayers are of a personal nature, and I do not want them overheard.'

William drew himself up to his full height and looked down his nose at the grocer. 'I am a friar, bound by the seal of confession,' he said indignantly. 'You can pray for whatever you like, safe in the knowledge that your words with God and His angels will never be repeated by me. Besides, I cannot leave pilgrims alone with the Hand of Valence Marie. They may become over-excited and try to make off with it – and then what would I tell the Chancellor?'

'Very well,' said Deschalers tiredly. He lowered himself to his knees, each movement painful and laboured. He hoped his plan would work – that his petition would be heard and his request granted – because everything else he had tried had failed. This was his last chance, and he knew that if the Hand of Valence Marie did not intercede on his behalf, then all was lost. He put his hands together, closed his eyes and began to pray.

Cambridge, late February 1355

When he first saw the well-dressed young man sitting on the lively grey horse, Matthew Bartholomew thought his eyes were playing tricks on him. He blinked hard and looked a second time. But there was no mistake. The rider, whose elegant clothes were styled in the very latest courtly fashion, was indeed Rob Thorpe, who had been convicted of murder two years before. Bartholomew stopped dead in his tracks and gazed in disbelief.

A cart hauled by heavy horses thundered towards him, loaded with wool for the fulling mill, and his colleague, John Wynewyk, seized his arm to tug him out of its way. It was never wise to allow attention to wander while navigating the treacherous surfaces of the town's main thoroughfares, but it was even more foolish when ice lay in a slick sheet across them, and a chill wind encouraged carters to make their deliveries as hastily as possible so they could go home.

'This cannot be right,' said Bartholomew in an appalled whisper, oblivious to the fact that Wynewyk had just saved his life. 'Thorpe was banished from England for murder. He would not dare risk summary execution by showing his face here again – not ever. I must be seeing things.'

'You will not see anything if you dither in the middle of this road,' lectured Wynewyk, watching the cart lurch away. 'Thomas Mortimer was driving that thing. Did you not hear what he did to Bernarde the miller last week? Knocked him clean off his feet – and right up on top of that massive snowdrift outside Bene't College.'

Bartholomew grudgingly turned his mind to Wynewyk's story. Mortimer's driving had become increasingly dangerous over the past few weeks, and he wondered whether it was accident or design that it had been Bernarde who had almost come to grief under his wheels – both men were millers, and they were rivals of the most bitter kind. Bartholomew supposed he should speak to the town's burgesses about the problem, because it was only a matter of time before Mortimer killed someone.

'Here comes Langelee,' said Wynewyk, pointing to where the Master of their College strode towards them. 'What is the matter with him? He looks furious.'

'Have you heard the news?' demanded Langelee as he

drew level with his Fellows. 'The King's Bench has granted pardons to Rob Thorpe and Edward Mortimer.'

Bartholomew regarded him in horror, although Wynewyk shrugged to indicate he did not know what the fuss was about. 'Who are these men? Should I have heard of them?'

Langelee explained. 'They earned their notoriety before you came to study here. Rob Thorpe killed several innocent people, and Edward Mortimer was involved in a smuggling enterprise that ended in death and violence.'

'Edward *Mortimer*?' queried Wynewyk. 'Is he any relation to him?' He nodded to where Thomas Mortimer's cart had collided with a hay wagon, causing damage to both vehicles. The hay-wainer was not amused, and his angry curses could be heard all up the High Street.

'His nephew,' said Langelee shortly. 'But the return of that pair bodes ill, for scholars and townsfolk alike.'

'So, it *was* Thorpe I saw just now,' said Bartholomew. 'But how did this come about? I thought they had been banished from England for the rest of their lives.'

'I thought they had been *hanged* for their crimes,' replied Langelee grimly. 'Not merely ordered to abjure the realm. But, from France, they managed to convince the King's Bench clerks that their sentence was overly harsh.'

'Perhaps they are reformed,' suggested Wynewyk. 'It is not unknown for folk to repent of their misdeeds after they are sent away in disgrace. You may be worrying over nothing.'

'We are not,' said Langelee firmly. 'They were dangerous two years ago, and they are dangerous now. I am on my way to discuss the matter with the Chancellor and the Sheriff, to see what – if anything – might be done to prevent them from settling here.' He strode away purposefully.

'He is exaggerating the seriousness of these fellows' return,' said Wynewyk, watching Langelee shoulder his way through the boisterous, cheering crowd that had gathered to watch the fist-fight between the miller and the hay-wainer. He glanced sidelong at Bartholomew. 'Is he not?'

'I do not think so,' replied Bartholomew soberly. 'I cannot imagine what Thorpe and Mortimer did to secure their pardons, but the fact that they are back means only one thing: trouble.'

That February saw the end of the worst winter anyone in Cambridge could remember. Screaming northerly winds had turned the river into an iron highway, and had deposited hundreds of tons of snow on to the little Fen-edge town, threatening to bury it completely. When milder weather eventually came, the drifts that choked streets and yards were so deep that it took many weeks for the largest ones to melt. The biggest of them all was the mammoth pile outside Bene't College on the High Street. This had turned to ice as hard as stone, and attacking it with spades proved to be futile work, so the citizens of Cambridge were obliged to let it disappear in its own time. It did so gradually, and people commented on its slowly diminishing size as they passed. Children played on it, using its slick sides for games, while some artistic soul caused a good deal of merriment by carving faces into it.

Weeks passed, until the drift dwindled to the point where people barely noticed it was there. Then, one morning, only the very base remained. It was old Master Kenyngham of Michaelhouse who discovered its grisly secret. He was walking to his friary for morning prayers, when he saw a dead, white arm protruding from it. He knelt, to whisper prayers for the soul of a man who had lain unmissed and undiscovered for so long. There was a piece of parchment clutched in the corpse's hand, so Kenyngham removed it from the decaying fingers, and read the message.

It was a note from a London merchant to his Cambridge kinsman, informing him of an imminent visit and detailing a plan to relieve a mutual enemy of some money. Kenyngham folded the parchment and put it in his scrip, intending to hand it to the Senior Proctor later. But first, there was a man's soul to pray for, and Kenyngham soon lost himself as he appealed to Heaven on behalf of a man he had never met.

Two weeks later, Kenyngham met Bosel the beggar, who made his customary plea for spare coins. The elderly friar emptied his scrip in search of farthings, and did not notice the forgotten parchment flutter to the ground. Bosel saw it, however, and snatched it up as soon as Kenyngham had gone. He peered at it this way and that, but since he could not read, the obscure squiggles and lines meant nothing to him. He sold it to the town's surgeon, Robin of Grantchester, for a penny.

Robin suffered from poor eyesight, and in dim light could not make out the words, either. He did not care what it said anyway, because parchment was parchment, and too valuable not to be reused. He scraped it clean with his knife, then rubbed it with chalk, and sold it for three pennies to Godric, the young Franciscan Principal of Ovyng Hostel. Robin went to spend his windfall on spiced ale at the King's Head; Godric walked home and spent the afternoon composing a moving and eloquent prayer, which he wrote carefully on the parchment.

Shortly before midnight, Godric rose and rang a small handbell to wake his students, then led them in a solemn, shivering procession through the streets to St Michael's Church, where he recited matins and lauds. When the office had been completed, he went to the mound in the churchyard that marked the place where his predecessor had been laid to rest a few weeks before. He scraped a shallow hole and laid the prayer inside, before bowing his head and walking away.

Bosel watched intently from the shadows thrown by a buttress. When Godric had gone, he moved forward, alert to the fact that Cambridge was a dangerous place at night and that beggars were not the only ones who lurked unseen in the darkness. He reached the grave and crouched next to it, hoping the Franciscan had buried something valuable – something that could be sold to raise a few coins for ale or a good meal. He was disappointed to discover parchment, and swore softly as he reburied it. He considered taking it to Robin, but only briefly. For all Bosel knew, the jumble of letters might comprise a curse, and only the foolish meddled with those sorts of things. He patted the earth back into place and wondered where he might find richer pickings that night.

As he pondered, he became aware that he was not the only one in the churchyard. He could hear voices as two people argued with each other. Knowing that conversations held among graves at the witching hour were unlikely to be innocent, and that witnesses might well be dispatched, Bosel shot back into the shadows, hoping he had not been seen. He waited, his body held so tensely that every muscle ached with the effort. When no cries of pursuit followed, he began to relax. Then he grew curious, wanting to know what business pulled folk from warm beds on such a damp and chilly night. He eased around the buttress carefully and silently, until he could see them.

He recognised both immediately. One was Thomas Deschalers the grocer, who was the wealthiest merchant in the town. He was also the meanest, although in the last couple of weeks he had deigned to toss Bosel a few coins, and had even taken to having bread and old clothes dispensed from his back door of a morning. The other was a popular Carmelite scholar called Nicholas Bottisham. Bosel liked Bottisham: he was generous, and never too busy to bless beggars if they called out to him. Bosel could not help but wonder what the gentle friar and the arrogant merchant could have to say to each other.

10

'I do not know about this,' Bottisham was saying uneasily. 'Even you must appreciate that it is an odd thing to ask me to do.'

'I know.' Deschalers sounded tired. 'But I thought—'

He stopped speaking abruptly when the night's stillness was broken by the sound of marching feet, the clink of armour and the creak of old leather.

'It is the night watch!' exclaimed Bottisham in an alarmed whisper. 'I do not want them to find me here with you, when I should be at my prayers inside. The answer to your question is no.'

Deschalers released what sounded like a groan. 'But I assure you, with all my heart—'

Bottisham cut across his entreaties. 'No – and that is the end of the matter. But I must go, or my colleagues will wonder what I have been doing.'

And then he was gone, leaving the grocer standing alone with his shoulders slumped in an attitude of defeat. Bosel pushed himself deeper into the shadows as Deschalers trudged past, sensing that this would not be a good time to make an appeal for spare change. The conversation was exactly the kind folk usually wanted to keep to themselves, and Bosel knew better than to reveal himself. He shuddered, supposing it was something involving money or power, neither of which Bosel knew much about. He decided to forget what he had seen. It was safer that way.

11

CHAPTER 1

Cambridge, March 1355

Thomas Mortimer the miller was drunk again. He had managed to climb on to his cart and take the reins, but only because his horses were used to his frequent visits to the town's taverns, and knew to wait until he was safely slumped in the driver's seat before making their way home. His fellow drinkers at the Lilypot Inn raised dull, blood-shot eyes from their cups to watch, but these were men for whom ale was a serious business, and the spectacle of an inebriated miller struggling into his cart did not keep their attention for long.

It claimed someone's, however. Brother Michael, the University's Senior Proctor and Benedictine agent for the Bishop of Ely, who taught theology at Michaelhouse when his other duties allowed, fixed the miller with a disapproving glare.

'If Mortimer were a scholar, I would have him off that cart and imprisoned for driving dangerously, not to mention public drunkenness,' he declared angrily. 'But he is a townsman, and therefore outside my jurisdiction. The Sheriff and the burgesses will have to deal with him.'

'They have done nothing so far,' said Matthew Bartholomew, Master of Medicine at Michaelhouse, who strode at Michael's side. 'He knocked his rival miller across that snowdrift outside Bene't College two weeks ago, and he will kill someone if he continues to drive when he can barely stand upright. The burgesses listened politely to my complaints about him, but said they do not want to offend the Mortimer clan by ordering Thomas off his cart.'

Michael shook his head in disgust. 'They are afraid that if they do, then the Mortimers will refuse to donate money for repairing the Great Bridge.'

The two scholars had just left Merton Hall, where they had taken part in a lively debate on the neglect of mathematics in academic studies, and were on their way to Gonville Hall. They had been invited to dine there by William Rougham, one of Bartholomew's medical colleagues. Bartholomew did not like Rougham, whom he found narrow-minded and dogmatic, but he felt obliged to suppress his feelings as well as he could, given that he and Rougham comprised exactly half of the total complement of physicians in Cambridge. So many medics had died during the plague that they were still in short supply, despite the best attempts of the University to train more.

It was a pleasant early spring day, with the sun dipping in and out of gauzy white clouds and trees beginning to turn green with buds and new leaves. A crisp breeze blew from the east, bringing with it the scent of freshly tilled soil from the surrounding fields. Bartholomew inhaled deeply, savouring the sweetness of the air at the northern outskirts of the town. A few steps ahead lay the Great Bridge, a teetering structure of stone and wood, and beyond this the air was far less fragrant. Fires from houses, Colleges, hostels and businesses encased Cambridge in a pall of smoke, almost, but not quite, strong enough to mask the stench of human sewage, animal manure and rotting rubbish that lay across the streets in a thick, fetid, greasy brown-black blanket.

The Great Bridge was heavily congested that morning. It was a Wednesday, and traders from the surrounding villages streamed towards the Market Square to sell their wares – sacks of grain and flour, noisy livestock, brown eggs

13

wrapped in straw, winter vegetables past their best, and rough baskets and mats woven from Fenland reeds. Agitated whinnies, baleful lows and furious honks and hisses expressed what the animals thought of the tightly packed, heaving throng that jostled and shoved to cross the river.

It was not just farmers in homespun browns or brightly clad merchants who wanted access to the town that day. The sober hues of academic tabards and monastic habits – the blacks, browns and whites of Dominicans, Carmelites, Franciscans and the occasional Benedictine – were present, too. Scholars from Michaelhouse, Valence Marie, Bene't College and countless other institutions were pouring out of Merton Hall to join the press, all anxious to be home in time for their midday meal.

As people pushed in their haste to be across the bridge, the crush intensified. A pair of tinkers with handcarts became jammed at the narrow entrance, and their irritable altercation was soon joined by others, who just wanted them to shut up and move on. Bartholomew watched the unfolding scene uneasily. The Great Bridge was not the most stable structure in the town, and collapses were not unknown. It was in desperate need of renovation, and he wished the burgesses would stop discussing how expensive it would be and just mend the thing.

'We will be late,' said Michael loudly, annoyed by the delay. 'And Gonville Hall might start eating without us.'

'The bridge should not be subjected to this level of strain,' said Bartholomew. His attention was fixed on the central arch, which he was certain was bowing under the weight of a brewer's dray and its heavy barrels of ale. 'It is not strong enough.'

'Rougham told me that the meal at Gonville today will cost a *whole* groat for each person,' fretted Michael, thinking about what he stood to lose if they took much longer to cross. 'He says there is a side of beef to be shared between just ten of us, not to mention roast duck, fat bacon and half a dozen chickens. *And* there will be Lombard slices to finish.'

'Did you see that?' exclaimed Bartholomew, pointing in alarm. 'A spar just dropped from the left-hand arch and fell into the water!'

'One of the carts knocked it off,' said Michael dismissively. He reconsidered uneasily. 'However, if it is going to tumble down, I hope it does not do so until we are over. I do not want to walk all the way around to the Small Bridges in order to reach Gonville. There will be nothing left to eat by the time we get there.'

Bartholomew regarded his friend askance, amazed that the monk could think about his stomach when they might be about to witness a disaster. Michael had always been big – tall, as well as fat – but his girth had expanded considerably over the last five years. Satisfaction with his lot as Senior Proctor – he was, by virtue of his own machinations, one of the most powerful men in the University – had occasioned a good deal of contented feeding. This meant that the tassels on the girdle around his waist hung a good deal shorter than they should have done, owing to the ever-expanding circumference they were obliged to encompass.

Michael had been to some trouble with his appearance that day, in honour of the debate and the meal that was to follow. His dark Benedictine habit was immaculate, and he wore a silver cross around his neck, in place of the wooden one he usually favoured. His plump fingers were adorned with jewelled rings, and his lank brown hair had been carefully brushed around his perfectly round tonsure.

By contrast, Bartholomew's black curls had recently been shorn to an uncompromising shortness by an over-enthusiastic barber, so he looked like one of the many mercenaries – relics of the King's endless wars with France – who plagued Cambridge in search of work. His clothes were patched and frayed, but of reasonable quality, thanks to the generosity of a doting older sister. His hands were clean, his fingernails trimmed, and frequent College feasts had not yet provided him with a paunch like the ones sported by so many of his colleagues. His profession as a physician saw to that, giving him plenty of exercise as he hurried around the town to visit patients.

'Here we are,' said Michael, grabbing Bartholomew's arm as their part of the crowd suddenly surged forward, much to the chagrin of people who were waiting on the other side. There were indignant yells and a considerable amount of vicious shoving that saw more than one bloodied nose. The monk thrust the toll-fee into the hand of a grubby soldier without breaking his stride.

'Walk near the edge, Brother,' advised the soldier, assessing the monk's bulk with a critical eye. 'You are less likely to drop through there, than in the middle.'

'Lord!' muttered Bartholomew, not liking the unnatural rocking motion under his feet as they began their traverse. 'We should have hired a boat.'

'They are all engaged,' replied Michael, nodding to where the rivermen were running a brisk trade below. Even boys with home-made skiffs were busy, ferrying small animals and light packs across the green, filthy water.

The Great Bridge was not very big, despite its grand name, and it did not take long to cross it, as they were forced to move quickly by the press from behind. Once on the other side, most people continued straight down Bridge Street, aiming for the Market Square, although some went to homes in the maze of alleys and streets that radiated out from the town's main thoroughfares. Bartholomew glanced behind him, still half expecting to see the bridge crumble beneath the mass of humanity. He noticed some folk entering the nearby Church of St Clement, and wondered whether they were going to offer thanks for a safe crossing.

'There is Thomas Mortimer again,' he said, as the miller's cart clattered towards them at a speed that was far from safe. He leapt back as it passed uncomfortably close before lurching towards the High Street. 'It is not yet noon. I know the Lilypot is popular with men who love their ale, but even they tend not to be drunk this early.'

'It is because the Mortimer family is so prosperous at the moment,' said Michael, aiming for Gonville Hall with single-minded purpose. 'Thomas owns the only fulling mill this side of Ely and his brother runs the town's biggest bakery. They are making a fortune, and Thomas has good cause to celebrate. Still, their success will cause trouble eventually: the other burgesses will resent their riches and there will be all manner of jealous rivalries. I am just glad it is not *I* who will be called upon to sort them out. I have my hands full with the upcoming debate.'

'The one on Saturday?' asked Bartholomew, increasing his pace to keep up with him. The monk did not usually walk fast, but was evidently prepared to make an exception when good food was waiting. 'When Michaelhouse will compete with Gonville Hall in the end-of-term debate – the *Disputatio de quodlibet*? Why should that take your time?'

'Because any large gathering of scholars means trouble for a proctor, as you well know. Even a serious academic occasion, like the *Disputatio*, may give rise to rioting or just plain bad behaviour.' Michael grinned, pushing his concerns aside for a moment as he considered another aspect of the occasion. 'Michaelhouse has not been invited to take part in a quodlibetical debate of this magnitude since the Death, and defeating Gonville will give me a good deal of pleasure. They are excellent scholars, and I shall enjoy pitting my wits against equal minds.'

'God's blood!' exclaimed Bartholomew, ignoring the monk's arrogant confidence. 'Mortimer has just driven into Master Warde from the Hall of Valence Marie. He

17

cannot control his cart in that state. You *must* say something before he kills someone, Brother – regardless of jurisdiction.'

'It is my jurisdiction now a scholar is involved,' declared Michael grimly, hurrying towards Mortimer's horses, which had been startled by the sudden and unexpected presence of a scholar under their feet, and were rearing and bucking.

Bartholomew hauled Warde away from the flailing hoofs, while Michael snatched the reins from Mortimer's inept hands and attempted to calm the horses.

'Watch where you are going!' Warde shouted furiously, fright making him uncharacteristically aggressive. He leaned close to the miller, taking in the bloodshot eyes and glazed expression, before pointing an accusing finger. 'You are drunk!'

'I am not,' slurred Mortimer. All three scholars were treated to a waft of breath thick with the fruity scent of ale as he spoke. 'I have only rinsed the dust from my throat. Ferrying bales of cloth from the quays to my fulling mill is thirsty work.'

Michael was unimpressed. 'Then rinse it with weaker ale,' he snapped. 'You cannot careen all across the street as if you are the only man using it.'

Infuriated by the reprimand, Mortimer snatched the reins from the monk and flicked them sharply so that the leather cracked across the horses' flanks. One reared again, then both took off at a rapid canter. Bartholomew watched them go, then turned to Warde. The Valence Marie Fellow was a tall man with yellow-grey hair that he kept well oiled with goose fat. He had a reputation for brilliant scholarship and boundless patience with his students, and the physician both liked and admired him.

'I have had a tickling throat for the past week,' said Warde with a rueful smile. 'But the shock of near-death under Mortimer's wheels has quite put it from my mind:

18

I no longer feel the urge to cough. Perhaps he has cured me. Or perhaps the prayers I have offered to sacred relics for my recovery have finally been answered. However, I can assure you that my relief has nothing to do with the potions Rougham prescribed for me. I should never have engaged him over you, Bartholomew.'

'Then why did you?' asked Michael bluntly. 'Matt is a much better physician.'

'Because Rougham was present when the malady first afflicted me,' said Warde apologetically. 'He offered me his services and that was that. I was stuck with him.'

Warde chatted about how he was looking forward to the forthcoming *Disputatio* for a few moments, then headed for St Clement's Church, where he said a special mass was being held to honour a much-loved saint. Bartholomew wanted to know which saint could attract the enormous congregation that was gathering, but Michael was impatient for food, and pulled him down the High Street towards Gonville Hall, where his whole groat's worth of meat was waiting. They had not gone far when there was a scream and a sudden commotion. Voices were raised and people began to run, converging on bodies that lay scattered in the road.

The first thing Bartholomew saw was Thomas Mortimer, sitting on the ground with his legs splayed in front of him and a startled expression on his face. Of the horses and cart there was no sign, and the physician assumed they had galloped off on their own. The second thing he spotted was the crumpled form of an old man with a broken neck. And the final thing was a fellow named Isnard, who lay in a spreading pool of blood.

'God damn you to Hell, Thomas Mortimer!' Isnard roared, trying to reach the bewildered miller and give him a pummelling with his fists. His face registered bemused shock when he found he could not stand, and he grabbed his bleeding leg with both hands. 'Look what you have done!'

Bartholomew knelt next to the old man, sorry to recognise him as the barber who had shorn him of hair just the previous day. The merest glance told him there was nothing he could do, so Michael eased him out of the way to begin his own ministrations, muttering a final absolution and anointing the body with the phial of chrism he kept for such occasions. Although Michael was a monk, rather than a priest, he had been granted special dispensation to offer last rites during the plague, and had continued the practice since.

Bartholomew turned his attention to Isnard, an uncouth bargeman who sang in Michaelhouse's choir. He was as tall as the physician but almost as broad as Michael, which made him a formidable opponent in the many brawls he enjoyed in the town's various taverns. He earned his living on the river, using his massive strength to service the boats that travelled through the Fens to supply Cambridge with grain, stone, wool and other goods. His thin hair was plastered in greasy strands across the top of his head, but this was more than compensated for by the luxuriant brown beard that hung almost to his belt.

'What happened?' Bartholomew asked, pushing away Isnard's hands so he could inspect the wound in his leg. It was a serious one, with splinters of bone protruding through the calf in a mess of gore and torn muscle. Bartholomew knew it could not be mended.

'I was talking to old Master Lenne when that drunken sot trampled us both into the ground,' yelled Isnard, outraged. He was not feeling pain, because the shock of the injury was still too recent. But he would, Bartholomew knew, and then the agony would be almost unbearable. One of Bartholomew's students, a lad called Martyn

Quenhyth, was in the crowd that had gathered to watch, so he sent him to fetch a stretcher. Isnard should be carried home before his anguish made him difficult to control.

'I did not,' said Mortimer, sobering up quickly as the seriousness of his situation penetrated his pickled wits. 'I was just moving along and they ran in front of me.'

'Lies!' bellowed Isnard. 'How could Lenne "run" anywhere? He is an old man!'

'Did anyone actually see what happened?' asked Michael, watching Bartholomew tie a tight bandage below the bargeman's knee to stem the bleeding.

'I did,' said Bosel the beggar, whose hand had been severed by the King's justices for persistent stealing, although he claimed its loss was from fighting in the French wars. He was unusually well dressed that morning, because some kind soul had given him new clothes. 'I saw Thomas Mortimer deliberately aim at Isnard and Lenne and ride them down.'

Bartholomew was sceptical. Bosel was not noted for his devotion to the truth, and might well stand as a witness against one of the wealthy Mortimer clan, just so he could later retract his statement – for a price. He had done as much before.

'Anyone else?' asked Michael, looking around at the crowd and apparently thinking along the same lines. Bosel would not make a credible witness.

There were shaken heads all around. 'But Mortimer *is* drunk,' added the taverner of the Brazen George. 'I know a man out of his senses from ale when I see one.'

'Not me,' persisted Mortimer, white-faced and uneasy. 'There was nothing I could do to avoid them. They just raced in front of my cart.'

'We did not!' objected Isnard hotly, wincing when Bartholomew tightened the bandage. 'See to Lenne, will you, Doctor? I saw the cart hit him, and he needs your

21

help more than I do. I know he gave you that fierce haircut, but you should not hold it against him. He no longer sees very well.'

Bartholomew said nothing, and concentrated on covering Isnard's exposed leg bones with a piece of clean linen in an attempt to protect the injury from the filth of the street. It was Michael who leaned down and put a comforting hand on the bargeman's shoulder.

Isnard's jaw dropped in horror when he understood what their silence meant. 'Lenne is dead?' he gasped in disbelief. 'Mortimer has *killed* him?'

'I have killed no one,' said Mortimer, coming slowly and unsteadily to his feet. No one made any attempt to help him. 'I am going to be sick.'

The spectators watched in distaste as the miller deposited his ale into the brimming gutters that ran down the High Street. Bending close to the drains' noxious fumes and unsavoury contents made him more ill than ever, and it was some time before he was able to stand, ashen-faced and trembling. He wiped a sleeve across his mouth, and eyed his audience defiantly.

'I am not drunk,' he persisted sullenly. 'I had an ale or two in the Lilypot, but I am not drunk.'

'Perhaps not now he has donated half a brewery to the gutter,' muttered Michael to Bartholomew. 'But I will swear in any court of law that he was unfit to drive a cart, and so will you.'

But all Bartholomew's attention was focused on Isnard, whose outrage had dissipated when his body had finally registered that it had suffered a grievous insult, leaving him cold, clammy and breathless. Bartholomew had seen men die from the shock of serious injuries, and he did not want Isnard to expire in the grime of the High Street. He glanced up briefly, silently willing Quenhyth to hurry with the stretcher.

The next person to arrive, however, was Sheriff Tulyet, a small, neat man with tawny hair and an elfin face that seemed inappropriate on the person who embodied the strong arm of secular law in the town. Many folk were deceived by Tulyet's youthful looks, but few remained so for long. He was an energetic and just Sheriff, and the fact that he was popular with everyone except criminals and malcontents said a good deal about the tenor of his reign.

'Who saw what happened?' he asked, taking in the scene at a glance: Lenne's body covered by the cloak of a kindly onlooker, Isnard writhing in his pool of gore, and Mortimer grim-faced and defiant. 'Who witnessed this accident?'

'It was no accident,' said Isnard between gritted teeth. 'He tried to kill us.'

'I saw,' piped up Bosel, enjoying himself. 'Thomas Mortimer is a murderer.'

'They ran under my wheels,' declared Mortimer. He glared around, challenging anyone to say otherwise. Bartholomew saw some folk look away, reluctant to engage in open conflict with a member of the influential Mortimer clan. The family could destroy smaller businesses simply by whispering a few carefully phrased sentences in the relevant places, and few townsmen were prepared to make an enemy of the likes of Thomas.

'Michael?' asked Tulyet hopefully. 'Matt? Did you see?'

He was disappointed when they shook their heads. Two men, braver or more foolish than the rest, stepped forward and began to clamour that the miller was drunk. One had seen the cart – *sans* driver – pelt down the High Street immediately afterward, but only Bosel claimed to have seen the accident itself. Bartholomew was inclined to accept Isnard's account – that he and Lenne had been talking at the side of the road when the cart had ploughed into them – but saw that Tulyet would be hard pressed to prove either side of the story. Tulyet questioned Mortimer carefully, but the man was determined not to bear the blame for the incident, and was sullen and uncommunicative. All he did was reiterate that the fault lay with Lenne and Isnard.

Eventually, Quenhyth arrived with the stretcher and three students to help carry it, and Bartholomew prepared to accompany the bargeman home. Isnard was beginning to shiver, so he removed his own cloak to cover him. He was pleased when Quenhyth and his cronies did the same without being asked.

'How much?' the student asked in a whisper. He began to gnaw at his nails, an unpleasant habit he had acquired as his studies at Michaelhouse became more onerous. Bartholomew gazed at him blankly, and Quenhyth stifled a sigh of exasperation. 'How much can you charge Isnard for our services? He will need a surgeon, so you can hire Robin of Grantchester and add that to the fee, too. Plus a little extra for your use of us as stretcher-bearers.'

Bartholomew gaped at him, scarcely believing his ears. 'This man sings in our College choir. And we do not haggle over fees with seriously injured people in the street anyway. It is not seemly.'

'Seemly!' sighed Quenhyth despairingly. 'I suppose this means *you* will pay for his salves and horoscopes, but we will not see a penny in return. Michaelhouse will never raise enough money to buy that book by Roger Bacon if you do not charge your patients properly.'

Bartholomew had had this particular discussion with Quenhyth before. The lad was not one of Michaelhouse's wealthier scholars, and regarded his teacher's casual attitude to fee collection as a personal affront. But it was neither the time nor the place for a debate about finances, and Bartholomew decided not to respond to his comments. Instead, he indicated that the students were to lift the stretcher. They staggered as they began the journey to the river: the bargeman was heavy.

'Give Rougham my apologies,' Bartholomew said to Michael as he prepared to follow. 'He will understand why I cannot dine with him at Gonville today. You should consider yourself fortunate, Brother: you can now eat two groats' worth of meat instead of one.'

'What of Isnard?' asked Michael, ignoring his friend's attempt at levity. He was fond of the gruff bargeman who had served in his choir for so many years.

Bartholomew lowered his voice so Isnard would not hear. While he believed in honesty where patients were concerned, and rarely flinched from telling them the truth, he saw no advantage in frightening folk into losing hope just before painful and traumatic surgery. 'He will lose his leg, and possibly his life.'

The stricken expression in Michael's eyes turned to something harder and more dangerous. 'Damn Mortimer! I will see he pays for this! I will bring the full force of the law down upon him.'

'You can try,' said Tulyet, overhearing. 'But you will not succeed. No one has admitted to *seeing* what happened – Bosel does not count – and Mortimer claims that Isnard and Lenne ran under his wheels. We will never prove who was at fault here, because we have no independent witnesses.'

'Someone must have seen something,' said Bartholomew. He gestured around him. 'The street was full of people.'

'Perhaps so, but no townsman will denounce a Mortimer – not if he values his business.'

'But Mortimer was drunk!' objected Bartholomew, indignant that the miller was about to evade justice on the grounds that his family intimidated people. 'He should not have been driving a cart, and it *is* his fault that Lenne is dead and Isnard may follow.'

'I know,' said Tulyet softly. 'And justice dictates that he should pay for it. But we have no case in law. I doubt whether Mortimer will be punished for this.'

'Then the law is wrong,' declared Bartholomew hotly.

'Yes, often,' agreed Tulyet sombrely. 'But it is all we have between us and chaos, so do not dismiss it too harshly.'

'And do not confuse it with justice, either,' added Michael acidly. 'They are not the same.'

'No, they are not,' said Bartholomew angrily. He turned and hurried to his patient's side as the first real cries of agony began to issue from the injured bargeman.

'You look tired, Matt,' said Michael the following day. It was dawn, and they had just celebrated prime in St Michael's Church. Their colleague Father William had conducted the ceremony, gabbling the words so fast that it was over almost before it had started. William was not popular with the students, because he was fanatical and petty, but they all admired his speedy masses.

Bartholomew and Michael took their places in the sedate procession of scholars that moved quietly through the gradually lightening streets, heading towards a breakfast of baked oatmeal and salted fish. They crossed the High Street and turned down St Michael's Lane, passing Gonville Hall as they went. Part of Gonville's protective wall had recently been demolished, because its Fellows intended to build a chapel in its place. A plot had already been measured out, marked with ropes and stakes, and foundation stones were laid in a long, even line. Judging by its dimensions, the church would be an impressive edifice once completed.

'Will Isnard live?' asked Michael quietly, when his friend did not reply.

'It is too soon to say,' replied Bartholomew, stifling a yawn. He had spent most of the previous night at the bargeman's house and had not managed more than an hour of sleep. 'His leg was so badly crushed that I was obliged to remove it below the knee. But it will be some days before we know whether he will survive the fever that often follows such treatment.'

'*You* amputated his leg?' asked Michael uneasily. 'God's teeth, you play with fire! You are not a surgeon, and Robin of Grantchester has already made several official complaints about you poaching his trade. You also seem to forget that cautery is not a skill held in great esteem by your fellow physicians; they claim you bring them into disrepute when you employ knives and forceps, instead of calendars and astronomical charts.'

'Isnard would be dead for certain if I had allowed Robin at him,' said Bartholomew, too weary to feel indignation that his three fellow physicians – Rougham of Gonville, Lynton of Peterhouse and Paxtone of King's Hall – should presume to tell him how to practise medicine.

'I know that,' said Michael impatiently. 'I was not thinking of Isnard – there is no question that you have done *him* a favour by dispensing with the unsavoury Robin – I was considering you. It was different when only you and Lynton were in Cambridge, and people could not afford to be particular. But now there are four of you, you must be more careful. Several of your most affluent patients have already left you.'

'I was relieved to see them go – it means I can give the remaining ones more time and attention. The rich are better off with Paxtone or Rougham anyway. They are good at calculating horoscopes while I am happier with people who have a genuine need.'

'Like Isnard,' said Michael, his thoughts returning to the stricken singer. 'He is one of my most loyal basses. Can I do anything to help?'

Bartholomew refrained from suggesting that he could ensure the choir – infamous for its paucity of musical talent – should practise well out of the ailing man's hearing, and shook his head. 'Say masses for him. You might try

27

reciting one for Thomas Mortimer, too, and ask for him to be touched with some compassion. He is a wealthy man, and could have offered a little money to see Isnard through the first stages of his illness.'

'But that might be construed as the act of a guilty man,' Michael pointed out. 'And Mortimer maintains the accident was not his fault. Did I tell you that I went to see Lenne's wife – widow – last night?'

'She has a sickness of the lungs,' said Bartholomew, recalling her soggy, laboured breathing from when her husband had shorn him of hair two days before. 'Who will care for her now he is gone? Widows sometimes take over their husbands' businesses, but she is too ill. Lenne was a barber, anyway, and shaving scholars and trimming tonsures is scarcely something she can do in his stead. The University would not permit it.'

'And neither would I!' exclaimed Michael in horror. 'God's blood, man! Women barbers would slit our throats because their attention is taken with the latest style in goffered veils or the price of ribbon. Barbers have always *been* men, and they should always *remain* men.'

'Barbers must be male. Surgeons must conduct cautery,' remarked Bartholomew dryly. 'I had no idea you were so rigidly traditional, Brother. How will we make progress if we remain so inflexible? Many of our greatest thinkers have been deemed heretics merely because they dare to look beyond that which is ordained and accepted, but they are nearly always proven right in the end. Take Roger Bacon, the Oxford Franciscan, who was persecuted for "suspected novelties" and his works censored some fifty years ago. These days everyone acknowledges the validity of his ideas.'

'Not everyone,' argued Michael, thinking about Bartholomew's medical colleague Rougham, who made no secret of his contempt for Bacon's theories. 'He is still regarded as anathema to many, although I noticed you reading his *De erroribus medicorum* the other day.'

'Paxtone of King's Hall lent it to me.' Bartholomew became animated, his tiredness forgotten at the prospect of discussing an exciting text with a sharp-minded man like Michael. 'Bacon relies heavily on Arabic sources, especially Avicenna's *Canon*, which, as you know, I regard as a highly underrated work. Regarding rhubarb, Bacon contends that—'

'You have never hidden your esteem for Arabic physicians,' interrupted Michael. 'And I know the one you admire over all others is your own master, Ibn Ibrahim. But not everyone believes foreign thinkers are as good as our own, and you should be more cautious with whom you discuss them.' He hesitated and shot his friend an uncertain glance. 'Did you mention rhubarb?'

'This is a University and we are scholars,' objected Bartholomew. 'Why should I suppress my ideas just because ignorant, narrow-minded men might not like them? It does not matter whether we agree, only that we discuss our theories so we can explore their strengths and weaknesses.'

'Matt!' exclaimed Michael in exasperation. 'That will be no defence when Rougham accuses you of heresy. I thought you had learned this, but now you insist on flying in the face of convention again. Rougham is jealous of your success: do not provide him with an easy means to destroy you.'

Bartholomew gazed at him in surprise. 'He is not jealous of me.'

'He does not like you, despite the superficial friendship you both struggle to maintain. He will make a poisonous enemy, and you should take care not to provoke him. Damn! That unbearable student of yours is waiting for us.'

The 'unbearable student' was Martyn Quenhyth. Quenhyth was a gangly lad of about twenty-two years, with a thatch of thick brown hair that he kept painfully short. He had a long, thin nose that dripped when it was cold, and sharp blue eyes. His hands were bony and always splattered in ink, and his nails were bitten to the quick. He was fervently devoted to his studies, and there was scarcely a moment when he was not reading some tome or other. This made him joyless, pedantic and dull, and Bartholomew's feelings toward him were ambiguous. On the one hand he admired the lad's determination to pass his disputations and become a qualified physician, but on the other it was difficult to find much to like in his humourless personality.

'He accused his room-mate of stealing again yesterday,' muttered Michael as they approached the student. 'Does he have a case? Is Redmeadow a thief?'

'If so, then he confines his light fingers to Quenhyth's belongings,' said Bartholomew, who was obliged to share a room with them both, since student numbers in the College had finally started to rise again after the plague. He liked Redmeadow, who was an open, friendly sort of lad with a shock of ginger hair, although he had a fiery temper to go with it. 'He has taken nothing of mine.'

'Isnard wants you again,' said Quenhyth, when Bartholomew reached him. 'I was about to go to him myself, but now you are here, I shall have my breakfast instead.'

'You can come with me,' said Bartholomew, deciding that if he was to forgo a meal, then Quenhyth could do so, too. He was not overly dismayed by the prospect of sacrificing breakfast. Michaelhouse fare had seen something of a downward turn in quality over the past ten days or so, and he knew he was not going to miss much. 'And Redmeadow, too. We are going to discuss fevers this week, and this will give you some practical experience. Roger Bacon asserts the superiority of experience over authority and speculation, after all.'

He shot a combative glance in Michael's direction and

the monk sighed, but declined to argue. If his friend wanted to play with the fires of heresy, and would not listen to advice about how not to burn himself, then Michael could do no more to help him. While Quenhyth sped across the yard to fetch his fellow student, Bartholomew leaned against the gate and surveyed the College that was his home.

The centrepiece was Michaelhouse's fine hall-house. It boasted a lavish entrance with the founder's coat of arms emblazoned above it, which opened to a wide spiral staircase that led to the hall and conclave above. Below were the kitchens and various storerooms and pantries. At right angles to the hall were a pair of accommodation wings, both two storeys tall and with sloping, red-tiled roofs. A wall opposite the hall made an enclosed rectangle of the buildings, and its sturdy oaken gate meant that the College was well able to protect itself, should it ever come under attack. There was a second courtyard beyond the first, but this comprised mostly stables, storerooms and lean-to sheds, where the servants lived and worked. Past that was a long strip of land that extended to the river.

Michael also decided to accompany Bartholomew, content to miss a Michaelhouse breakfast on the understanding that they ate a better one in a tavern later. He was just asking for more details about Isnard's health when there was a sudden commotion in the kitchens. First came a screech of rage from Agatha the laundress – Agatha was the College's only female servant, and she ran Michaelhouse's domestic affairs with ruthless efficiency – and then a cockerel crowed. Within moments, the bird came hurtling out of Agatha's domain in a flurry of feathers and flapping wings, followed by the laundress herself, who was brandishing a long carving knife. Agatha was an intimidating sight at any time, but being armed and angry made her especially terrifying.

'I will chop off your head next time, you filthy beast!' she bellowed, waving the weapon menacingly but declining to enjoin an undignified chase that the bird would win. It fluttered to a safe distance, fluffed up its feathers, then crowed as loudly as it could. Agatha started towards it, furious at being issued with what was clearly a challenge.

'Leave him alone!'

Walter the porter, who owned the cockerel, was out of the gatehouse and steaming across the yard, intent on rescuing his pet from the enraged laundress. He was a morose man, who seldom smiled and who cared for nothing and no one – except the annoying bird that had made an enemy of almost everyone who lived in the College. It crowed all night, keeping scholars from their sleep; it slipped into their rooms when they were out and left unwelcome deposits on their belongings; and it terrorised the cat, which people liked because it was friendly and purred a lot. The cockerel was not friendly, and did nothing as remotely endearing as purring.

'Keep that thing away from the hens I am preparing for dinner,' Agatha yelled at Walter. 'It is a vile, perverted fiend, and if I catch it I shall serve it to you stuffed with eel heads and rhubarb leaves.'

Michael turned to Bartholomew in alarm. 'Should we allow her control of our kitchens if she has the ability to devise dishes like that?'

'You would not dare to stuff Bird!' howled Walter in fury. 'I will kill you first!'

'You could try,' snarled Agatha, her voice dropping to a low, dangerous growl. She still waved the knife and was clearly ready to inflict serious damage with it, preferably on something avian.

Bartholomew stepped forward quickly. 'Agatha, please. No harm has been done, and Walter will try to keep his bird out of your way in future.'

'He had better do more than try, if he does not want me to wring its neck,' she hissed, before turning on her heel and stalking back inside. The cockerel watched her with its pale, beady eyes and released a triumphant cackle. Fortunately for all concerned, the sound of smashing pottery came from the scullery at that point, and Agatha was more interested in what had been broken than in prolonging the duel with her feathered opponent.

'Bird knows how to look after himself,' said Walter to Bartholomew with considerable pride. 'She will never catch him, no matter what she says.'

'She might,' warned Bartholomew. 'I have seen her move like lightning in the past, and Bird is becoming over-confident. You should lock him away if you do not want him cooked.'

Walter strode to the tatty creature and scooped it under his arm. If anyone else had tried to do the same, there would have been a frenzy of flailing claws and snapping beaks, and Bartholomew marvelled that Walter had made a connection with such a surly beast. He supposed that each of them must have recognised a kindred spirit.

'There now, Bird,' Walter crooned, kissing the top of its feathered head with great tenderness. 'You are safe now. I will not let anyone stuff you – and especially not with eels and rhubarb.'

'I do not blame Agatha for wanting to dispense with Bird,' said Michael, as the porter entered his gatehouse and slammed the door behind him. 'It ate a page from the *Insolubilia* I am writing the other day – the part where I expand on dialectic being the only science to prove the existence of God. All that brilliance, and it ended up in the gullet of that foul creature.'

Bartholomew was not amused when Quenhyth arrived not only with Redmeadow, but with Rob Deynman, too. Deynman was a student tolerated at Michaelhouse because his father paid extra fees, but he was becoming an embarrassment, because he was the oldest undergraduate in the University and would never pass his disputations. Bartholomew had also learned from bitter experience that the lad could not be allowed near patients, either. That morning, however, he did not have the energy to send him on a different mission, so Deynman formed part of the small procession that hurried along Milne Street on its way to Isnard's house.

'There is that strange woman again,' said Deynman, pointing towards the churchyard of St John Zachary. 'She arrived here two or three weeks ago, and does not know who she is. People say she is looking for a lover who died in the French wars.'

Bartholomew followed the direction of his finger and saw a dirty, huddled figure sitting atop one of the tombs, rocking herself back and forth. She was so encased in layers of rags that it was impossible to tell what she looked like, but he could see long, brown hair that had probably once been a luxurious mane, although it was now matted with filth, and a white, pinched face that had a half-starved look about it. She was singing, and her haunting melody cut through the noise of the street, its notes sad and sweet above the clatter of hoofs and the slap of footsteps in mud.

'Then she will not find him here,' said Quenhyth unsympathetically. 'She should visit Paris or Calais instead. We should hurry, Doctor. Isnard's summons sounded urgent.'

'She looks familiar,' said Bartholomew, pausing to look at her and ignoring Quenhyth's impatience at the delay. The student was hoping they would tend Isnard and still be back at Michaelhouse in time for breakfast; being impecunious, he tended to be less fussy about what he ate, especially when it was free. 'But I cannot place her face.'

'You cannot know her,' said Deynman. 'She is a stranger here.'

'She should go to the Canons at St John's Hospital,' suggested Redmeadow, ready to foist the problem on to someone else. The kindly Canons often found a bed and

34

a meal for those who were out of their wits, and all budding physicians knew they provided a quick and easy solution for some of their more inconvenient cases.

'I took her there last week,' said Quenhyth, grabbing Bartholomew's sleeve in an attempt to drag him away. 'She was in the Market Square talking to some onions, and it occurred to me that there might be something amiss with her wits.'

'Such an incisive diagnosis,' muttered Redmeadow. 'She talks to onions, and it crosses his mind that she might be addled.'

Quenhyth did not dignify the comment with a reply, and continued to address Bartholomew. 'I escorted her to the Canons, but she ran away from them the next day. They told me she will leave Cambridge when she realises that whatever she is looking for is not here, and will head off to haunt some other town. They say they have seen many such cases since the plague.'

Bartholomew pulled away from Quenhyth, not liking the way his student had taken to manhandling him on occasions. He rummaged in his scrip and found some farthings. 'Give her these,' he said to Deynman. 'Or better still, go with her to Constantine Mortimer's shop, and ensure she buys bread – not ribbons or some such thing.'

'But by that time you will have finished Isnard's treatment,' cried Deynman in dismay. 'And I will not have seen what you did.'

'Go and help her, Deynman,' said Bartholomew softly, moved by the sight of the pitiful creature who rocked and sang to herself. 'She needs you.'

Reluctantly, Deynman did as he was told. Bartholomew saw him bend to speak to her, then politely offer his arm, as he might to any lady in his rich father's house. Physician Deynman would never be, but he had better manners and a kinder heart than his classmates. Bartholomew was about to resume his journey to Isnard when Deynman issued a shriek of horror.

Bartholomew's blood ran cold. The woman had seemed more pathetic than violent, and he had thought she was not the kind to harm anyone who might try to help her. But he could have been wrong – and if he were, then he had forced Deynman to pay the price for his misjudgement. He stumbled across the ancient graves towards them, fearing the worst. But it was not Deynman who had come to grief; it was Bosel the beggar. The alms-hunter lay curled on his side in the long grass of the churchyard, his skin waxy with the touch of death.

'Poisoned?' asked Michael in surprise. He watched Bartholomew examine the beggar's corpse as they waited for the Sheriff to arrive. 'Are you sure? Who would poison Bosel? He is harmless.'

'You would not think that if you were one of the people he had burgled,' said Bartholomew. 'Or if you were Thomas Mortimer, and had him claiming you deliberately ran over Lenne and Isnard.'

'You think Mortimer killed Bosel?' asked Michael. He rubbed his chin, nodding to himself. 'Ridding yourself of an inconvenient witness *is* a powerful motive for murder.'

'I thought he had more sense, though,' said Bartholomew, prising open Bosel's mouth to show Michael the discoloured tongue and bloodied gums. 'He must have known he would be the obvious suspect.'

'Desperate men are not always rational,' replied Michael, looking away quickly before he lost the illicit early breakfast he had eaten in his room before mass that morning. Bosel's mouth was not a pretty sight. 'But Thomas is constantly drunk these days. I am surprised he could carry out a murder using as discreet a means as poison.'

'His family, then,' said Bartholomew. 'His brother

Constantine and all those nephews and cousins. Still, I am surprised. Poisoning Bosel is an utterly stupid thing to do.'

Michael agreed. 'Poor Bosel. I shall miss his insolent demands for spare change on the High Street. What killed him?'

'He ate or drank something caustic that burned his mouth and innards,' said Bartholomew. 'It would not have been an easy death.'

'She might have killed him,' suggested Quenhyth, nodding to where Deynman was sitting on a tomb with his arm around the shoulders of the madwoman. It was not quite clear who was comforting whom, and Deynman seemed to be deriving as much relief from the warm, close presence of another living person as was the woman herself. 'She was discovered next to his corpse, after all.'

'She does not have the wits,' said Michael, although Bartholomew remained sceptical. His alarm when he had thought she might have harmed Deynman was still bright in his mind.

'She says she was keeping his body company,' said Redmeadow, eyeing her uneasily, as if he did not know what to believe. 'She claims she found him at dawn this morning, and did not want him to be alone. She was waiting for a priest to come and relieve her of her vigil. She told me Deschalers the grocer gave Bosel his new clothes, though. Perhaps that is significant.'

Bartholomew did not see why it should be. 'Bosel was a beggar, and people were always giving him things. It is how he made his living.'

'I do not see Deschalers poisoning him to get them back, either,' said Michael, surveying what had once probably been some decent garments, but that had become soiled and ragged in Bosel's possession. He glanced up and saw the Sheriff striding towards him. 'But this is *his* problem, not mine. The victim here is a townsman.'

Tulyet listened in silence to Bartholomew's opinion that Bosel had died from ingesting something highly caustic. The physician pointed out an empty wineskin and a pool of vomit near the body, which he thought indicative that Bosel had died fairly soon after swallowing the substance. He did not possess the skill claimed by some of his medical colleagues to determine an exact time of death, but a lump of bread in Bosel's scrip was unmistakably the kind handed out by the Canons of St John's Hospital at seven o'clock each evening. Therefore Bosel had died later than seven. The body was icy cold, suggesting it had been dead several hours. Tulyet bullied and cajoled Bartholomew until he had the physician's best guess: Bosel had probably died late the previous evening, most likely before midnight.

Tulyet frowned. 'Did he do this to himself? Is he a suicide?'

'I do not see why,' said Bartholomew. 'First, he had no funds to buy poison. And secondly, I imagine he was going to demand money from the Mortimers – by offering to retract his story about the incident with Lenne and Isnard. His future was looking rosy.'

'It was,' agreed Tulyet thoughtfully. 'The obvious conclusion is that Thomas Mortimer did this: mixed poison with wine and gave it to Bosel to drink. However, if Bosel was murdered between seven and midnight, then Mortimer is innocent. He was at a meeting of the town burgesses during those hours, discussing repairs to the Great Bridge. I know, because I was there.'

'One of his family, then,' said Michael. 'God knows, there are enough of them. And do not forget that they now include his nephew, Edward, whom we know is a killer.'

'Edward was at this meeting, too,' said Tulyet. He grimaced. 'And so was young Rob Thorpe.'

'Thorpe and Edward,' mused Quenhyth, who was listening uninvited to their discussion. 'The two felons who were found guilty by the King's Bench but who then secured themselves pardons.'

'Quite,' said Tulyet bitterly. 'Two ruthless criminals given the liberty to roam free in *my* town. I have enough to worry about, without watching them day and night.'

'You should not have recommended them for a King's Pardon, then,' said Michael tartly. 'I made some enquiries about that, and learned it was a letter from the Sheriff of Cambridgeshire that tipped the balance in their favour. Without that letter, they would still be in France.'

Tulyet shot him a withering look. 'That may well be true, but *I* was not Sheriff when their case came under review. Stephen Morice was. *He* was the one who claimed the town had no objection to their release, not me.'

'Do you think Thorpe and Edward killed Bosel?' asked Michael of Bartholomew, ignoring the Sheriff's ire that he should be blamed for something his predecessor had done.

Tulyet raised his eyebrows and spoke before the physician could reply. 'I have just told you they were both in a meeting last night. How can they be responsible?'

'Because you do not need to be present when your victim dies of poison,' Michael pointed out. 'They could have given Bosel the doctored wine hours before they went to this meeting.'

Tulyet considered, then nodded towards the madwoman. 'In my experience the person who finds a murdered corpse is often its killer, and *she* seems to have no rational reason for being with Bosel. Do I know her? She looks familiar.'

'Where would she find the money to buy wine and poison?' asked Michael. 'And why kill Bosel when she is a stranger in Cambridge, with no reason to harm any of its inhabitants?'

'How do you know she had no reason to harm Bosel?' asked Bartholomew reasonably. 'We know nothing about her, not even her name. And she is out of her wits, so is

39

not rational. She may have killed him because she thought he was someone else.'

'Shall I arrest her, then?' asked Tulyet. 'I will, if you think she is guilty.'

'I do not know,' said Bartholomew, unwilling to condemn anyone to the Castle prison. It was a foul place, full of rats and dripping slime. 'She might be telling the truth – that she found the body and did not like to leave it alone until a priest came.'

'Perhaps she *stole* the wine,' suggested Tulyet, reluctant to dismiss a potential culprit too readily. 'Or Bosel did – and got more than he bargained for. Unfortunately, I am too busy to look into this myself. Repairs to the Great Bridge begin today, and I must be there to supervise.'

'Why?' asked Michael curiously. 'That is the burgesses' responsibility, not yours.'

Tulyet's face was angry. 'Because the burgesses, in an attempt to cut costs, want to use the cheapest labour available: the prisoners in my Castle. That is why we had that meeting last night. I objected very strongly, but I was outvoted on all sides, so debtors, thieves and violent robbers will be set free to work on the bridge this very afternoon. I need to make sure they do not try to escape – or that my soldiers will know how to stop them, if they do.'

'*When* they do,' muttered Bartholomew.

'It is about time the bridge was mended,' said Michael. 'It almost collapsed when I last used it.'

'It has been subjected to some *very* heavy loads recently,' agreed Tulyet. 'But, besides watching forty able-bodied villains, I am also obliged to keep a close watch on Thorpe and Edward. I am sure they came here intending mischief. I shall have to delegate Bosel's murder investigation to Sergeant Orwelle.'

'Orwelle is a good man,' said Bartholomew, although he thought it a pity that Bosel was to be deprived of the

40

superior talents of the Sheriff. 'He will do his best to solve this crime.'

'And he has a limited number of suspects,' added Michael. 'Thomas Mortimer and his clan are the only ones with a known motive.'

'Well, there is her,' said Tulyet, pointing at the woman. 'However, I have a feeling you are right: Bosel's death probably does have something to do with the Mortimers. Bosel's evidence was not worth much, but without it I have nothing.'

Bartholomew and Michael left the Sheriff, and resumed their walk to Isnard's house with Quenhyth and Redmeadow trailing behind them; Deynman had been charged with taking the woman to St John's Hospital. They passed through the Trumpington Gate, then cut down the narrow lane opposite the Hall of Valence Marie, which was rutted with water-filled potholes deep enough to drown a sheep. Isnard's home was on the river bank, overlooking the Mill Pool.

The bargeman's residence was not in a good location. It was near both the Cam and the King's Ditch, both of which were stinking open sewers that contained all manner of filth. Being by the Mill Pool did not help either, since the current slowed there, causing the foulness to linger rather than being carried away. The pool was fringed with reeds and, in the spring and summer, Bartholomew imagined the bargeman would be plagued with swarms of insects. The house was near the town's two largest water-mills, too, and, although Bartholomew supposed their neighbours would grow used to the rhythmic clank and rumble of their mighty wheels, he did not think he would ever do so. As he picked his way along the muddy path to Isnard's home, he studied them.

The King's Mill was a hall-house located a few paces upstream from the Mill Pool. It spanned an arm of water that had been artificially narrowed to make it run faster and stronger. Its vertical wheel was of the undershot style, designed so that water struck its lower blades to set it in motion. The power generated was transferred to the mill itself by means of an 'axle tree' – a shaft connected to a series of cogs and wheels. It was not just the swishing, clunking sound of the wheel as it turned that was so noisy, but the rattle of the machinery, too.

Standing a short distance from the King's Mill was Mortimer's Mill, owned and run by the man who had injured Isnard. It was smaller than its competitor but just as noisy, and a good deal more filthy. The King's Mill ground grain for flour, but Mortimer's Mill had recently been converted for fulling cloth, a process that entailed the use of a lot of very smelly substances, all of which ended up in the river. The bargeman would be able to see Mortimer's enterprise from his sickbed, and Bartholomew wondered what he thought as he lay maimed and fevered, while the author of his troubles continued with the work that was making him a very wealthy man.

As Bartholomew listened to the repetitive rattle coming from the King's Mill, he became aware that it was slowing down. There was not as much water in each of the wheel's scoops, and the busy sound of its workings faltered, as though it had run out of energy. By contrast, Mortimer's Mill was operating at a cracking pace, and, if anything, was going even faster. He saw people hurry from the King's Mill and start to inspect their wheel, as if they could not understand why it had lost power. He watched their puzzled musings for a moment, then turned to enter his patient's home.

The house was poor and mean. Its thatched roof was in need of repair, and plaster was peeling from its walls, exposing the wattle and daub underneath. A chamber on the ground floor held a table, a bench, a hearth and a shelf for pots; an attic, reached by a ladder, was where Isnard usually slept. Since the bargeman's injury meant he could not climb the steps, Bartholomew had carried his bedding downstairs the previous day.

The physician was fully expecting him to develop a fever that might kill him, and was surprised, but pleased, to discover that the burly bargeman had not succumbed. He was even more surprised to find him sitting up and talking to a visitor – a man named Nicholas Bottisham, who was Gonville Hall's Master of Civil and Canon Law. Bottisham was regarded as one of the finest scholars in the University, possessing a mind that retained facts and references and made him a superb disputant. He had recently taken major orders with the Carmelites, and his new habit was still pristine. His complexion was florid and uneven, as a result of a disfiguring pox contracted in childhood, and his hair was cut high above his ears in a way indicating that Barber Lenne had been at it. He stood when Bartholomew, Michael and the two students entered.

'You are a popular man, Isnard,' said Bottisham, picking up his cloak from the table. 'I shall leave you, before you have so many guests that your walls burst and your house tumbles about your ears.'

'Thank you for coming,' said Isnard, reaching out to take the man's hand. 'It was kind.'

'I will come again tomorrow,' promised Bottisham. 'And I shall visit old Mistress Lenne. I will see she is looked after until her son arrives from Thetford, just as you ask.'

'And what about Thomas Mortimer?' asked Isnard, his voice angry. 'Will you detain him in a dark alley and chop off his legs with an axe? I asked you to do that, too.'

Bottisham smiled indulgently. 'You can do that yourself, when you are better.'

Isnard grinned without humour. 'It will give me something to look forward to. I will teach him that he cannot

43

drive when he is full of ale, and kill honest old men as they stand chatting in the streets. Thank God Bosel is prepared to stand up and tell the truth.'

Bartholomew and Michael exchanged a glance. Isnard did not notice, but Bottisham was an observant man and immediately sensed something amiss.

'Has Bosel retracted his statement already?' he asked in dismay. 'I did not think Mortimer would act quite so soon. I assumed he would wait to see what kind of case the Sheriff put together before spending money on bribes that might not be necessary.'

'Bosel will not be bribed by Mortimer,' predicted Isnard confidently. 'He will tell the truth. I have already made sure of that by offering three groats more than Mortimer's highest price.' He smiled in satisfaction at his foresight.

'Bosel is dead,' said Michael bluntly. 'He will not be telling the "truth" for anyone.'

'Mortimer murdered Bosel, so he cannot speak for me?' asked Isnard, aghast.

'The Sheriff says Mortimer was at a meeting all last night, so cannot be responsible,' said Michael. 'He will have to make his case without Bosel.' He did not add that Tulyet considered this impossible.

'I will dispense a little justice of my own, then,' said Isnard, wringing his bed-covers furiously. 'I will not lie here with Lenne *and* Bosel slain, and let Mortimer get away with it.'

'Not yet,' said Bartholomew, concerned that Isnard might persuade some crony to help him leave his sickbed too soon, resulting in a third death.

Isnard shook his head, already spent and too unwell to sustain his temper for long. 'I am full of words, and not the type to stalk merchants and take axes to them.' Bartholomew said nothing, knowing he was exactly that kind of man – or had been, when in possession of all his limbs. 'But I mean what I say about justice. I *will* see Mortimer punished for what he did, even if it means visiting the King himself to put my case.'

'I will tell you how to go about it,' offered Bottisham generously. 'The law is complex, and there are certain procedures you must follow. But your physician is waiting to tend you, and I should not linger here and make a nuisance of myself. Rest, Isnard. I will pray for you.'

He patted the bargeman's shoulder, nodded a friendly farewell to Bartholomew and Michael, and squeezed past Quenhyth and Redmeadow to reach the door.

'I am delighted to see you looking so well,' said Michael, plumping himself down on Isnard's single bench with such force that Bartholomew thought it might break. 'When I heard you had summoned Matt this morning, I assumed you had taken a turn for the worse.'

'I need something for the itching, Doctor,' said Isnard sheepishly. 'I am sorry to drag you from your breakfast, but it could not wait. It is driving me to distraction.'

'Itching?' asked Bartholomew, assuming that now Isnard was confined to his bed, he was unable to escape the fleas that flourished in his filthy blankets. Cleansing the house of all the small creatures that bit and sucked blood would be an imposing task, and Bartholomew was not sure it could be done.

'My foot,' whispered Isnard hoarsely. 'It itches something fierce.'

'Scratch it, then,' suggested Redmeadow helpfully. He flexed one of his hands, revealing some lengthy nails. 'I will do it for you, if you like.'

'No, the *other* one,' said Isnard, still in a whisper, as though he considered it unlucky or dangerous to speak in a normal voice about a limb that was no longer attached.

'You mean the one that is gone?' asked Michael warily. 'How do you know it is itching? I doubt Matt told you what

45

he did with it. He usually declines to share such ghoulish information.'

'It itches,' persisted Isnard stubbornly. 'And I do not mean from the river, or wherever he disposed of it. I mean it itches at the bottom of my leg, where it used to live.'

'I have heard such complaints before,' said Bartholomew, aware that Michael was looking around for evidence that Isnard had been drinking. He recalled an archer in France telling him the same thing about an amputated arm. 'It is not unusual to imagine a limb is still there for some time after it has been removed. And I did not throw it in the river, by the way. People drink from that.'

'But what can I do about it?' asked Isnard, distressed. 'I cannot think about anything other than this itch, and yet I cannot put an end to it. Will it last for the rest of my life? If so, I do not think I can stand it.' His voice was unsteady.

'I can dig it up and give it a good scratch, if you like,' offered Redmeadow, trying hard to be useful. 'That might cure you.'

'He needs a purge,' countered Quenhyth with great conviction. 'A tincture of linseed fried in fat should put an end to his miseries. Or perhaps mallow leaves stewed in old ale.'

'It might put an end to him, too,' said Bartholomew. 'I do not want his humours unbalanced by purges. He needs to gain strength from his food, not lose it by vomiting.'

'A clyster, then,' said Quenhyth with unseemly relish. 'I can prepare a potion of green camomile, salt, honey and lard, and you can squirt it into his anus and cleanse his bowels.'

'I do not like the sound of this,' said Isnard uneasily. 'My bowels are my own affair, and not for others to explore as they please.'

'I quite agree,' interposed Michael, the expression on his face indicating that he found the discussion distasteful.

He changed the subject. 'Why was Bottisham visiting you, Isnard? I did not know the two of you were acquainted.'

'I regularly haul barges for his College – Gonville,' replied Isnard. 'And Master Bottisham has always been kind to me. He came to ask if there was anything I need, but, apart from strong ale, which Doctor Bartholomew says I cannot have, I am well looked after by my neighbours.'

'I prescribed a clyster for Master Bernarde the miller when he had an aching elbow,' said Quenhyth sulkily. 'It worked very well.'

Bartholomew gaped at him. 'You did what?'

'You were out inspecting corpses with Brother Michael,' said Quenhyth, becoming defensive when he saw his teacher was shocked. 'What am I supposed to do when a patient comes wanting help? Send him away empty handed?'

'Yes,' said Bartholomew in exasperation. 'And then tell me, so I can visit him myself. You must *not* dispense medicines to my patients. You are not qualified, and you do not have enough experience to start giving out remedies of your own.'

'I have been watching you for *six months*,' objected Quenhyth, making it sound like a decade. 'And I am a quick learner. I know more than you give me credit for.'

'But still not enough,' said Bartholomew. 'But I will not argue with you. Either you do as I say or you can find yourself another teacher.'

'I will obey you,' said Quenhyth in the kind of voice that indicated he considered it an immense favour. 'But I was only trying to help.'

'Then go back to Michaelhouse,' said Bartholomew wearily. 'And do not "help" without my permission again.'

'I do not want *him* tampering with my personal places, thank you very much,' said Isnard after Quenhyth had gone. 'He can take his green camomile and lard and shove them up his own arse.'

47

'I am sorry, Isnard,' said Bartholomew. 'And I cannot help with your itch, either. I do not know what can be done to alleviate it.'

Isnard sat back with a grimace and folded his arms. 'Do not worry about that, Doctor. I am already cured. The notion of that boy loose on my bowels has quite put the itch out of my mind.'

CHAPTER 2

'And there were doucettes and a rose pudding to follow,' enthused Michael gleefully the following Saturday, as he walked with Bartholomew and Michaelhouse's Master of Civil Law, John Wynewyk, to the Church of St Mary the Great. 'Along with more Lombard slices than I have ever seen in one place, although I prefer the almond variety to the date.'

'We will be late,' warned Wynewyk, more interested in the debate they were about to engage in than his colleague's detailed analysis of the repasts he had enjoyed at various academic and religious institutions during the week. 'I do not want Gonville to win the *Disputatio de quodlibet* by default, just because we fail to arrive on time.'

'All right,' muttered Michael, not pleased to have his culinary reminiscences cut short. 'I am going as fast as I can. I thought you would be interested in what is eaten at the high tables of other Colleges, since you hold Michaelhouse's purse strings these days. Gonville keeps a remarkably fine table, and Michaelhouse . . . well, Michaelhouse does not.'

'Langelee trusts me to spend our funds sensibly,' said Wynewyk primly. 'That means peas for pottage and flour for bread, not cream and sugars for custards.'

Although the monk complained constantly that Michaelhouse's fare was inferior to that of other institutions, and his colleagues had learned to take his grumbles with a grain of salt, Bartholomew thought his gripes were currently justified. For some unaccountable reason the standard of

College food had plummeted dramatically during the last two weeks, and even the least discerning scholars had been prompted to comment on it. Bartholomew supposed that Wynewyk had been obliged to use the funds usually earmarked for victuals for some other – doubtless equally deserving – purpose, and just hoped the situation would not be permanent. It was not pleasant to be hungry all the time.

He was about to ask, when there was a clatter of hoofs behind them. With the memory of Isnard's shattered leg fresh in his mind, Bartholomew darted to one side of the road, with his friends not far behind; even the obese Michael could move quickly when life and limb were under threat. A horse galloped past, too fast for a narrow thoroughfare like St Michael's Lane. It reached the end of the street and its rider wheeled it around, to return at a more sedate trot.

'Rob Thorpe,' said Michael heavily when he recognised the culprit. Wynewyk immediately raised his hood and bowed his head, and Bartholomew saw that Thorpe's reputation had gone before him. Even men like Wynewyk, who had not been in Cambridge when the lad had embarked on his spree of violence, were unwilling to attract his attention. 'So, it is true. You have indeed decided to return to the town you used so badly.'

Thorpe had changed during the two years that he had been in exile. He was no longer a bony, gangly youth with immature fluff framing a childish face. He was a man, with a man's strength and a man's confidence, even though he was not yet twenty. He was clean shaven, and wore a close-cut quilted tunic with buttoned sleeves – called a gipon – over which was thrown a shoulder-cape fastened with a gold pin. His hose were soled, rendering shoes unnecessary, and his hood turban was one of the most elaborately decorated Bartholomew had ever seen. It comprised a triangle of scarlet worsted with a hole for the head, and the two ends fell elegantly over his shoulders in the fashion currently popular at the King's Court.

'I have been meaning to pay you a visit, monk,' said Thorpe insolently. The smile that played around his full, red lips did not reach his eyes. His gaze shifted to Bartholomew, and he bowed his head in a gesture that was more insulting than polite. 'And you, too, Bartholomew, although I did not think you would still be here.'

'Where else would I be?' asked Bartholomew, a little surprised by the statement.

'I thought you would have been burned at the stake for using unorthodox and dangerous remedies,' Thorpe replied nastily. 'But perhaps people are more forgiving these days. Times change, I suppose.' The bitterness in his voice was unmistakable.

'What do you want?' demanded Michael curtly. 'You must know you are not welcome in Cambridge. You were found guilty of several vicious murders, and you are fortunate you were not hanged. You are not the kind of man we want in our town.'

'I have come to visit old friends,' replied Thorpe, unruffled by the monk's hostility. His eyes were spiteful as he addressed the physician. 'I intend to pay my respects to *your* family soon – your sister Edith and her husband Oswald Stanmore. I am sure they will be delighted to see me after all these years.'

'"All these years"?' echoed Michael in disbelief. 'It has only been twenty-six months.'

Bartholomew knew delight would be the last thing on his family's mind if they were visited by Thorpe. Stanmore was a wealthy clothier, and Thorpe had been one of his apprentices. He and Edith had taken the lad into their house and treated him like a much-loved son. Their sense of betrayal when they discovered they had nurtured a killer was still not forgotten.

'You will have to wait for that pleasure,' said Bartholomew, relieved that they were away and did not plan to return to Cambridge for some weeks. With luck Thorpe would be gone by then. 'They are not here.'

Thorpe shrugged, although Bartholomew sensed he was disappointed. 'It does not matter. I have been waiting for a long time to reacquaint myself with my old master and his wife, so a few more days are nothing. When did you say they will return?'

'I did not,' replied Bartholomew coolly. 'But Huntingdon is a long way from here, so I doubt it will be very soon.'

'Huntingdon is *not* far,' flashed Thorpe with sudden anger. '*France* is a long way from here – and that is where *I* was condemned to go. No one would speak for me at my trial – not my father, not the Stanmores, and not you scholars. I will repay you all for that.'

Michael raised his eyebrows. 'No one spoke for you, because you were guilty – by your own admission. You cannot blame others because you were caught and punished. You are a man now, so act like one, and accept responsibility for what you did.'

Thorpe became smug. 'But my case has now been reviewed by His Majesty's best law-clerks. I have been granted a King's Pardon – which means no one can hold those crimes against me ever again.'

Michael was unimpressed. 'I shall hold crimes against whomever I like. However, I do not want to talk to you when I have important matters to attend. Move that miserable nag out of my way and let me past.'

They all looked around as a second horseman arrived, also riding too fast for the small lane. Bartholomew's heart sank when he recognised him, too, and Wynewyk huddled even deeper into his cloak.

'Edward Mortimer,' said Bartholomew, taking in the

sober clothing and soft features of the exiled baker's son – the second of the two felons to be pardoned and permitted to return to the scene of his crimes. Like Thorpe, Mortimer had grown sturdier and stronger during the time he had been away. Bartholomew remembered him as a dreamy lad, bullied by his domineering father, but there was no weakness in his face now. It was cold, hard and determined, and Bartholomew saw the malleable youth had long gone.

Michael was puzzled as he looked from one felon to the other. 'You two did not know each other before the King's Bench ordered you to abjure the realm – on the same day, but in separate trials – so why are you together now? Is it because no one else will entertain your company?'

Thorpe's eyes glittered at the insult, and Bartholomew suspected Michael had touched a raw nerve. Mortimer simply smiled.

'I belong to a large and powerful family, Brother; they are always pleased when another Mortimer swells their ranks. My father, uncles and cousins are thrilled to have me back.'

The jealous glance Thorpe shot his way confirmed to Bartholomew that the younger man's kin had indeed been less than pleased about *his* return. The physician understood why. Thorpe's father was Master of a large and wealthy College, and would not want a murderous son hovering in the background, spoiling his chances of promotion. For Mortimer it was different: his family was rich, influential and not afraid to consort with those on the fringes of legality. Edward was doubtless telling the truth about his reception: the Mortimers would be only too happy to swell their ranks with a seasoned criminal.

'I have no wish to linger here,' said Thorpe, affecting indifference to the discussion. He forced a grin at Mortimer. 'I will buy you an ale at the Lilypot.'

With a mock salute, he kicked hard at his horse's sides. It reared, then cantered up St Michael's Lane and turned towards the Great Bridge, scattering pedestrians as it went. Bartholomew heaved a sigh of relief when Mortimer followed, and realised his heart was pounding, not because he was afraid, but because the pair brought back memories of an adventure he would sooner forget. He watched them leave with a sense of foreboding. Neither seemed reformed by exile; on the contrary, they appeared to be nastier than ever.

'The infamous Thorpe and Mortimer,' said Wynewyk, rubbing his hands together as though the encounter had chilled him. He pushed his hood away from his face. 'The town has been full of talk about their misdeeds ever since they arrived back. I looked up their trial in the Castle's records, and, as an expert on civil law, I can tell you there is no doubt at all that their conviction was sound. The evidence against them was irrefutable.'

Michael nodded. 'I cannot imagine how they managed to persuade the King's clerks to review their sentences, or why a Pardon was granted.'

'I suppose money changed hands,' said Wynewyk. 'That is what usually happens in cases like this. But it is odd that they should arrive in Cambridge just before Bosel the beggar – chief witness against Mortimer's uncle – should be murdered. I doubt it is coincidence.'

'Dick Tulyet said they were both at a meeting of the town's burgesses when Bosel died,' said Michael, although his eyes were troubled. 'And I do not see why they would pick on Bosel anyway.'

'Because he was poor and friendless, and no one will invest too much time or energy in hunting his killers,' suggested Bartholomew. 'It is entirely possible that Bosel was an experiment – to see what would happen when they committed their first new murder. All their alibi from Tulyet does is tell us they were not present when Bosel actually ingested the poison.'

Michael sighed. 'Dick thinks they may have persuaded that madwoman to give it to him, but I disagree. She seems too witless to entrust with such a task.'

'I have heard so many rumours about that pair that it is difficult to separate fact from fiction,' said Wynewyk, beginning to walk again. 'What really happened? Are they the Devil's spawn, as Agatha the laundress claims? Or are they poor misguided children, as Master Kenyngham would have me believe?'

'Neither,' replied Bartholomew. 'They are just men who killed without remorse or hesitation, solely to realise their own plans for revenge and riches.'

'They were caught – thanks to some clever investigating by me – and confessed to their crimes,' elaborated Michael rather smugly. 'Did you know that Thorpe's father is Master of the Hall of Valence Marie? It is hard to believe: a high-ranking scholar spawning a murderer.'

'Master Thorpe is the man who first found the sacred Hand of Valence Marie,' mused Wynewyk, changing the subject. 'I heard the Hand came from a local saint, and is imbued with great power.'

'The Hand was hacked from the corpse of a simpleton,' corrected Bartholomew firmly. 'It is *not* imbued with any kind of power, sacred or otherwise.'

'That is not what most folk believe,' argued Wynewyk. 'It is stored in the University Chest in the tower of St Mary the Great, and people petition it all the time. Many of them have had their prayers answered. To my mind – and theirs – that makes it a genuine relic.'

Bartholomew was exasperated when he turned to Michael. 'I told you to destroy the thing three years ago, Brother. You had the chance: you could easily have tossed it into the marshes. But you insisted on keeping it, and now it is too late. It has become an object of veneration – again.'

'Again?' asked Wynewyk. 'It has been worshipped before?'

'Briefly,' said Bartholomew. 'When it was first dredged from the ditch outside Valence Marie. But we proved beyond the shadow of a doubt that it was hacked from Peterkin Starre – because his corpse happened to be available at the time – and it is not and never has been sacred.'

'The fascination with it will not last,' insisted Michael, although he sounded uneasy. 'These things come and go, and what is popular today is forgotten tomorrow. And anyway, it is not my business to decide what should and should not be destroyed. I pass that responsibility to the Chancellor.'

Bartholomew laughed in disbelief. 'I am not a complete innocent, Brother! Everyone knows Chancellor Tynkell does exactly what you say, and there is only one man who determines what happens in the University these days: you. If you wanted these bones destroyed, they would have vanished by now.'

Michael grinned, unabashed by the reprimand and amused that his friend had so accurately described his relationship with the Chancellor. Tynkell was indeed becoming a figurehead, with Michael holding the real power. Tynkell had expressed a desire to resign and allow Michael to take the reins, since he was already making most of the important decisions, but the monk demurred. He liked things the way they were – it was useful to have someone to blame when anything went wrong.

'Tynkell does listen to my advice,' he confessed modestly. 'But destroying the Hand would have been an extreme reaction – and one that could never be reversed. I thought it might come in useful one day, and that it would be safely anonymous in the University Chest.'

'Not safely anonymous enough, apparently,' grumbled

Bartholomew, unappeased. 'Wynewyk is right: there are always pilgrims around the tower these days. It will not be long before we have a wave of religious zeal to quell, and there is no reasoning with folk once they have decided upon issues of faith. The Hand has always been dangerous. Look what happened to Thorpe's father over the thing.'

'What?' asked Wynewyk, intrigued. 'Anything to do with his son?'

'No, nothing like that,' replied Bartholomew. 'But, as you just said, Master Thorpe was the one who found the Hand in the ditch outside his College. The King and the Bishop of Ely were so angry with him for starting what might have become a powerful cult that they forced him to leave Valence Marie and take a post at a grammar school in York.'

'York,' said Wynewyk with distaste. 'I have heard it smells of lard. But Master Thorpe is not in York. He is here, in Cambridge.'

'He was reinstated after a series of appeals to the King,' said Bartholomew. 'Apparently, his successor was not gentlemanly enough, and kept wiping his teeth on the tablecloth during meals.'

'Nasty,' said Wynewyk with a fastidious shudder. 'The Bishop of Norwich does that, too.'

'Since then, Master Thorpe has impressed everyone with his diligence and scholarship,' continued Michael. 'He is a changed man, but, unlike his son, *he* has changed for the better.'

Wynewyk became aware of the passing time with sudden alarm. 'We should not be reviewing ancient history now, my friends. We should be debating with the scholars of Gonville and, unless we hurry, they will assume we are too frightened to meet them. The honour of Michaelhouse is at stake – we must run.'

*   *   *

St Mary the Great was the town's largest and most impressive church. Its chancel had recently been rebuilt, replacing the narrow pointed lancet holes of an earlier age with great windows full of delicate tracery. These fabulous arches, so vast and open that it seemed they would be incapable of supporting the weight of the roof above them, allowed sunlight to flood in and bathe the building with light and warmth. The coloured glass that had been used in places caught the sun's brilliance and accentuated the scarlets, golds and emeralds of the wall paintings.

Over the last few weeks Bartholomew had noticed more and more people praying outside the church, and there were often folk kneeling on the roughly paved ground by the tower. There were three there that morning, busily petitioning the Hand that languished in the University Chest just above their heads. One was John of Ufford, a son of the Earl of Suffolk, who was learning law so he could forge himself a career at Court. He was a pleasant enough fellow, with a perfectly straight fringe of dark hair over his eyes. He nodded a greeting as the Michaelhouse men passed, raising one hand to touch a sore on his mouth as he did so.

'If you leave it alone, it will heal more quickly,' said Bartholomew, unable to help himself. The lesion looked as though it was played with constantly, and he knew it would only disappear if it was granted a reprieve from the sufferer's probing fingers.

'I am praying to the Hand of Valence Marie,' said Ufford. He looked frightened. 'This sore might be the first sign of leprosy, and I need the intervention of a powerful saint to help me.'

'It is not leprosy,' said Bartholomew, wondering whether Rougham had been talking to him. The Gonville physician had a nasty habit of diagnosing overly serious ailments in his patients so that he could charge them more for their 'cures'.

'No?' asked Ufford with sudden hope. 'Are you sure?'

'If you keep your fingers away from it, and do not smother it with salves, you will notice a difference in a week. It needs clean air and time to heal, nothing more.'

He followed Michael and Wynewyk inside the church. It was packed to overflowing. Public debates were important occasions – particularly the end-of-term *Disputatio de quodlibet* – and representatives were present from every College and hostel, many wearing the uniform of their institutions. There was the black of Michaelhouse and the dark blue of Bene't, mixed with paler blues and greens from places like King's Hall, Valence Marie and Peterhouse. Among them were the blacks, browns, greys and whites of the religious Orders, and the whole church rang with the sound of voices – some arguing amiably, others more hostile. Although debates were designed to bring scholars together in an atmosphere of learning and scholasticism, they were also often used as excuses to re-ignite ancient feuds and hatreds, and Bartholomew noticed that Michael had arranged for a large contingent of beadles to be present, too.

'There you are,' said Ralph de Langelee, Master of Michaelhouse, when he spotted his three colleagues. His barrel-shaped soldier's body cut an imposing figure, and other scholars gave him a wide berth as he shoved his way through them. He was no one's idea of an academic, with a mediocre intellect and only a hazy grasp of the philosophy he was supposed to teach, but he was an able administrator, and a definite improvement on his predecessor. 'I know I told you not to arrive too early – to dull your wits in mindless chatter while you wait for the *Disputatio* to begin – but I did not expect you to cut it this fine.'

'Not knowing whether your opponents will arrive is a sure way to unsettle the enemy,' said Michael comfortably, glancing towards the place where the scholars of Gonville Hall had gathered.

'Well, *I* was beginning to think you had decided not to come, too,' said Langelee, a little irritably. 'And Gonville have been claiming that their minds are too quick for us, and we have decided to stay away, rather than risk a public mental drubbing.'

'We shall see about that,' said Wynewyk, grimly determined. 'The likes of Gonville will not defeat *me* in verbal battle!'

Langelee started to move towards the dais that had been set up where the nave met the chancel. 'Do not underestimate Gonville, Wynewyk: they are very good. We are not talking about Peterhouse here. Well, are you ready? Have you spent the morning honing your debating skills on each other, as I recommended?'

'We do not need to practise,' declared Michael immodestly. 'Although, I confess I have not taken part in a major *Disputatio de quodlibet* since the Death.'

'The subject you three will be asked to debate could be anything – theology, the arts, mathematics, natural philosophy, even politics,' said Langelee, as if his Fellows might not know. 'That is the meaning of *quodlibet*: "whithersoever you please".'

'Thank you, Master,' said Michael dryly. 'I am glad you told us that.'

Bartholomew ignored the monk's sarcasm. He was looking forward to the occasion, and was honoured that Langelee had chosen him to stand for Michaelhouse. 'These debates are opportunities for us to express opinions and ideas with a freedom not always possible within the rigid constraints of more formal lectures,' he said.

The others regarded him uneasily. 'I hope you do not intend to say anything that might be construed as heresy,' said Langelee. 'I should have thought of this before inviting you to represent us. I had forgotten your penchant for anathema.'

'He will not say anything inappropriate,' said Michael firmly, fixing his friend with the kind of glare that promised all manner of retribution if he was disobeyed. 'Spouting heresy will see Michaelhouse disqualified, and none of us want that – nor do we want inflammatory remarks to spark a riot.'

Langelee arrived at the dais, and looked his three Fellows up and down before sighing in exasperation. 'I told you to dress nicely, Bartholomew, and you have turned up looking like a pauper from Ovyng Hostel.'

'This is my best tabard,' objected Bartholomew indignantly. He glanced down at the stained and crumpled garment. 'But I had to visit Isnard earlier, to change the bandages on his leg, and some—'

'No details, please,' said Langelee firmly. 'If you are to stand near me for the next two hours, I do not want to know the origin of any peculiar smells. Still, I suppose I can rest easy knowing you have clean fingers.' He started to chuckle, convinced as always that Bartholomew's obsession with rinsing his hands after dealing with bloody wounds and decaying corpses was an unnaturally fastidious fetish.

Michael saw that his friend was about to begin a lecture on hygiene, so he intervened hastily, nodding to where the scholars of Gonville Hall were waiting. 'We are supposed to be arguing with them, not each other. We should start, or they really will think we are afraid of them.'

'Michaelhouse will see these upstarts off,' proclaimed Wynewyk fiercely. He cleared his throat and looked uneasy. 'At least, we stand a fighting chance if the Chancellor selects a decent Question.'

'That is why I chose you three to argue on our behalf,' said Langelee. 'You are our best lawyer; Michael's knowledge of theology surpasses anyone's except gentle old Kenyngham's – but he lacks the killer instinct necessary for this kind of event; and Bartholomew can cover the sciences. Gonville will crumble before our onslaught.'

'They will,' vowed Wynewyk with keen determination. 'I prayed to the Hand at a special mass held in St Clement's Church last Wednesday, and asked it to let us win. So, what with our wits and the intervention of a saint, victory will be ours for certain.'

The atmosphere in the church was one of excited antici-pation. Every scholar from Michaelhouse was present, standing on the left of the dais. To the right were the scholars of Gonville, who were mostly priests dressed in habits of brown or white. Bartholomew glanced at the assembled faces in the nave, recognising many; some were friendly, others were not. None were indifferent: everyone had chosen a side. The end-of-term *Disputatio* was an impor-tant occasion, because students had been scarce since the plague and the College that won it could expect more applicants. It was not just simple intellectual rivalry that made this particular debate such an intense affair: there were financial considerations, too.

Someone waved to Bartholomew, making encouraging gestures. It was Thomas Paxtone, who had recently arrived at King's Hall to take up an appointment as Regent Master of Medicine. After so many years with only the conserva-tive Peterhouse medic Master Lynton, it was a pleasure to have Paxtone in Cambridge. Bartholomew wished he felt as positive towards the second arrival, Rougham of Gonville; although they both maintained an outward show of cordiality towards each other, there was active dislike festering beneath their veneer of civility.

Chancellor Tynkell ascended to the dais when he saw all parties were present, and an expectant hush fell over the assembled scholars. Bartholomew was some distance away, but he could still detect the stale odour that always emanated from the University's figurehead. Tynkell believed that any form of washing was dangerous, and avoided contact with water if he could. It was rumoured that he did not even like Holy Water on his skin, a tale that had given rise to some wild speculation about his religious beliefs. Bartholomew knew nothing about Tynkell's personal theology, but he did know that the man was plagued by all manner of digestive complaints. When he had had the temerity to suggest that if the Chancellor rinsed his hands before meals he might lead a more healthy life, Tynkell had promptly dismissed him and hired Rougham instead.

'Good morning,' announced Tynkell in his reedy voice. He rubbed his stomach, indicating that he was suffering from whatever he had last eaten. 'This is the last of our public debates this term, and the outcome of today's *Disputatio de quodlibet* will determine which of the Colleges may lay claim to owning the University's strongest and best disputants. You will be aware that the "Scholars of the Holy and Undivided Trinity, the Blessed Virgin Mary and St Michael" *and* the "Scholars of the Hall of the Annunciation of the Blessed Virgin—"'

'If he means Michaelhouse and Gonville, then why does he not say so – simply?' demanded Deynman in a loud whisper that had the scholars of Gonville howling in derisive laughter and his Michaelhouse colleagues ready to teach them a lesson for their poor manners. Langelee went to silence Deynman, to ensure he did not embarrass them with further outbursts.

'Lord!' muttered Michael, looking around him uneasily. 'I hope this does not degenerate into a brawl. Being Senior Proctor is not easy at the best of times, but it is worse when we have five hundred war-thirsty scholars packed into a confined space.'

'You cannot ban public debates because scholars

squabble,' said Bartholomew, suspecting that Michael would like to do just that. 'And not everyone is spoiling for a fight, anyway. Some are here because they want to hear a good argument.'

'Have you heard what the Question might be?' whispered Wynewyk, as Tynkell launched into a tedious account about who had won quodlibetical disputations in the past. 'It would be beneficial to think out some of our arguments in advance.'

'I have not,' said Michael haughtily. 'That would be cheating. You know perfectly well that the Question is kept in strictest secrecy, and that Tynkell is very careful about it. Believe me, I had a good look in his office last night after he had gone home, but I could find nothing.'

'I have decided that Master Warde of Valence Marie will preside,' intoned Tynkell. This was no surprise. Warde was considered one of the best mediators the University had, and was known for his integrity and even-handedness. He was a good choice.

Warde had apparently anticipated that he would be selected, because he was already waiting. When he heard his name, he climbed stiffly on to the dais and stood next to the Chancellor. Bartholomew saw him wince when he moved, and supposed he was still bruised from when Thomas Mortimer had knocked him down the previous Wednesday. He recalled the flailing hoofs and the miller's drunkenness, and supposed Warde should consider himself lucky to be alive, given what had happened to Lenne and Isnard a few moments later. Warde began to cough, and Tynkell was obliged to hammer on his back until he stopped.

'What is the Question?' called Langelee, bored with the ponderous preliminaries and keen for the event to begin in earnest. 'What will they be discussing?'

'Damn this tickle!' rasped Warde. There were shocked intakes of breath from those scholars in religious Orders who disapproved of cursing in church. 'It is driving me to distraction.'

'It is driving *us* to distraction, too,' mumbled a grey-haired Fellow called Thomas Bingham, also from Valence Marie. 'You keep us awake at night with it, and it disrupts our teaching during the day.'

'The Question is as follows,' announced Tynkell. There was absolute silence in the nave. He took a breath, relishing the fact that he had everyone's attention: it was not often that academics listened *en masse*. '*Frequens legum mutato est periculosa.*'

'A too frequent change in the law is dangerous,' translated Bartholomew under his breath. 'I am not the best person to take part in this particular affray. Most of what I know of the law I find contemptible. It fails to prosecute Thomas Mortimer for killing Lenne, and it sells pardons to convicted felons.'

'You cannot withdraw,' said Wynewyk in alarm. He gestured to the other Michaelhouse Fellows who had gathered to discuss the topic in low, excited voices. 'Father William, Clippesby or even Langelee himself might offer to take your place. And then Gonville would defeat us for certain.'

'This is a good topic for you,' said Michael to the lawyer. He shot Bartholomew a stern look. 'But you must keep your opinions about our legal system to yourself. We will lose points if you launch into a tirade, no matter how much you long to expose the law's idiosyncrasies. But do not worry: the three of us will do the subject justice.' He sniggered. 'If the words "justice" and "law" can be uttered in the same sentence, that is.'

'We will lose for sure if you make jokes like that,' said Wynewyk irritably. 'Do not—'

Tynkell clapped his hands. 'Commence!'

Wynewyk was the first to speak, and Bartholomew was

impressed, as always, by his colleague's precise logic. The scholar from Gonville who stepped forward to refute his points was Bottisham, the kindly Carmelite lawyer who had visited Isnard two days before. He spoke well, without recourse to the scornful viciousness some scholars employed when attacking their opponents' reasoning. Michael argued against Bottisham, and in turn was refuted by Gonville's second speaker, Richard Pulham. Pulham was a fussy little Cistercian, with the largest ears Bartholomew had ever seen on a man. When the Master of Gonville was away from Cambridge, which he was most of the time, the running of his College usually fell to Pulham, who held the post of Acting Master.

Then it was Bartholomew's turn. He found Pulham's points easier to refute than he had anticipated, and felt he comported himself fairly respectably. Debating in front of hundreds of sharp-minded scholars certainly helped to hone the wits, he thought. The last person to speak was Gonville's William Rougham. Rougham allowed himself the luxury of a sneer before he began, as if he considered his fellow physician's logic seriously lacking.

Rougham was not an attractive man, either physically or in terms of his personality. He had lank black hair that was smoothed over a shiny pate, and a close-shaven beard was obviously intended to conceal the absence of a chin. His teeth were large, brown and decayed, so that his breath smelled, and Bartholomew often wondered why he did not pay a surgeon to remove the offending fangs before they rotted and fell out of their own accord. In terms of scholarship Rougham was pedantic and trivial, and Warde was obliged to reprimand him several times for making bald statements, rather than using logic to underline his points. Rougham became flustered, and finished speaking somewhat abruptly.

Once the main arguments had been laid out, the debate

gained momentum and Bartholomew was forced to focus hard, lest Gonville slipped an invalid statement past Michaelhouse. The scholars in the nave cheered when one College scored a particularly cunning point, and time flew past. Bartholomew's head began to ache from the effort of intense concentration, and from the noise and heat inside the building. But eventually Warde raised his hand to indicate that the Question had been sufficiently discussed. He held up a waxed tablet on which he had been keeping a tally and, once again, there was an excited hush among the scholars.

'This was a close-run battle, with clever and elegant postulations and refutations from both sides. However, the arguments of one College were slightly superior and more succinct than those of the other.'

He stopped speaking and began to cough. There was an audible sigh of irritation throughout the church, and Michael stepped forward to thump his shoulders, rather vigorously considering the man was about to make an important judgement that reflected the honour of Michaelhouse.

'An excess of phlegm,' announced Rougham, seizing the moment to engage in a little self-promotion. 'An inconvenient problem, for which *I* prescribe a syrup of honey and boiled nettles.'

'I tried that,' wheezed Warde. 'And it did not work.'

'Then I shall suggest something stronger later,' said Rougham shortly, not liking the fact that Warde had just denounced his cure as ineffectual in front of most of the University. 'But let us return to the business in hand. You were about to announce the winner.'

'Yes,' said Warde, his eyes watering furiously, either from coughing or from Michael's slaps. 'I declare the winner is—' He faltered a second time when there was a commotion near the west door.

All heads turned at the rattle of spurred feet on the flag-stones, and an agitated whispering broke out. The man who caused the disturbance was cloaked, and had not bothered to remove his sword, as was customary when entering religious houses. He elbowed his way through the throng to the dais.

'Now what?' murmured Michael uneasily. 'I see from his livery that he is from the papal court in Avignon. Why would the Pope send a message to anyone in Cambridge?'

'Perhaps Innocent the Sixth is dead, and we have another French puppet in his place,' suggested Bottisham, not without rancour. 'This schism between Avignon and Rome is a ridiculous state of affairs. It is time the papacy was wrested from French control and returned to Rome, where it belongs.'

Warde agreed. 'We are at war with the French, and it is not fair that they should exert power over us through the Church in this way.'

'Which one of you is Chancellor Tynkell?' asked the messenger in a clear, ringing voice. 'And Richard Pulham, Acting Master of Gonville Hall?'

The two men stepped forward unwillingly. In an age when it was easy to make accusations of treason and heresy – but far more difficult to prove innocence – no one liked being singled out for special attention from a man like the French Pope.

'I have news from Avignon,' said the messenger in a voice that was loud enough to be heard at the other end of the town. Bartholomew sensed he was enjoying himself, with his dramatic entrance and town-crier-like pronounce-ments. 'From John Colton, the Master of Gonville Hall, who, as you know, has been engaged on important busi-ness in the papal curia.'

'Hardly!' muttered Michael in Bartholomew's ear. 'Colton's only "important business" has been to further his own career by following Bishop Bateman of Norwich all over the world. When Bateman went to Avignon in the King's service, there also went Colton. The man is like a leech.'

Bartholomew refrained from pointing out that Michael was in the service of a bishop himself, and might well follow him to Avignon, if he thought it might be worth his while.

'Colton wishes me to inform you that Bishop Bateman is dead,' said the messenger. 'He was murdered – perhaps *poisoned* – at Avignon on the sixth day of January this year.'

The death of the popular Bishop of Norwich was a significant event in Cambridge, even though the town was officially under the jurisdiction of the Bishop of Ely. People were saddened by the news, especially since Bateman's demise was rumoured to have been at the hand of an enemy. The scholars of Gonville were especially distressed, because the Bishop had been instrumental in founding their College, and had been generous to them with his time and his money. Bateman would be missed, and most scholars felt the world was a poorer place without him in it.

The atmosphere in the church changed after the announcement, and the excited discussions about whether Michaelhouse or Gonville were better disputants were forgotten as scholars exchanged reminiscences of Bateman's gentleness and integrity. Bottisham was affected particularly. His face was grey and sad, and Bartholomew thought he had aged ten years within a few moments.

'I cannot tell you how much we will miss him,' he said to Bartholomew. Rougham was nearby, and came to join them. 'I hope Gonville will not flounder now he is not here to protect us.'

'I do not see why it should,' said Bartholomew, surprised that Bottisham should think his College so frail. 'It is well established, with its own endowments and properties to pay for its running. Michaelhouse lost its founder within three years, but we are still here.'

'However, we are talking about a superior institution when we discuss Gonville,' interposed Rougham haughtily. 'Not some run-down place like Michaelhouse.'

Bartholomew gaped at him, thinking it was small wonder that so many academic institutions were at each other's throats if they made a habit of issuing such brazen insults. Unwilling to allow such rudeness to pass unremarked, he addressed Rougham icily. 'Our theologians are second to none, and Wynewyk is one of the best civil lawyers in the country.'

'Michaelhouse is a mixture of good and bad,' said Rougham, his voice equally chilly. 'Suttone, Kenyngham, Wynewyk, Clippesby – and even the hedonistic Michael – are acceptable. Langelee and William are not. You *would* be, if you paid more heed to traditional wisdom and less to heretical notions invented by men like Roger Bacon.'

'I was most interested in Bacon's analysis of the rate of time-drift at the equinox,' said Bottisham hastily, hoping to prevent a quarrel. 'He calculated that the removal of a day from the Julian calendar every one hundred and twenty-five years – rather than the Gregorian adjustment of three days in every four hundred – will hold the equinox steady.'

'Fascinating,' said Rougham nastily. 'And why did Bacon imagine we would be interested in such irrelevant matters?'

'Probably because you need an accurate calendar to calculate horoscopes,' retorted Bartholomew, knowing the great store Rougham set by determining courses of treatment based on the alignment of the heavenly bodies – something Bartholomew had long since decided was of little practical value. It felt good to catch the man in an inconsistency.

Bottisham intervened a second time when he saw Rougham's eyes narrow in anger. 'Wynewyk tells me you prescribed him an excellent potion containing essence of rhubarb to strengthen his bowels, Bartholomew. I have suffered from a—'

'I would never allow a patient of mine to consume rhubarb,' interrupted Rougham disdainfully. 'It leads the bowels to empty completely and without control. Besides, it is poisonous.'

'I use the stems, which are safe in small amounts,' argued Bartholomew. 'Rhubarb is no different from any other commonly used ingredient: a little is beneficial, too much can cause harm. The same is true of lily of the valley, for example, which we all use to ease the heart – but it can stop one dead, if a patient swallows too much.'

'You should not be discussing dangerous compounds here,' said Chancellor Tynkell, advancing on them on a waft of bad air. Instinctively, all three scholars took a step backwards. 'Not with poor Bishop Bateman dead from such a mixture.'

'We do not know for certain he was poisoned,' Bottisham pointed out. 'The messenger said it was rumour, not fact. Still, I am told some poisons are impossible to detect once swallowed, so perhaps someone killed him with one of those.'

'I suppose *you* know about such substances?' said Tynkell to Bartholomew, stepping closer while the physician tried to hold his breath. 'Which poisons to use in those sorts of circumstances?'

'I do not,' replied Bartholomew, feeling as though Tynkell was trying to recruit him for something sinister. A man like the Chancellor had plenty of enemies, and Bartholomew hoped he had not decided that what worked in Avignon would be suitable for use in Cambridge, and intended to employ a personal poisoner on his staff. He was aware that Rougham and Bottisham were eyeing him curiously, puzzled and intrigued by Tynkell's questions.

'What kind of poison killed Bateman, do you think?' pressed Tynkell, his attention still firmly fixed on Bartholomew.

'I really have no idea,' said Bartholomew, wishing the Chancellor would talk about something else. It was clear from the expression on Rougham's face that he thought Tynkell might have some specific reason for asking his rival physician about such matters, and Bartholomew did not want him to leave with the impression that Michaelhouse men knew all about potions that could kill.

'Well, think about it, and if anything occurs, let me know,' said Tynkell, moving towards Michael and Langelee, who were conversing in low, serious voices. Bartholomew took a deep breath of untainted air, then became aware that Rougham and Bottisham were regarding him with distinct unease.

'It is odd that he should choose to ask *you* about the nature of Bateman's death,' said Rougham bluntly, making it sound like an accusation.

'I cannot imagine why he did that,' said Bartholomew, unsettled.

'I can,' said Rougham. 'You alone of the Cambridge physicians read the kinds of books where such information might be found. You know more about poisons than the rest of us put together.'

'Take me home, Rougham,' said Bottisham, when he saw Bartholomew draw breath to take issue. 'Bateman's death has distressed me, and I need to lie down.'

Rougham began fussing around his colleague, making loud, confident proclamations about the remedies he prescribed for shocks, while Bottisham turned to Bartholomew and winked. Bartholomew smiled, grateful that he had been spared from wasting more time with a man of narrow vision like Rougham. He was about to leave the church when he saw himself summoned by a peremptory flick of Michael's fat, white hand. He disliked the way Michael brandished his plump digits and expected people to come scurrying, so he ignored him. He did not get far, however. As he passed the place where the monk conferred with Langelee and Tynkell, a powerful hand shot out and grabbed him. He tried to free himself from Langelee's vicelike grip, but it was impossible without an undignified struggle. The Master of Michaelhouse was a very strong man.

'We are talking about Thorpe and Mortimer,' said Michael, ignoring Bartholomew's irritation at being manhandled. 'Chancellor Tynkell made some enquiries in Westminster, regarding why they were pardoned. The official reason is that there was some question about the legality of the evidence that convicted them. That is why they have been declared free men again.'

'But they both confessed to what they did – murder and theft!' exclaimed Langelee, outraged. 'I heard them myself. And Wynewyk, who is an excellent lawyer, said there was no legitimate argument for overturning their convictions.'

'Apparently, the Mortimers wanted to clear the family name, so decided to appeal against the verdict,' explained Tynkell. 'The law-clerks contacted the Sheriff of Cambridgeshire, and asked for more details. Unfortunately, the Sheriff at the time was not Tulyet.'

'It was Morice,' snarled Langelee, railing at the combination of circumstances that had led to an injustice. 'That corrupt vagabond was Sheriff for a brief period last year.'

'It seems the Mortimers paid Morice to sign a letter urging the clerks to clemency,' Tynkell went on. '*Then* the clerks cooked up their excuse about the evidence being inadmissible. Rumour has it that gold changed hands there, too. So, the upshot is that Thorpe and Mortimer were able

73

to buy a King's Pardon. I thought they would stay away – that a sense of shame would prevent them from showing their faces here – but I was wrong.'

'They may kill again,' warned Langelee, as if he imagined the others needed to be told.

'They will not find it easy,' said Michael. 'My beadles and Dick Tulyet's soldiers will be watching their every move. But we will not be able to do so for long.'

'Why not?' asked Langelee. 'Because you need your peace-keepers for other duties?'

'Because the Mortimers have threatened to sue if we harass their Edward,' explained Tynkell. 'We cannot afford to pay huge sums in compensation because his liberty is being curtailed.'

Bartholomew gazed at him. '*His* liberty? What about the liberty of the people who are dead because of him and Thorpe? This is not justice!'

'No, but it is the law,' said Tynkell flatly. 'None of us want that pair in our town, but they have the King's Pardon, and there is nothing we can do about it.'

'But this is preposterous!' exclaimed Langelee furiously. 'They are criminals!'

Tynkell sighed. 'You are not listening, Master Langelee. The law is not about who is the criminal and who is the aggrieved. It is about enforcing a set of rules. And those rules have just put Thorpe and Mortimer in the right.'

Bartholomew started to walk home, Tynkell's words echoing in his mind. He could not believe that self-confessed killers were not only free to wander where they liked, but were enjoying protection by the very laws that should have condemned them. He was grateful his sister and brother-in-law were away, and hoped Mortimer and Thorpe would have tired of their sport and left before they returned.

He had not travelled far when he saw the town's wealthiest merchant, Thomas Deschalers, riding along the High Street on an expensive-looking horse. Despite his fine, jewel-sewn clothes, the grocer looked ill, and Bartholomew's professional instincts told him there was something seriously amiss with his health. Oddly, the madwoman who had discovered Bosel's corpse was trailing behind him. Bartholomew studied her, noting her flat, dead eyes, and wondered what she and Deschalers planned to do together. They were odd bedfellows, to say the least.

Deschalers reeled suddenly, and something slipped from his hand to the ground. He righted himself, then gazed at the thing that had fallen, as though asking himself whether retrieving it was worth the effort. Since the woman did not attempt to help, Bartholomew went to pick it up for him. It was a leather purse, heavy with coins and embossed with the emblem that represented Deschalers's wares: a pot with the letter D emblazoned across it. This distinctive motif was also engraved in the lintel above the door to his house, and it often appeared on the goods he sold.

'Thank you,' said Deschalers, taking the purse gratefully. 'I would have had to dismount to get that, and I do not know whether I have the strength.'

'You could have asked her,' said Bartholomew, indicating the woman, whose dirty hand rested on the grocer's splendid saddle. She regarded him blankly, and he realised that his earlier sense that he knew her had been wrong. There *was* something familiar about her face and the colour of her hair, but the familiarity was simply because she reminded him of someone else. However, the woman who looked similar hovered just outside his memory.

'She is slow in the wits,' said Deschalers. 'It would have been just as much trouble to make her understand what I wanted as to collect it myself. I do not have the will for either.'

'You are unwell?' asked Bartholomew, since Deschalers seemed to expect such an enquiry.

'Very,' said Deschalers. 'Rougham says I will recover my former vigour, but I know that whatever is rotting inside will soon kill me. I do not think any physician in England can help me now, not even one who flies in the face of convention to affect his cures. But thank you for the offer, anyway.'

'You are welcome,' said Bartholomew, who would never have done any such thing. First, he seldom saw eye to eye with the laconic, aloof grocer and suspected Deschalers would be a difficult patient, arguing over every scrap of treatment and advice. Second, Rougham would not appreciate the poaching of his wealthiest patient. And third, Bartholomew knew Deschalers's self-diagnosis had been correct: he already walked hand in hand with death, and no physician could snatch him back.

Deschalers rode on with the woman in tow, and Bartholomew watched him acknowledge Rougham and Bottisham with a weary wave as he passed. Rougham called something about a new tincture of lavender that he claimed would make the grocer a new man, but Deschalers shot him a bleak look that made him falter into silence. Sickness made Bartholomew think of Isnard, who had been stricken with a mild fever earlier that morning. He recalled his concern, and started to stride towards the Mill Pond.

'Slow down, Matt!' came a breathless voice from behind him. He turned to see Paxtone, the Master of Medicine from King's Hall, hurrying after him. 'I have been chasing you all along the High Street, shouting your name, and you have ignored me completely.'

Bartholomew smiled. He liked Paxtone, who was merry faced with twinkling grey eyes and rosy cheeks, like russet apples in the autumn. He was a large man, although not as big as Michael, and usually moved slowly when he walked, as if his weight was too much for the joints in his knees and he needed to proceed with care lest they collapse. But he had a sharp mind and was willing to listen to some of Bartholomew's more exotic medical theories, even if he did not usually agree with them.

Paxtone held Bartholomew's arm, and used it as a prop while he recovered his breath. 'You were racing along like Thomas Mortimer's cart,' he gasped.

'That was what I was thinking about,' said Bartholomew. 'Mortimer escaping justice because Bosel is dead. His nephew buying a King's Pardon.'

'My College's lawyers discussed those King's Pardons at length yesterday. They concluded that if we appeal against them, we are essentially saying that His Majesty is wrong – and that might be construed as treason. We will be fined far more than we can pay, just to teach us never to challenge the royal courts, no matter how wicked and corrupt their decisions.'

'It is a depressing state of affairs.'

'It is an appalling state of affairs, but a decision has been made in the King's name, and we must live with the consequences. I heard you were instrumental in catching Thorpe and Edward Mortimer, so you had better be careful of them.'

'I played a very small part in their downfall. There were others who did far more to bring them to justice than me – Michael, my brother-in-law, Sheriff Tulyet, Master Langelee, various soldiers from the Castle, and even Michael's grandmother, Dame Pelagia.'

'They were overheard bragging to some of Edward's cousins in the Market Square the other day. They said they intended to repay *everyone* who played *any* role in their capture. Your name was among the many they listed, so do not think they have forgotten whatever it was you did. It is a pity you allowed your book-bearer to accompany your sister to Huntingdon. If you ever needed his ready sword it is now.'

'I can look after myself.'

Paxtone patted his arm. 'I know. But you can allow a friend to show a little concern. Remember that if anything happens to you, I shall be left with Lynton and Rougham – and neither of *them* will discuss Arab medicine with me.'

Bartholomew smiled. 'We can learn a great deal from the Arab world. For example, did you know that there is a hospital in Egypt that can house *eight thousand* patients simultaneously? It teems with physicians, apothecaries and folk to cater to the patients' daily needs. If a man is sick in the stomach, then a physician who knows about stomachs will tend him. If he has a hardened spleen, then the physician who studies spleens will come.'

'I do not think that is a good system. Your expert in spleens may concentrate on the one part of the body he loves to the exclusion of all else, and ignore other, more serious, ailments.'

'Perhaps,' admitted Bartholomew. 'But I would like to know more about this place – how many inmates are cured and how many die. However, for now, I am only going to visit Isnard.'

'I heard *you* performed his surgery,' said Paxtone disapprovingly. 'You must not demean yourself by undertaking such base tasks. Would you sharpen your students' pens or replace the wax on their writing tablets? No! And you should not dabble in cautery, either. It is a filthy business, and best left to the likes of Robin of Grantchester, who is a filthy man.'

'Exactly,' said Bartholomew, irritated that Paxtone should preach at him. 'That is why so many of his patients do not survive his operations. I do not want Isnard to die, when I know I can save him.'

'We should not argue,' said Paxtone, seeing he was close

to overstepping the boundaries of their friendship. 'I am only trying to warn you. I do not want Rougham to use your fascination with surgery to discredit you. He is jealous of you, and would love to see you fall from grace.'

'That is what Michael says, but he can have no quarrel with me. I have done him no harm.'

'Let us discuss Isnard instead,' said Paxtone with a sigh, seeing they would not agree. 'What method did you employ to prevent the fever that usually follows the removal of a limb? Did you attempt to rebalance the humours by purging and bleeding?'

'Yes and no,' said Bartholomew. 'It *is* important to restore the balance of humours, but my teacher Ibn Ibrahim maintained that this is best achieved by a poultice of yarrow and ensuring the injury is free to drain. Tightly wrapped wounds fester, because they trap evil humours. Rather than drawing them off by purges, I find it is better to let them ooze away of their own accord.'

Paxtone was sceptical, and they were still debating the issue in a friendly way when they reached Isnard's house. Bartholomew tapped on the door, aware of voices within. Isnard had more visitors. He was surprised to see Walter, Michaelhouse's porter, there with his cockerel tucked under his arm.

'I thought Isnard might like to see Bird,' said Walter, standing when the physicians entered. 'He often brings a smile to a sick man's face.'

'I am not sick,' said Isnard, who was sitting up in his bed and looking more hale and hearty than the pallid Walter. 'I am temporarily incapacitated.' He pronounced the last two words carefully, evidently unused to them. 'At least, that is what Master Bottisham says. Robert de Blaston the carpenter is going to make me a leg of wood. He is even carving a foot on it, with proper toes.'

'Good,' said Bartholomew, easing away from Walter when

he became aware that the cockerel had fixed its mean little eyes on him, evidently sizing him up as something to peck.

'Thank you for bringing him, Walter,' said Isnard. 'But next time, I would prefer a wench. Even Agatha would do. I have not set eyes on a woman for five days now, and I am desperate.'

'Is there anything else?' asked Walter archly, offended that Bird should be regarded as second best to a woman. Walter had no time for ladies, which was why he was so well suited for life in a College like Michaelhouse, where, with the exception of Agatha, they were forbidden to enter.

'Yes,' said Isnard. 'I would like to hear the choir. Can you ask Michael to bring them? I have a fancy for a little music.'

'You are wrong,' murmured Paxtone to Bartholomew. 'The man is not healing after all. In fact, he is deranged and out of his wits. I can think of no other explanation for anyone willingly subjecting himself to the unholy caterwauling that passes for music among the Michaelhouse choir.'

'Bishop Bateman's death will be a blow to Gonville Hall,' said Michael, not without malice, after the noon meal the following day. 'His patronage was useful, and they will miss it now he has gone – especially since they have just started to build that chapel.'

He was sitting in the conclave at Michaelhouse, a pleasantly comfortable chamber with a wooden floor and tapestries that took the chill from the stone walls. The College's books were housed both there and in the hall, attached to their shelves by thick chains to ensure no one made off with them; books were rare and expensive, and no institution risked having them stolen. Each week, one of the Fellows was detailed to dust them and conduct an inventory, to make sure none were missing.

Because the weather was still cold for the time of year, the conclave's window shutters were closed, even though it was the middle of the day. The fire in the hearth sent a homely orange glow around the room, accompanied by the earthy scent of burning peat. There had once been glass in the windows, but a series of accidents had resulted in too many breakages, and Langelee had finally thrown up his hands in despair, claiming that the College could not fund repairs each time there was a mishap. Michaelhouse's Fellows were forced to make a daily choice between a light room that was cold, or a dark one that was warm.

The Fellows often gathered in the conclave on Sundays, to while away the hours until it was time to eat or sleep, while the students tended to claim the larger, but less comfortable hall next door. Michaelhouse had eight Fellows, including the Master, and all were present that afternoon. Some were trying to read by the flickering light of a wall torch, and others were just enjoying the opportunity to relax after a morning of masses.

Langelee occupied the best chair, not because he was Master, but because he was strong and better equipped to seize it in the customary post-prandial scramble for seats. The elderly Gilbertine friar Kenyngham perched next to him, staring into the flames as he recited a prayer, wholly oblivious to the desultory conversations that were taking place around him. On Langelee's other side, the gloomy Carmelite Thomas Suttone was informing Wynewyk that the plague would return in the next year or so, and kill everyone it had missed the first time round. Wynewyk was pretending to be asleep.

Bartholomew and Michael sat at a table together. Bartholomew was sharpening the knives he used for the surgery of which his colleagues so disapproved, while Michael studied the message Master Colton of Gonville

Hall had written to Chancellor Tynkell regarding the death of Bishop Bateman, looking for inner meanings that were not there. Meanwhile, the Dominican John Clippesby, who was Master of Music and Astronomy, watched the physician intently, like a cat waiting at the hole of a mouse. It was common knowledge, not only at Michaelhouse but throughout the town, that Clippesby was insane, largely because he held frequent and public conversations with animals and dead saints. His insanity did not usually induce bouts of unwavering scrutiny, however, and Bartholomew found it disconcerting. He tried to ignore him.

'How will Gonville pay for their fine chapel with Bateman dead?' asked the Franciscan Father William with spiteful satisfaction. He was the last of the Fellows, and occupied a comfortable wicker chair opposite Clippesby. He answered his own question gleefully. 'They will not, and they will be left with a scrap of bare land and a few foundations for ever.'

William had once been Michael's Junior Proctor, but had performed his duties with such enthusiasm and vigour that even peaceful and law-abiding scholars were not safe from fines and imprisonment. Everyone had heaved a sigh of relief when he had been 'promoted' to Keeper of the University Chest. However, while most scholars were relieved to see him occupying what they considered a harmless post, Bartholomew was concerned. It was William who had revived interest in the dubious Hand of Valence Marie, using his new authority to rescue the so-called relic from the depths of the Chest and bring it back to the public's attention by putting it on display.

'Gonville's chapel will be a very grand building,' said Wynewyk, interrupting Suttone's tirade about the plague. 'It will have similar dimensions to one I saw in Albi, in southern France.'

'Pride is a terrible sin,' proclaimed Suttone in his

sepulchral voice. 'It was pride that drove the scholars of Gonville to build themselves a chapel, and God is showing them the error of their ways by taking away the man who might have paid for it.'

'I do not follow your logic,' said Bartholomew, looking up from his knives. 'Are you saying God does not approve of chapels being built? If that is the case we should raze St Michael's to the ground, and conduct our offices in the graveyard instead.'

Suttone glared at him. 'That is different. Michaelhouse men are not hedgerow priests!'

'Neither are the scholars of Gonville. They are only doing what our founder did for us thirty years ago. What is wrong with a College wanting its own chapel? Would *you* like to be in a position where you had to vie for space with half a dozen other institutions in St Mary the Great?'

'Gonville's building is sinful,' persisted Suttone staunchly. 'And it is pride and false humility that will have the Death yapping at our heels again. You mark my words.'

'It is a pity Warde declared Gonville the winner of the *Disputatio* yesterday,' said Kenyngham, aiming to prevent a squabble. He abhorred discord and was always trying to keep the peace in his College – which was no mean feat when there were belligerent and opinionated men like William, Suttone and Langelee to contend with, to say nothing of the lunatic Clippesby. Bartholomew glanced up from his whetting and saw the Master of Music and Astronomy still staring at him. He went back to ignoring him, hoping the Dominican would soon fix his manic gaze on something else.

'We were shamefully wronged by Warde,' said William angrily. 'Even the most stupid of mediators must have seen that *we* had superior arguments and that *we* debated with better skill.'

'Warde is from Valence Marie, so what do you expect?'

83

said Suttone glumly. 'I imagine Gonville bribed him to grant them the victory.'

'They did not!' exclaimed Bartholomew, laughing at the notion that Gonville would stoop to such a low trick – and that Warde would accept the offer. 'It was a perfectly fair contest, and Warde was right: Gonville did outperform us yesterday.'

'Gonville won because the Question was about law,' grumbled William. 'It was an unfair choice on Tynkell's part, because all Gonville's scholars, with the exception of Rougham, are lawyers.'

'Gonville played us very fairly,' argued Bartholomew. 'They used Rougham as one of their disputants – and he is not a lawyer, as you pointed out. They could have supplied three lawyers, not two and a physician. What is wrong, Clippesby?' He was unable to stand the unblinking gaze any longer. 'You are making me nervous, and I do not want to slip and cut myself.'

'I do not know why you possess knives,' said Clippesby coldly. 'You are supposed to be a physician, not a surgeon, so you should not need such implements. The rats by the river told me that you severed the bargeman's leg on Wednesday night. It is not natural.'

'The rats are right, Matt,' said Langelee from the hearth. 'You should not perform surgery. First, it is forbidden for those in holy orders to practise cautery, and second, Robin of Grantchester will accuse you of poaching his trade again. We do not want a dispute between you and him to spill over and become a fight between scholars and townsfolk.'

'I am not bound by the edicts of the Lateran Councils,' said Bartholomew, referring to a writ of 1284 that forbade clerics to practise surgery. 'I am not a monk or a friar. And what would you have had me do? Wait for Robin to finish his ale at the King's Head, while Isnard bled to death?'

'Isnard would be dead for certain if Robin had got at

him,' agreed Wynewyk. 'Matt saved his life, so leave him alone, Clippesby.'

'Now there are four physicians in Cambridge, you should be more careful, Matt,' advised Michael, not for the first time. 'You have an odd reputation with your penchant for knives, and you will lose more customers to Paxtone and Rougham if you do not watch out.'

'What are they like?' asked Langelee conversationally. 'As medical men? I have met them both, of course, and Paxtone seems a decent fellow, although I did not take to Rougham.'

'Rougham is ambitious and aggressive,' stated William in his uncompromising manner. 'I do not like him.' He folded his arms, as if he considered the discussion over now that he had had his say. This was one of the reasons why he was never allowed to represent Michaelhouse at debates.

'Paxtone is a good physician,' replied Bartholomew. 'But Rougham tends to dismiss any theories that are not written down in Latin or Greek.'

'Does he slice his patients up with sharp knives?' asked Langelee meaningfully.

'No,' said Bartholomew, becoming tired of pointing out that his most important duty was to save or cure a patient, and if that involved surgery, then it was his moral obligation to offer that choice. The patient could always decline the treatment, if he did not want it.

'Then neither should you,' said Langelee. 'I do not want you accused of witchcraft. It would be embarrassing for the College if you were put to death or exiled for unseemly practices.'

'I will bear it in mind,' muttered Bartholomew, sharpening his knives more vigorously and sorely tempted to practise a little surgery on some of his colleagues.

*   *   *

'Has everyone heard the news about the town's mills?' asked Michael that evening, after Langelee had produced a cask of wine as an unexpected Sunday treat, and the Fellows were in a more mellow frame of mind as they relaxed in the conclave. Bartholomew's knives were back in his bag, and he was scanning a tract on the Book of Job by the famous scholar Robert Grosseteste – which was sufficiently uncontroversial to offend no one.

'What about them?' asked William drowsily. He had drunk twice as much as everyone else, and it had had a soporific effect on him. This suited his colleagues very well.

'There is a dispute brewing between them over water,' said Michael. 'I detect Edward Mortimer's hand in it personally, because his uncle's fulling mill and the King's Mill worked perfectly harmoniously together until *he* came back.'

'Edward Mortimer and that Thorpe are always together,' said Clippesby, who had a sleepy grass-snake in his lap. 'A ram at the Market Square said they are lovers, although I do not know whether to believe him. However, the Gonville cat, who gets around at night, informed me that Master Thorpe of Valence Marie will not have his son in his College. Young Thorpe is living with the Mortimers.'

'Is he now?' mused Michael. Clippesby was often in possession of valuable information, although the sources he claimed for it were invariably improbable. Most of his conversations sounded like the ramblings of a deranged mind, but experience had taught the monk that Clippesby was often well informed, so he usually made some effort to distil the truth from the wild fantasies that encased it.

'Master Thorpe told *me* he was appalled when his son appeared at Valence Marie and demanded to be welcomed home,' said William, not to be outdone with the gossip. 'He had no hand in obtaining the King's Pardon, and he wants no part of his boy.'

'I visited Master Thorpe yesterday,' said Langelee, joining in the competition to see who had the most news. 'He said the Mortimers had told him they planned to get a King's Pardon for his son and Edward, but he did nothing about it, because he sincerely believed that the King had no reason to grant one – their guilt was too clear. But he underestimated the power of bribery.'

'The Mortimers *did* bribe the King's Bench clerks,' said Clippesby. 'One of the swans – who flies near Westminster at this time of year – told me he saw gold changing hands.'

'Poor Master Thorpe,' said William. 'His son is a dangerous man, and it took real courage for the father to disown him. I would not want someone like young Thorpe angry with *me.*'

Michael nodded, a little impatiently. 'He is brave. But none of this has any relevance to what I am trying to tell you about the mills. We all know that the King owns the King's Mill, and that a profit-making guild called the Millers' Society leases it from him.'

'The Millers' Society comprises the apothecary Lavenham and his hussy wife Isobel, Cheney the spice merchant, Deschalers the grocer and Bernarde the miller – miserable sinners, every one,' said Suttone, who enjoyed listing people who would die when the plague next came. 'And Mayor Morice.'

'*Mayor* Morice!' spat Langelee in disgust. 'I could not believe it when that dishonest scoundrel was elected. Look what happened when he was Sheriff! He was so brazen with his corruption that it took my breath away.'

'It is *his* fault that Thorpe and Edward are back,' agreed William. 'He accepted gold from the Mortimers, in return for a letter saying our town had no objection to the pardons being issued.'

Michael gave an irritable sigh, to indicate that their interruptions were interfering with his tale. He spoke loudly. 'So, we have the King's Mill, leased from the King by the Millers' Society. And Mortimer's Mill – owned by Thomas Mortimer – is *upstream* from it. And we all know that Mortimer's Mill was recently converted from grinding grain to fulling cloth.' He gazed around, pursing his lips, as if he imagined he had made a significant point.

'So?' asked William eventually. 'What of it?'

Michael grimaced at his slow wits. 'Fulling needs more water than grinding corn – or so I am told – and the Mortimers keep diverting water for the process, so the King's Mill cannot operate. They refuse to settle the matter amicably, so it has gone before the King's Bench for a decision.'

'Then doubtless there will be more bribery taking place as we speak,' said Langelee acidly. 'It seems to me that the King's clerks will make any decision you like, as long as you have the funds to pay for it. I knew they were corrupt, but—'

'What did you think of my sermon this morning?' interrupted William. They had discussed the subject of corruption among the King's officers at length that afternoon, and he was bored with it. However, he was proud of his work in the church earlier that day, and clearly felt that some compliments were in order.

'It did not dwell sufficiently on the Death,' replied Suttone immediately. 'It is our duty to point out that it *will* return, and that we will all die unless we repent of our sins.'

'I repent every day,' said William, the tone of his voice indicating he did not think he had much to confess. 'And folk are growing tired of hearing about the Death each Sunday. They want something more inspiring, and my oration today was just that. They need to hear about the fire and brimstone of Hell.' William knew far more about Hell than Bartholomew felt he should have done.

'It was about how God killed a man called Uzzah for daring to touch the Ark of the Covenant,' said Clippesby. 'I was listening to you, William. The oxen carrying the Ark stumbled, and Uzzah tried to stop it from falling to the ground. He was struck dead for his audacity, but the oxen survived, so it was a tale with a happy ending.'

'I do not think the cattle are relevant to the story,' said William stiffly. 'My point was that anyone who does not treat sacred objects with respect and reverence will be similarly struck down. They will end up roasting in the Devil's cauldrons, surrounded by screaming demons with—'

'You were referring to the Hand of Valence Marie,' interrupted Michael distastefully. 'Your message was quite clear: anyone who disbelieves in the Hand's power is ripe for holy vengeance.'

'Precisely,' said William comfortably. 'I would not like my colleagues to vanish in a column of fire for treating holy relics with disrespect.' He shot a meaningful look in Bartholomew's direction.

'I have every respect for holy relics,' replied Bartholomew, tired of being the one always accused of heresy and irreverence. 'I would never dare touch a real one. But the Hand is *not* a real one – it belonged to Peterkin Starre. You were using your sermon as an opportunity to tout for business: you want folk to visit the relic, so you can charge them to see it.'

'Yes,' agreed William, pleased with himself. 'Many folk flock to it with their prayers and petitions, and I am keen to give others the opportunity to—'

There was a knock at the door, and Quenhyth entered. The student marched across the conclave, heading for Bartholomew. There was a book under his arm that he made sure everyone noticed, so they would know that while the other students were chatting or playing games in the hall, he had devoted himself to more serious pursuits.

'The reading of academic texts on a Sunday is forbidden,' snapped William when he saw it. 'You will be bound for Hell if you disregard the proscriptions for this most holy of days.'

'It is a theological text,' replied Quenhyth virtuously. With one hand he proffered it for the Franciscan to inspect, while the other went to his mouth for the nails to be gnawed. 'It is an analysis of the Question: Let us debate whether the Body of Christ became different after His soul separated from it.'

'You do not need texts to answer that question, boy,' growled William. 'I can tell you. No.'

'A most eloquent argument, Father,' said Michael drolly. 'Gonville must be quaking in their boots in anticipation of meeting that kind of incisive logic at the next *Disputatio*.'

William nodded his pleasure at the compliment, and folded his arms. 'However, I *have* read that particular text, as it happens. Well, not the whole thing, I admit – I just went straight to the end and looked at the conclusion. I do not waste my time reading silly twists and turns, not when there are heretics to unveil and the University Chest to protect.'

'I see you chose well in becoming a scholar,' said Wynewyk, raising his eyebrows in amusement. 'Why would a theologian bother with "silly twists and turns" in a scholarly debate?'

'Quite,' agreed William, the irony quite lost on him.

'Sergeant Orwelle is here, sir,' said Quenhyth to Bartholomew, bewildered by the exchange. His literal mind rendered him no better with irony than did William's. 'There has been an incident at the King's Mill, and you are needed. He says Brother Michael should come, too, since one of the fatalities might be a scholar.'

'*One* of the fatalities?' queried Michael, reaching for his cloak. 'I do not like the sound of this.'

CHAPTER 3

Bartholomew and Michael hurried along streets that were dark grey with dusk. It was a cold evening, and the physician could see his breath pluming in front of him as he walked. He wondered whether there would be a frost that night. The previous winter had been one of the coldest anyone could recall, when snows had choked the roads and sealed the town from the outside world for days. The river had frozen, too, and the town's watermills had been unable to operate, because the millers were afraid the ice would damage their machinery. This had driven up the price of flour, and people had died of starvation before winter had finally loosened its frigid grip.

There was a stiff breeze that Sunday evening, which meant the smoke that rose from hundreds of fires was blown away, rather than hanging over the town in a choking pall. Bartholomew could see the first stars appearing in the dark-blue sky and, when he breathed deeply, he detected not only the sulphurous stink of the marshes that lay to the north, but the more pleasant scent of early spring. He had seen primroses near Isnard's house earlier that day, little lemon spots on a scrubby bank.

Sergeant Orwelle led the way. He was a grizzled veteran of the French wars, who usually worked at the Trumpington Gate, where he screened any strangers who wanted access to his town. The gate was not far from the King's Mill, so Bartholomew supposed someone had run to him for help when the 'incident' – whatever that was – had unfolded.

'What happened?' he asked as they went, with Orwelle

setting a cracking pace that had the overweight Michael gasping for breath. Bartholomew wondered whether Orwelle's haste was because casualties needed urgent medical assistance, or whether he simply wanted to be back at his familiar post and out of the cold. 'An accident?'

'I would not say that,' replied Orwelle, rather obtusely. 'But then I know little of these things.'

'What things?' panted Michael.

'The dead. You know,' said Orwelle mysteriously.

Bartholomew began to have misgivings about the whole venture. There was a good deal of heavy machinery in a mill, and he had been called to some very unpleasant crushing accidents in the past. He skidded to a standstill.

'Are you sure I am needed? I deal with the living, not the dead. If I have a sinister reputation for performing the odd surgical operation, then that is not going to be made better by my exploring mangled bodies at this hour of the night.'

'You are the University's Corpse Examiner,' pronounced Orwelle uncompromisingly. 'Everyone knows that. You are supposed to look at their deceased. It is your job.'

'It is not!' exclaimed Bartholomew indignantly, appalled that the occasional helping hand he gave to Michael should be seen as an official position. 'I am a physician!'

'You are both,' said Orwelle, unmoved. They had reached the Trumpington Gate. 'This is where we part company, gentlemen. I have no desire to see *that* again.'

'You are looking into the murder of Bosel the beggar,' said Michael, dabbing his sweaty brow with a piece of white linen, as he embarked on another subject. Bartholomew was not the only one who was unwilling to see what awaited him at the King's Mill. 'What have you learned so far?'

'Nothing, despite the fact that I have questioned virtually everyone in the town over the last two days.' Orwelle sounded dispirited. 'Sheriff Tulyet says I should investigate

92

Thorpe and Edward Mortimer, because they are known killers.'

Bartholomew rubbed his chin. 'It would be stupid to start murdering people as soon as they arrive, and they are not fools. Perhaps someone killed Bosel in the hope that they would be blamed.'

Orwelle was appalled. 'But there are hundreds of folk who want that pair gone from our streets! I will never narrow it down to one suspect.' He sighed, and became even more gloomy. 'The Sheriff says I should look at *Thomas* Mortimer, too, because Bosel threatened to be a witness against him. He also suggested I probe the affairs of the madwoman – Bess – who arrived here a few weeks ago.'

'Who is she?' asked Michael. 'And why did you let her into our town, if you thought she might be dangerous?'

'She is not dangerous,' said Orwelle with great certainty. 'And she did not kill Bosel, either. She came mumbling something about finding a lost lover. She is clearly out of her wits, and I thought she might be able to beg a few pennies here before she moves on, poor lass. She is too addled to know about poisons. But it is cold out here, and there is a fire in the gatehouse.' Without another word, he turned and strode away, leaving the two scholars to complete the short journey alone.

'Orwelle is right about your duties as Corpse Examiner,' said Michael, as they passed Peterhouse and began to walk towards the mill, which was a black mass against the darkening sky. 'In fact, I discussed the matter with Tynkell only last week, and we have decided to make the post a permanent one, with a proper stipend.'

'Good,' said Bartholomew with feeling. 'You can offer it to Rougham. He can chase after you in the dead of night looking at sights no physician ever ought to be asked to see. He may even enjoy it.'

'I do not want Rougham,' said Michael. 'I want you. Rougham's mind is too closed to allow him to be of use to me – and do not suggest Paxtone, either. He is a pleasant fellow, but he is unimaginative, and would probably faint if I showed him a corpse.'

'I will not do it,' said Bartholomew firmly. 'It would mean I am never free to refuse you.'

'You never refuse me anyway,' Michael pointed out. 'So you may as well be paid for your trouble. The Chancellor is willing to provide fourpence for every corpse examined. At that rate, it will not take you long to earn enough to buy Roger Bacon's *De erroribus medicorum.* You have wanted a copy of that ever since Paxtone lent you his, and I hear Gonville intends to sell theirs.'

'Buy me the Bacon now, and I will inspect all the corpses you like for the next year,' said Bartholomew, after a moment's thought. 'Rougham disapproves of *De erroribus*, because Bacon uses Arabic sources. He may destroy it, just to prevent student physicians from becoming tainted with ideas that did not originate with Christians.'

'Have you pointed out that Aristotle, Plato and Socrates were not Christians either?' asked Michael archly. 'And that their philosophy forms the basis of nearly all our teaching?'

'He says they are different, although he will not explain why. You know what zealots are like, Brother. They are so convinced that they are right they cannot – or will not – accept the validity of any arguments that contradict their beliefs.'

'The word for them is "bigots",' said Michael. 'And there are far too many of them in this University, especially among the religious Orders. It is astonishing how friaries attract those kind of men. There are fewer in monasteries, like those of my own Order, of course. But you say you will examine bodies for a year if I buy the Bacon for you?'

'From now until next Easter.'

'Done,' said Michael, thinking that he had secured quite a bargain. 'But we are at the King's Mill, and it seems there is a sizeable deputation waiting to greet us.'

'Listen,' said Bartholomew as they made their way along the narrow path that led from the lane to the mill. 'What can you hear?'

'Nothing,' said Michael, cocking his head on one side.

'Quite,' said Bartholomew. 'The wheel is not turning. They must have hauled it clear of the river.'

Considering it was late – well past eight o'clock – and a time when most folk were retiring to their beds, a large number of people were silhouetted against the torch-lit interior of the King's Mill. Bartholomew saw that most of the men who invested in the venture – the Millers' Society – were there, all apparently determined to know what effect the unwelcome presence of a corpse in the premises they rented might have on their finances.

One figure stepped forward, evidently considering himself their spokesman. It was Stephen Morice, a sly, disingenuous man, who had enjoyed a recent short but disastrous reign as Sheriff. He was brazenly corrupt, and everyone had been stunned when he had been elected Mayor that spring. Bartholomew suspected that buying the requisite number of votes had cost him a good deal of money. Morice was a swarthy man, with bright blue eyes, and a black moustache and beard that concealed thin lips. He was slightly hunched, as though he spent a lot of time writing, but Bartholomew knew he would never bother with anything so unproductive when there were folk to be blackmailed and justice to be sold.

'You took your time,' Morice remarked unpleasantly, as they approached. 'Why are you so late?'

'Who else is here?' asked Michael, peering into the

gloom. 'Why are they not by their firesides or in bed, like all honest folk at such an hour? Have guilty consciences lured them out?'

'The Millers' Society has a lot of money tied up in the King's Mill,' replied Morice testily. 'How could we sleep without knowing what was going on? Would you retire to *your* feather mattress without first ensuring that your hard-earned gold was safe?'

'Safe from what?' asked Michael.

'Safe from wicked men trying to prevent our mill from operating,' snapped Morice impatiently, as though the answer should have been obvious. 'The most serious crime committed here is not murder, Brother. It is sabotage.'

'And we know exactly who is responsible,' added Gilbert Bernarde the miller, coming to join them. Of all the Society, Bernarde had the most to lose, since his entire livelihood was based on the efficient running of the mill; for the others, it was simply a way of seeing a good return on money already made. Bernarde was of stocky build, and possessed far too many teeth for his mouth: they clustered against each other like drunken soldiers. The ball of his right thumb was flattened from years of testing the dressing of his millstones, and he had a persistent dry cough from the dust he inhaled on a daily basis. He always carried a large bunch of keys on his belt, as if he imagined flaunting such an impressive collection made him an important person.

'Who do you think is responsible?' asked Michael, always ready to listen to accusations that might lead to a speedy solution – although he would, of course, make up his own mind about their validity.

'The Mortimers, of course,' replied Bernarde, as if he considered Michael a simpleton for asking. 'They want to put me and my mill out of business. Did you hear that Thomas tried to kill me with his cart last month? He knocked me right on top of that massive snow bank outside Bene't College – before it melted, of course.'

'There was a corpse inside that, you know,' said Morice conversationally. 'Sheriff Tulyet told me. A man died there around Christmas, and remained covered by drifts until Master Kenyngham of Michaelhouse happened to notice a hand sticking out. No one knows who he was.' He shuddered. 'A corpse on the High Street all those weeks!'

Bernarde nodded. 'They say his indignant soul cries out on windy nights, angry that it took us so long to find him. However, I heard no wailing when Mortimer knocked me clean off my feet and on to his frozen tomb. All I heard was my ears ringing from the impact of my head on the ice.' He addressed Michael. 'Did *you* know about this? It was attempted murder!'

'It is a pity you did not tell the Sheriff, then,' said Michael coolly. 'It might have helped Lenne and Isnard. There was no icy bank to save *them* from Mortimer's thundering wheels.'

'A lone man does not take a stand against the Mortimers,' said Bernarde. 'Look what happened to Bosel the beggar, when he tried to speak out. But tonight's business is different: I have the Millers' Society on my side this time, and even Mortimer cannot silence us all. Besides me and Morice, there is Deschalers the grocer and Cheney the spicer. Cheney is over there.' He indicated a portly man with a red hat and matching face, who was staring uneasily at the stationary waterwheel.

'Do not forget Lavenham and his wife Isobel,' added Morice, indicating the couple who stood next to the spicer. 'Lavenham may be a newcomer to our town, but he is a wealthy fellow.'

Lavenham the apothecary was a tall, angular man with a weather-beaten face, keen grey eyes and silver hair. He was not, however, from the Suffolk wool village, but from

Norway, and his name – selected randomly, as far as Bartholomew could tell – was intended to make people believe he was local, on the grounds that some folk declined to take their business to foreigners. Unfortunately for Lavenham, the ploy would never work as long as he continued to speak eccentric English with an almost unintelligible accent.

His English wife Isobel was soft and voluptuous, with moist red lips and a predatory manner. Bartholomew's students always argued about who should collect his medicines from Lavenham's shop, and he knew it was not because they wanted to converse with the Norwegian. His own feelings towards her were ambiguous: he admired her spirit, but distrusted her sincerity. However, since she sold the ingredients he needed for his remedies, he was obliged to develop a working relationship with her, although it was sometimes difficult to repel some of her more determined advances.

'So, what happened inside the mill?' he asked. 'Who is dead? Orwelle said it might be a scholar.'

'We are not sure,' replied Morice mysteriously. 'Look for yourself.'

He gestured that they should enter the mill, a sturdy affair with a reed-thatched roof and wattle-and-daub walls. About a third of the building held the machinery that drove the millstones against each other, and the rest was used for stacking waiting grain, or was given over to the bins and equipment employed for weighing and sifting the finished product. Bartholomew had once been inside when the wheel was running and had been almost deafened by the clanking of wooden gears and the gush of water, but now it stood eerily still. Only the hiss of the river through its centre broke the silence.

He pushed open the door and stepped across the threshold. The instant he did so, dust caught at the back of his throat and made his eyes feel gritty. Next to him Michael sneezed. The mill was well lit, with several torches burning in sconces along the walls, ready for those occasions when the miller was obliged to operate in the dark in order to meet the demand for flour.

'Will you show us the way?' Bartholomew called to Bernarde, wanting someone to take them directly to the scene of the crime. He did not want to waste time blundering around a building he did not know in search of some undefined 'incident'.

'Look near the wheel,' recommended Morice, making no move to comply. 'We will stay here and wait for the Sheriff.'

'I will lead you,' said Bernarde unhappily, pushing past the Mayor to enter his domain. 'Seeing *them* will serve to remind me to take care when I work among the wheels and cogs.'

With considerable misgivings, Bartholomew and Michael followed him to the room that housed the machinery. Then the physician understood exactly why the others had been reluctant to accompany him. Two men lay tangled among the gears, both dead. It was not a pleasant sight, with skin split like overripe fruit and bones protruding from where they should not have been. Bartholomew heard Michael's sharp intake of breath as he backed away.

'That one is stuck between the pit wheel and the wallower,' said Bernarde, pointing to the man caught near the shaft that connected the waterwheel to the mill's internal workings. He indicated the other, who was trapped next to one of the two pairs of millstones. 'And he is between that timber pinion and the bed-stone. God knows how it happened. I always disengage the machinery at night – I disconnect the wheel from the wallower. That means the wheel continues to turn, but the machinery itself does not operate. I never forget to do it, so someone

99

must have re-engaged it later. It is not difficult to do, and requires no special skills – although inexperience cost these poor fellows their lives. However, while I can understand one man's clothes becoming snagged and it dragging him in, two at the same time is almost impossible. I disengaged the machinery *and* stopped the wheel as soon as I heard it.'

'Heard what?' asked Michael. He moved back and sat on a pile of grain sacks, his face pale in the torchlight. 'One killing the other?'

'The difference in sounds,' explained Bernarde. 'There was a change in pitch as the wheel turned, which made me sure someone had engaged the machinery. And there were two odd thuds. I hurried from my house to investigate and I found them here, like this.'

'Who are they?' asked Michael.

'I have not looked,' replied Bernarde with a shudder. 'No one should have been in here without my permission. Mills are delicate, and are not for anyone to wander around as they please.'

'It does not look very delicate to me,' said Michael, looking at the heavy stones and robust timbers.

'It is *very* delicate,' countered Bernarde firmly. 'That is why it takes a miller with experience and skill to keep one functional. Not everyone can do it – you only need to see the inferior flour many others produce to know *that*!' He shook his head and gave the corpses an angry stare. 'Who knows what damage they have done to my wallower and pinions with their blood and guts!'

'So, what happened?' asked Michael hurriedly, declining to hear more on that particular topic. 'There are two victims, so I suppose one killed the other, and then was dragged into the machinery as he gloated over his crime?'

'That seems likely,' agreed Bernarde. 'Mills can be dangerous places for those who do not understand them.

100

It is not unknown for a piece of clothing to be caught, and its owner pulled—'

'I suppose the cause of death is obvious, at least,' interrupted Michael hastily, taking a piece of linen from his scrip and wiping his face. 'I do not need a Corpse Examiner to tell me that mill machinery and the human body do not make good bedfellows.'

'Actually,' said Bartholomew, leaning over the first body and trying to keep his tabard from trailing in the gore, 'the cause of death is not obvious at all.'

Michael sighed. 'I know you have a penchant for grisly details, Matt, but I really do not need to know which part was crushed first. It will be irrelevant to my enquiries, and will provide me with information I would rather not have. I shall be haunted by this sight for nights to come as it is.'

'I am not sure either died from crushing,' said Bartholomew, clambering over a pile of empty sacks to reach the second body. 'They may have been killed by this.'

He held the head of the second corpse so that Michael could see what he had found. Protruding from the roof of the mouth was a long, thin nail, which had penetrated the palate and been driven deep into the brain above.

Michael stared at Bartholomew, his eyes huge in the gloom of the mill. Bernarde pushed forward to see, too, then stood back, scratching his head in puzzlement.

'Are you sure this is what killed them?' asked Michael, eyeing the nail protruding from the first corpse's mouth and then going to inspect the similar injury on the second.

'The crushing wounds you see are mostly to limbs and, despite how they look, would not have been quickly fatal. You say you came as soon as you heard the change in the noise the wheel made, Bernarde, which suggests you were very quickly on the scene. If they had suffered these injuries alone – without the nail – you would have seen at least one of them alive.'

'They were both dead,' said Bernarde firmly.

'So, what happened?' asked Michael of Bartholomew. 'Are you saying they died from stabbing, and fell into the machinery after?'

'That would be my guess,' said Bartholomew. 'It could not have been the other way around, because the moving parts would have made it difficult for the killer to put the nail in the right place.' He knelt next to the nearest corpse to assess how deep the metal pin had gone. It was embedded very firmly, and he supposed it had been applied with considerable force. 'I have never seen anything like this before.'

'Nasty,' said Michael, looking away as Bartholomew tugged the nail clear. It was long and sharp, and there were several others just like it on a shelf near the door, so it was clear the killer had used whatever weapon was easily to hand. The monk indicated one of the bodies with the toe of his boot. 'He is wearing the habit of a Carmelite. Do you recognise him?'

Bartholomew took a torch from the wall and held it closely to the man's face, to be certain before he spoke. There was a good deal of blood, and it was difficult to make out the features of either victim. 'I thought so,' he said sadly. There was only one man he knew who had taken holy orders so recently that his habit was new and unstained. 'It is Nicholas Bottisham of Gonville Hall.'

'No!' exclaimed Michael, white-faced. 'Bottisham? Are you sure? There must be some mistake!'

'There is not, Brother,' said Bartholomew quietly.

Michael swallowed hard. 'I liked him, despite the fact that his arguments were largely responsible for our defeat in yesterday's *Disputatio*. I hope Gonville does not assume we killed him because we lost. I do not want a riot and more blood spilled. Who is the other?'

'Deschalers,' said Bartholomew, after a few moments with water and a cloth. 'The grocer.'

'Thomas Deschalers is a member of the Millers' Society,' said Bernarde, shocked. 'But neither he nor the others ever come here. All our meetings are held in the Brazen George, because they dislike flour on their fine clothes – as you will find out tomorrow when you look at your own garments. I cannot imagine why Deschalers should be here.' He rubbed his hand across his mouth, unsettled and distressed. 'He has not been well recently. Perhaps sickness addled his mind.'

Bartholomew recalled how ill the grocer had looked the previous day. 'Rougham was his physician,' he said, thinking about what Deschalers himself had told him. 'I can ask whether the sickness was one that might lead a man to do odd things, but I doubt it was. It sounded more like a canker – agonising and debilitating, but unlikely to cause a loss of wits.'

'The Mortimer clan are rough men, especially now Edward is back,' said Bernarde uneasily. 'You know we have written to the King, to complain about them diverting our water? Perhaps they have decided to use force to take what they want, instead of relying on the King to make a decision. Perhaps they killed Deschalers.'

'The Mortimers seem to have done rather well out of the King so far,' remarked Bartholomew. 'He sold Edward a pardon.'

'Not the King,' said Bernarde sharply. 'His clerks. *They* are the corrupt ones, not His Majesty. We rent this mill from the King, and I do not want treasonous comments muttered in it, thank you very much. I do not want him to take it away from me – or to find against us in favour of the Mortimers in this dispute about water.'

'Never mind that now,' said Michael. He heaved himself up from his sacks and walked unsteadily to Bottisham's body, where he knelt and began to fumble for the holy oil he kept in his scrip. Bartholomew and Bernarde were silent as he said his prayers, accompanied only by the whisper of water under the wheel and the distant hoot of an owl. When the monk had finished with Bottisham, he went to do the same for Deschalers.

'I am sorry, Brother,' said Bernarde softly when the monk eventually completed his sorry task. 'I did not know Bottisham well, but he was a kind man. He visited Isnard the bargeman several times after his accident, and took him spare food from Gonville Hall's kitchen.'

Michael looked away, and when he spoke, there was a catch in his voice. 'This has not been a good week. First, there was Master Lenne and Isnard, and now there is Bottisham.'

'And Deschalers,' added Bartholomew. While he had not much liked the haughty grocer, he was still saddened that he had died in such a manner, especially given that he had been so ill. But then he thought about Bottisham, and was sorrier still. The lawyer had been courteous and compassionate, and Cambridge would be a poorer place without his gentle, kindly humanity.

Michael took a deep breath to pull himself together. He coughed as dust caught in his throat, and gratefully accepted a gulp of the strong wine Bartholomew kept in his bag for medicinal purposes. He tried to speak, coughed again, and drained what was left in the flask. He handed the empty container back to his startled companion, cleared his throat, and began to speak, becoming businesslike in an attempt to disguise his distress.

'The question we must answer is why a wealthy and fastidious town merchant should be found dead in a mill with a lawyer from Gonville. If Deschalers's was the only body here, I would say you could be right, Bernarde: the Mortimers did away with him. But his death makes no

104

sense when combined with the murder of poor Bottisham. He is not a member of your Society, is he?'

Bernarde shook his head. 'Gonville scholars patronise other mills.'

Michael wiped his forehead with his linen and went to sit on the sacks again. 'Since both these men died in an identical manner, we must assume their deaths are related. It cannot be coincidence. But what is their connection?'

'They have known each other for a long time,' said Bartholomew. He had spent some of his childhood in Cambridge, whereas Michael hailed from Causton in Norfolk and had only lived in the town for a decade or so. 'I vaguely recall a legal matter many years ago, which threw them together.'

Michael raised his eyebrows. 'Can you be more precise? What kind of legal matter? What was it about? And when?'

'A long time ago,' repeated Bartholomew helplessly. 'I recall my sister talking about it, but I do not remember the details. You must ask someone else.'

'It was something about a contested field,' said Bernarde, scratching his head as he, too, searched distant memories. 'Deschalers hired Bottisham to prove that he owned some piece of land, but they lost the case. Is that the incident you mean, Bartholomew? It *was* years ago. I imagine they would have forgotten about it by now.'

'You are probably right,' admitted Bartholomew. 'An ancient lawsuit will have no bearing on what happened today. You will need to look elsewhere for your answers, Brother.'

'So, what else can you tell me, then?' asked Michael. 'Other than that they were both murdered by some deranged killer, who then hurled their corpses into the machinery?' He sounded angry.

But Bartholomew could add little more. He was deeply repelled by the grisly nature of the crime, although he had been careful to maintain an outwardly professional indifference; revealing his own shock would not have helped Michael. He was also disturbed by the disrespectful way the bodies had been treated, and was aware of a burning desire to see the perpetrator brought to justice. However, none of this meant he could tell the monk anything useful to catch the killer – or killers – and all he could do was speculate.

'Perhaps Deschalers and Bottisham were pushed into the machinery to hide the fact that they had been murdered?' he suggested tentatively. 'Master Bernarde said it had been disengaged for the night, which suggests someone restarted it for a reason.'

'But it did not work,' countered Michael. 'You saw almost immediately what had happened with the nails.'

'But it might have done, had Bernarde not rushed here so quickly and stopped the wheel to prevent further damage to the bodies.'

'Did you see anyone leaving?' asked Michael of Bernarde. 'Or hear anything else?'

'I heard another change in pitch as I was running towards the mill,' replied Bernarde, still scratching his pate as he struggled to remember. 'That must have been the second body hitting the cogs. When I reached the outside door, it was open, so I locked it behind me as I came in . . .'

'You locked yourself inside?' interrupted Michael. 'Why did you do that?'

Bernarde shrugged. 'Habit, I suppose. This is a large building, and my apprentices and I always lock the door when we are in it alone. There is a lot of valuable grain in here – and it is especially valuable now, at the end of winter, when supplies are low and demand is high.' He jangled the large bunch of keys that always hung at his belt.

'So, once the door was locked, the killer could not have escaped from inside?' asked Michael.

'No,' said Bernarde. 'But that assumes he was in here when I arrived, and he was not. No one was – other than Deschalers and Bottisham – and I saw no one leave.'

'Is there another door?' asked Bartholomew. 'Or a window?'

Bernarde shook his head. 'All the windows are shuttered for the night. You can see for yourselves that they are all barred from the inside. That front door is the only way in or out.'

'But you said you heard the second body fall when you were running towards the mill,' Bartholomew pointed out. 'That means the killer *was* still inside when you arrived, or you would have seen him come through the door. He must have been here – there are a lot of places to hide.'

'No one was here,' said Bernarde firmly. 'And there are not as many hiding places as you might think, because everywhere is full of grain right now. Also, we would be able to see footprints in the dust if someone had dashed away to hide, and you can see there are none – other than our own. The only place a third party could have been is here, in this chamber, and then I would have seen him.'

'So,' concluded Michael. 'The killer was here when you raced towards the mill, because you heard him performing his gruesome work, but he was not here when you arrived? He did not leave through the door, or you would have seen him, and there is no other way out?'

'That is correct,' said Bernarde firmly. He had the grace to look bemused. 'It is odd, is it not?'

'Very,' agreed Michael, eyeing him in an unfriendly manner. 'If not impossible.'

'Then perhaps there was no killer,' suggested Bartholomew. 'Perhaps we were right with our first theory: that Bottisham and Deschalers killed each other.'

Michael and Bernarde started to argue. The monk was

107

certain Bottisham was too gentle to turn killer, while Bernarde maintained that Deschalers would have hired someone else to commit murder and would not have done it himself. Bartholomew listened to them and became increasingly troubled. No matter how the situation was presented, there was no mistaking the fact that a scholar and a townsman had been murdered. He hoped their deaths would not pre-empt a bloody battle between town and University. He turned his attention to the bodies again. He did not like the notion of them remaining in the machinery overnight, so he began the unpleasant process of extricating them.

Bernarde watched, presumably only to ensure no harm came to his 'delicate' equipment, because he did not offer to help. Nor did Michael, who immediately embarked on a search of the premises so that he would not have to see what was being done. Fortunately, neither victim was heavy – Bottisham because he was small and Deschalers because he had been ill – and Bartholomew found he could manage alone. It was an awkward struggle, though, and involved the use of knives and a saw at one point, but eventually he had them laid side by side on the dusty floor, covered with sacking.

'This is puzzling,' he said, when he had finished. 'I wonder how it could have happened.'

'What do you mean?' snapped Michael, concealing his grief with irritability. 'You have already told us about the nails.'

'Yes, but *how*? I cannot see Deschalers meekly standing still while Bottisham fiddled around in his mouth, looking for the right spot, no matter how ill he was feeling.'

'Are you saying Bottisham killed Deschalers?' asked Michael uneasily, glancing at Bernarde, who was nodding in satisfaction. 'Not the other way around?'

'It would have taken considerable force to do this – not

just to ram the nail into position, but to hold the victim still in the first place. I am not sure whether Deschalers had that kind of strength left. But Bottisham was a gentle man, and I do not see him committing such a vile crime, either.'

Michael was pensive. 'But Bernarde's testimony has ruled out the possibility of a third party killing them both, so logic dictates that one must have committed a double crime: murder, then suicide. We must determine who is the victim and who is the killer.'

'There is no way to know, Brother.' Bartholomew gave a helpless shrug. 'I have no idea how to find out what really went on here.'

Bartholomew wanted to go home after the gruesome discoveries in the mill; he was shocked by what had happened and needed some time alone with his thoughts. But Michael had other ideas. His distress was turning to an ice-cold anger, which was galvanising him into action, and Bartholomew could see him become more determined to solve the crime with every step that led them away from the crushed corpses. The monk declined to answer the questions rattled at him by the waiting members of the Millers' Society, and stalked along the dark lanes towards the Trumpington Gate. He hammered on it until Orwelle allowed him through, then strode to Gonville Hall. He wanted to inform its scholars that Bottisham had died in mysterious circumstances before they heard it from other sources: he wanted to gauge their reactions.

He was to be disappointed. Word of the incident had already reached Gonville, and nearly all its Fellows had gone to take the shocking news to the Carmelite Friary. Only one, John of Ufford, was home, and his response on learning about the untimely loss of a much-loved colleague was to set off for St Mary the Great, where he said he would pray to the Hand of Valence Marie for Bottisham's soul. Michael watched him go with narrowed eyes.

'That Hand is enjoying far more popularity than is right. I must have words with William.'

'It was stupid to make him Keeper of the University Chest,' said Bartholomew, fully agreeing with him. 'He is honest – there is no question of that – but he is not to be trusted with anything religious. He is a fanatic, and that sort of zeal can be contagious, like a virulent fever that strikes all in its path.'

'That is a good analogy,' said Michael. 'This devotion to the Hand is indeed like an ague that rages out of control and against all reason.'

They fared no better at Deschalers's house on Milne Street. Deschalers had been widowed during the plague, and he lived alone, although there had been rumours of lovers in his past. However, with the exception of Bess the madwoman, whom Bartholomew had seen trailing after him the day before, it seemed Deschalers had forsaken women. Even Michael, who listened to more town gossip than he probably should have done, had heard no tales of current sweethearts.

'There is no one here, either,' said the monk irritably, thumping on Deschalers's handsome front door for the third time.

'Who were you expecting?' asked Bartholomew. 'He had no family. Well, there is his niece Julianna, but she does not live with him.'

'Servants,' replied Michael. 'I want to question *them* about his state of mind this evening. Was he anxious or agitated, as a man planning a murder and suicide might be? Did he mention a secret meeting in the unlikely venue of the King's Mill? Did he contact Bottisham, or did Bottisham call him? And I want to know more about their ancient dispute – the one you recall only vaguely.'

110

'Someone is in,' said Bartholomew, watching a shadow pass across one of the upstairs windows with a candle. 'Knock again.'

Michael hammered a fourth time, hard enough to make the sound reverberate along the street, so that lights began to appear in the houses of Deschalers's neighbours. Immediately to the left was Cheney the spicer's home, and Bartholomew saw him open a window to see what the noise was about. He was shirtless, but still sported the red hat he had worn when he had been with the other members of the Millers' Society earlier. Someone called for him to return to bed, and Bartholomew recognised the stridently insistent tones of Una the prostitute. The house on Deschalers's right was owned by Constantine Mortimer – Edward's father – but, although lights flickered briefly in one chamber, no one was curious enough about furious bangs to come and investigate.

Eventually, Michael's pounding was answered by an elderly, stooped man who carried a candle. He wore the same livery as Deschalers's apprentices, a red tunic emblazoned with the grocer's distinctive motif of a pot with the letter D inside it. He cupped his ear when Michael asked to be allowed in, then informed the monk that he had no wish to become a student, thank you, because Michaelhouse had a reputation for serving small portions at mealtimes.

'What?' asked Michael, bemused. 'I have not come here to recruit you, man! I am here to ask you about your master, Thomas Deschalers.'

'I am fond of pigeon,' said the servant. 'But you have to watch the bones at my age.'

'I see,' said Michael, pushing past him to reach the shadowy interior of the merchant's house. 'Hand me the candle.'

'I do not eat dog,' said the servant indignantly. 'The hair might get trapped in my throat.'

'Lord!' muttered Michael, snatching the lamp and climbing the stairs to the large room on the upper floor that Deschalers used as an office. 'Please shoot me, Matt, when I reach the point where I make rambling statements about food all the time.'

'I shall hire a crossbow for tomorrow, then,' replied Bartholomew. 'What are we doing here, Brother? We cannot search Deschalers's house in the middle of the night – especially with no credible witnesses. People will say we came here to see what is worth stealing.'

Michael sighed, looking at the shelves with their neatly stacked piles of documents, and at the table, where more parchments had been filed by pressing them on to spiked pieces of wood. 'I do not know what I hoped to find. A suicide letter, perhaps, or something telling us why he murdered Bottisham, then killed himself.'

'Cat is something I have never enjoyed,' burbled the servant. 'It tastes too much like ferret.'

'We do not know that is what happened,' warned Bartholomew. 'I know you would rather have Deschalers than Bottisham as the killer, but we cannot draw that conclusion with the evidence we have. But there is no note here, Brother, and we should leave. I do not know why you expected one, when you know Deschalers could not write.'

'He hired a clerk,' said Michael. 'All the merchants do.'

'You do not dictate a suicide letter to a clerk,' Bartholomew pointed out. 'He would have to report it to someone, or run the risk of being charged as an accessory to a crime.'

'Of course, the finest flavour of all comes from grass-snake,' continued the old man, following them down the stairs again. 'But Master Deschalers did not like me bringing them into the house. One escaped once, you see, and frightened his lover. Then he was hard-pressed to explain to her husband why she had fainted in his bedchamber.'

112

'I can well imagine,' said Michael wryly. 'I would find it a challenge myself.'

'It was Katherine Mortimer,' said the servant, his wrinkled face creasing into a fond, toothless smile. 'She was the best of them all, and he loved her the most. She was fond of stewed horse, in—'

'Katherine Mortimer?' interrupted Bartholomew, startled. 'Constantine the baker's wife, who died two years ago?'

The old man nodded. 'She was the mother of that murderous Edward, who struts around the town so proud of his evil deeds. The King should never have pardoned him. It is not right.'

'It is not,' agreed Bartholomew. 'But when did Deschalers have this affair with Katherine?'

'More than a year before her death,' replied the servant. 'He was heartbroken when she decided their liaison was too risky and told him it was over. I could see her point: her husband lives next door and, while it was convenient to have her close by, there was always the risk that they would be caught.'

'*I* caught them,' said Bartholomew, frowning as a memory surfaced all of a sudden. 'I saw him entering her house in the middle of the night sometimes, when I was called out to tend patients. It was always when Constantine was away. I assumed Deschalers was being neighbourly – making sure she was all right on her own.'

Michael gazed at him. 'Did you? That was naïve, even by your standards!'

The servant cut across Bartholomew's defensive reply. 'My poor master was never the same after she threw him over. When she died, he grieved far more deeply than her husband did. He—'

'What was that?' asked Bartholomew, as an odd rattle sounded in the chamber above, followed by a heavy thump. 'There is someone else in here!'

He darted back up the stairs and looked into the office, but it was empty. Then he saw that the window in the adjoining bedchamber was wide open. He ran across to it and leaned out, just in time to see a figure drop to the ground and make his escape down the narrow alley that led to the river. Without thinking, Bartholomew started to follow, but his cloak caught on a jagged part of the shutter and he lost his balance trying to free it. His stomach lurched when he saw he was about to fall – and it was a long way to the ground. He flailed frantically, but there was nothing to grab. With infinite slowness, he felt himself begin to drop.

He did not go far. With almost violent abruptness, a hand shot out of the window above his head and hauled him roughly towards the sill, which he seized with relief. For a moment, he did nothing more than cling there, aware of a slight dizziness washing over him at his narrow escape. While the fall would probably not have killed him, it certainly would have resulted in broken bones.

'Thank you, Brother,' he said unsteadily. 'There is no point giving chase now. Whoever it was will have reached the river, and there are too many places for him to hide. Give me your hand.'

'Crow pie is one of my favourites,' said the servant, reaching out to help the physician clamber through the window again. The monk was not there, and Bartholomew was surprised that the elderly man had possessed the strength to save him; he was obviously less frail than he looked. 'Is that what you were doing out there? Looking for crows? You should be careful. You might have fallen.'

Bartholomew tumbled over the sill and climbed to his feet, leaning against the wall while he caught his breath and tried to regain his composure. He smiled wan thanks at the retainer, then followed him down the stairs to where Michael was talking to an old woman in the room where Deschalers received his guests – a pleasantly large chamber with comfortable chairs and dishes of dried fruits set out for those who were hungry.

'Did you see anyone?' the monk asked of his friend.

Bartholomew nodded. 'But he escaped through the window. I tried to follow, but it was not a good idea.' He smiled his thanks at the old man a second time.

'Crows,' said the servant to the old woman. 'He was after the crows that roost on the chimney.'

'Did you get one?' she asked keenly. 'Crow pie is delicious, especially if you add cabbage.'

'I do not eat cabbage,' said Michael superiorly. 'How can any right-thinking man enjoy something that is popular with snails?'

'I wonder who it was,' said Bartholomew, still thinking about the intruder. 'It was not someone with a legitimate purpose, or he would not have been skulking around in the dark. It was probably the same shadow I saw when you first started knocking, too.'

'It is suspicious,' agreed Michael. 'Particularly given what happened to Deschalers tonight. I would be inclined to say it might have been his killer, but Bernarde's evidence tells us that is not possible. Deschalers's murderer was either Deschalers himself or Bottisham.'

'Deschalers was a merchant,' Bartholomew pointed out soberly. 'Who knows what secrets he harboured or marginal business he conducted? The burglar may have nothing to do with his death.'

'Minced fox has an unusual flavour,' declared the old man with considerable authority. 'But it leaves an unpleasant aftertaste in the mouth.'

'So does your master's untimely death,' murmured Michael softly.

The tinny little bell in the Carmelite Friary was chiming for the night office of nocturn by the time Bartholomew

115

and Michael returned to Michaelhouse. The College was silent, and most scholars had been asleep in bed for at least four hours. Two lights still burned. One gleamed in the chamber Deynman shared with two Franciscan novices called Ulfrid and Zebedee, who were notorious for enjoying the night hours and emerging heavy-eyed for the obligatory masses at dawn. The second was in the conclave, where Bartholomew imagined Langelee and Wynewyk would be going over College accounts, or perhaps Suttone or Clippesby was preparing lectures for the following day. The physician was exhausted, but since he knew his teeming thoughts would not allow him to sleep, he accepted Michael's offer of a cup of wine while they discussed the events of the night.

Michael's room-mates were a pair of sober Benedictine theologians, but they were keeping a vigil in St Michael's Church for Lenne, so Michael had the chamber to himself that night. The monk had done no more than present his guest with the smaller of his two goblets, when Walter poked his head around the door.

'The Sheriff is here to see you,' said the porter, trying to keep his cockerel from entering by blocking its path with his foot. 'Should I let him in?'

'Of course you should let him in!' exclaimed Michael, horrified at the notion of influential townsmen being kept waiting on the doorstep. 'We can hardly discuss our work in the street.'

Walter was unmoved. 'Father William says we should not allow seculars in, so I am only doing what he says. But as long as you are certain the Sheriff is welcome here, then I shall admit him.'

He closed the door and they heard his footsteps echo in the yard as he walked to the gate. The hinges squeaked, then came the sound of voices kept low out of consideration for those sleeping. A dog barked far in the distance.

Suddenly, Walter's cockerel gave a brassy and prolonged trill. There was a chorus of weary groans as scholars awoke. Bartholomew heard Deynman shouting at it, and Walter howling something threatening in reply.

There was a tap on Michael's door, and Tulyet was ushered inside. He looked tired: keeping peace in the violent Fen-edge town was not easy. The town hated the University for its arrogance and superiority, and scholars despised merchants and landlords for trying to cheat them at every turn. It was an uneasy and volatile mix, and Michael and Tulyet worked hard to keep it under control. Both men knew the deaths of Bottisham and Deschalers might well tip the balance, and lead to fighting and riots as both sides accused each other of the crime. Tulyet listened in grim silence as Bartholomew summarised his findings.

'So, what do you think happened?' he asked, flopping on to the stool near the hearth and helping himself to Michael's wine. He raised his eyebrows in surprise at its quality. Michael was a man of impeccable and expensive tastes when it came to selecting clarets for his own consumption.

'Deschalers and Bottisham were killed by nails through the palate,' replied the monk bluntly.

'I am impressed you spotted that; I had eyes only for their mangled limbs,' said Tulyet. 'I have just come from the King's Mill, and Bernarde is having great difficulty cleaning his millstones. I shall have to tell my wife to buy flour elsewhere for the next few days. I do not want bits of Bottisham and Deschalers in my daily bread.'

Michael shuddered involuntarily. 'Those poor men! God only knows what happened tonight. At first, we thought a third party had killed them both, but that seems impossible in the light of Bernarde's testimony. The only logical conclusion is Matt's: that one killed the other and then himself – although it is an odd means of suicide, to say the least.'

117

'Very odd,' agreed Tulyet. 'Is it even possible?'

'Just,' said Bartholomew. 'By a desperate man. I can only assume he put the nail into position and then hurled himself into the moving engines to ensure it was driven home.'

Michael shuddered at the image. 'However, you say there is no way to determine who was the murderer and who was the victim?'

'They were both victims, Brother,' said Bartholomew softly. 'No matter what we discover.'

Michael sighed and took a gulp of wine from the physician's cup. 'I do not suppose you recall details of some ancient dispute that threw Bottisham and Deschalers together, do you, Dick?'

Tulyet frowned. 'There was something about a field, now you mention it. But it happened too long ago for me to remember the outcome. Why do you ask? Do you believe a long-forgotten argument may have led one to kill the other?'

Michael shrugged helplessly. 'I do not know what to think. Poor Bottisham.'

'Poor Deschalers,' said Tulyet immediately, seeing where the monk's sympathies lay. 'He was arrogant, but he did not deserve to die like that. But what makes you think Bernarde is not the killer? Has it occurred to you that he might be lying about what he saw and heard, as he rushed to see what was making the odd noises in his property?'

'Bernarde is not the killer,' said Michael with great conviction. 'For one very good reason: he would never make such a mess in his beloved mill. I do not see him lying to protect the culprit, either. I think he would have told me if he had seen someone running away after the second thump.'

Bartholomew agreed. 'He did seem affronted by the damage.'

118

Tulyet swirled the wine around in his cup. 'But Bottisham and Deschalers could not have killed each other with nails during a fight. It would be improbable to the point of impossible. And I do not accept the notion of a suicide pact, either: it is too neat. Therefore, I think you are right: the only plausible option is that one killed the other, then dispatched himself in a fit of sorrow.'

'Then who was the killer and who was the victim?' asked Michael.

Tulyet turned to Bartholomew. 'There was nothing on the bodies to help you determine that?'

'Not a thing,' said Bartholomew. 'I think they died at more or less the same time – both were warm when we arrived. Also, remember that Bernarde heard two thumps – bodies dropping into the workings – within a short period of each other once the machinery had been engaged.'

'Is it possible to drive a nail into your own palate, then throw yourself into the gears and cogs?' asked Tulyet.

'You could stand *near* the machinery when applying the nail, so you would fall into it,' replied Bartholomew, trying not to show his distaste for the discussion. He knew the various possibilities had to be investigated, but he did not like doing it when Bottisham was one of the victims. He forced himself to continue. 'It would be a good way to make sure you die – insurance against the nail missing its mark or you not having the strength to drive it home.'

Tulyet winced, and looked back at his wine. 'Deschalers has been ill recently – weary and listless. I doubt he had the strength for murder, so I am inclined to think Bottisham is the culprit.'

'No,' said Michael, still unwilling to believe the kindly Bottisham would kill. 'Deschalers is a more convincing suspect. He was clearly up to something sinister, because someone invaded his house the moment he died.'

'He was a wealthy man,' Tulyet pointed out. 'And he

lived alone. His house will be the target of every thief in the town until his heirs come to organise his affairs – including the forty felons who have been detailed to repair the Great Bridge. You cannot read anything significant into your encounter with that intruder.'

They were silent for a while, thinking about the deaths and the seemingly impossible task of discovering what had happened. They knew they stood on the edge of a chasm: Tulyet had already made the assumption that the scholar was the killer, while Michael was inclined to view the townsman as the villain. Others would do the same, and the situation needed to be handled very carefully if they did not want more deaths and violence.

'What happens now?' asked Bartholomew eventually. 'A townsman's death must be investigated by the Sheriff, and a scholar's by the Senior Proctor. But they are the same case. What happens if your conclusions contradict each other?'

'We must ensure they do not,' said Tulyet soberly. 'At all costs. Neither of us wants a riot over this. Therefore, I suggest *you* conduct this investigation, Brother – Deschalers's death as well as Bottisham's. I trust you to be impartial, and I promise to bide by whatever conclusion you draw. That will eliminate some potential for dispute, at least.'

'Very well,' agreed Michael, although he did not look happy. 'As long as you are willing to explain to Deschalers's fellow merchants why you have delegated the business to me.'

'That is easy,' said Tulyet bitterly. 'I am obliged to spend most of my time watching the criminals working on the Great Bridge. *And* I must keep an eye on Rob Thorpe and Edward Mortimer. I barely have time to breathe, let alone look into what may be a complex murder.'

'Can you not use your soldiers for that?' asked Michael, who would have set his beadles on tasks that sounded so time-consuming and dull.

'I dare not abandon the villains. Two slipped past my sergeants only this morning, and would have escaped if I had not been there to catch them. And nor will I abandon my surveillance of Thorpe and Mortimer until I know what they plan to do. It would not surprise me to learn that *they* had arranged the deaths of Bottisham and Deschalers.'

'Really?' asked Michael eagerly, ignoring the fact that they had just reasoned a third party involvement was impossible. 'That would be a neat conclusion. Why? Would it be because Deschalers once had an affair with Edward's mother, and Edward wants revenge on the man who sullied her virtue?'

Tulyet was startled. 'I doubt it! Edward encouraged Katherine's various liaisons, because they made her happy – and he liked to see his mother happy.'

'You are not surprised to hear that Deschalers and Katherine were close?' asked Bartholomew.

Tulyet shrugged. 'Katherine and my wife were friends, and I have known about her relationship with Deschalers for years. He was deeply hurt when Katherine decided it was too risky to have a lover in the house next door – the affair meant far more to him than it did to her. She soon found herself a replacement, but he never did. Apparently, *you* kept running into them, Matt, and Katherine was afraid you might say something to her husband.'

'But she was not afraid her son might tell?' asked Michael curiously.

Tulyet shrugged a second time. 'Edward detested his father, so was only too pleased to see him made a cuckold. So, if he did arrange for Deschalers to die, it would not have been over Katherine.'

'What, then?' asked Bartholomew. 'Is there another motive?'

'None that I know – other than to make trouble between town and University by having a scholar and a merchant murdered in the same place. He hates us, because we were instrumental in his capture. What better way to avenge himself on Sheriff and Senior Proctor than to present us with an unsolvable crime? We will look incompetent, and it will bring about riots at the same time.'

Michael was thoughtful. 'I thought they would be here for a week or so, try to dispatch one or two "enemies", and then disappear when they see everyone is watching them. But they seem intent on staying and making careers for themselves.'

Tulyet agreed. 'They are settling in more comfortably than I would like – even attending meetings of the burgesses. Edward refused to work in his father's bakery, and is helping at Mortimer's Mill instead. Meanwhile, Thorpe has been accepted into Gonville Hall to study. He tried his luck at Valence Marie first, but *his* father declines to have anything to do with him.'

'He had the gall to apply to Michaelhouse, too,' added Michael. 'Damned cheek! Pulham told me that Gonville had accepted Thorpe because he offered to sew altar cloths and chasubles for their new chapel. He learned how to make them during his apprenticeship with your brother-in-law, Matt.'

Bartholomew was troubled. 'Why not ask them to leave Cambridge, Dick? No one wants them here – with the exception of the Mortimer clan, of course. And perhaps now Gonville.'

Tulyet looked pained. 'How can I? They have the King's Pardon. If I were to banish them, then I am effectively saying that the King was wrong to invite them back to England. And that is treason. So, there is nothing I can do unless we actually *catch* them committing a crime.'

'Damn Constantine Mortimer!' said Michael. 'He was the one who purchased these pardons.'

Tulyet shook his head in despair. 'The Mortimers are

already quarrelling with the Millers' Society over the issue of water, and I am sure Edward has turned the dispute more bitter. The Millers' Society thinks Bottisham and Deschalers were murdered in connection with the dispute, although I do not see why.' He scrubbed at his eyes, frustrated by so many questions and so few answers.

They were silent again, as each tried to envisage a solution that would fit the evidence. How did one man come to drive a nail into the palate of another? Did he choose that method because he hoped it would be undetectable once the machinery had done its work? Was he hoping both deaths would be seen as accidents? But whatever solution Bartholomew devised merely left him with more questions, and he saw he would not solve the riddle until he had more information.

Tulyet reached for his cloak. 'Thorpe and Mortimer are still drinking in the King's Head, so I cannot stay here too long, lest they make trouble. You know what a volatile place *that* is.'

'They are there now?' asked Bartholomew, startled. 'But it is the middle of the night!'

'If Thorpe is now a scholar, then I can fine him for being in a tavern,' said Michael, downing the last of the wine and preparing to carry out his duty immediately.

'No,' said Tulyet, putting out a hand to stop him. 'He is trying to antagonise us, to see how far he can go. The best thing you can do is have a word with Gonville, and see if they will dismiss him. If all the Colleges refuse to house him, he may move on – perhaps to Oxford.'

'You assume he wants to study,' said Michael. 'But he is no more eager to learn his Aristotle than Edward is to become a miller. They have other reasons for inflicting their presence on us.'

'True,' said Tulyet. 'They were found guilty of all manner of crimes – most of which they freely admitted. But their guilt will not prevent them from wanting revenge on us all.'

'I do not understand,' said Bartholomew tiredly. 'How can they want revenge when they know they are in the wrong?'

'Because they were caught,' said Tulyet. 'And *that* rankles.'

Michael and Bartholomew returned to the King's Mill early the following morning to inspect the building in daylight. It was William's turn to recite the daily mass again, and he shot through the office at such a speed that there was ample time to visit the mill and search for clues among its dusty corners before teaching began at eight o'clock. They explored every crack and crevice in the rambling building, but to no avail: there was nothing to help them ascertain what had caused Bottisham and Deschalers to die in such bizarre circumstances. Bartholomew rubbed a hand through his hair in frustration, wanting desperately to find something that would tell him what had happened, but not knowing where else to look or what else to do.

'You see this dust?' asked Bernarde, pointing to a thick, even layer of grainy-grey powder that lay across the floor. 'It has not been disturbed since my boy swept it last night. Watch.'

He took a few steps across it, keys bouncing importantly at his waist, and Bartholomew saw his footprints quite clearly as they left a distinctive trail behind him.

'We always sweep the floor before retiring for the evening,' Bernarde went on. 'Then we bag up the dust and sell it at a reduced rate to the lepers at Stourbridge. The only footprints when I arrived last night were the ones made by Bottisham and Deschalers, as they came in through the door and made for this end of the building. These have now been overlain by our own. But you can see for yourselves that no one went anywhere else to hide – as you suggested yesterday. There would be marks leading to his hiding place, and there are none.'

'So, this really does discount the possibility of a third party,' said Bartholomew, disheartened when he saw the miller was right. There were no trails leading to dark corners, and the killer would have been seen had he remained in the chamber with his victims. 'Unless he escaped before the second body fell . . .'

'Not possible,' countered Bernarde immediately. 'I left my house very quickly after I heard the machinery engage, and I would have seen anyone leaving. I am sorry, Doctor, but there were only two men here last night: Bottisham and Deschalers.'

Bartholomew wandered outside, to see whether there were windows or cracks that might be used to effect an escape, but mills suffered from interested rats and tended to be fairly well sealed. There was no other exit, except a gate high on the upper floor that was used to hoist sacks of grain to the storage bins. But Bartholomew knew this had been barred from the inside the previous night, because he had seen it himself. He sat on the river bank and looked across the Mill Pool to Isnard's cottage. Bottisham's pleasant face kept swimming into his thoughts.

'Bernarde *could* have killed one or both of them,' he said, when Michael joined him.

The monk glanced behind him, to ensure the miller was not listening. 'You would not say that if you heard the fuss he was making about bits of bone in his pinions – whatever they are. He is furious about it. Besides, Deschalers was a member of the Millers' Society, and I do not see why Bernarde would do away with a colleague and an investor.'

Bartholomew rubbed his hands together, noting that they were deeply impregnated with pale dust. 'Do you think Bottisham killed Deschalers, and then Bernarde stabbed Bottisham in revenge? Bernarde then could have thrown them both in the workings to confuse us.'

'I have just interrogated Bernarde's boy, who is slow witted and an uneasy liar, and he corroborates his father's story very convincingly. Bernarde left his house just as he says – after the change in the wheel's pitch alerted him to the fact that something was not right. I do not see why Bottisham should kill Deschalers anyway.' Michael sighed miserably. 'None of this makes sense. I hate cases where I am obliged to investigate the death of a man I liked. They make me feel guilty when my enquiries do not proceed as quickly as they should.'

'Then I suspect we will both be feeling guilty about this one, Brother,' said Bartholomew. 'I cannot imagine where we will begin.'

Michael gave a wan smile. 'You plan to help me? That is good news. I do not think I will be able to solve this alone.'

They were about to leave the mill and return to Michael-house, when they saw they were not the only ones keen to explore the scene of the crime in the cold light of day. Members of the Millers' Society assembled as the sun began to rise and the day lost the delicate silver shades of early dawn. Mayor Morice was there with the burly Cheney, while the Lavenhams stood arm in arm nearby, listening to Bernarde's assurances that most of the gore had been removed from those parts of the mill that mattered.

'I assume you have finished now?' asked Morice, approaching Michael. 'We cannot allow the mill to stand idle any longer. We have twenty sacks of grain left from yesterday, and we are expecting a consignment from Valence Marie this morning. Their flour is almost completely exhausted, and we have promised that their corn will be milled by this evening.'

'Then they will have to buy some from the Market Square

126

instead,' said Michael coolly, not about to be bullied by Mayor Morice. 'I am conducting a murder investigation, and that takes precedence over any trading agreements you might have.'

Morice's expression was disdainful. 'Although one of the bodies was a scholar's, this mill is not University property and you have no right to tell us what to do. It will start working in an hour.'

'We will see what Dick Tulyet says about that,' argued Michael. 'He—'

'Tulyet should be ashamed of himself,' spat Morice in disgust. 'He told us this morning that *you* will be looking into Deschalers's death on his behalf. Delegating to scholars! That would not have happened when *I* was Sheriff.'

'It is because of the Great Bridge,' said Cheney uneasily. 'He needs to watch the felons – and Mortimer and Thorpe. I am just as glad to see him doing that, and—'

'There are a lot of things that would not have happened when you were Sheriff, Morice,' retorted Michael icily, ignoring the spicer. 'And a thorough investigation was one of them. However, I *have* finished here, so the mill's reopening depends on whether Bernarde feels his equipment is properly cleaned.'

'I asked the Hand of Valence Marie to bless it,' Bernarde told his assembled colleagues. 'That should take care of any lingering evil spirits. And I spent most of the night washing blood and lumps from the cogs, so the wheel should run smoothly now.'

'Never mind that,' said Isobel de Lavenham. 'What about the parts that grind the corn? We do not want complaints that our flour contains meat as well as grain. We might be fined!'

There were dismayed mutterings at that prospect, and Bernarde was enjoined to go back inside and check his

127

millstones. The miller declared that he and his boy had been scrubbing them for hours, and that he was more concerned about expensive damage to his delicate mechanisms than about stray fingers in the flour. The debate raged back and forth until Bernarde told them exactly how much it would cost to repair a damaged spur wheel or a wallower. Then it stopped. Bartholomew was disgusted with them all for thinking more about profits than the death of one of their colleagues – and of Bottisham.

Now seriously worried that the incident might affect him financially, Morice turned on Michael and pointed an accusing finger. 'It was a waste of time summoning you last night. All we have done is ensure you begin one of your ponderous enquiries, which will interfere with every aspect of our lives. You detest townsfolk, and an opportunity like this will give you the excuse you crave to make a nuisance of yourself.'

'I do not detest townsfolk,' replied Michael calmly. 'It is you I do not like.'

'We had no choice,' replied Cheney, his local burr conciliatory as he addressed the Mayor. He was flushed that morning, and Bartholomew could smell wine on his breath. 'Bernarde was obliged to tell someone in authority that two bodies were in his mill.'

'What I want to know is what Bottisham was doing here in the first place,' said Isobel unhappily. 'Deschalers I can understand: he had a key – and he had every right to inspect the property he invests in, no matter what the time of day or night. But Bottisham did not.'

'Did Deschalers invite him, then?' suggested Cheney thoughtfully. 'Were they meeting for some reason? I thought they tended to avoid each other.'

'What do you know about that?' pounced Michael. 'Were they enemies?'

'I am not certain,' replied Cheney, glancing around at

his companions, who shrugged. 'I recall something bad happened between them, but it was a long time ago.'

'Bottisham be the rascal,' said Lavenham hotly, pushing his apothecary's hat back on his head. His accent was pronounced that morning, and agitation about the state of the mill seemed to deprive him of the ability to speak good English. 'He be one with crime. Deschalers he not.'

'We shall see,' said Michael. He turned to Bernarde. 'What time did you close the mill last night?'

'About seven o'clock,' replied Bernarde. 'I locked the door myself, after my boy had finished sweeping. And it was empty,' he added, anticipating Michael's next question. 'And the machinery was disengaged as I told you – the wheel was still turning, but the millstones were not. However, it is simple to start them up again. Even a scholar would be able to work out what to do.'

'Who has access to your key?' asked Bartholomew, ignoring the slur.

'Me and my boy,' replied Bernarde, jangling the metal on his belt. 'My wife did, but she died of the Death, as you know, Doctor – you tried to save her. But we are not the only ones with keys: Morice, Cheney and Lavenham all have one, as did Deschalers.'

'Why is that necessary?' asked Bartholomew.

'It is stipulated in the Millers' Society charter,' explained Cheney. 'I have never understood why, but we keep them anyway.' He rummaged about his plump person and produced a key made from ancient black metal. 'Here is mine.'

'There was one like that in Deschalers's scrip,' said Bartholomew to Michael. 'I saw it when I examined him last night. I assumed it was for his house, but it seems I was mistaken.'

'I carry mine never,' declared Lavenham. 'My wife, he cares for these thing.'

'It is at home, locked in the cupboard where we keep our strongest medicines,' said Isobel. Her smile became predatory. 'I can show you, if you like, Brother.'

'I will take your word for it,' said Michael primly.

'Mine is here,' said Morice, and Bartholomew heard the tinkle of metal as he fumbled on his belt. 'So, they are all accounted for. What does this tell you, Brother? What have you deduced by asking who has these keys?' His jeering tone made Bartholomew want to punch him.

'It has allowed me to conclude that Deschalers probably came here willingly, and that he used his key to let himself in,' replied Michael, less aggravated by the Mayor's insulting manners than the physician. 'And the fact that it was in his scrip – rather than on a belt or a chain around his neck – indicates he was not in the habit of carrying it, but that he took it specifically to come here last night.'

'So?' demanded Morice, irritated that the monk could indeed make inferences from the results of his questioning. 'What does that mean?'

'It *means* he intended to come here,' said Michael. 'And that Bottisham is unlikely to have arranged it, because Deschalers was the one with the key.'

'So, Isobel was right,' said Cheney thoughtfully. 'The real question we should ask is what was *Bottisham* doing here, not Deschalers. Bottisham was a scholar, after all, and not the sort of man with whom Deschalers would normally deign to fraternise.'

'And he was from Gonville Hall,' added Morice meaningfully.

'Why is that significant?' asked Michael.

Cheney replied. 'Because Gonville are representing Mortimer's Mill – our rivals – in the case we intend to bring before the King. We are suing them because they keep stealing our water.'

130

Morice's expression was smug. 'But we will win this case, because some of our profits go to the King – and the King is not a man to let the Mortimers interfere with the contents of his coffers.'

Bartholomew was sure he was right. The King was always in need of money, and would not let the Mortimers deprive him of what seemed to be a fairly regular and easy source of income. He would be almost certain to find in the Millers' Society's favour. However, the scholars of Gonville were skilled and clever lawyers, as he had seen for himself in the *Disputatio*. It was possible that the Mortimers' case was not so hopeless after all.

'You are not in a position to make comments about the integrity of others, Morice,' countered Michael acidly. 'I understand it was an endorsement from *you* that allowed King's Pardons to be issued to Edward Mortimer and Rob Thorpe.'

'Nonsense,' said Morice calmly, and if he was concerned that his colleagues were regarding him uneasily, then he did not show it. 'That had nothing to do with me. It must have been a forgery. These Westminster clerks are good at that sort of thing. They learn such skills in the universities.'

Bartholomew put his hand on the monk's shoulder, to prevent the caustic retort he was sure was coming. They needed answers, not an argument with a man who could barely speak without uttering some falsehood. 'But if Gonville's clerks intend to represent the Mortimers, then it is *very* odd that Deschalers should be in this mill with Bottisham – a Gonville scholar,' he said.

'Very,' agreed Cheney. 'It looks as though Deschalers was consorting with the enemy. However, we must remember that he was a clever man, and may have been trying to make some sort of arrangement to our advantage. I do not think his liaison with Bottisham necessarily implies he was doing something that might harm the Society.'

'I am not so sure,' said Bernarde worriedly. 'If he was being honest, then why not meet Bottisham during the day, in a tavern or a church? You are wrong, Cheney. The fact that Deschalers was here alone in the dark with Bottisham indicates that he *was* up to no good as far as I am concerned.'

'He was probably buying shares in the Mortimers' enterprise,' said Morice angrily, quick to condemn. 'And that would have weakened our case. Damn the man! What was he thinking of?'

They continued to bicker, so Bartholomew went inside the mill again, thinking he should conduct a final search if it was going into action in an hour. Once the waterwheel started to turn, any remaining evidence would quickly be obliterated. He felt under considerable pressure to find something, but although he exhausted himself by frantically hauling bags of grain this way and that as he hunted for clues, his Herculean efforts went unrewarded.

When he had finished, he stood still, trying to catch his breath. The complex mess of gears and cogs had been scoured and lovingly coated with grease, while the millstones had been scrubbed spotlessly clean. Bernarde's boy was still working on them, and Bartholomew thought no one need have concerns about finding body parts in their bread. As the great wheel was lowered into the water to commence its work, Bartholomew dropped to his knees and began one last, desperate inspection of the floor, ignoring the splinters that stabbed his hands as he groped under sacks and bins.

Bernarde's apprentices started to arrive, tripping over him and treading on his fingers, and at last he was forced to concede defeat. He stood again, thinking that Michael's assumptions must be correct: Deschalers had indeed met Bottisham after dark, when he knew the mill would be locked. It would be an ideal location for an assignation he did not want anyone to know he was having. But why? Was Morice correct: that the grocer had been trying to strike some sort of bargain with a man who was legally representing his adversary? Or was it nothing to do with the mill dispute, and the two men had other things to discuss?

'There is nothing here, Brother,' he said, when Michael came to join him. The monk regarded him with amusement, and when he looked down he saw his clothes were covered in dust, giving him a ghostly appearance. He brushed irritably at his tabard, raising a cloud of white. 'I hope it does not rain today, or I will find myself encased in pastry.'

'No,' said Michael, after a moment of serious thought. 'You need butter and lard to make pastry, so you will be encased in glue. What do you think of them, Matt? The Millers' Society, I mean?'

'They are like all merchants – there is good and bad in each. Except Morice, of course. There is no good whatsoever in him. He is unashamedly corrupt, and is motivated purely by self-interest.'

'What of the others? Cheney? The Lavenhams?'

'Cheney is pompous, but decent enough. Lavenham is as untrustworthy an individual as I have ever met. He knows I re-weigh the medicines he sells me, so he has stopped cheating me now. Isobel is very popular with my students, because she seduces them each time they visit her shop.'

'And what do you think about this dispute with the Mortimers over water?'

'I think they should resolve the issue like rational men. I do not approve of rushing to the King each time there is a squabble. The Mortimers should be careful about how much water they divert, and the Millers' Society should devise some sort of timetable to avoid clashes. It cannot be that difficult. They worked perfectly well together until recently.'

'Things are always difficult when there are large amounts of money at stake,' said Michael soberly. 'And there is plenty of money in milling.'

CHAPTER 4

On Mondays Bartholomew taught in the mornings, then took his three senior students – Quenhyth, Redmeadow and Deynman – with him when he visited his patients. But his mind was full of Bottisham and Deschalers as he ate the bowl of oatmeal Agatha had saved for his breakfast, and he wondered whether he should abandon his academic duties and concentrate on the murders instead. But he could think of nothing to do that would move the enquiry along, and his students were waiting. Reluctantly, he went to the hall and led a discussion on the Greek physician Galen's short treatise on barley soup. After the midday meal, he collected his three students and set off to see his patients, Bottisham's death still playing heavily on his mind.

The arrival of Rougham and Paxtone in Cambridge had relaxed the pressure on him considerably, and he now had a list of patients he felt was manageable. Most of the folk who had abandoned him were wealthy, and preferred the newcomers' willingness to calculate horoscopes and concoct potions to help them recover from the after-effects of too much food and drink. Bartholomew was left with the town's poor, whom the others would not have deigned to advise anyway, although Paxtone offered free consultations on Wednesday evenings.

Although a shorter list of people wanting his services was a blessing, Bartholomew soon discovered that the ones who summoned him invariably could not pay him or buy the medicines he recommended. While he was not overly concerned about the loss of income for himself – his basic

135

needs were provided for by his College stipend – he was unhappy about the fact that there were folk suffering just because they could not afford to purchase what they needed to make them well. Sometimes he received donations from generous colleagues, but more often than not he was obliged to pay for the remedies himself or watch his patients try to recover without them.

That day, he was summoned to the home of a woman with an excess of choler in the stomach, and knew she would be much more comfortable if she drank a solution of chalk and charcoal, mixed with poppy juice. But the patient was Una, one of the town's more desperate prostitutes, and she needed to spend her meagre earnings on bread and rent; medicine was an unthinkable luxury. He glanced around her hovel, noting the holes in the roof, the gaps in the wall, and the mean little fire in the hearth.

He asked for a sample of urine, then showed the students how to assess it for various maladies. All three scribbled notes furiously on scraps of parchment. Redmeadow dropped his pen in his desperation to write, and had to grovel on the floor to retrieve it from under a bench. As he stretched out his hand, he exposed the sleeve of his tunic, and Bartholomew saw it was ingrained with dust and dirt. Bartholomew assumed he had been earning extra pennies by drudging for Agatha in the kitchens. Like Quenhyth, Redmeadow was not a wealthy student, and was often obliged to undertake menial tasks in an effort to make ends meet.

'I saw you last night, Doctor,' said Una mischievously, when the consultation was over and the students started to argue among themselves about the reason for the sudden decline in Michaelhouse victuals. They paid her and their teacher no attention.

'I saw you, too,' Bartholomew replied, smiling as he sat on the bench. 'Or rather, I heard you. You were at Cheney's house. Incidentally, he fed you acidic wine that upset your humours. You should demand a better-quality brew from him in the future.'

She grimaced. 'I wondered why he took his own claret from a different jug. But I watched you go inside Deschalers's home, and I saw someone else run out a little later. Did you startle a burglar? I am not surprised someone chanced his hand. Deschalers's house will offer handsome pickings, and the whole town knew he was not in a position to defend his property last night.'

'The burglar climbed out of a window at the back,' said Bartholomew. 'Then he made good his escape down the alley that leads to the river.'

'No, he left through the front door,' argued Una. 'After you and the fat monk had gone inside. I saw him with my own eyes – although Cheney's wine made me feel as though I had six of them.'

'Perhaps he doubled back,' said Bartholomew, thinking she had probably seen Michael or the elderly servant. Or perhaps she had confused the sequence of events, and had watched the burglar entering the house rather than leaving it.

'Perhaps.' She winced and put a hand on her stomach as she was gripped by another spasm of pain. 'This hurts, Doctor. There must be *something* that can relieve it. I hear you always carry strong wine to use as medicine. Will you give me some of that?'

'It would make you worse,' said Bartholomew. He left her house, fuming silently that rich merchants could have whatever they liked, while Una would not eat that day if she did not secure herself some customers. It was unjust, and he fully empathised with the growing unrest among folk who were clamouring for better pay and wanting to narrow the gap between rich and poor. He recalled the disturbances in Ely the previous summer, when men had risked the King's displeasure by instigating insurrection among the peasantry.

He was still fretting about the problem when he met a messenger with an order to attend Tynkell at the Church of St Mary the Great. Quenhyth, Redmeadow and Deynman immediately began to speculate about why an august personage like the Chancellor should want Bartholomew to visit him. Bartholomew hoped it was nothing to do with the curious discussion about poisons they had had after the *Disputatio de quodlibet*. He doubted it was anything to do with the mill deaths, because Michael would have answered any questions arising from that.

'Perhaps Tynkell wants you to take his place,' suggested Quenhyth sycophantically. 'He has been in office for three years now, and he may have decided it is time for a change.'

'I think Brother Michael might have something to say about that,' said Redmeadow. '*He* intends to be the next Chancellor. And chancellors are elected, anyway. It is not for Tynkell to appoint one.'

'Perhaps he is with child and knows you are better with women's matters than Rougham and Paxtone,' suggested Deynman.

Bartholomew regarded his cheery-faced student warily, while the other two students clutched each other in helpless laughter. 'How could Chancellor Tynkell be pregnant?'

Deynman blushed furiously. 'Surely you do not need me to explain that process? It happens when a husband and his wife come together, and—'

'That is not what I meant,' interrupted Bartholomew, amused by Deynman's prim notion that the making of children occurred only between married couples. 'I was referring to the fact that Tynkell is a man – and men do not bear children.'

'Some do,' said Deynman, round-eyed. 'I read it in Aristotle last night. He said that the sex of hermaphrodites is determined by whether they prefer the clothing of males or females. Although Tynkell was baptised a man, he obviously prefers wimples and gowns, and he will soon bear a child.'

Not for the first time, Bartholomew thought how dangerous a little knowledge could be in the mind of someone like Deynman. He struggled to explain in words he thought the lad might comprehend. 'Aristotle actually said that hermaphrodites should be considered men or women depending on their ability to copulate – nothing to do with clothes or bearing children. But why have you attributed this particular condition to Tynkell?'

'He is always rubbing his stomach,' said Deynman, as though no further explanation were necessary. He glanced at his teacher, saw his confused expression, and hastened to elaborate. 'Labour pains. All pregnant women have them.'

'I see,' said Bartholomew cautiously, aware that Redmeadow and Quenhyth were almost in tears as they attempted to suppress their amusement. 'Is that all?'

'And because he never bathes,' said Deynman earnestly. 'He does not want anyone to know of his circumstances, because, as a woman, he would not be permitted to be Chancellor. By never bathing – and thus never revealing any minute portion of his flesh – he ensures his secret remains safe.'

'Except from you,' said Bartholomew, wondering how he would ever solve the problem that Deynman had become. At some point the student was going to realise that he could study for the rest of his life and still not be good enough to pass his disputations, and then he would leave Cambridge and descend on some unsuspecting settlement to ply his 'skills'. Not all physicians completed their University studies, and there were many who had never attended a school at all. However, Deynman could honestly say that he had studied longer than most, and prospective patients would be impressed. Bartholomew felt a sudden stab of fear, knowing it was only a matter of time before Deynman did someone some serious harm.

'Why are Una's humours unbalanced?' asked Redmeadow, wiping his eyes and attempting to bring the discussion back to the patient they had just visited. 'Is it because she spends too much time romping with men she does not know?'

Bartholomew applied himself to answering, noticing how Quenhyth and Deynman hurried to emulate Redmeadow, and extract scraps of parchment from their scrips and jot down notes. He talked about the delicate balance of humours in the stomach, and how Una had an excess of acid bile that needed to be brought under control. Redmeadow and Deynman listened, then lagged behind when they felt they had heard enough. Quenhyth, however, was still full of questions.

'You did not suggest bleeding. When there is an excess of evil fluids, then surely the best recourse is to drain them away?'

'Bleeding will not reduce the amount of bile in the stomach,' argued Bartholomew. 'And purges that cause vomiting will bring pain. A compound of chalk and charcoal would soothe the caustic humours and allow them to reduce naturally.'

'Is this what Galen recommends?' asked Quenhyth, scribbling furiously.

'Galen suggests cutting around any intestine ulcerated by black bile,' said Bartholomew. 'But I do not think such a drastic step is necessary in Una's case.' And he had no wish to be reprimanded by his colleagues again for employing surgical techniques.

'What about a poultice of henbane?' asked Quenhyth, shaking his pen in an attempt to relieve a blockage. Ink splattered across the sleeve of Bartholomew's tunic. 'You mentioned yesterday that Arab medicine makes good use of plants like henbane, which are poisonous but which can be used as cures by the cautious.'

'By the very cautious,' warned Bartholomew, scrubbing at the spots and making them worse. 'Henbane slows the brain and reduces the sensation of pain. No physician prescribes it lightly, and most only do so as a last resort. Too much will kill, while too little will not achieve the desired effect. Lily of the valley can also be used to soothe pain, but again it is essential to determine the precise dosage, or it will not work. Personally, I would not use either. They are too dangerous.'

'Henbane,' said Quenhyth, underlining what he had written with several firm strokes. He glanced up and pointed at the black splatter on Bartholomew's tunic. 'Agatha will not be pleased when she sees that. Ink is not easy to remove.'

Before he arrived at St Mary the Great, Bartholomew emptied his scrip and found a few pennies – the last of his stipend for that month. Hoping there would not be some unforeseen emergency that would require him to pay for something else, he handed them to his students and instructed them to buy ground chalk and poppy juice from the apothecary. Quenhyth demurred, virtuously claiming that he did not want to be seduced by the salacious Isobel, so the others suggested he scavenge charcoal from the blacksmith instead. Bartholomew promised to show them how to mix the potion for Una later, when they were all back at Michaelhouse.

The Chancellor's office in the University Church was spacious and functional, with a bench running along the length of one wall, and shelves overflowing with parchments and scrolls. A large table stood in the middle, also piled high with documents, and the whole room was sharp with the daylight that flooded in through one of the beautiful perpendicular glazed windows.

Bartholomew was surprised to discover Michael already there, comfortably settled with a goblet of warmed wine. The monk was telling Tynkell how to sell one of the University's unoccupied houses, and the Chancellor was busily writing his instructions down. The rumours were true about how much power Michael had accrued in his capacity as Senior Proctor, Bartholomew thought. It was clear from the way they interacted that Michael was in charge.

'Ah, Bartholomew,' said Tynkell, waving a grime-impregnated hand to indicate that the physician should enter. Bartholomew obliged, and wondered how Michael could stand the stale odour that emanated from the Chancellor's long-unwashed person. He supposed the monk considered it a small price to pay for the kind of influence he had inveigled for himself. 'We wanted to see you.'

He offered the physician some of the wine that was mulling over the fire. Bartholomew accepted, but was not impressed by the fact that Tynkell's aversion to water seemed to extend to his goblets, too. There was a ring of brown scum on the rim from the lips of previous drinkers, and its outside was sticky from greasy fingers. Tynkell sat again, and Bartholomew discovered he had been holding his breath while the Chancellor was close. Meanwhile, Michael kept his nose in his goblet, and the physician saw he was using it much as he might employ a pomander.

'You are filthy,' said Tynkell to Bartholomew in an aggrieved tone of voice. He pointed to the ink stains on the physician's sleeve. 'Look at that! It is no example to set to your students.'

Bartholomew heard Michael snigger into his wine.

'Agatha will wash it tonight,' he said, wishing he had the nerve to point out to the Chancellor that he had seldom encountered such brazen hypocrisy.

'I am not telling you to resort to extremes,' said Tynkell hastily. 'You just need to buy a tabard with long sleeves. Then no one will notice your dirty tunics. I recommend Isobel de Lavenham, who has a nimble needle and offers good rates.'

'I have done nothing about the deaths of Bottisham and Deschalers since we were at the King's Mill this morning,' Michael said to Bartholomew, his voice taking on a curious, echoing quality as it came through the cup. 'I was obliged to pay a visit to the King's Head, because Thorpe – now flaunting himself as a scholar – made trouble there, and I do not want him to be the cause of a riot between students and apprentices.'

'No,' agreed Tynkell, rubbing his stomach and wincing. 'That must be avoided at all costs. Do you think *they* murdered Deschalers and Bottisham, Brother?'

'It is possible,' said Michael.

'I am not so sure,' said Bartholomew. 'Bernarde would have seen them.'

'Such details are not important,' said Tynkell firmly. 'I want the perpetrator of this monstrous crime in a prison cell as soon as possible. We can work out their motives and methods later, when the danger is no longer stalking our streets. We cannot afford to dally with this, Brother.'

Michael's expression hardened. 'I know that. However, I need clues in order to solve the mystery, and they have not been forthcoming. Unfortunately, at the moment, the most likely theory is that Bottisham killed Deschalers, then did away with himself in a fit of remorse, and—'

'No!' exclaimed Tynkell. 'That cannot have happened! Not a scholar murdering a townsman! That would cause a riot for certain – especially since the victim was wealthy.

The burgesses would appeal to the King for justice, and God knows where that might lead.'

'We do not know what took place,' said Bartholomew, also reluctant to believe that the gentle Bottisham would kill Deschalers. However, he was painfully aware that if Deschalers could not summon the energy to retrieve a dropped purse, then he certainly would think twice about attempting to stab a fit and healthy scholar and throw him in the workings of a mill. 'But we will try to find out.'

'You must do more than try,' snapped Tynkell. He rubbed his stomach a second time, grimacing with the pain. 'Since you are here, Bartholomew, I am suffering acutely from that complaint we discussed a month ago – an excess of bile in the spleen, you said.'

Bartholomew immediately thought of Deynman's theory, and drank some wine in an attempt to compose himself. He looked the Chancellor up and down, aware that he was actually a very unusual shape. 'Bile in the spleen can be uncomfortable,' he managed eventually.

'I hope I am not being poisoned,' Tynkell went on nervously. 'As Bishop Bateman was poisoned in the papal court at Avignon.'

'So *that* is why you asked me about poisons at the *Disputatio*,' said Bartholomew, greatly relieved. 'You thought someone might be using a toxin that is giving you gripes in the stomach. I thought you wanted the information so you could use it on an enemy.'

Tynkell regarded him icily, while Michael's green eyes grew as huge and round as those of an owl. 'Have a care, Matt,' he muttered. 'Accusing the Chancellor of plotting to murder his adversaries is no way to further your University career.'

'I asked those questions because I have been unwell for so long,' replied Tynkell stiffly. 'Bishop Bateman was also ill for some time, and it occurred to me that someone

144

might be feeding me a noxious, slow-acting substance to bring about my death.'

'In that case, you should eat only from dishes shared by your colleagues, and never accept gifts of food and wine,' suggested Bartholomew. 'I wish you had mentioned this on Saturday. Our discussion gave Rougham entirely the wrong impression.'

Tynkell was not interested in the damage he might have done to Bartholomew's reputation. 'You are the University's Senior Physician, so of course I consulted you about my concerns. Who else should I ask?'

'I do not think anyone is poisoning you,' said Bartholomew, although it crossed his mind that the Chancellor might well be poisoning himself – with his powerful personal odours. 'But you should discuss this with your own physician, not me.'

'I do not know what to do about these gripes,' Tynkell went on, ignoring the advice. 'I summoned Rougham first, then Paxtone, and they were both very thorough. Rougham composed a horoscope, and Paxtone wrote out details of a dietary regime involving beet juice that he said would have me better within a week. But I am not better, and I prefer your unorthodox treatments to their conventional ones: your cures work, and theirs do not.'

Bartholomew hid a smile. 'So, are you abandoning them to return to me?'

'I have not been well since I defected,' admitted Tynkell. He hesitated, never a man to be decisive. 'But perhaps I could keep all three of you. What do you think of that?'

'I think you will find yourself given a lot of contradictory advice,' replied Bartholomew, amused by the proposition. 'You will compromise, and take the most appealing cures from each of us, and you will probably end up feeling worse.'

'I thought you would say that,' said Tynkell. 'But I know

how to resolve this conundrum. I shall have my horoscope from Rougham, my eating plan from Paxtone, and my medicine from you. Then I shall offend no one – Gonville, King's Hall or Michaelhouse.' He beamed, and Bartholomew saw that compromise and an unwillingness to offend was probably the root of his success as Chancellor – along with the fact that Michael made the real decisions.

'We did not ask you here for a consultation,' said Michael. He pushed a parcel across the table, an oblong shape wrapped in cloth. 'This is for you, on the understanding that you accept the official post as Corpse Examiner for the next year, as you agreed last night.'

Bartholomew gaped at him. 'You did not waste any time!'

'I believe in striking while the iron is hot,' replied Michael smugly. 'Purchasing Bacon's *De erroribus medicorum* from Gonville was the first thing Chancellor Tynkell did this morning, and drawing up an official document to seal our pact was the second. Sign here.'

'No,' said Bartholomew, reluctantly pushing the book away. 'I had better take the fourpence per corpse instead. I realised this morning that I need the money more than a book.'

'I suppose you want it to buy medicines,' said Michael, regarding his friend astutely. 'And since most of your rich patients have abandoned you in favour of Paxtone and Rougham, you find yourself short of funds, and your patients are without the benefit of your generosity. I wondered how long it would take before you discovered that the wealthy have their uses.'

'I have no choice but to opt for the fourpence,' said Bartholomew tiredly. 'I waste my time if I recommend medicines that cannot be purchased. I may as well not bother to visit the sick at all.'

'But this Bacon cost ten marks,' said Tynkell, aggrieved. 'Now you say you do not want it?'

'I did not say I do not want it,' said Bartholomew. 'I said I needed the coins more.'

'Take the book,' said Tynkell, thrusting it so hard across the table that Bartholomew had to leap forward to catch it before it fell. 'You can consider it a long-term loan from the University to Michaelhouse – as payment for services already rendered. And you shall have your fourpence per corpse, too. You had better submit an invoice monthly, because if you send me one every time a body is discovered, I will be doing nothing other than processing your demands.'

Bartholomew regarded him suspiciously. The University was not noted for its largess, and he did not want to accept something that would later come to cost a good deal more. 'A loan? Why?'

'To ensure we keep you,' said Tynkell. 'You are not the only one who wants this newly created post: Rougham is also interested in fourpence per corpse. But Brother Michael would rather have you. In fact, he organised the whole thing specifically for your benefit.'

'He did?' asked Bartholomew, startled. He saw Michael scowl at the Chancellor, but Tynkell was not to be silenced.

'You should not hide your good deeds, Brother. It will do your reputation no harm for folk to know you occasionally act with compassion. Your friend has lost his wealthy patients, so you decided to help him with his predicament. I thought twopence per corpse was ample, but you insisted on more.'

'It is a business arrangement,' said Michael stiffly, disliking the notion that he should be seen as someone who acted out of the goodness of his heart. He preferred to be seen as a cunning and ruthless manipulator. 'Nothing more, nothing less.'

'Thank you, Michael,' said Bartholomew sincerely.

'Sign here,' snapped Michael. Bartholomew took the

147

pen and wrote his name, feeling as though he were making a pact with the Devil. Michael smiled in grim satisfaction. 'Good. Now you are legally bound to inspect any corpse I discover for the next year.'

'The first thing we must do is visit Gonville and ask why Bottisham was in the King's Mill last night,' said Michael, as they left the Chancellor's office. Both took deep breaths, grateful to be away from the aromatic presence. 'Then we will go to Deschalers's house and see whether his apprentices or servants have anything more meaningful to tell us than recipes for rat custard and stoat soup.'

'I agreed to examine corpses for you, Brother,' said Bartholomew warningly. 'But that does not mean I am at your beck and call to help with all your murder investigations from now on.'

Michael slapped his friend on the shoulder. 'That is better, Matt. I was beginning to think there was something seriously amiss when you agreed so readily to become my Corpse Examiner. No terms, no conditions – it was most unlike you. But here you are, complaining as usual, and I see all is well. However, you did offer to help me with Bottisham's investigation.'

'I will,' promised Bartholomew, not sure what he could do on that front, much as he had liked the Gonville lawyer. It was depressing to have no encouraging leads. 'But first, I must visit Isnard, and then I promised to show my students how to mix a potion for Una. She has a sore stomach again.'

'It is all the claret she drinks,' remarked Michael. 'It is too little like wine and too much like vinegar. That is what ails her.'

'I imagine she would not be able to carry out her professional duties if she did not have some strong drink inside her – and then she would starve for certain. Come with me. She likes you.'

148

'They all do,' said Michael, leaving Bartholomew wondering who was meant by 'all' and how the monk had interpreted 'likes'. 'But not if Quenhyth is going, too. He is the least likeable student in the University, and I do not know why you are so patient with him.'

'Because he may make a good physician one day. He works hard and, although he will never be a popular healer, he may become an effective one, and that is all that really matters.'

'If you say so. We are beset by unpleasant young men these days: Thorpe, Mortimer, Quenhyth. Damn! I should have held my tongue. All three of them are suddenly coming our way.'

Bartholomew saw he was right. Thorpe and Edward Mortimer were striding along the High Street from the direction of the Great Bridge, while Quenhyth and Redmeadow were making their way up St Michael's Lane from the College. Bartholomew was tempted to duck into the nearest church and avoid them all, but Michael was not so squeamish. He bared his small yellow teeth in a grin of false welcome as the two felons drew level, watching them exchange nudges and glances, and clearly intent on aggravation. The students reached them at the same time, and stood behind Bartholomew, expressing silent solidarity.

'You two caused a lot of trouble in the King's Head last night,' said Michael without preamble. 'You should be careful. You are not popular, and taverns have a reputation for unsolved murders.'

'No one would dare harm us,' said Mortimer smugly. 'We enjoy the protection of the King. If anything happened to us he would descend on Cambridge, and every man, woman and child would learn they had crossed the wrong /man.'

'That may be true,' said Michael. 'But the patrons of taverns are not noted for their forward thinking while in

149

their cups. They strike first, and think about the consequences later. Having the King impose heavy fines will not help you if you are dead, will it?'

'We heard about Bottisham and Deschalers,' said Thorpe, when his friend declined to answer. A malicious grin curled the corners of his mouth and he winked at Mortimer, coaxing a smile from him. 'What were they doing together in the mill in the middle of the night?'

'You tell me,' said Michael, resisting the temptation to react with anger. He shot Bartholomew a glare: he could see the physician was less sanguine about the matter, and looked ready to respond with curt remarks. 'Have you heard rumours?'

'Oh, plenty,' said Thorpe. 'But I would not repeat them to you. I hear you are easily shocked.'

'Where were you last night?' demanded Michael. '*Before* you arrived at the King's Head?'

The two men exchanged expressions of feigned horror, and Mortimer placed one hand on his chest, to indicate that the implied accusation had wounded him. 'You think we killed them?'

'Well, someone did,' replied Michael.

Thorpe sneered. 'You should watch where you aim your accusations, Brother. They are offensive, and I may sue you in a court of law for an apology.'

Michael was about to reply when there was a sharp snap, followed by a rattle. Someone had thrown a stone. His eyes narrowed, and he studied the mass of humanity that moved up and down the High Street. Who had thrown the missile? Was it the troublesome Franciscans from Ovyng Hostel, a clutch of whom had just emerged from St Michael's Church? Was it Robin of Grantchester, aiming his pebble at Bartholomew for operating on Isnard's leg? Or was it one of the many folk who glanced uneasily at Thorpe and Mortimer as they passed, most too afraid to make an open protest about their unwelcome presence?

'That was Cheney,' whispered Bartholomew. 'I saw him.'

'At me?' asked Michael, wondering whether the Millers' Society did not trust him to investigate the murder of one of their own and had intended to prevent him from doing so.

'At Mortimer, I suspect – for being one of the clan stealing the King's Mill water.'

'Why do you insist on remaining here?' asked Michael, addressing the two felons, who seemed to care little that they were on the receiving end of hostile looks from the passing populace. 'You must know that folk are not pleased to see you, and I cannot imagine what it must be like to live in a place where everyone is longing for you to leave.'

'It is just like France,' said Mortimer expressionlessly. 'We were not welcome there, either, because we are English. It is not so different here.'

'We have scores to settle,' said Thorpe, fixing his glittering eyes on Bartholomew. 'We were accused of and punished for heinous crimes.'

'That is because you were guilty,' said Michael.

'Maybe so, but that is irrelevant,' said Thorpe. 'The King's Pardon says we are forgiven now. And I want compensation.'

'Money?' asked Bartholomew, wondering how many corpses he would have to examine before he had earned enough to send them on their way. 'Is that what you want?'

'In part,' said Thorpe. 'But we deserve to be compensated in other ways, too, for the unjust suffering we endured.'

'It was not unjust,' Bartholomew pointed out reasonably. 'You confessed.'

'I *said* that is irrelevant!' snarled Thorpe, taking a step towards the physician that could only be described as menacing. Quenhyth shrank back in alarm, but Redmeadow held his ground. His hand dropped to the knife he carried in his belt. Bartholomew saw the lad's jaw tighten with anger, and hoped he would not lose his temper.

'It is not irrelevant,' said Bartholomew quietly. 'You cannot start demanding vengeance from people just because you committed felonies and were caught.'

'Now we have the King's Pardon, we can do what we like,' countered Mortimer. 'This town is going to pay handsomely for our two years' banishment. And so is that vile old woman. It was *her* testimony that sealed our fate. The justices listened to her as though she was one of God's angels.'

'What vile old woman?' asked Bartholomew, puzzled. He had not attended the young men's trials himself, because there were so many other witnesses with first-hand knowledge of their crimes that he had not been needed.

'The nun,' elaborated Thorpe. 'The one with the long nose and the brown face, whom everyone thought was so wonderful. She was nothing but a wizened hag, and she had no right to tell people we did all those things – even if we did them.'

Bartholomew glanced at Michael, whose mouth was set in a hard, thin line. 'I sincerely hope you are not referring to my grandmother,' said the monk coldly. 'Dame Pelagia is a noble lady, so I advise you to keep a civil tongue in your head when you mention her.'

'Dame Pelagia,' said Mortimer, pronouncing the name with satisfaction, pleased to see that he had discovered a weak spot in Michael's armour. 'That was the harridan's name. Everyone said she was one of the King's agents, although I do not think it was true. The King is not so desperate for spies that he is obliged to scour nunneries, looking for withered old crones to serve him.'

Michael lunged suddenly and had Mortimer by the throat before the man knew what was happening. The

152

monk's bulk was deceptive, and he could move like lightning when required. 'If I hear you mention her name with disrespect again, I will have you arrested – King's Pardon or no.' He shoved Mortimer away with considerable vigour, then wiped his hands on the sides of his habit, as though they were stained with something nasty.

Mortimer shrugged, quickly recovering his composure and his balance. 'Is she here?'

'No,' said Michael shortly.

'There are a number of folk we shall visit now we are free,' said Thorpe silkily. 'She is one of them. I will see Bartholomew's sister and her husband, too. They were far too quick to throw me to the wolves.'

'They stood by you longer than you deserved,' said Bartholomew, grateful they were away.

'And my father,' added Thorpe. 'He wants nothing to do with me – he will not even accept me into his own College. I was obliged to apply to Gonville instead.'

'We will have words with you two at some point, too,' said Mortimer with icy menace, gazing first at Michael and then Bartholomew. 'In some quiet, secret place, where we will not be overheard.'

'Are you threatening us?' demanded Michael, speaking loudly enough to gather an audience. 'Are you saying you mean to lure us into a remote place and dispatch us? If so, then no one will need to look far for the culprits. Look at how many people heard you.' He gestured to at least a dozen folk – scholars and townsmen – who were listening with rapt interest.

Mortimer saw he had been outmanoeuvred, and declined to take the conversation further. He nodded a farewell to the monk, and the cold light in his eyes made Bartholomew's blood run cold. Thorpe was less willing to admit defeat, and opened his mouth to say something else, but Mortimer took his arm and pulled him away. Unlike his younger friend, he was intelligent enough to see that nothing more could be gained from prolonging the encounter – but that a good deal might be lost.

'Their absence has made them bitter as well as dangerous,' said Bartholomew, watching them walk away. 'I wish they were not here.'

'You are not alone,' said Michael gravely. 'There have been all manner of complaints about them, but unfortunately nothing serious enough to warrant prosecution. Dick was right: if we expel them without irrefutable and incontestable evidence, it will appear as though we are criticising the King's Pardon. His Majesty will not like that, and it should be avoided at all costs.'

'What sort of complaints?' asked Bartholomew.

'About their manners, for a start,' said Quenhyth, back at Bartholomew's side now the two louts had gone. 'Edward especially is rude and overbearing. You are right to include him in your investigation into the deaths of Deschalers and Bottisham.'

'Why do you think he is part of that?' asked Michael.

Quenhyth looked superior. 'It is *obvious* that he and his friend are the culprits, and common sense dictates that you must arrest them immediately.'

'But they have learned to fight, so challenge them with care,' added Redmeadow, who had been in Cambridge when the pair had first come to public attention. 'They were apprentices, so they already knew how to brawl, but in France they were taught how to use swords and knives.'

'How do you know?' asked Michael, fixing him with a steely glance. 'Have you been listening to gossip in taverns, and thus breaking University rules?'

'*I* have not,' said Quenhyth sanctimoniously. 'I would never do such a thing.' He looked smugly at his discomfited colleague.

Redmeadow blushed, but shook his head. 'A tavern is

154

not where I witnessed their newly acquired fighting skills. It was near St Mary the Great. They picked a quarrel with Ufford from Gonville Hall – or perhaps he picked one with them. Regardless, Ufford was lucky they did not kill him.'

'Ufford is a son of the Earl of Suffolk,' said Michael thoughtfully. 'He has been well trained in the knightly arts and should know how to take care of himself.'

'Quite,' said Redmeadow, nodding vigorously. 'That is why I was surprised when they defeated him. I would have nothing to do with them, if I were you, Doctor. Leave them to the Senior Proctor.'

'Thank you very much,' said Michael flatly.

There was a glorious sunset that evening. Bartholomew and Michael walked through the kitchens to where the College grounds stretched in a thin strip down to the river. The part nearest the door was planted with herbs and vegetables; some of the beds were dug ready to receive annual seeds and bulbs, while others were the kind that grew all year. The herb garden, Agatha's pride and joy, was laid out in neat squares, each section containing a different kind of aromatic or edible plant. She was less interested in the vegetables, and their management was left to the cook and his two assistants. One was there now, hoeing a space for the powerful little leeks she used to disguise the taste of meat that was past its best.

Behind the vegetable plots a gated wall separated the cultivated part of the garden from the orchard. The orchard was one of Bartholomew's favourite places, mainly because only he and Michael ever seemed to use it. The fruit – largely apples and pears, but some cherries and plums – was harvested each year, but for the most part the trees were left unattended. The cook occasionally directed one of his helpers to cut the grass, which was gathered, dried and used as hay, but such activities were infrequent, and

155

the fragrant little wood was invariably deserted and peaceful.

Near one of the walls, an old apple tree had fallen, and its sturdy trunk formed a pleasant bench for any scholar wanting a little tranquillity, away from the hubbub in the conclave and hall. It was sheltered from the prevailing wind, but placed to catch the best of the sun, and Bartholomew loved the way the branches swayed above him and created dappled patterns on the grass with the sunlight.

It was pleasant to sit there that evening, despite the fact that the end of the day brought cooler temperatures and a wind that was biting. The distant sun was a glowing orange orb that lit the clouds in layers of purple and scarlet. The sounds so characteristic of dusk were beginning: the hoarse yell of a baker selling the last of his wares, the clatter and creak of carts making their way home, the weary voices of labourers returning from surrounding fields, and bells chiming for vespers. Bartholomew could hear the great bass of St Mary the Great, followed by the cracked treble of St Botolph's.

Michael shivered. 'I do not know why you wanted to sit out here, Matt. It is freezing.'

'It is peaceful,' countered Bartholomew. 'Besides, William is ranting in the conclave about some lecture he heard today. He claims the speaker's points were wrong, because he was a Dominican – and being a Dominican rendered him incapable of rational argument. I do not want to listen to that sort of rubbish. I would rather be out here.'

'William in full flow does change matters,' agreed Michael, pulling his cloak more tightly around his shoulders. 'But we should not stay here long. We both need a good night's rest, if we are to be alert and perceptive when we interview the Gonville Fellows tomorrow. I did not like the fact that they refused to speak to me today.'

'They were praying, Brother,' said Bartholomew, who

did not think it odd at all for Bottisham's colleagues to spend the day of his burial on their knees. 'And they declined to break their vigil out of concern for his soul.'

'Yes, yes,' murmured Michael, knowing he was right. 'We shall speak to them in the morning, and I shall have my answers. Perhaps it was just as well. I was tired and sluggish today when we interviewed Deschalers's apprentices, and I need to be sharp for the men who defeated us in the *Disputatio*. The workmen told us nothing of relevance, and I do not want Gonville to do likewise, just because I am too weary to see through clever lies.'

'The apprentices were not lying, Brother – they really do know nothing of any relevance. But you are right about being tired today. It was difficult to sleep last night. I kept thinking about Bottisham – and Deschalers, of course. But Bottisham was harder . . . because I liked him, I suppose.'

Michael nodded. 'I was restless, too. And attending Bottisham's requiem this afternoon sapped the last of my energy. It was a sad business. I saw you there, with Master Warde of Valence Marie.'

'He kept coughing,' said Bartholomew, who had used the distraction to take his mind off the fact that they were burying someone of whom he had been fond. 'Have you learned anything about what might have happened in the King's Mill last night from other sources?'

Michael banged his fist hard against the trunk, making Bartholomew jump. It was unlike the monk to be openly emotional. 'No! But it is not from want of trying. I interviewed the Millers' Society – Morice, Cheney, Bernarde and the Lavenhams – but learned nothing I did not already know.'

Bartholomew closed his eyes, and it crossed his mind that they might never discover the truth about the deaths. They were silent for a while, each thinking about the bodies in the mill. Eventually, Michael spoke again.

157

'Did I tell you Sergeant Orwelle has still not managed to find out who killed Bosel? He asked for my help this afternoon. No witnesses have come forward, and he cannot decide whether it is because there are none, or because they are too afraid to speak.'

'Has he taken Dick Tulyet's lead, and narrowed his list of suspects to Thorpe and the Mortimer clan? And that odd woman?'

'That woman – Bess – barely recalls her own name, let alone whether she murdered someone. Perhaps you could talk to her, and see whether you can make sense of what she says. You have a way with the insane. You should do, given the practice you have in dealing with Clippesby.'

'Tomorrow, after Gonville,' offered Bartholomew, content just to lean against the wall and watch the sunset. 'Will it count as a consultation for the Corpse Examiner, and earn me fourpence?'

Michael glanced at him sharply before realising he was being teased. When the gate creaked, his expression hardened. 'Here comes Quenhyth, to pester you with questions again. Is no time sacred to the boy? Can he not even allow you a few moments of peace at the end of the day? He is worse than a wife!'

'He is all right,' said Bartholomew. 'He is just keen to learn.'

'I am sorry to disturb you, sir,' said Quenhyth, approaching with his hat held in his hands. 'But Sheriff Tulyet has asked you to go to his house. His son has had an accident.'

'God's teeth!' swore Bartholomew in annoyance. 'Not Dickon again! This will be the third time they have summoned me in as many weeks, and Dickon is not the easiest of patients.'

Michael agreed. 'The boy is a monster. I do not envy you your duty, Matt, not even for a goblet of Dick Tulyet's fine wine.'

'You will not come with me, then?' asked Bartholomew, disappointed. 'It would be good to have reinforcements.' He did not add that it would be especially good to have someone of Michael's size when dealing with Tulyet's fiendish brat.

'I will not,' said Michael firmly.

'I will,' offered Quenhyth. 'The messenger said something about a dried pea in the ear, and we learned about ears last week. I shall fetch your bag – assuming that Redmeadow has not been in it, stealing its contents, like he takes my ink and parchments.'

'Redmeadow is not a thief,' said Bartholomew, not looking forward to the imminent battle with Tulyet's infant son, or to having Quenhyth with him while he did it.

Quenhyth gave him a look that indicated *he* knew better. They set off, and Michael accompanied them as far as the Jewry, an area that had earned its name because it had once housed a number of Jewish moneylenders. They had been expelled from the country the previous century, although not before the King had confiscated all their property. When the monk stopped opposite King's Childer Lane and claimed he had business nearby, Bartholomew was suspicious. The woman he secretly loved lived in the Jewry, and he suspected Michael planned to visit her and take advantage of the fact that she kept an excellent cellar, a good kitchen and cushioned benches around a pine-scented fire. He enjoyed spending evenings with Matilde himself, and was envious that Michael should be able to do so while he was obliged to see Dickon. He watched the monk stride into the maze of tiny alleys with considerable resentment.

Quenhyth chattered as they walked the remaining distance to the handsome house on Bridge Street, where the Tulyets lived. Bartholomew listened reluctantly, not especially interested in the diagnosis that Cheney's partiality to blood pudding rendered him choleric, or in the intelligence that Deynman had been seduced by Isobel de Lavenham. However, he was interested in the news that Deynman had been the butt of jokes following his announcement of Chancellor Tynkell's pregnancy, and was determined to prove himself correct. He closed his eyes: preventing Deynman from doing something dreadful to the University's figurehead was yet another task for which he would have to find time.

He was about to approach Tulyet's house when he saw a lonely figure standing on the Great Bridge. Because it was almost dark, the bridge was deserted, and the felons who were repairing it had been escorted back to the Castle. The figure was Bess, and she leaned over the scaffolding-swathed parapet in a manner that was far from safe. The way she stood, cupping her face in her hands, jogged his memory so sharply that his hand froze halfway to the door.

'Katherine Mortimer!' he exclaimed suddenly. 'That is who Bess reminds me of.'

'One of the Mortimer clan?' asked Quenhyth, who had not been in the town when the baker's wife was still alive. 'Bess has Edward's colouring, I suppose.'

'Katherine was his mother. The likeness has been nagging at me ever since I first saw Bess. It is just a coincidence. Bess is too young to be Katherine – and I was with Katherine when she died, anyway. But the likeness is uncanny.'

'Perhaps they are related,' suggested Quenhyth. 'And that is why Bess came here from London.'

'London?' asked Bartholomew. 'Is that where she usually lives?'

'So she says. It is a big city, with thousands of inhabitants, so it is possible. But perhaps she came here because her addled wits reminded her that she has kin in the town.'

'What do you think is wrong with her?' Bartholomew asked, curious to know whether his student would remember what he had been taught about ailments of the mind.

'Melancholy?' asked Quenhyth. 'Perhaps she is about to jump.'

'Then we should stop her,' said Bartholomew, hurrying towards the bridge.

'We should not,' said Quenhyth, snatching at his sleeve and missing. He sighed and ran to catch up. His teacher tended to move very quickly when he thought someone needed his help. 'We should let her choose her own destiny, sir. She is clearly unhinged and deeply unhappy, so why should we condemn her to more misery by forcing her to live?'

Bartholomew regarded him askance. 'Do you know what the Church teaches about suicide? And what it teaches about those who stand by and do nothing while it happens?'

'I know what *you* think,' countered Quenhyth. 'You do not always condemn suicide when you think the victim has good reason for ending his life. And you do not always commit him to a grave in unhallowed ground, either. I know exactly how Father Ailred of Ovyng perished – he was a suicide, without question – but he lies peacefully in St Michael's churchyard.'

Quenhyth was right, and Bartholomew saw he would lose that particular argument. He turned his attention to Bess. He approached slowly and took her hand when he was close enough, so he could ease her away from the edge of the bridge. She regarded him with her flat black eyes, and then settled her gaze on Quenhyth.

'Where is my man?' she asked softly.

'I do not know your man,' said Quenhyth stiffly, evidently loath to be addressed by someone who was addled. 'When did you lose him?'

'He has gone away,' she whispered. 'Many moons ago. He went, and he never came back.'

'I am sorry for you,' said Quenhyth, not sounding at all

sympathetic. 'But you should step away from the bridge, madam. It is narrow, and a cart might come past and spray you with filth.'

'Filth,' said Bess blankly.

'Muck,' elaborated Quenhyth helpfully. 'Dirt. Sewage. You know.'

'I know,' replied Bess distantly. 'Have you seen my man? He went away.'

'She is raving,' said Quenhyth to Bartholomew, impatient to be away. 'You have saved her from death, so we should leave her, and go to see Dickon before he pushes the pea so far into his ear that you will need to remove it through his nose.'

'We cannot leave her alone,' objected Bartholomew. 'Perhaps the Canons at the Hospital of St John will take her again. She seems distressed this evening, and I do not want her to harm herself.'

'Do you know where he is?' asked Bess, looking from Bartholomew to Quenhyth with desperation in her eyes. 'Please take me to my man.'

'What is his name?' asked Bartholomew gently.

'My man,' echoed Bess softly. 'He has a name. He has gone away.'

'And so should we,' said Quenhyth, growing even more impatient. 'Give her a penny, sir. She can go to the King's Head and buy a bed in the stable loft.'

'I do not have a penny,' said Bartholomew, feeling his empty purse.

Quenhyth regarded him in disbelief. 'But we have visited seventeen patients over the last five days. They must have paid you something.'

'Do you have one I can borrow? I will return it as soon as I am paid.'

'You will forget,' cried Quenhyth, clutching his bag protectively. 'You care so little for your own money that you place scant importance on that belonging to others, too. But I am short of funds myself at the moment, and had to borrow from Deynman today. I was going to talk to you about a loan from one of the College hutches. I have no spare pennies to lend you.'

Bartholomew rifled through the contents of his medical bag, to see whether there was something that might be sold in order to raise the needed money. Or perhaps he could offer the landlord of the King's Head a free consultation in exchange for a bed and a meal for Bess.

'I have a penny,' said Bess, reaching into the wrappings around her unsavoury person and producing a groat. 'See? It is a pretty thing, is it not? It has the King's face on it.'

'Very pretty,' said Bartholomew, pushing her hand back into her clothes and hoping no one else had seen it. A groat was a lot of money, and Cambridge was no place to flaunt coins, especially at dusk. Shadows writhed and slunk in dark doorways, where thieves waited to prey on the unwary and vulnerable. 'Put it away, and do not show it to anyone else.'

As he glanced around, he became aware that a solution was at hand. Matilde was walking towards him, in company with the carpenter Robert de Blaston and his wife Yolande, who were staying with her. Their own house had collapsed during heavy winter snows, and Matilde had offered the family a home until it was rebuilt. Bartholomew was surprised to find himself maliciously gratified that Michael had had a wasted journey, if he had intended to visit her.

'Matthew!' Matilde exclaimed in pleasure, breaking away from the Blastons and coming to greet him. The couple lingered, unwilling to leave her at a time when decent folk were already inside their houses and the town became the domain of a rougher, more dangerous breed of people. Matilde's eyes strayed to Bartholomew's shorn hair. 'Oh, dear!'

'Lenne's handiwork,' said Bartholomew. 'I was probably his last customer.'

'Just as well,' he heard Yolande mutter.

'I heard about the deaths in the King's Mill,' said Matilde to Bartholomew. 'Poor Bottisham. You must be upset, because I know you liked him. But I have been worried that you might become embroiled in another of those nasty plots.'

'What do you mean?' asked Bartholomew, grabbing Bess's arm as she made to return to the Great Bridge. Her attention had wandered and she was muttering about flying over the pretty water. He supposed Quenhyth was right, and she did intend to hurl herself over the edge, although he did not know whether it would constitute a deliberate attempt to end her life, or whether her wits were too scrambled to understand the consequences. Either way he intended to prevent it.

'I mean there are rumours that the murders relate to the quarrel between the Millers' Society and the Mortimers.'

'They might,' agreed Bartholomew. 'Although I am not sure how.'

'Well, there is the fact that Bottisham was one of the lawyers the Mortimers hired to present their case, for a start. You do not need me to tell you that the whole thing stinks of corruption and malice, Matthew. You should take care.'

'I will,' promised Bartholomew, although he felt he had no real cause for concern. He had nothing to do with either side in the dispute, and did not care who won the case that had been taken to the King.

'I have something for you,' said Matilde, turning to the carpenter and gesturing that he should pass her the basket he carried. She rummaged inside it and produced a package. Curiously, Bartholomew removed the protective cloth to reveal a scroll.

'Trotula!' he exclaimed in delight, turning it this way and that in an attempt to decipher some of the words in the failing light. It was a good copy, illustrated lovingly by some scribe who had taken pride in his work. 'Her musings on childbirth.'

'I thought you would like it,' said Matilde, smiling at his pleasure. 'It may come in useful soon, because Yolande has just informed me that she is pregnant again.'

'Again?' asked Bartholomew, regarding the woman in awe. It would be her eleventh. He looked at the scroll, then, with great reluctance, handed it back to Matilde. 'I cannot accept this. It probably cost a good deal of money, and I do not have a penny.'

'It is advance payment for the services you might soon render to Yolande,' said Matilde firmly, pushing it back at him. 'Do not refuse me, Matthew. I do not want to employ Rougham in your stead, and I might have to, if you will not accept your dues.'

'Do not hire him for poor Yolande,' said Quenhyth fervently. 'Rougham knows nothing about women's problems.'

'Then thank you,' said Bartholomew, although he suspected Yolande would need no help from him. She might require a midwife briefly, but she was strong and healthy, and he did not expect anything to go wrong with so experienced a mother. 'I shall treasure it. But I need another favour. I do not want to leave Bess alone, but I have been summoned to attend Dickon . . .'

'You want me to give her a bed,' surmised Matilde. She smiled. 'I am sure we can find a corner, although my little home is very crowded these days with an additional two adults and ten children under my roof. Another visitor arrived today, too. We are crammed inside like herrings in a barrel of salt.'

'Who?' asked Bartholomew, wondering whether he

should be jealous. Matilde's past life was a mystery to him; it was rumoured that she had been lady-in-waiting to a duchess before being dismissed for entertaining one too many courtiers at night. Matilde gave the impression that she found such stories amusing, and enigmatically refused to say whether or not they were true.

Matilde gave him a mischievous smile that made his heart melt, then cocked her head and started to laugh. 'You will need to come for a drink when you finish with Dickon, Matthew. I can hear the little angel screaming from here!'

Bartholomew watched her walk away with Bess and the Blastons, then turned back to the Sheriff's house. It was a sumptuous affair, with walls made from stone, rather than the more usual wattle-and-daub, and boasted a new roof that stood proudly above the rough reed thatches of its neighbours. It was three storeys high, and the Tulyets and their only son had enough room to claim a sleeping chamber to themselves, an almost unimaginable luxury when there were servants and retainers to be housed and a steady stream of visitors claiming hospitality.

Bartholomew knocked on the door, but the enraged screeches that emanated from within were so loud that he was obliged to hammer another three times before a harried maid finally heard him over the commotion. He was about to follow her inside when a tiny movement at the corner of his eye caught his attention. He spun round, and saw Thorpe leaning against a doorway, half hidden by shadows.

'What are you doing there?' he demanded, unsettled by the man's sudden appearance.

Thorpe uncoiled himself and jerked a thumb in the direction of Tulyet's home. 'I was passing and heard a racket. I was curious to know what is going on. Will Brother Michael offer his services in the form of reinforcements tonight? It sounds as though you might need a burly arm.'

Bartholomew grimaced. 'Dickon only fights battles he is sure he can win.'

'Very wise,' said Thorpe, giving one of his unpleasant grins before walking away towards the town centre. Bartholomew watched him go in puzzlement, but Dickon's shrieks reached a new level in volume and the maid appealed to him with desperate eyes, so he pushed Thorpe from his mind and entered the small hell that comprised Dickon's domain.

'Thank God,' said Tulyet shakily, when Bartholomew was shown into the solar. 'I do not think I can stand much more of this. He is in pain, but we do not know what to do.'

Young Dickon, a child of just over three years of age, was perched on his mother's knee. His little face was scarlet with the effort of producing the ear-splitting screams that were having exactly the effect he wanted on his long-suffering parents. Adults fluttered around him, trying to calm him with kisses and sweetmeats, while the little hellion learned how he might manipulate them even more efficiently in the future.

Dickon already knew he could achieve almost anything with a tantrum, and had recently realised this could be taken to new heights if his doting parents thought he was hurt, too. As a consequence, Bartholomew was frequently summoned to treat minor bruises and scratches that most children would not have noticed, and an increasingly imaginative array of 'accidents' that included invisible splinters, an alleged surfeit of carrots, and an array of bizarre objects inserted into various orifices – although none embedded deeply enough to cause genuine pain. Dickon was not stupid.

'You say there is a pea in his ear,' shouted Bartholomew over the howls, kneeling next to Mistress Tulyet and taking the lad's head to tilt it gently towards the light. Dickon's reaction was instant and predictable. He twisted quickly, and his sharp little teeth clicked in empty air, just as the physician jerked his hands away.

'Dickon!' exclaimed Tulyet in horror. 'You know you must not bite!'

Dickon began to scream again, this time because his attack had been thwarted and he was angry. Meanwhile, his mother petted and fussed over him, believing the shrieks were a result of the mishap with the pea. Bartholomew was baffled. Tulyet was astute when it came to dealing with the felons who came his way, and was seldom taken in by their lies and deceits. The physician had no idea why he did not apply the same rules to his son. As a baby, Dickon had been snatched by blackmailers, and his parents had coddled him ever since. They were now reaping the rewards of spoiling a boy who had needed a firmer hand.

Tulyet spread apologetic hands. 'I am sorry, Matt. He is beside himself with agony and does not know what he is doing.'

Bartholomew thought Dickon knew exactly what he was doing. He took the child's head in a firmer grip. There was an immediate struggle, with Dickon screeching his outrage when he saw he could not escape. His face turned from red to purple.

'You are hurting him!' cried Mistress Tulyet, trying to prise Bartholomew's hands from her son.

'I am not,' replied Bartholomew, releasing his patient and wondering whether he would be obliged to wait until the brat fell asleep before removing the pea. It would not be a difficult operation, and would have taken only a moment with any other child. He sat back on his heels and considered his options, most of which involved sending the parents from the room, and a gag. Rescue – for patient and physician – came from an unexpected quarter.

'Dickon,' said Quenhyth brightly, kneeling next to the boy. 'Would you like a rat?'

Dickon's wails stopped abruptly. 'Rats bite,' he said. But he was clearly interested. His screeches did not resume, and he waited for Quenhyth to elaborate.

'This one will not,' said Quenhyth, gesturing to the horrified parents that he did not have a real rodent in mind. 'And it will have a tail as long as a dog's. Would you like to see?'

'Give,' said Dickon, thrusting out a hand that was sticky from the treats his mother had been feeding him ever since he had first looked her in the eye and pressed the pea into his ear.

'Here,' said Quenhyth, reaching into his bag – modelled rather obviously on the one Bartholomew carried – and withdrawing an object that was all stick legs and clumsily sewn fur. 'I was making this for my little brother, but you look like a lad who will appreciate a rat.'

'Give,' ordered Dickon again, chubby fingers stretching for the prize.

'It has proper eyes,' said Quenhyth, flaunting the object just out of Dickon's grasp. He reached into his bag a second time and pulled out a length of twine that had been woven to look uncannily like the tail of a rodent. 'All I need to do is attach this, and it will be finished. What do you say?'

Dickon squirmed out of his mother's arms, aiming to snatch the toy, but the student had anticipated such a move. He stood up quickly, and Dickon found himself unable to reach. He opened his mouth for another of his monstrous shrieks.

'No,' said Bartholomew sharply, before he could start. 'You cannot have it if you screech.'

Dickon's mouth snapped shut, eyes fixed on the toy that dangled so tantalisingly close. It was not an attractive thing,

169

and Bartholomew thought normal children might have found it a little frightening. But Dickon was not a normal child. He was fascinated by the ugly wooden frame, inexpertly covered with fur salvaged from an old winter cloak. The four legs were of different lengths, the snout was long, thin and mean, and the eyes – made from polished stones – glittered in a way that was sinister. There was also a set of improbably large teeth, which had been fashioned from scraps of metal scavenged from the blacksmith's forge and then hammered into its jaws.

'You should not let him have that,' said Bartholomew, thinking that Quenhyth had probably gone to some trouble to make it. It would not last long with Dickon, who tested new toys by hurling them against walls or dropping them from upstairs windows. 'You are unlikely to get it back in one piece.'

'I do not think my brother will like it, actually,' admitted Quenhyth ruefully. 'It did not turn out the way I expected. It ended up looking a trifle . . . demonic.'

'It certainly has,' said Tulyet, regarding it uneasily.

'I have been carrying it about for weeks now,' Quenhyth went on. 'It seems a shame to throw it away, since it took me the best part of four Sundays to make. I am happy for Dickon to have it.'

'It is very kind,' said Mistress Tulyet gratefully. 'It has already distracted him from his pain, and he has stopped that terrible crying.'

'Thank God,' muttered Bartholomew. He edged closer to the boy again, ready to retreat if the brat tried to bite, kick, scratch, thump or pinch. He had suffered enough bruises from Dickon in the past to be cautious, even when it appeared his attention was captured by something else. 'If you want the toy, Dickon, you must sit on your mother's lap and tilt your head to one side. Quietly.'

Dickon regarded Bartholomew venomously, knowing

170

that the pea was about to be removed, and that it might result in a little discomfort.

'Let him have the toy first,' suggested Mistress Tulyet. 'He will sit still while he inspects it.'

'No,' said Bartholomew. Once Dickon had the rat in his possession he would never do as he was told. 'Pea first, rat second.'

Dickon's expression was murderous, but he crawled on to his mother's knee and put his head to one side. Bartholomew selected a tiny pair of forceps and had secured the pea before the lad had even taken a breath to bray his displeasure. Dickon eyed the pulse in astonishment, and Bartholomew saw the realisation register that he would have to find another excuse if he wanted to indulge in more bad behaviour that evening. The lad wriggled away from his mother and dashed to Quenhyth.

'Give,' he said firmly.

'Do you want it to have a tail?' asked Quenhyth. Dickon nodded slowly. 'Then you will have to wait while I sew it on. Sit with me by the hearth, and watch.'

To Bartholomew's surprise, Dickon squatted by Quenhyth as meekly as a lamb, and there was blessed silence while he watched the tail being appended. Tulyet heaved a sigh of relief.

'I was beginning to think we might be up all night with the poor child. I shall pay your student as much as I give you for this consultation, Matt. I shall always be in his debt.'

Bartholomew smiled. 'It means Dickon will be his first official patient, and not one he will easily forget.' He did not mean it as a compliment.

Grateful that another domestic crisis was over, Tulyet turned the discussion to town affairs, while Quenhyth and Dickon sat by the fire and Mistress Tulyet watched with a doting smile. Bartholomew noticed the servants were not nearly so soft-hearted. They exchanged glances indicating that *they* knew exactly how to deal with small, calculating fiends who frightened their parents and threw the whole household into disarray.

'I am worried about Mistress Lenne,' said Tulyet, pouring Bartholomew some wine. 'She was ailing anyway, but her husband's death under Mortimer's cart has hastened her journey to the grave.'

'Her son will be here soon,' said Bartholomew, thinking about what Bottisham had told him – before he had met his own grisly end. He also recalled that Bottisham had been visiting both Isnard and the old woman, helping them with small, practical donations of money and food. He hoped someone else would take up where he had left off, and realised yet again what a good man the lawyer had been.

'It is not right,' said Tulyet bitterly. 'Mortimer was clearly drunk, yet I am powerless to bring him to justice. Bosel was a poor witness, but at least he was something. Without him I have no case.'

'Orwelle thinks no one will ever be charged with Bosel's murder, either.'

'It looks that way. If Mortimer had not been at that town meeting, I would have arrested him immediately. But I saw him with my own eyes – and what better alibi can he claim than me?'

'I told you: he may have given Bosel the poison earlier in the day. Bosel drank it in the evening, but Mortimer may have passed it to him much sooner.'

Tulyet disagreed. 'We are talking about Bosel here, Matt. He would not have waited before consuming a gift of wine. First, he would not have had the self-control, and second, he would have been afraid that someone would take it from him, if he did not swallow it immediately.'

Bartholomew knew this was true. Bosel was not the only

172

beggar in Cambridge, and if any of them had seen him with wine they would have demanded a share – or would have taken it by force.

'Still,' mused Tulyet, 'perhaps Thomas will lose his lawsuit against the King's Mill. That would hurt him far more than a mere charge of murder.'

'How will the King investigate the mill dispute?' asked Bartholomew, wanting to talk about something other than murderers who might go unpunished.

'Four men will be appointed as commissioners, and they will reach a verdict based on an impartial assessment of the facts. Whatever they decide will be law in the King's name.'

'Will these men be the same ones who pardoned Thorpe and Edward? Because if so, then justice will have nothing to do with their decision. Whoever offers the largest bribe will.'

'Now, now, Matt,' admonished Tulyet mildly. 'Watch what you are saying. I do not want my son's physician hanged for treason. But how is Michael faring with the other business – Deschalers and that scholar . . . what was his name?'

'Bottisham,' said Bartholomew, displeased that the Sheriff had forgotten. 'Nicholas Bottisham. And Michael is not faring at all. He has learned nothing to help him unravel the mystery.'

'Then I hope he has better luck tomorrow. There are already rumours in the town that Deschalers was murdered by a scholar, and ill-feeling is beginning to fester. Cambridge will be in flames if he does not have a culprit soon.'

Bartholomew and Quenhyth took their leave of the Tulyets with grateful thanks ringing in their ears. Quenhyth hummed happily, and Bartholomew saw the student was pleased with himself – because of the Tulyets' adulation as well as the much-needed donation of funds. Bartholomew congratulated him on his performance, and was surprised to see him blush as he admitted a talent for dealing with children. Bartholomew decided he would take Quenhyth with him the next time he was summoned to tend Dickon. Perhaps he could eventually relinquish him as a patient, since Dickon's ailments were never anything a student could not handle. The future began to look brighter.

They parted company at the Jewry, where Bartholomew tried to guess the identity of the visitor to whom Matilde had alluded, hoping he would not be obliged to exchange pleasantries with one of her former lovers. He dragged his feet a little as he made his way to her home, apprehension mounting as he drew closer. She owned a handsome, albeit small, house that stood near the crumbling church of All Saints in the Jewry. He knocked on her door with some trepidation, and was ushered in by Matilde herself, who smiled her pleasure at his arrival. She gestured that he was to precede her into the comfortable ground-floor chamber where she entertained her guests.

The room was crammed full of people, with children perched on every knee, lap and available scrap of floor, and several adults sitting on the cushioned benches that ran around the walls. Michael was squashed uncomfortably between Yolande and her husband. He had a goblet of wine in one hand and Yolande's smallest baby in the other. He was clearly nervous of the tiny scrap of humanity – not that his large hands might damage it or make it cry, but that something might leak through its swaddling clothes and leave a stain on his habit. He held it at arm's length, like a man showing off a prize vegetable. The child surveyed the room from its unusual vantage point with startled eyes.

At first, Bartholomew could not detect any unexpected visitor in the sea of faces that greeted him. Then he realised that every single person, regardless of age or sex, was facing in one direction, towards a figure who sat in the

174

seat of honour next to the blazing hearth. It was almost as though no one else existed; even the baby's great blue orbs were drawn that way.

An old lady sat there, small, slight and almost swallowed up by an array of cushions and blankets. Yet she was upright and spry, and exuded the sense that here was a woman of great strength and determination. Her emerald eyes were unreadable, but unmistakably intelligent, and she had a large hooked nose. Bartholomew recognised her immediately and a sense of foreboding flowed through him. Matilde gestured to the old woman with an elegant hand.

'You remember Dame Pelagia, I am sure, Matthew,' she said. 'She is Michael's grandmother, and the King's best and most famous agent.'

'Lord!' breathed Bartholomew, as he fought to remember his manners and make a bow that was suitably low and deferential. It would not do to offend a woman like Dame Pelagia with inadequate shows of obsequiousness, even inadvertently. 'Now the corpses will start piling up.'

Dame Pelagia's elderly appearance was deceptive, and her hearing was just as sharp as it had been when she was a comely young maiden some sixty years before. Her smile was enigmatic and impossible to interpret.

'Do not complain, Matthew,' she replied, her green eyes, so like Michael's, gleaming with mischief. 'My grandson tells me you need all the fourpenny fees you can get.'

175

CHAPTER 5

The following morning, Bartholomew visited the small house on Shoemaker Row, near the Market Square, where Lenne's widow lived. Michael went with him, on the understanding that the physician would then accompany him to interview the Fellows at Gonville Hall.

The Market Square was noisy and colourful that day. Apprentices were everywhere, carrying goods in barrels, sacks, crates and buckets, clad in liveries to advertise their masters' businesses. Customers weaved among them – haughty retainers from wealthy households, friars and monks from religious houses and the University, and wide-eyed peasants from the surrounding villages. The air rang with sound, and Bartholomew and Michael had to shout to make themselves heard above the yelling of traders, the clatter of hoofs, the squealing of pigs headed for Butchery Row, and the furious barking of a dog. The acid stench of old urine from the tanneries and the rank, sickening aroma of decaying offal from the slaughterhouses was especially pungent that morning, making Bartholomew's eyes water so that he could barely see where he was walking.

Shoemaker Row was a narrow, congested lane that was inhabited mostly, but not exclusively, by cobblers. Its largest building was Ely Hall, rented by a contingent of Benedictine monks from nearby Ely Abbey, while the Lenne home was one of the smallest, comprising a single ground-floor room with a lean-to kitchen at the back.

The red ribbon that had fluttered outside the house, to tell passers-by the nature of Lenne's profession, had been

176

taken down, probably by other barbers keen to secure his customers for themselves. When a feeble voice answered Bartholomew's tap, he pushed open the door and entered, squinting against the sudden sting of smoke and waiting for his eyes to become accustomed to the gloom. Mistress Lenne lay on a pallet, dangerously close to the fire.

'I keep expecting him to come home,' she whispered as Bartholomew crouched next to her. Michael busied himself by taking a broom handle to the flue in the roof, in an attempt to clear some of the choking pall that rose from the peat faggots in the hearth. 'I think I hear him chatting outside with his customers, and that he will come in to tell me the gossip.' Her eyes filled with tears.

'How is your chest?' asked Bartholomew, not knowing what to say, so taking refuge in practical matters. 'Does it still ache when you breathe?'

'They say he was drunk when he murdered my husband. Thomas Mortimer, I mean. Is it true, Doctor? Did he ride him down as though he was a dog, and then laugh at the damage he had done?'

'He did not laugh,' replied Bartholomew truthfully.

'But he did not cry, either,' she said bitterly. 'He just lied to protect himself. Sheriff Tulyet tells me that he cannot charge him with my husband's murder, because Bosel is dead. Mortimer has not even said he is sorry.'

She turned away, tears leaving silvery trails in the soot that dusted her cheeks. Bartholomew took her hand and held it while she sobbed. When she quietened, he helped her to sit up and drink a syrup of angelica he had prepared the previous evening, which he thought would soothe the racking cough that left her gasping for breath. Then he eased her under the covers again, and sat with her while Michael sang soft, haunting ballads. Eventually, she dozed.

Michael was silent when they left, closing the door gently, so it would not wake her. Bartholomew took a deep breath, wondering whether he would ever become inured to some aspects of life as a physician. He glanced around, in the hope that one of his students might be nearby, because he wanted someone to be with her when she woke again. He was in luck: Quenhyth was tugging insistently at the sleeve of Cheney the spicer, while informing him that his handwriting was the best in Michaelhouse, and that his rates for writing trade agreements were very low. Quenhyth was usually to be found at his studies, and Bartholomew had seldom seen him doing anything else. He listened with interest to the conversation that followed.

'I do not need another clerk,' snapped Cheney. 'I already have Redmeadow.'

'But he steals,' said Quenhyth. 'So, if you notice items missing, and you require a clerk whose honesty is beyond question, you will know where to come. To me.'

'All the University's scribes steal,' said Cheney matter-of-factly. 'It is a grim reality – and the reason why no sensible merchant ever leaves one unattended in his home or near anything valuable.'

'Oh,' said Quenhyth, deflated. 'Well, I am no thief, I promise you, Master Cheney. My father is a wealthy merchant, just like you, and he taught me right from wrong.'

'If he is wealthy, then why are you scribing for pennies?' asked Cheney, not unreasonably.

'He pays my fees and board,' explained Quenhyth. 'But the food has recently become inedible at Michaelhouse, and we are all obliged to buy victuals from elsewhere. That requires money.'

'True,' muttered Michael, watching the spicer waddle down the street, leaving a disconsolate Quenhyth behind him. 'Buying supplies to supplement what Michaelhouse provides has become a necessity of late. *We* have friends who give us meals – do not look startled, Matt. You have

178

dined out at least four times recently – but Quenhyth has not, and must win his victuals by scribing instead.'

'Have you spoken to Wynewyk about this?' asked Bartholomew, hoping Quenhyth did not decide to practise medicine for money if he could not secure work by writing.

'He says food prices are increasing – they always do at the end of winter – so we must economise.' Michael was disgusted. 'The words "economise" and "food" should never be used in the same sentence. They are anathema to each other, like "small" and "portion".'

Bartholomew waved to catch Quenhyth's attention, and told the student he wanted him or Redmeadow to visit Mistress Lenne three times a day until her son arrived from Thetford. Quenhyth nodded, eager to accept the responsibility. He took parchment and a pen from his scrip and wrote down his teacher's instructions, doing so flamboyantly, in the hope that his literary skills might attract customers.

'None of this is fair,' said Michael bitterly, when Quenhyth had gone. The visit to Mistress Lenne had distressed the monk. 'Look what Thomas Mortimer has done! He killed *two* people with his careless driving, because that old woman will not last long now her husband is gone. He was lucky Isnard is built like an ox, or there might have been three.'

'Isnard is recovering well,' said Bartholomew, wanting to say something to cheer him. 'He is pestering Robert de Blaston to finish carving his new false leg. When he has mastered its use – which he anticipates will only be a matter of an hour or two – he plans to visit Mortimer.'

'Then thank God wooden legs take time to make,' said Michael fervently. 'Isnard has a black temper, and Mortimer is likely to enrage him with his uncaring attitude. But we should visit Gonville before any more time passes. We must resolve this business with Bottisham and Deschalers, and—'

'There he is,' interrupted Bartholomew, pointing to where Thomas Mortimer lurched through the market stalls with various packets and parcels in his arms. One fell, and an urchin had scampered forward and stolen it before his wine-addled brain had even registered that it had dropped. 'He is drunk again, and it is barely past dawn.'

Michael's expression turned into something dangerous. 'His brother Constantine is with him. Shall we ask them why they have inflicted such suffering on our town with the careless driving of carts and the buying of pardons for killers?'

'I do not think that is a good idea, Brother,' said Bartholomew, thinking it was likely to instigate a brawl. Many scholars were indignant about what had happened to a member of a University choir, and might well grab the opportunity to mete out justice with their fists. Meanwhile, the Mortimer clan employed a large number of apprentices, all of whom would fight to protect their masters' good name.

But Michael was not listening. He strode up to the Mortimer brothers and beamed falsely at them. Bartholomew's heart sank, and he saw he should not have taken the soft-hearted monk to visit Mistress Lenne. While Michael liked to give the impression that he was cool and dispassionate, few things enraged him as much as injustice and suffering among the poor. Bartholomew sensed the ensuing confrontation was going to be an unpleasant one.

'Good morning,' said Michael, addressing the reeling miller. Thomas Mortimer promptly lost the rest of his parcels and looked down at them with a bemused expression, trying to work out what had gone wrong. 'Surely it is too early for wine? I have only just had breakfast.'

180

'That is from last night,' said Constantine, snapping his fingers at an apprentice, ordering him to retrieve the fallen items. 'Thomas has had no wine this morning.'

Constantine the baker was a fighting cock of a man, who had once been notorious for his vicious temper and bullying manners – a smaller version of his brother Thomas. But his son's exile and the death of his wife Katherine had affected him deeply, and rendered him milder and sadder. He was still loyally devoted to his numerous cousins, aunts and nephews, but he was not quite as pugilistic as he had once been.

'That makes it all right, then,' said Michael caustically. 'It is perfectly natural for a man to imbibe so much wine that he is still drunk after a night in his bed. Still, at least he has the sense not to do his shopping in a cart.'

'Lenne was an accident,' said Constantine wearily, as though tired of repeating himself. 'Everyone makes it sound as though Thomas did it on purpose. He cannot help it if careless peasants stray across the streets without warning.'

'And if people do not shut up about it, then the town can look elsewhere for money to repair the Great Bridge,' slurred Mortimer nastily. 'I am not giving good silver to help a gaggle of ingrates!'

Bartholomew saw that a number of Mortimer apprentices, all wearing distinctive mustard-yellow livery, were gathering. He tugged on Michael's arm, to pull him away. He disliked brawling and, although he was angry enough with Thomas and he would enjoy punching the man, he had no intention of being drawn into a fight in which he was so heavily outnumbered. Michael shook him off.

'Did you see this "accident" yourself?' the monk asked archly. Constantine shook his head. 'Then how do you know what happened? Thomas certainly did not, and he was driving!'

'We have business at Gonville, Brother,' Bartholomew

whispered urgently, trying again to pull the monk away. 'We need to exonerate Bottisham from these accusations before there is trouble.'

'Then tell me why you arranged for Edward to be pardoned,' ordered Michael, when neither Mortimer responded to his question. He freed his arm firmly enough to make Bartholomew stagger. 'Why did you want him back, after all he did?'

Constantine flushed and looked down at his feet. 'Partly because my son's conviction was a slur on the Mortimer name. And partly because it was *my* fault that he turned to evil ways – I drove him to crime with my temper. I thought I could make amends by bringing him home.'

'And that has not happened?' asked Michael. He grimaced in disgust when Thomas toppled backwards and would have fallen, if his apprentices had not darted forward and caught him.

Constantine shook his head. 'Edward refuses to live with me. Nor will he resume his baker's training. His mother would not have been pleased.'

'She is here, you know,' said Thomas, his arrogance suddenly replaced by fear. 'I saw Katherine near the Great Bridge, and she *looked* at me. She is back from her grave to haunt us. I had to visit the Hand of Valence Marie, and pay a shilling to ask for its protection from her troubled spirit.'

'He saw Bess,' explained Constantine, when he saw Michael assume it was the wine speaking. 'That madwoman who is here to look for her husband. She gave me a turn when *I* first saw her, too. The likeness between her and my wife is uncanny – even Deschalers commented on it, and he *never* spoke to me about Katherine. He was always too ashamed for making me a cuckold.'

'Did Katherine have a younger sister?' asked Bartholomew, thinking that Deschalers had not been the kind of man to feel shame for enjoying himself with another man's wife. It seemed more likely that the grocer had never mentioned Katherine because the memory had been too painful for him.

'Katherine was an only child,' replied Constantine. 'She hailed from the Fens, whereas Bess comes from London. Their similarity is coincidence, nothing more. They are not related.'

'Edward will become a miller, like me,' rambled Thomas; he had already forgotten the scare 'Katherine' had given him. He cast a triumphant look in his brother's direction, so Bartholomew surmised it was a source of discord between them. 'And together we shall siphon water away from the King's Mill until it is dry.'

'Why would you do that?' asked Bartholomew, puzzled. 'There is enough to run both.'

'There *was* enough for both, when Thomas was grinding corn,' explained Constantine. 'But fulling needs far more water.'

'So the Millers' Society can go and hang themselves,' declared Thomas thickly, trying to fix the physician in his sights. He blinked hard and stood swaying, while his apprentices tensed, ready to catch him again. 'The scholars of Gonville Hall will see them off. Lawyers are cunning and scholars are cunning. So a scholar–lawyer will be *very* cunning.'

'Is that why you hired Gonville?' asked Michael curiously. 'Because you think them more sly than the town lawyers?'

'Well, it is true,' said Constantine. 'We cannot lose this case, because the forfeits would be fierce – loss of our mill, heavy fines, legal costs. It does not bear thinking about.'

'Do you know why one of your Gonville lawyers – Bottisham – should have been with Deschalers at the King's Mill on Sunday night?' asked Michael, seizing the opportunity to advance his investigation a little. 'You heard what happened?'

'Stabbed, then thrown on to the millstones,' said Constantine. He shuddered. 'I have seen mills working, and that would not be a pleasant way to die. But if Bottisham was meeting Deschalers on our behalf, then he said nothing of his plans to us. You must ask Bernarde and his cronies about it. After all, it was in *their* mill that this tragedy occurred.'

'What are we going to do about Edward?' asked Bartholomew when he saw the Mortimers knew – or would reveal – nothing about Bottisham's death. 'Even *you* have no control over your son, and the whole town is waiting for him to do something terrible. We must act before someone is hurt.'

'But I do not know what to do!' cried Constantine. His sudden wail startled physician, monk and miller alike. 'God forgive me! I thought I was doing the right thing when I bought their pardons – Edward asked me to help Thorpe, too, because his father had disowned him. But I did not know how much they had both changed.'

'He is no longer the malleable boy you knew?' asked Michael.

'He is not, and I do not like what he has become. He unnerves me with his vengeful glowers and spiteful comments. If I could go to the King and tell him I had made a mistake, I would. But Edward said he would kill me if I did that.'

'Did he now?' asked Michael thoughtfully, wondering whether threats of murder might be sufficient to see the pardons withdrawn.

'More than once.' Constantine lowered his voice so his brother would not hear, although Thomas was leaning so heavily against a staggering apprentice that Bartholomew thought he might have passed out. 'The combination of Thomas's drinking and Edward's resentful fury is not a good one. I am afraid: for me, for my bakery, for my

184

brother and for his mill. I shall have to go to the Hand of Valence Marie, and pray for its help.'

'I doubt that will do any good,' said Michael bluntly. 'The best way to ensure no one is hurt is to prevent trouble in the first place. Do you have *any* idea what Edward and Thorpe might be plotting? If you do, then we may be able to thwart it, and we can rectify this miscarriage of justice that *you* have brought about.'

'The Hand will answer our prayers,' slurred Thomas, struggling over his words as though his tongue belonged to someone else. 'Young Hufford of Honville Gall has been praying for days for a cure. And he has one.'

'A cure for what?' asked Bartholomew warily. He hoped rumours were not about to circulate that the Hand had healing powers, because then the spread of the cult would be unstoppable.

'For a sore on his mouth,' explained Constantine.

'Oh, that,' said Bartholomew, relieved. 'It healed naturally – the Hand had nothing to do with it.'

'Never mind this,' said Michael impatiently. 'What about Edward's plans?'

'Edward barely speaks to me,' said Constantine bitterly. 'And he is destroying our family by making us take sides against each other – brother against brother, cousin against cousin. We were solidly loyal before he arrived, but now we argue all the time. We will lose all our power and influence in the town if we allow our clan to fragment – and then where will we be?'

'Where indeed?' mused Michael thoughtfully.

Once Constantine had struggled away with his reeling brother, Bartholomew and Michael fought their way through the Market Square towards Gonville Hall. But Bartholomew found himself reluctant to go, unaccountably afraid he might learn something that would disappoint or shock him about the scholar he had so liked and admired. It would not be the first time an investigation had revealed a seemingly good man to be something rather different, and he realised his work for Michael had turned him from someone naturally trusting to someone uneasy and suspicious. He walked slowly, aware that Michael was matching his reduced pace and was probably assailed with the same concerns.

'You must be pleased to see your grandmother,' he said, yawning. He wished he had spent less of the previous night reminiscing with the old lady, and more in his own bed. 'Were you expecting her?'

Michael smiled fondly. 'No, but I am not surprised she is here. She played an important role in convicting Edward Mortimer and Thorpe, and she is not a woman who likes loose ends. She came to see for herself what was happening.'

'It is a pity she did not prevent the pardons from being issued in the first place. From what I hear, the King listens to her and never does anything she believes to be imprudent or wrong.'

'Unfortunately, she was in Avignon when the matter went to the King's Bench clerks. She only heard about it when it was too late to do anything. She was not pleased, I can tell you!'

Bartholomew could well imagine, and was wryly amused with himself for feeling safer now the old lady was there. Dame Pelagia was elderly and slight, but her deceptively frail figure concealed a core of steel, a raw and ruthless cunning, and a rather shocking talent for throwing knives. Bartholomew had come to understand Michael's fondness for intrigue and deception far better once he had met his formidable forebear. He stopped to fiddle with a strap on his boot, knowing it was a deliberate ploy to delay what he was certain was going to be an unpleasant interview at Gonville.

'What was she doing in Avignon?' he asked. He had

been under the impression that she had retired from her long and distinguished service as the King's best agent. Then it occurred to him that Bishop Bateman had been poisoned in Avignon.

'She has always liked France,' replied Michael, airily vague. 'And she has spent a good deal of time there in the past. She told me she had a desire to see it again.'

Bartholomew did not respond immediately. England had been at war with France for the past twenty years, and he suspected her sojourns there had been spent implementing plots and intrigues – all designed to harm France and benefit England. He wondered whether the conflict might have ended a good deal sooner, had the likes of Dame Pelagia not been on hand to stir it up.

'So, who killed Bishop Bateman?' He glanced up at Michael. 'It was not her, was it?'

Michael regarded him with astonishment. 'Of course not! If she had killed anyone, it would have been the French ambassador, who was refusing to listen to Bateman's terms for peace.'

'But Bateman was not a successful diplomatist,' said Bartholomew. He stood up and started walking again. 'Perhaps the King wanted rid of him, without the inconvenience of saying why.'

'Well, if he did, my grandmother did not oblige him,' said Michael stiffly. 'She does not murder well-regarded prelates.'

The tone of his voice suggested she might well dispatch a couple of unpopular ones, though, and Bartholomew supposed the haughty and irascible Bishop of Ely had better watch himself if Dame Pelagia was back in the country.

'Here is Gonville,' said Bartholomew, deciding to end the discussion before it ranged too far into uncharted waters. 'We should not discuss the murder of their founder when they might overhear us.'

187

'Especially if you accuse my grandmother of doing it,' said Michael huffily.

'Are you not concerned for her?' asked Bartholomew, knocking at Gonville's gate. He did so tentatively, and his soft tap was unlikely to be heard by any but the most sharp-eared of gatekeepers. 'Thorpe and Mortimer seem to blame her for their exile, and I am worried about the fact that she has chosen to stay with Matilde. If they attack Dame Pelagia, then Matilde may be hurt.'

'She only intends to impose herself on Matilde for one night,' said Michael. 'She has other arrangements for the rest of her stay here.'

'Where?' asked Bartholomew. He regarded the monk uneasily. 'Not at Michaelhouse?'

Michael snorted his laughter. 'Of course not! How could she stay in a College that only admits men? I know her disguises are legendary, and she could pass herself off as a travelling academic, if she was so inclined. But she is almost eighty years old, and she yearns for a little comfort in her old age. She will stay with Mayor Morice.'

Bartholomew was unable to prevent himself from gaping. 'With Morice? But why?'

'Because he has the best house in Cambridge, why else? His corruption has made him a rich man, and he can offer a high level of accommodation that is unavailable else-where. Deschalers would have been her first choice – he was wealthier still – but she can hardly claim his hospitality now he is dead.'

'Does Morice know who she is?'

'He knows she has the ear of the King, and that is enough for him to welcome her. Morice has many enemies – folk he has cheated and deceived over the years – so his house is sturdily built and protected like a fortress. It is a very safe place for her to be.'

Bartholomew did not know what to think. Perhaps news

of Morice's brazen dishonesty had reached royal ears, and Dame Pelagia had another, more sinister, reason for demanding the Mayor's hospitality. It also occurred to him that it had been Morice's letter to the King's Bench that had tipped the appeal in Mortimer and Thorpe's favour, and had gone a long way towards getting them their royal pardons. He wondered whether Morice would survive the visit, or whether he would die in some mysterious accident before his enigmatic guest finally took her leave of the town.

Michael hammered on the sturdy oaken gate, seeing no one was going to reply to the physician's polite raps. They exchanged an unhappy glance while they waited, neither looking forward to the task of prising personal secrets from Bottisham's friends.

Gonville Hall comprised two stone mansions linked by a central gatehouse. The upper floor of the smaller house held the College library, which Bartholomew coveted – Michaelhouse's 'library' comprised a couple of shelves in the conclave and hall. Gonville's books were housed in a handsome room that boasted polished wooden floors and a hearth where there was nearly always a fire. The chamber was usually peaceful, since teaching was conducted in the hall below, and Bartholomew imagined it would be an excellent place to study, away from distractions.

Adjacent to the library were the foundations for the new chapel. Bartholomew could see them through gaps in the wood of the gate. It was to be a substantial structure, and he wondered how it would be funded now that Bishop Bateman was dead.

Michael pounded on the gate yet again, claiming no College had the right to keep the Senior Proctor waiting. There was a grille set in the door, and Bartholomew saw it open very slowly, as if the person peering out did not want the visitors to know they were being examined. It did not escape Michael's attention, however.

'Let me in,' he ordered, thrusting his large face close to the opening. 'I have come to talk to you about Bottisham.'

'Brother Michael,' said the watcher with relief, and there were loud clicks as a key was turned in a lock. 'I am sorry. But one cannot be too careful these days – what with pardoned exiles strutting around freely.'

'You are wise to be cautious,' said Michael, easing himself through the gate. Bartholomew followed, and watched while the scholar secured it again. 'I heard what happened to you.'

The scholar on gate duty that day was John of Ufford. Bartholomew recalled Redmeadow telling him that Mortimer and Thorpe had picked a fight with Ufford, and folk had been surprised when he was trounced. Ufford was the son of an earl, and therefore trained in the arts of swordplay, battle tactics and horsemanship. The fact that the two exiles had beaten him said a good deal for the skills they had learned in France. Ufford had a cut on his nose, and was limping. The sore on his mouth had all but healed, though, and Bartholomew supposed he had taken his advice about its care when they had met before the *Disputatio de quodlibet*.

'I was not even doing anything,' said Ufford indignantly. 'I was outside St Mary the Great, thanking the Hand for not letting me contract leprosy, when they started to pick on me. I drew my dagger, thinking the sight of it would see them off, but they pulled out their own and I was defeated.' He shook his head, as if he could not imagine how such a thing had happened.

'Then you must have been dismayed when you learned Thorpe had inveigled himself a home in your own College,' said Michael.

Ufford grimaced. 'I was not dismayed – I was furious! But, fortunately for all concerned, Thorpe is rarely here.

190

I think he just wanted to prove to his father that he could secure his own place in the University. It is common knowledge that Valence Marie refused to accept him.'

'Where is your Master?' asked Michael, looking around at a College that appeared to be deserted. 'We need to ask him questions about Bottisham, and I was told all the Fellows would be here today.'

'Master Colton is – was – with Bishop Bateman at Avignon,' replied Ufford. 'He has been the Bishop's chief clerk for some years now. Their relationship is rather like the one you enjoy with the Bishop of Ely, Brother – except that Colton does not spy for Bateman, and you probably do not want to be your bishop's replacement.'

Michael stared at him, amusement glinting in the depths of the green eyes that were so uncannily like his grandmother's. 'You speak very plainly, Ufford! However, I assure you that I do not *spy* for the Bishop of Ely, nor would I refuse his see, should it ever be offered to me. But I had forgotten Colton is away. How do you manage without him?'

'We are used to his absences, and the College is run very ably by Acting Master Pulham.'

'I see,' said Michael. 'It must have been a bitter blow for you to learn of Bateman's death.'

'Very bitter,' agreed Ufford. 'He was a good man, and generous to us. But you are in luck, Brother. Here are my colleagues now, back from their devotions at St Mary the Great.'

Bartholomew watched Ufford open the gate a second time, to allow the scholars of Gonville Hall inside. They were a neat, sober group, older than those at most other Colleges and hostels, because they had been selected by Bishop Bateman himself – and Bateman had a preference for established scholars over young students. His reasons were

191

understandable: older men were less inclined to join in the frequent brawls that marred the town, and so were less likely to bring his institution into disrepute.

Bartholomew recognised all the Fellows at the head of the procession, and a few of the students behind. Leading the way was Acting Master Pulham with his Cistercian habit and colossal ears, while Rougham the physician was close on his heels. Next came a gentle friar called Henry of Thompson, who hailed from a famous college of priests in south Norfolk. Finally, there was a nobleman named Henry Despenser, who was said to be destined for great things in the Church.

'Brother Michael,' said Pulham genially. 'I am sorry we were not available to see you yesterday. Come to our library for a cup of warmed ale. And while we are there, you might care to inspect a tome or two. We sold Bacon's *De erroribus medicorum* to the Chancellor yesterday, and you might be interested in other items we have for sale.' He sounded hopeful.

'You are selling your books?' asked Bartholomew, who would rather have starved than part with one of his own. He thought about the large and extravagant meals for which Gonville was famous, and wondered why they did not economise on food instead. 'Why?'

'Just the few we do not use,' replied Pulham. 'To raise funds for our chapel.'

'We will soon have the books from Bateman's private library,' said Rougham boastfully. 'He is certain to have remembered us in his will. So, we are ridding ourselves of rubbish we would never consider using anyway – like the Bacon, and the Trotula scroll I sold to that whore.' He glanced at Bartholomew out of the corner of his eye, so the physician was sure his words were intentionally insulting on two fronts: Bartholomew's fondness for unorthodox medicine and for Matilde.

192

He rose to the bait, ignoring Michael's warning elbow in the ribs. Some discourtesies were simply too grave to be ignored. 'No gentleman slanders a lady's good name,' he said coldly. 'Your slur reflects more poorly on you than it does on her.'

Rougham glowered. 'Are you questioning my breeding, sir?' he demanded archly.

'If your breeding is reflected in your manners, then I am,' replied Bartholomew. 'It is—'

'Warm ale, did you say?' interrupted Michael, in an attempt to prevent a quarrel. He wanted the Gonville Fellows' co-operation in the matter of Bottisham's death. 'In the library?'

'This way,' said Pulham hastily, indicating the direction with his hand. But Rougham was not to be silenced.

'Trotula is foreign rubbish,' he said, following the Acting Master across the yard, although he had the sense to let the matter lie regarding Matilde. 'I only ever use Latin or Greek texts in my classes.'

'They are foreign,' Bartholomew pointed out.

'*Ancient* Greece was very different to the Greece of today,' said Rougham haughtily. 'And Trotula was from Salerno.' The tone of his voice made it sound akin to Sodom or Gomorrah. '*Her* medical knowledge was confined to adultery and poisoning. Just like the Arabs, in fact.'

Bartholomew gazed at him, somewhat startled. Rougham knew Bartholomew's own teacher had been an Arab – many of the 'unorthodox' treatments he had learned from Ibn Ibrahim had actually been known in the eastern world for centuries – and so his comments were clearly intended to be offensive. The expression on Rougham's face was challenging, but Bartholomew quickly suppressed the raft of tart responses that flooded into his mind, and decided to ignore the man. He assumed Rougham was just in a bad mood, and his inflammatory statements were not worth arguing over – especially if to do so would interfere with the investigation into Bottisham's death.

They entered the library, and sat on the benches that had been placed around the walls. A fire was burning in the hearth, and the room smelled of peat smoke, polished wood and ancient parchment. It was an agreeable aroma, and one that reminded Bartholomew of his Oxford days, when he had studied long hours in the library at Merton. If he closed his eyes, he could imagine himself back there, unplagued by worries like purchasing medicines for impoverished patients, bitter rival physicians, and the violent deaths of colleagues. It was peaceful; the only sounds were the crackling of the fire and the occasional rustle of a page turning.

Pulham fussed over jugs and goblets, then presented his guests with cups so full he was obliged to carry each in both hands, gnawing at his lower lip as he concentrated on not spilling any.

'As you have probably surmised, we are here to talk about Bottisham,' said Michael, when he had drained his goblet dry to prevent accidents. He did not approve of liquids near books. 'We are deeply sorry about what happened to him. He was a kindly man, and he will be missed.'

'Kindly?' asked Rougham icily. 'How do *you* know what he was like?'

Bartholomew wished the man would go away, since he was not prepared to be polite. 'He gave me a gold noble to buy medicine for Godric of Ovyng Hostel a few weeks ago. Godric was bitten by a dog and the wound festered, but Ovyng did not have the money for salves. Bottisham has been helping Isnard and Mistress Lenne, too.'

Rougham stared at him angrily. 'I did not know any of this. Why was *I* not called to attend this Godric? And why did Bottisham dispense funds to help men from other hostels, when we have a chapel to build?'

Bartholomew saw he should have remained quiet about Bottisham's quiet generosity. Most men would have been impressed to learn that someone they knew had acted in an anonymously charitable manner, but Rougham seemed intent on being antagonistic that morning. Bartholomew decided it would be better for everyone if he did not dignify the man's curt questions with a reply.

'Bottisham *was* a good man,' said Pulham. He smiled at Rougham in an attempt to placate him. 'Perhaps he left us something in his will. Then we can rid ourselves of young Thorpe.'

'You should not have accepted Thorpe as a student,' said Michael. The monk had changed the subject, reluctant to begin an interrogation in which he would demand to know whether Bottisham had been involved in something sinister that had led to his odd death in the King's Mill. 'His presence in your College will only end in tears.'

'He was persistent,' explained Pulham. 'He was determined to become a scholar, so I thought we may as well take his fees, since we are currently short of funds. He offered to sew us an altar cloth and chasuble if we took him. Besides, he does not want to *live* here, just to study occasionally.'

'You will find yourselves the losers,' warned Michael.

'*I* certainly did,' muttered Ufford, touching the cut on his nose.

'Did you make an official complaint about this attack on you?' asked Michael. 'To the Sheriff or one of my beadles?'

Ufford pulled a disagreeable face. 'There was no point. I am a lawyer, and I know any King's Pardon is absolute. Complaints about Thorpe or Edward will just be seen as sour grapes. They are untouchable. Look what else they did to me.'

He pulled up his tabard to reveal a knee that was bruised

and swollen. Bartholomew winced, knowing such an injury would make walking painful.

'They stamped on it, when I was down,' said Ufford, the indignation in his voice making it clear what he thought of their ungentlemanly conduct.

'You did not tell me why they picked on you,' said Michael. 'Did you say something to antagonise them? They are spoiling for a fight, so it would not be difficult to do.'

'I was praying to the Hand,' said Ufford resentfully. 'They had no right to resort to violence. I gave them no cause to do so – ask anyone. Several Michaelhouse students saw what happened. They will tell you I was an innocent victim of a gratuitous attack.'

Michael was disapproving. 'I know the Hand is revered in some quarters, but I did not imagine the scholars of Gonville Hall to be among its foolish admirers.'

'We are not,' said Pulham firmly. '*Most* of us know it came from Peterkin Starre the simpleton.'

'The Hand is imbued with healing powers,' argued Rougham, fixing his colleague with an angry glare. 'I often send my patients there when all else fails. Some have been cured instantly. Look at Ufford. He was on the verge of leprosy, but has been reprieved by the Hand's intervention.'

'Why should Thorpe and Mortimer object to your prayers to the Hand?' asked Bartholomew of Ufford. He was proud of himself for not telling Rougham that his diagnosis was absurd.

'Thorpe was telling people that the Hand should not be locked away in the University Church,' replied Ufford. 'He said it should be somewhere more public. Foolishly, I ventured the opinion that it was all right where it was, and that it should not be moved. St Mary the Great is a fine, strong church, and Father William is an honest guardian, who never refuses anyone access to it – scholar or townsman.'

196

'Thorpe fought you over the location of a false relic?' asked Michael incredulously.

'No, Brother,' replied Ufford gravely. 'He fought me over the Hand of Valence Marie. It is *not* a false relic, and in time it will make Cambridge a site of great pilgrimage.'

'Sweet Jesus!' muttered Michael.

'If the Hand is so powerful, then why is your nose cut and your leg swollen?' asked Bartholomew archly, although the question was really aimed at Rougham. 'Surely, you should be cured?'

'I have not been to visit it since the attack,' explained Ufford simply. 'Rougham calculated my horoscope and he says it is not safe for me to leave the College for another two days.'

Rougham looked smug. Bartholomew thought Ufford would have benefited more from a poultice of powdered knapweed root and warm beeswax, but he held his tongue.

'The Hand did not intercede for Deschalers,' said Pulham to Rougham. 'Even I could see that he had the taint of death about him. He told me you recommended a private audience with the relic, but afterwards, he became more ill than ever.'

'He had a canker in the bowels,' said Rougham. 'I did suggest a visit to the Hand, but his sins must have been too great, for his prayers went unanswered. I knew he was not long for this world, although it is unfortunate he was deprived of his last few weeks by a nail.'

'I agree,' said Michael. 'Was he depressed about his condition, do you think?'

'You are asking whether I believe Deschalers was so distressed about his impending death that he murdered Bottisham and killed himself,' surmised Rougham, who had evidently heard about the lack of a third party in the King's Mill when the two men had died. 'And the answer is yes. He was weak from his illness, but he could have mustered enough strength to perform one last act of violence. It is the only viable solution, because Bottisham cannot have murdered Deschalers.'

'I heard they died from nails penetrating their brains via their mouths,' said Pulham distastefully. 'I do not see Bottisham inflicting that sort of injury – or any other, for that matter – on anyone. It seems an odd way to choose for a suicide. What was Deschalers thinking of?'

'It does sound improbable, and I speak from my experience as a *medicus*,' agreed Rougham. 'I suppose the man must have used a nail on Bottisham, then felt obliged to dispatch himself in a like manner. Suicides are rarely rational in their thoughts as they prepare to die. He probably saw some contorted logic in his decision that is impenetrable to a sane mind.'

Bartholomew conceded that he was probably right, and the twisted reasoning of a deranged mind had led one of the two men to kill his enemy and then himself in this bizarre manner. He could think of no other explanation that made sense.

'I heard Gonville will represent the Mortimer clan in their argument about water with the King's Mill,' said Michael, changing the subject. 'Is it true?'

Pulham nodded. 'We shall miss Bottisham's incisive mind, though.'

'Why have you chosen to support the Mortimers over the Millers' Society?' asked Michael. 'Do you have shares in their venture, or have they promised to become benefactors?'

'No,' said Rougham shortly. 'We took their case because they offered to pay us well.'

Ufford gave a rueful smile. 'And because we are tired of seeing men like Deschalers, Morice, Cheney and Lavenham have their way in the town. They are all wealthy, yet they dabble in milling to make themselves richer still.

It is time they learned they cannot always have what they want.'

'But the Mortimers are wealthy and greedy, too,' Michael pointed out. 'And Thomas killed an innocent man by driving a cart when he was drunk. They are scarcely blameless.'

'Bottisham was shocked by that,' admitted Pulham. 'I imagine that is why he visited Isnard and Mistress Lenne: to ease his troubled conscience.'

'But *you* see no problem in representing them?' asked Michael.

'Not really,' replied Pulham. 'The Mortimers have been appealed by the Millers' Society, and they need legal representation. That is the sum of our relationship with them: they are clients. We do not accept or decline folk on the basis of their moral standing; that is for God to decide.'

'Damn it all!' exclaimed Ufford, who had been gazing out of the window. '*He* is here. Who gave him a key?'

Bartholomew went to look, rashly handing his still-brimming goblet to Michael to hold. He saw Thorpe open the gate and saunter across the yard, whistling to himself. If the young man knew his new colleagues did not like him, he did not seem to care. He strutted confidently to the library door.

'I did,' said Rougham defensively. 'He is entitled to one, because of the fees he pays. He is not here often anyway, so it does no harm. Make yourself scarce, if you want to avoid him.'

Ufford scowled, not liking the notion that he should be obliged to 'make himself scarce' because his colleagues had decided to house a ruffian. But he was in no condition to fight, and it was not long before he slunk out of a door at the back, clearly furious.

'Thorpe,' said Michael, as the man entered the library.

199

He lifted Bartholomew's cup in mock salute and downed its contents in a single swallow. 'What a pleasant surprise.'

Thorpe was not pleased to see Michael. He pulled a disagreeable face, then went to sit at the carrel he had been allocated, slouching against the wall and ignoring the philosophical text that lay open in front of him. He shuffled restlessly for a few moments, then abandoned his pretence at scholarship, and started for the door. Bartholomew wondered if he had come with the express purpose of baiting Ufford, since he had clearly not come to study.

'Is that it?' asked Michael, as he watched Thorpe return the book to its shelf. 'Is that the sum of your learning for the day? You will not pass your disputations like that!'

'My disputations are not until summer,' replied Thorpe. 'That is a long way in the future.' The expression on his face indicated he felt a lot could happen before then, and that he thought it unlikely Michael would ever have the opportunity to savage him in the debating hall.

'Why do you want to become a scholar?' asked Michael conversationally. 'Are you attracted to philosophy or the sciences? Or do you simply enjoy the company of erudite men, like me?'

'No, I do not enjoy the company of men like you,' replied Thorpe ambiguously.

'Your father must be proud,' probed Michael, knowing that mention of the kin who had disowned him would annoy Thorpe.

'He has not said so,' replied Thorpe stiffly. 'Not yet.'

'Where is our new altar cover?' demanded Rougham, breaking into their discussion. 'You have not shown us the cloth you intend to use yet, and it might not be suitable.'

'In time,' said Thorpe coolly. 'There are more pressing matters to attend first.'

He left as abruptly as he came, leaving Bartholomew

uneasy and unsettled. Thorpe had not enrolled at Gonville to study, so he obviously had something else in mind. The possibilities were many and all unpleasant.

'I do not like that young man,' said Pulham worriedly. 'Brother Michael is right: we should tell him to leave. Everyone says he is dangerous, so why should we have him in our College?'

'I do not like him, either,' said Thompson the priest, speaking for the first time. 'There is something about him I find distasteful. I do not judge others on rumour and speculation, so I base my assessment on my own interpretation of his character: he is not a good man, and he will bring us trouble we cannot afford. I recommend we repay his fees and ask him to go.'

'We have already spent his fees on timber for the chapel,' replied Rougham shortly, displeased to be outvoted on all sides. 'He must remain until at least the summer. So, since we cannot undo what has been done, I suggest we abandon this tedious subject and discuss something more appropriate for learned men in a Cambridge College.'

'Then you can tell me why you are convinced of the authenticity of the Hand of Valence Marie,' suggested Michael. 'I cannot understand how you, intelligent men, should believe that thing is real.'

'I have already told you: *we* do not,' said Pulham. 'Only Rougham and Ufford are believers. Thompson, Deschalers and I see it for what it is: the illegally severed limb of Peterkin Starre.'

'No one is saying it did not come from Peterkin,' replied Rougham impatiently. 'However, Father William – a devout Franciscan from your own College, Brother – says Peterkin was a saint.'

'Does he?' asked Pulham, aghast. 'I thought he had more sense than to fabricate tales like that. Who knows where they will lead? You should stop him, Brother.'

201

'Oh, I shall,' vowed Michael with grim determination.

'The Hand is holy,' persisted Rougham. 'It effects miraculous healings.'

'Name one,' said Bartholomew. 'Other than Ufford's "leprosy".'

'There was an incident just today,' flashed Rougham. 'Una the whore petitioned for an end to the ache in her guts, and was rewarded by a cure that was virtually instant.'

'I gave her medicine this morning,' said Bartholomew. 'She must have felt better after taking it.'

'An Arab potion, I presume,' said Rougham, his voice dripping with contempt. 'Well, I can tell you for a fact that *that* rubbish would not have worked. What was in it, anyway?'

'Charcoal and chalk, which are hot and moist to counteract the cold dryness of black bile, mixed with poppy juice. It is not an Arab potion, but one known to English physicians for centuries.'

'You gave her burned wood and stones?' demanded Rougham in horror. 'My God, man!'

'They are ingredients recommended by Dioscorides,' said Bartholomew tartly. 'Not to mention Galen and Hippocrates.'

'Did you actually see her take your "remedy"?' asked Rougham, not wanting to argue against the great Greeks, so changing the line of his attack. 'Because, if you did not, then I imagine she took one look at it, and decided against pouring it in her innards.'

'I left Redmeadow and Quenhyth to do that.'

'Redmeadow!' spat Rougham. 'He is as loathsome a vermin as I have ever encountered. I would never have accepted such a student at Gonville!'

'Why not?' asked Bartholomew, startled by the man's vehemence. Redmeadow did not usually induce a strong dislike in people.

'He is inefficient and careless,' snapped Rougham. 'I gave him a penny to fetch me some catmint from Lavenham the apothecary. But he brought me calamint instead. Fool!'

'They are both used for similar ailments,' said Bartholomew, thinking Rougham was over-reacting. 'A confusion between calamint and catmint is unlikely to prove overly disastrous. Bacon said that—'

'Bacon!' Rougham pounced with distaste. 'A heretic!'

'He was not a heretic,' said Bartholomew. He reconsidered. 'Although, I confess I am sceptical of his theories regarding the *secretum secretorum* – the fabled remedy for all ills, which is also alleged to restore youth to the aged. That seems a little fabulous to me.'

'Really,' said Rougham flatly. 'You only mentioned that because you know it is the *only* aspect of Bacon's work that I find remotely believable.'

'Surely not!' exclaimed Bartholomew, who had known no such thing. 'The notion of a *secretum secretorum* flies in the face of all reason! How could there be such a phenomenon? All empirical evidence indicates that it is nothing more than wishful fancy.'

'Your contention does not surprise me, given that you also dismiss the holy power of relics,' said Rougham icily. 'But you came to discuss Bottisham, not the Hand.'

'True,' agreed Michael. He took a deep breath, knowing the unpleasant part of the interview could be postponed no longer. 'Were any of you aware that Bottisham and Deschalers knew each other?'

'Of course,' sighed Rougham. 'Deschalers was a grocer and Bottisham's duties as a Fellow included purchasing our College's victuals. They did a lot of business together.'

'What can you tell me about Bottisham? Did he have any enemies who might wish him harm? Or a lover who—'

'No,' said Pulham firmly, before he could continue. 'I knew you would do this: rummage through Bottisham's personal affairs in search of scandal. But you will not succeed, Brother. There were no shameful secrets in his past. He had just taken holy orders with the Carmelites, and his life was blameless. He was the victim here, not the perpetrator.'

'We do not know who killed whom yet,' said Michael carefully.

'Bottisham was *not* the villain,' stated Rougham. 'He was a good man – gentle and kind – and he would never hurt anyone. I have already told you that Deschalers could have summoned the strength to kill, so the case is closed as far as I am concerned. Deschalers killed Bottisham, then made an end of himself in a fit of remorse.'

'If Bottisham was so gentle and kind, then why would Deschalers want him dead?' asked Michael.

Rougham glared at him. 'There are all kinds of possible explanations. Deschalers might have mistaken Bottisham for someone else. Or perhaps Deschalers did not intend to kill anyone, and the whole thing was an accident. Who can say?'

'You do not "accidentally" drive a nail into a man's brain,' said Michael. 'And every member of the Millers' Society thinks Bottisham is the killer – that he followed Deschalers into—'

'No!' cried Thompson, distressed. 'Bottisham would never do such a thing! How can you even think it? I thought you liked him.'

'I did – do,' said Michael tiredly. 'But if we want to solve this crime, then we must explore every possible angle, and – unfortunately for those of us who admired him – that means prying into aspects of his life that he might have preferred to keep to himself.'

'I have already told you that you will be disappointed if you go that way,' warned Pulham angrily. 'Bottisham had no sordid secrets.'

'We all have something we would rather no one else knew,' said Michael softly. 'I have been Senior Proctor for long enough to learn that, at least.'

'Bottisham believed Deschalers was a wicked man,' said Pulham, raising a hand to prevent another enraged outburst from Rougham. 'He often commented that he was corrupt and nasty. We saw that side of Deschalers for ourselves, when he promised funds for our chapel and then withdrew them at an inconvenient time. Remember that, Thompson?'

Thompson turned to Michael and Bartholomew. 'About two years ago, Deschalers offered Gonville a donation that would have gone a long way to raising our chapel walls, if not the roof, too. But, just as the work was about to begin, he withdrew the entire amount. I was sure the whole thing was engineered to embarrass Bottisham.'

'There was also some ancient quarrel involving a field,' said Michael. 'Do you know anything about that?'

Thompson nodded. 'Deschalers owned a field in Chesterton, but the Bigod family said it was theirs. Deschalers took the case to the King's Bench, and employed Bottisham to argue for him. Bottisham lost, and Deschalers was angry, because he believed his claim was solid.'

'And was it?' asked Michael. 'Solid?'

'It appeared to be, on parchment. But courts do not always operate on the principle of justice and right, as you have no doubt observed. Bribes change hands. Bottisham was honest, and would never have indulged in such corruption. I imagine that was at the heart of their schism.'

'Deschalers lost his field because Bottisham refused to negotiate a bribe?' asked Bartholomew.

This time, it was Pulham who nodded. 'Deschalers was furious that he had lost land, just because Bottisham refused to compromise his personal integrity. And they were enemies thereafter.'

'But Bottisham's anger was passive,' added Thompson. 'He was not a man to engage in noisy and public quarrels. Deschalers was more vocal, and the distasteful incident of the withdrawn funds is just one example of sly tricks designed to hurt Bottisham. Bottisham genuinely believed Deschalers wanted to bury the hatchet when he offered us that donation. We should all have known better.'

'We should,' agreed Rougham. 'So, you can dig and pry all you like, Brother, but you will never find anything sinister or corrupt in Bottisham's past. He is sinless, and he was ruthlessly murdered by a man who hated him. Deschalers is your killer, and that is that.'

Bartholomew was relieved when the monk stood to leave, bringing the uncomfortable interview to a close.

'Thank God that is over,' said Michael vehemently, as he and Bartholomew left Gonville Hall. 'You cannot imagine how distasteful it was, demanding to know nasty secrets about poor Bottisham.'

Bartholomew felt he could imagine very well, and thought it – combined with Rougham's inexplicable hostility – made for one of the least pleasant encounters he had ever endured at another College. He started to turn right, towards Michaelhouse, but the monk had other ideas, and he found himself steered to the left instead. 'Where are we going?'

'To Deschalers's house. I have already spoken to his apprentices, and today I want to talk to the servants. We learned virtually nothing from Gonville, so we had better hope we hear something useful from Deschalers's people, or we shall be at a dead end again.'

'Tulyet told me that Deschalers was a very private man, so I doubt you will learn much from servants. And he had no close friends – not since the plague took them, at least.'

'Rougham does not like you,' remarked Michael,

changing the subject. 'And the feeling is mutual. I have seldom seen such a disgraceful display of sniping and snapping.'

'It is a pity,' said Bartholomew. 'Physicians are not so numerous in Cambridge that we can afford to spurn each other's company, and yet I find Rougham a deeply repellent man. He seemed much worse today than usual, though. We have always managed a show of civility in the past.'

'He invited you to dine last Wednesday,' said Michael thoughtfully. 'Yet, just a week later, he can barely stand to be in the same room as you.'

'Perhaps he was offended that I amputated Isnard's leg instead of eating with him.'

'Physicians are often called away from pleasant social occasions by their patients. I am sure he understands that. No, Matt, his antagonism goes a lot deeper than a missed meal. He was accusing you openly of holding fast to heretical ideals. I told you to be careful of him with your casual approach to what he considers anathema, and I was right. You have clearly done something to tip him over the edge and shatter the illusion of tolerance between you.'

'Perhaps he is angry with Redmeadow over the catmint episode, and holds me responsible. But here comes a physician who is fair-minded and pleasant company: Paxtone from King's Hall.'

'Matthew!' exclaimed Paxtone, his round features breaking into a smile. 'I was hoping to see you. Rougham is selling all Gonville's medical books that are not by Greeks, and I have purchased the writings of Lanfrank of Milan on surgery. I would value your opinion. Will you visit me later?'

'I would like to come now,' said Bartholomew unhappily. 'But I am going to Deschalers's house, to see if we can discover why he and Bottisham were found dead together.'

Paxtone shuddered. 'Poor souls! What have you learned

so far? It grieves me to say so, but Deschalers did not harm Bottisham – he was too ill. And since Bernarde the miller says they were the only two people there, then it stands to reason that Bottisham must have killed Deschalers. But Bottisham did not seem like the kind of man to kill . . .' He trailed off uncomfortably.

'He was not,' said Bartholomew, more sharply than he intended. 'Besides, Rougham was Deschalers's physician, and he disagrees with you. He says Deschalers *was* strong enough.'

Paxtone pursed his lips, to indicate with silence what he thought of Rougham's diagnosis. 'Then perhaps one of them was fed some potion that made him different in character. I have read that the Italians know how to make such compounds. You should ask whether Thorpe and Mortimer went anywhere near Italy during their exile.'

Bartholomew stared at him, wondering whether the answer could be that simple. It would certainly fit the physical evidence – that only Deschalers and Bottisham were present when they died and that one had killed the other. But would Thorpe and Mortimer have orchestrated such a thing? He concluded that they might, because it would set University against town and lead to chaos and disorder. What better way to avenge themselves on a place they felt had wronged them?

'Or perhaps Thorpe and Mortimer had nothing to do with it,' Paxtone went on. 'Perhaps someone *wants* them blamed, so they can be re-exiled.'

'It is possible, I suppose,' said Michael thoughtfully. 'The whole town would be delighted to see the back of them. But Bottisham's life is a huge price to pay.'

Paxtone patted his arm. 'I do not envy you your investigation, Brother. I shall go to the Hand of Valence Marie and ask it to help you.'

'*You* believe in its power, too?' asked Michael with a

groan. He began to walk away. 'I feel I am one in a slowly dwindling minority who does not feel compelled to revere the damned thing.'

With an apologetic smile for the monk's brusqueness, Bartholomew left Paxtone and followed Michael along Milne Street to Deschalers's luxurious home. Michael knocked at the door. It was opened by the old servant, who showed them into the tastefully decorated chamber on the ground floor that they had visited before. Michael's attempts to question him were met with puzzled looks or odd statements about exotic foods, and it was not long before the monk abandoned the interrogation. The man either did not know anything, or was not prepared to be helpful; Bartholomew suspected the former, because nothing much seemed to catch his attention unless it involved eating. As soon as he had gone to fetch someone else to see to them, Michael – another man obsessed with his diet – homed in on the dishes of dried fruits that had been left for visitors, determined to scoff as many as possible as a small act of revenge against a household that yielded so little in the way of clues.

'Oh,' came a voice as the door opened and a woman swept in. 'It is you two.'

Michael almost choked on his apple ring, although he should have anticipated that the grocer's untimely death would result in the appearance of the woman generally acknowledged to be his heir. Julianna Deschalers, his niece, had become his sole surviving kin after the plague had claimed all the others. She was tall, with a mass of fair hair that was coiled into plaits at the sides of her face. Her clothes were expensive and decorated with silver thread, and she held herself with the confident poise of someone used to having her orders obeyed. Bartholomew had met her before, and considered her headstrong and boorish.

'Madam,' said Michael, recovering from his surprise and

bowing. Bartholomew did likewise, although he did not think she warranted such courtesy.

'I am well, thank you,' Julianna replied, in answer to the question she obviously felt they should have asked. 'And so is my child.'

'Child?' echoed Bartholomew, startled. 'Who is the father?'

'That is not a question you should ask a respectably married woman,' she replied indignantly. 'But you know the answer anyway. My daughter's father is Ralph de Langelee. He is Master of your College and he *was* my husband – until we agreed that our marriage should be annulled. You know I was pregnant when I married him, because you were both at our wedding. But I have remarried now – thankfully. It was not many weeks before Langelee decided he would rather frolic with men in a College than enjoy normal sexual relations with his wife.'

'I hardly think—' began Bartholomew, although the Master's manly reputation needed no protection from him. There did not exist a more vigorous and practised lover, according to the many prostitutes who seemed intimately acquainted with his performances.

'Never mind that,' she interrupted impatiently. 'I am now married to Edward Mortimer.'

'Edward Mortimer?' asked Bartholomew, shocked. 'The exile?'

She glared at him, angry at his reaction of horror when she obviously felt congratulations were in order. 'How many other Edward Mortimers do you know?'

'None, thank God,' said Bartholomew, before he could stop himself.

She glared again. 'I was looking for a husband, and my uncle mentioned that Edward had recently acquired a King's Pardon. Edward is heir to a great fortune, and so am I. So it was a good match. My name is Julianna *Mortimer*, now.'

'Lord!' breathed Michael, sitting down heavily in a delicate chair. Something cracked, and she scowled at him. 'But you were betrothed to Edward once before, were you not? Before he was banished?'

She bent to inspect the chair, and did not seem very interested in answering him. 'Yes, I was. But I thought him a weakling then, and not worthy of me. However, he is a *real* man now. He learned at Albi, in the south of France, during his exile. I like him a lot better now he is no longer a silly boy.'

'I am sure you do,' said Bartholomew, thinking that a self-confessed killer would be very attractive to a woman like Julianna, who seemed to like rough, unmannerly men.

She grabbed one of the chair's legs and gave it a vigorous tug. She was a strong woman, and Michael was obliged to grab a windowsill to stop himself from being jerked off it. There was another snap, and she straightened with a satisfied expression. 'There; that should do it. Edward plans to demand compensation from the town for the agonies it caused him with this nasty banishment. Did he tell you that?'

There was an ominous groan from the chair, and Michael leapt to his feet. 'But he cannot win such a case. He has been *pardoned*, which is not the same as being deemed innocent. He cannot claim compensation in those circumstances.'

'Well, you are wrong,' said Julianna firmly. 'He will be paid *lots* of money, and we will both have a wonderful time spending it.' She clapped her hands in delight at the prospect.

'Sweet Christ!' grumbled Michael under his breath. 'What have we done to deserve her?'

'What are you mumbling about?' demanded Julianna immediately. 'I had forgotten how you academics mumble. It is an unattractive habit. Why can you not speak at a normal volume?'

'Tell me about your uncle's death,' said Michael, wanting to ask his questions and leave.

'I will inherit *everything*,' sang Julianna happily, twirling on her heels like a child. 'Edward was *so* pleased when I told him. He must have forgotten I was Uncle's sole heir.'

'I imagine that is unlikely,' muttered Michael acidly. He saw Julianna scowl because she could not hear him, and raised his voice again. 'I was not referring to the disposal of your uncle's worldly goods. I want to know why he went to the mill with Nicholas Bottisham.'

'I do not know anything about that,' said Julianna carelessly. 'It is very sad, of course.' She arranged her features into something that approximated grief, which Bartholomew could see was far from genuine. 'Of course, he had been ill for some time.'

'With a canker of the bowels,' said Bartholomew.

'With a wasting sickness,' corrected Julianna primly. 'We do not mention bowels in this gentle household. It is not polite.'

'How long was he ill?' asked Michael. 'Weeks? Months? A year?'

'A few months,' she replied. 'That was why I came to live in Chesterton – that pretty little village just to the north of here – after Christmas. I wanted to claim my inheritance as soon as he died, you see. You cannot be too careful these days, what with thieves and killers at large.'

'Did you ever see your uncle with Bottisham?' asked Bartholomew, declining to mention that one such thief and killer was her new husband. 'Did Bottisham visit him or send him messages? Do you know anything about the funds promised for Gonville's chapel, which were later withdrawn?'

'Uncle never donated anything to *Gonville*,' declared Julianna, pronouncing the name with considerable disdain. 'He occasionally gave money to Bene't College, which he

212

helped to build. But he was not interested in helping other halls and hostels.'

'So Bottisham never visited your uncle here?' clarified Michael.

'I did not say that,' replied Julianna. 'I said Uncle did not donate money to Gonville. Bottisham did come here occasionally, because Uncle was the town's best grocer. Many scholars do business with him, and Bottisham was no different.'

'Did he come alone?' asked Bartholomew. 'Or were there other Gonville men with him?'

'I do not know,' replied Julianna with a bored sigh. 'I have not been living here with him, have I? I have a house in Chesterton, where I reside with my husband and my daughter. And Rob Thorpe on occasion, although I do not like him.' Her face took on a sulky expression. 'When he is present, Edward ignores me, and all they do is sit together and scheme.'

'What do they talk about?' asked Michael, exchanging a glance with Bartholomew. Perhaps she would tell them what the pair intended to do in Cambridge.

'Plotting,' replied Julianna guilelessly. 'Planning. You know the kind of thing.'

'Enlighten me,' invited Michael.

'They have been deciding what they will do,' said Julianna slowly, as though speaking to her infant daughter. 'They agreed that Edward will work for his uncle – Thomas the miller – and Rob *was* going to study with his father. But his father will not have him, so he went to Gonville instead.'

'But why?' asked Bartholomew uneasily. 'Do they envisage staging some sort of revenge?'

'I expect so,' said Julianna, with a shrug to indicate she did not care. 'They do not tell me the details, and I am not interested in their dull discussions anyway. But I thought you came here to talk about my uncle. You should try catching whoever broke into his house the night he died. That might help you with your investigation into his sad death.' She was unable to suppress a grin, knowing what that 'sad death' meant for her future.

'He was burgled?' asked Bartholomew, although he knew the answer to that: he had seen the fellow himself. 'What was taken?'

'Nothing, as far as I know, but documents were tampered with. They did not steal the will though, thank the Lord!'

'Who would be interested in his documents?' asked Michael.

'I have no idea, but you should find out. I do not like the rumours circulating that say poor Uncle murdered this scholar. I am sure it was the other way around.'

CHAPTER 6

Bartholomew remained haunted by Mistress Lenne's haggard, distraught face, so went with Redmeadow and Quenhyth to see her the following morning after prime. Redmeadow pulled his writing tablet from his bag and provided the physician with a detailed résumé of what had been said when he had visited her the previous evening. There was nothing of import, and Bartholomew had the impression that the old lady had become impatient with the student's ponderous enquiries, and had wanted him to leave. It was not a bad sign: irritation was better than bleak hopelessness.

He and the students left the Lenne house, and turned towards the High Street. When they drew near St Mary the Great – with Redmeadow regaling Quenhyth with a rather fanciful theory about how Bishop Bateman came to be poisoned in Avignon – Bartholomew spotted two familiar faces among the throng that had gathered to pay homage to the Hand. Paxtone and Wynewyk stood close together, holding what seemed to be an intense discussion.

Bartholomew was surprised, since he had never seen the Michaelhouse lawyer and the King's Hall physician together before. He started to walk towards them, intending to pass the time of day, but Paxtone happened to glance up and see him. He grabbed Wynewyk's arm and hauled him towards the Trumpington Gate. Wynewyk stole a quick look behind him as they went, and walked even faster when he saw Bartholomew was watching. The physician stared in total mystification, wondering what had induced such odd behaviour in two people he regarded as friends.

'There is Master Warde from the Hall of Valence Marie,' said Redmeadow, pointing in the opposite direction. 'He was the fellow who robbed us of victory in the *Disputatio de quodlibet*. It was a bad decision. Michaelhouse was much better than Gonville.'

'We were not,' said Bartholomew. 'Bottisham argued very elegantly, and so did Pulham.'

'Rougham was rubbish, though,' said Quenhyth, gnawing at a fingernail. 'I do not like him. He shouted at Redmeadow, just because he fetched calamint from the apothecary the other day, not catmint.' His voice was smug, as though *he* would not have made such a basic mistake.

'He can be brusque,' said Bartholomew. He watched as Warde hacked helplessly, struggling to catch his breath. 'Warde has had that cough for a long time now.'

'He is being treated by Rougham, and we all know how ineffective *he* is as a healer,' said Quenhyth. 'You are much better.' He flashed an ingratiating smile, and Bartholomew winced.

'Lord!' exclaimed Warde hoarsely, as their paths converged. 'This tickling throat will be the death of me. I have had it a full ten days, and it still shows no sign of abating. I have tried everything – even a potion from Egypt that Deschalers the grocer sold me before he died.'

'What kind of potion?' asked Bartholomew. 'And how do you know it came from Egypt?'

'Deschalers told me Arabs use it when desert sand clogs their lungs, although it tasted like a simple syrup of honey and acid fruits to me.' Warde shook his head sadly. 'It is a terrible business with him and Bottisham. I was fond of them both. I cannot imagine what happened to them, or why they should have been together in the King's Mill.'

'Nor can we,' replied Bartholomew. 'But they had an ancient disagreement over a field, then Deschalers pretended he was going to give Gonville money for their chapel but withdrew it at the last moment – to embarrass Bottisham, apparently. We also know that Bottisham planned to represent the Mortimers in the mill dispute – against Deschalers and the Millers' Society.'

'The situation was more one-sided than that,' said Warde, coughing again. 'Bottisham held no ill feelings for Deschalers; he told me so himself. But Deschalers harboured them for Bottisham. Deschalers was protective of his possessions, and did not like losing a field that was his by rights.'

'Was it his by rights?'

Warde nodded. 'Oh, yes. I reviewed the evidence when Bottisham accepted the case, some twenty years ago now. But the other claimant bribed witnesses. Deschalers wanted to do the same, but Bottisham refused. Deschalers was bitter about Bottisham's incorruptibility, and said a lawyer's principles should not come between a man and his property. I can see his point: he lost a valuable piece of land because Bottisham refused to employ tactics used openly by other clerks.'

'Do you think this festered, and Deschalers decided to have his revenge while he still could?' Bartholomew was sceptical. He did not really believe Rougham's assurances that the dying man had mustered the physical strength for a final act of vengeance.

Warde shrugged. 'I do not know. However, I must point out that most men who are mortally ill avoid committing sins close to the time when their souls will be weighed. Perhaps it was not *Deschalers* who killed Bottisham, but a member of the Mortimer clan.'

'Why?' asked Bartholomew. 'Bottisham was going to work for them, as one of their lawyers.'

'Quite,' said Warde. 'And who wants a clerk so scrupulous that he will lose a case before resorting to dishonesty? However, I have heard that no one else was in the mill when Deschalers and Bottisham died, so I am doubtless wrong in my speculations. What did you think of my lecture at Merton Hall last Wednesday?'

'The one about the neglect of mathematics in academic studies?' asked Bartholomew, casting his mind back to the lively debate that had taken place the morning before Isnard and Lenne were crushed by Mortimer's cart. 'You are right: mathematical principles underlie our most basic philosophical tenets, and we should ensure our students are well versed in their application.'

'Because of that lecture, Doctor Bartholomew is going to talk about Euclid's *Elementa* all day,' said Quenhyth to Warde, clearly less than happy about the prospect. 'Particularly the theory that parallel lines will never meet, even in an infinite universe.'

'Good,' said Warde, rubbing his hands over his oily yellow hair and coughing a little. 'There is nothing like the *Elementa* to drive cobwebs from the mind.'

'*God* must be able to make parallel lines meet,' said Redmeadow thoughtfully. 'He is omnipotent, after all, and it cannot be that hard to do.'

'I imagine He has better things to do than confound Euclidean geometric universals,' said Warde. A smile took the sting from his words. 'Hah! There is Rougham. I must consult with him again about my cough.'

Rougham was in a hurry. He strode along the street in a flurry of flapping sleeves and billowing cloak, showing all who saw him that here was a man with important business to attend. It gave the impression that he was much in demand, and that patients who secured *his* services were gaining the attention of a man who knew what he was about. He carried a thick book by Galen, to indicate that he was learned as well as busy, but was not burdened down with battered bags full of potions and knives, like a common surgeon. Despite the fact that his rapid progress indicated that he had not a moment to spare before descending on his next lucky customer, he was prepared to stop and talk to Warde.

'The syrup of blackcurrants did not work?' he asked, making a show of consulting his book, although Bartholomew was certain Galen never mentioned this particular fruit in his analysis of foods with medicinal qualities. He said nothing, but Quenhyth was not so prudent.

'Galen does not talk about blackcurrants in that,' he declared, tapping a bony, ragged-nailed finger on Rougham's tome. 'He discusses black*berries*, but not black*currants*.'

If Quenhyth expected Rougham to be grateful for having his mistake pointed out in front of a patient, he was to be disappointed. 'What do you know about physic, boy? You do not even know the difference between calamint and catmint.'

'That was not me,' objected Quenhyth indignantly. 'It was Redmeadow. But that is beside the point. There is nothing about blackcurrants in Galen.' He turned to Bartholomew. 'Is there?'

'We should be on our way,' said Bartholomew tactfully. 'We can talk about Galen as we go.'

'No!' cried Quenhyth stubbornly. 'I am right. Tell him!'

'Do you see this boy?' roared Rougham suddenly, addressing the people who were nearby. Some stopped to listen, and Warde began to cough in agitation, uncomfortable with the scene Rougham was about to create. Redmeadow simply turned and fled, and Bartholomew wished he could do the same. 'He thinks he is a great physician who can challenge his betters. But I advise you all to let him nowhere near you, because he will kill you with his inexperience and foolishness.'

Quenhyth's normally pallid skin flushed a deep red. 'I will not! I am—'

'An imbecile,' said Rougham, cutting through the student's stammering objections. 'A dangerous fool. Take my warning seriously, friends, or he will bring about your deaths with false remedies.'

'No,' said Bartholomew quietly, moved by the tears of humiliation that spilled down Quenhyth's downy cheeks. 'He will make a good physician one day, and he is right about the blackcurrants. Galen does not mention them.'

'I said black*berries*,' asserted Rougham loudly. He opened the book and pointed to a spot on the page, waving it far too close to the physician's face for him to be able to read it. 'Here. Do you see that? You are as bad as your dithering, blundering student.'

He snapped the book closed and stalked away. Quenhyth gazed after him, tears staining his face and his hands clenched at his sides. He was shaking so much that Bartholomew put an arm around his shoulders, but Quenhyth knocked it away. Seeing the show was over, people began to disperse, some laughing at the sight of physicians quarrelling publicly.

'He did say blackcurrants,' said Warde kindly to Quenhyth. 'And he recommended black*currant* syrup to me.' He turned to Bartholomew. 'Does this mean I asked Lavenham for the wrong thing?'

'Someone spoke mine name?' asked the apothecary, who happened to be passing with Cheney the spice merchant and Bernarde the miller. Their heads were down, as though they had been deep in serious conversation. 'I here.'

'I need a potion of black*berries* for my cough,' said Warde. 'Do you have one?'

'I give blackcurrant,' said Lavenham in surprise. 'Blackberry now? You want all black potions future? Bartholomew give black medicine for black bile. Charcoal for Una the prosperous—'

'Una the *prostitute*,' corrected Bernarde, jangling his keys. 'She is not prosperous at all.'

'She should charge her customers more, then,' said Cheney, as though the solution to Una's poverty was obvious. 'These women call themselves the Guild of Frail Sisters, but then they cheat themselves by charging ridiculously low amounts for their services.'

'They cannot demand too much,' said Bernarde. It seemed he, too, was intimately acquainted with the Frail Sisters' economic shortcomings. 'Or men would just take what they could not afford. That happened with flour after the Death – people had no money, so they stormed the mill and stole what they needed. The Frail Sisters will not want that to happen to them.'

'And there is issue for quality,' added Lavenham knowledgeably. 'Una do not ask much, because she not good. Not like Yolande de Blaston, who ask more, and is very good when she can be got.'

'We should go,' said Bartholomew, reluctant to become engaged in a public discussion about the town's prostitutes. 'Come on, Quenhyth.'

'Rougham did not have to do that,' sniffed Quenhyth, as he and Bartholomew left the burgeoning conversation about the town's Frail Sisters and their value for money. Warde waited for it to finish so that he could order Rougham's next ineffective remedy. Although syrups were good for coughs of short duration, Bartholomew felt Warde's had lingered long enough to warrant something more powerful, and hoped Rougham would soon prescribe a remedy that might work.

'Rougham was unkind,' he agreed. 'But do not take his words to heart.'

'He confused me with Redmeadow,' said Quenhyth in

a broken voice. 'That is the only explanation. I do not see why else he should attack me.'

'There is Bess,' said Bartholomew, hoping to distract him from his misery. 'Shall we talk to her, and see whether she is more rational today?'

'No,' said Quenhyth, beginning to weep again. 'I do not want to talk to anyone. I want to go to our room and hide. If you had not stepped in, he would still be abusing me now. I hate him! How can I visit your patients now? They will laugh at me and say I am not fit to be in their presence!'

'They will not,' said Bartholomew firmly. He took a phial from his bag that contained medicine for Isnard. It had to be delivered daily, because the bargeman had already tried to swallow a month's worth in the mistaken belief that a larger dose would speed his recovery. 'Take this to Isnard and ensure he takes it. Then check his pulse and ask him how he feels. If you conduct his daily examination, then I will not need to visit him today.'

Quenhyth's eyes shone with sudden pride. 'You trust *me* to see him? Alone?'

'You have watched me for a week now, and you know what to do. Hurry. He will be waiting.'

'Thank you,' said Quenhyth, scrubbing his wet face with his sleeve. He gave a venomous glower in Rougham's direction. 'I look forward to the day when I qualify. *Then* we shall see who knows more about Galen and blackcurrants!'

Bartholomew returned to Michaelhouse, where he spent the rest of the morning and much of the afternoon discussing Euclid's *Elementa* with a class that was not nearly as enthusiastic about geometry as its teacher. Redmeadow made a nuisance of himself by insisting that God could make exceptions to any universal laws of physics, and then demanded to know whether the Holy Trinity added up to

180 degrees, like one of Euclid's triangles. Bartholomew became exasperated by the interruptions, and longed to order him to leave God out of the debate. But Father William was listening, and he knew what would happen if the fanatical Franciscan heard him make such a remark.

Bartholomew left the hall feeling drained, and walked to the fallen apple tree in the orchard, thinking that a few moments with Bacon's *De erroribus medicorum* might restore his equilibrium. However, when he arrived, the gate was open, and he saw through the trees that Wynewyk was already there, also seeking some peace after three hours of teaching in a hall crammed with noisy, querulous undergraduates. Since he did not want to intrude on another's solitude, Bartholomew walked farther into the orchard and found a sheltered spot among some bare-twigged plum trees.

He had not been reading for long when he heard the gate rattle. Assuming Wynewyk was leaving, and not comfortable under the plum tree anyway, Bartholomew decided to reclaim the apple trunk. He closed his book and strolled through the orchard, relishing the scent of early blossoms and the hum of a bee as it sailed haphazardly towards the hives at the bottom of the garden.

However, Wynewyk was not leaving; he was answering a knock at the small gate that opened on to St Michael's Lane. Bartholomew watched him remove the stout bar that secured it, then take a key from his scrip to deal with the lock. He had been on the verge of calling to him, but, without knowing why, he hesitated. Instead of striding forward, he slipped behind a flourishing gooseberry bush and peered through its bright new leaves. Wynewyk opened the door and ushered someone inside, looking surreptitiously up and down the lane before closing it again. For some reason, he did not want anyone to know that Paxtone of King's Hall was visiting him.

'Well?' he asked eagerly. 'Do you have it?'

'Not yet,' replied Paxtone. 'It is proving more difficult than I imagined, because they keep changing their minds. We may have to abandon it altogether.'

'No!' groaned Wynewyk. 'Not after all our planning!'

'Matt saw us today, you know,' said Paxtone worriedly. 'He looked right at us – and he will be even more suspicious if he catches us together again. We *must* be more careful.'

'And whose fault was that?' objected Wynewyk. 'We could have brazened it out if you had not panicked and fled like a guilty criminal.'

Paxtone sighed. 'I wish we had never started this. I am not good at subterfuge and secrecy.' An expression of alarm suddenly crossed his homely features. 'I hope he does not mention any of this to Brother Michael! I do not want *him* after me!'

Wynewyk glared at him. 'Michael is too busy to bother with us. Besides, I did not put myself through all this inconvenience to give up now. We *will* persist.'

'Very well,' said Paxtone unhappily. 'But it will not be easy. Rougham foils me at every turn, and is making a damned nuisance of himself. I may be forced to take some radical steps.'

'Well, be careful,' said Wynewyk. 'If the merest whisper of this gets out, all our labours will have been for nothing. I do not want Rougham to spoil our fun.'

'Do not worry about him,' said Paxtone meaningfully. 'But I cannot stay here – I am expected at Valence Marie. Be sure to close this gate properly after I leave. We do not want a small thing like an improperly secured door to give away our secret.'

Wynewyk ushered the physician into the lane, then closed the gate and barred it, before walking back to the apple tree. He collected the tome he had been reading, and tucked it under his arm. As he walked away, Bartholomew saw a severed chain dangling behind him, indicating it was a library book – and one that had been forcibly removed from its moorings, too. When he had gone, Bartholomew stared at the apple tree unhappily, wondering what wrongdoings the ancient bark had just witnessed.

Bartholomew was bothered by what he had seen in the orchard, but Michael was dismissive when he was told what had happened, and pointed out that there might be any number of innocent explanations. Bartholomew tried not to think about it, although a disagreeable nag at the back of his mind kept reminding him that there was unexplained business of a potentially sinister nature involving two people he liked. It was not a pleasant sensation.

'It is time you and I visited the fabled Hand of Valence Marie, Matt,' said Michael. There was still an hour before the evening meal. 'I saw a large number of people lining up to be admitted to its presence earlier today, and I want to see it for myself.'

'Perhaps we can steal it while William's back is turned, and throw it in the river,' suggested Bartholomew petulantly. 'That would put an end to this nonsense.'

'It might put an end to us, too,' said Michael, beginning to walk up St Michael's Lane. 'I do not want to be summarily hanged by a mob for depriving the town of its sacred relic. You must try to control your thieving impulses for now – although I may make use of them later, when we will not be the obvious culprits.'

'Your grandmother would be better than me,' said Bartholomew, suspecting that the old lady would think nothing of outwitting the likes of Father William and making off with the University's treasure with no one any the wiser.

'True, but I do not want to ask her,' said Michael. 'She

will think me a fool, unable to steal relics in his own town. I do not want her telling the King that her grandson is lacking in the requisite skills.'

'Requisite for what?' asked Bartholomew, trying to imagine which career opportunities in the King's service might list thievery as an essential qualification.

'This and that,' replied Michael vaguely. 'But you see my point, Matt. No man wants his grandmother to see him as an inadequate burglar.'

'Heaven forbid,' said Bartholomew. He saw a familiar figure walking slowly along the High Street, reaching out a dirty hand to stop all who passed and asking everyone the same question. Most simply shook their heads and went about their business; others were less happy about being waylaid by such a filthy creature. Bess grabbed Bartholomew's arm with fingers that were long, bony and surprisingly strong.

'Have you seen my man?'

'No,' said Bartholomew. 'Have you eaten today? Do you still have money to buy food and a bed for the night?'

She ignored him, and moved on to Michael. 'Have you seen my man?'

'What does he look like?' asked Michael. 'Tall, short, fat, thin?'

'He is gone,' she whispered. 'And I am looking for him.'

'Do you know the Mortimer family?' asked Bartholomew, wondering whether Constantine had told the truth when he had said Bess was no relation of the dead Katherine.

'Do they know where he is?' she asked.

Her voice was flat, and Bartholomew thought she was probably too addled to recognise her man, even if she did manage to locate him. Without waiting for his reply, she headed for Deynman and Redmeadow, who were out for a stroll before the evening meal. She put her question, and Bartholomew listened to Deynman explain that he knew her from when she had discovered Bosel's body. She waited until he had finished speaking, then went to talk to someone else.

'She does not remember Bosel,' said Michael, as Deynman joined them, hurt that his kindness should have been so quickly forgotten. 'Why did you ask whether she knows the Mortimers, Matt? Do you think one of *them* is the fellow she hunts so ardently?'

'I asked only because of her resemblance to Katherine,' said Bartholomew.

'It is an uncanny likeness,' agreed Michael. 'A few days ago, I asked you to examine Bess and tell me whether she might be feigning madness to disguise her real identity as a killer. Did you do it?'

'I have had several conversations with her, Brother, but I can tell you no more now than when I first met her – except that she has been here for a month or so, and that she came from London. Her insanity *seems* real to me, but I would not stake my life on it. I am not good with ailments of the mind, and find it hard to distinguish genuine cases from false ones.'

They watched Bess accost Bernarde the miller, who shoved a coin into her hand without breaking stride. She stared at it blankly, then dropped it in the mud of the street. Next, she seized Clippesby of Michaelhouse. The Dominican listened carefully, then recommended she ask the town's cats about her husband's whereabouts, on the grounds that they were more knowledgeable about such matters than people.

'I cannot listen,' said Redmeadow, starting to walk away with Deynman in tow. 'Witnessing a conversation between mad Master Clippesby and addled Bess is more than anyone should be asked to do. We are off to see the Hand of Valence Marie. Father William has promised us a private viewing.'

'Good,' said Michael, catching up with them. 'He can show it to us at the same time.'

'But then it will not be private,' objected Deynman.

'You will not notice us,' promised Michael, patting the student's arm. 'We will be quiet. But why are you so keen to see the thing? Surely you know it is not genuine?'

'Actually, I think it is,' said Deynman seriously. 'Father William says that more than two hundred people have been to see it, and we all know that two hundred people cannot be wrong.'

Michael gave him a sidelong glance to indicate that *he* had no such faith in the populace's ability to determine such matters. He led the way to St Mary the Great, where a line of about twenty folk were waiting. The relic appealed to the wealthy as well as the poor, which made for a curious mixture of supplicants. Cheney the spicer was next to grizzled Sergeant Orwelle, while Yolande de Blaston and the wealthy Isobel de Lavenham stood side by side.

'We were here first,' called Cheney, as Michael pushed past them to enter the church. 'You must wait your turn. It is only fair.'

'He is right,' agreed Isobel, pouting her voluptuous red lips. 'You must stand here, next to me.'

'I am not a penitent,' replied Michael haughtily. 'I have business with the Chancellor.'

'Very well, then,' said Yolande coolly. 'But I would not like to think you were pushing in.'

'The Hand of Valence Marie is for everyone,' said Orwelle. 'We all have important reasons for being here. I have come to ask for help with Bosel's murder, since I am getting nowhere on my own – and it has been a week now. I need some divine assistance, or the Sheriff will think me incompetent.'

Michael smiled sweetly and entered the airy interior of

228

the church with Deynman, Redmeadow and Bartholomew behind, all uncomfortable with Michael's lies. Without the slightest hesitation, Michael made straight for the spiral staircase that led to the tower, and climbed to the first floor, where Tynkell was busily filing documents on nail-spiked pieces of wood.

'I am finding it difficult to work with folk clattering up and down the stairs all day long,' he grumbled as Michael entered. Bartholomew and the students hovered on the stairs outside, loath to be in a room containing the odorous Chancellor, especially a small one in which the windows did not open. 'I am beginning to wish you had never created the position of Keeper of the University Chest for William. The Hand lay forgotten and buried until *he* came along and resurrected the thing.'

'I know,' said Michael grimly. 'You should have removed it from the Chest before he took charge. But the deed is done now, and we shall have to live with your blunder.'

'How are you, sir?' asked Deynman, looking directly at the Chancellor's stomach before the man could object to Michael's brazen blame-shifting. 'The life inside you, I mean?'

Bartholomew's heart sank when he realised Deynman was about to try to prove Tynkell was a pregnant hermaphrodite. While Redmeadow sniggered softly, the physician flailed around for ways to stop him before the situation became embarrassing. But nothing came to mind.

Tynkell regarded the student uneasily. 'The life inside me?'

'You know,' said Deynman earnestly.

Tynkell cleared his throat, then shot a glance at Bartholomew to indicate he would like some help. 'Well enough under the circumstances,' he replied carefully, when the physician did nothing to oblige.

'Good,' said Deynman brightly, giving Bartholomew a

hard nudge, to ensure his teacher had noticed that the Chancellor did not deny the charge. 'Do feel free to call on Doctor Bartholomew, should you require a physic for your condition. Or on me, of course.'

'Right,' said Tynkell, becoming flustered and busying himself with his parchments.

'I know these things can be awkward for men . . . for *people* like you,' said Deynman, pressing his point relentlessly. 'But I can be very discreet, and I am shocked by very little these days.'

'I am glad to hear it,' replied Tynkell. He swallowed hard, uncomfortable with an interview loaded with double meanings he did not understand. 'Have you come to see the Hand?'

'I shall say a prayer for you,' said Deynman generously. '*People* in your condition need them.'

Bartholomew bundled his student up the stairs with Redmeadow giggling uncontrollably behind him, but then wondered whether he should have let the conversation run its course. If Deynman was sent down for claiming the Chancellor was the wrong sex, then it would solve one problem. Hopefully, Deynman's father would not allow him to practise medicine if he ended his academic career in disgrace, and hundreds of prospective patients would be spared. Bartholomew wished he had not been so hasty to defend Tynkell's sensibilities.

William was just ushering Bernarde the miller out, when Bartholomew, the students and Michael arrived at the University Chest on the floor above the Chancellor. Bernarde enquired after the investigation into the mill deaths, but did not seem surprised when the monk informed him there was nothing new to report.

'There are folk downstairs who have been waiting for hours,' said William, when Bernarde had gone. 'It would not be fair to allow my own colleagues to petition the Hand before them. Take your place in the queue.'

'Bernarde has not been waiting for hours,' Michael pointed out. 'I saw him not many moments ago, hurrying along the High Street and shoving coins at Mad Bess when she tried to waylay him.'

'He is different,' replied William, unperturbed that he had been caught out in an inconsistency. 'He made a substantial donation for the privilege – something I am sure you do not intend to do.'

'How much do you usually charge?' asked Bartholomew curiously, thinking that Yolande would be unlikely to afford the sort of payment Bernarde – or Isobel, Cheney or even Orwelle – might make.

William raised his shoulders. 'It depends on the individual. They give what they can – or what their consciences dictate they should. Some folk pay nothing at all, because they are too poor, while others pay in gold. It is between them and God.'

'And you,' said Bartholomew, indicating a box on the windowsill that was full to overflowing.

'I am merely the collector,' said William loftily. 'And do not look so disapproving, Matthew. Some of this will be used to pay *you*, when you are next required as Corpse Examiner. The University is doing rather nicely from the revenues raised by the Hand.'

'How nicely?' asked Michael suspiciously.

William looked smug. 'Well, just yesterday I had three pennies from Rougham, a groat from Lavenham the apothecary, and a skin of wine from Warde of Valence Marie. And you enjoyed some of that wine yourself last night, Brother, so do not tell me I should not have accepted it.'

'But you should not,' exclaimed Michael. 'God's teeth, man! Do you not see how dangerous this might become?

231

You cannot accept bribes and bring them to Michaelhouse. This must stop!'

'But I have secured six pounds over the last few weeks!' cried William, horrified that his foray into commerce might be about to meet an abrupt end. 'And every penny has gone into the University Chest – I keep a record, if you want to see it. And what shall I say to the folk who come? That the University has decided no one is allowed access? Do you not see that would be equally dangerous?'

'He has a point,' said Bartholomew to Michael. 'Now this has started, it may be difficult to stop.'

'Damn it, William,' muttered Michael. 'You have unleashed a monster.'

'It was a monster *you* should have destroyed a long time ago,' said Bartholomew, thinking the monk should bear some responsibility for the situation. It had been *his* decision to keep the Hand, and *he* had promoted William to Keeper of the University Chest, knowing the Hand was in it. It did not take a genius to predict what William was sure to do with it.

'You would not believe the things I have heard folk tell the Hand,' said William, hoping to convince Michael that the relic had its uses. 'Deschalers came, before he died. He was one of the first merchants to visit.'

'What did he say?' asked Bartholomew, grateful that William had added the caveat 'before he died'. He did not like to imagine the Hand petitioned by the dead, as well as the living.

'He prayed for forgiveness,' said William. 'I am bound by the seal of confession, so cannot give you too many details. But he prayed for Bottisham, and he asked for a cure for his own ailment. He told the Hand it was his last hope, and said he hoped his plan would work.'

'I am glad you did not reveal *too many* details,' muttered Bartholomew; William had been rather free with what had,

232

after all, been a genuine confession and should have been kept confidential.

'Did he pray for Bottisham in the kind of way that indicated his victim would soon die?' asked Michael keenly, constrained by no such moral dilemmas. 'And exactly what was this plan?'

'He prayed for lots of people, but for Bottisham in particular. I do not recall him saying he *planned* murder obviously, or I would have stopped him. But he did not say he was *not*.' William pursed his lips, as though Deschalers not mentioning a crime was as damning as an admission.

'And the plan?' asked Michael.

The friar shrugged. 'I am sorry, Brother. I did not hear that bit. He spoke too softly.'

'Let us see this Hand, William,' said Michael wearily. 'And then we will leave you in peace.'

'It is in its reliquary,' said William, indicating a handsome box that stood on the table in the centre of the room. It was a beautiful thing, covered in precious stones and delicately carved.

'That box contains a piece of the True Cross,' cried Michael, shocked. 'Have you shoved Peterkin Starre's severed limb on top of what is a genuine relic?'

'The box was empty when I did an inventory of the University Chest's contents,' said William, unperturbed by Michael's horror. 'Since it has not been opened in years, I am inclined to believe that the True Cross was never there in the first place – or it was stolen so long ago that the thief is long since burning in Hell. It seemed a shame to have a glorious reliquary with no relic, so I put the Hand in it instead. I *could* show you the Hand, but I usually keep it locked away. It does not do to allow the peasantry to become too familiar with sacred objects. It might send them insane.'

'I am not a peasant,' said Michael indignantly. 'Nor will

I start baying at the moon because I set eyes on a few dead fingers.'

William cast him the kind of glance that indicated he was not so sure, but bent over the box and, with great reverence, removed a satin parcel that held the yellow-white bones. They were exactly as Bartholomew remembered, with sinews cleverly left to hold the hand together – except for one place where they had broken and were mended with a cunningly concealed pin. The bones were huge, and belonged, without question, to the simpleton whose gigantic corpse had provided a convenient source of material for men who had thought Cambridge needed a relic of its own. The little blue-green ring it wore was still there, too – a cheap thing, but pretty enough.

'There!' breathed Michael. 'The bones that caused us so much trouble when wicked men used them for their own vile and selfish purposes. They look just as they did two years ago, when they brought about so much unhappiness and tragedy.'

'They are causing us problems now, too,' said Bartholomew, somewhat accusingly. 'The University should not be taking money from folk to visit them. It is not right.'

'If you stop now, you will learn the true meaning of trouble,' warned William. 'People like the Hand. They believe it has the power to answer their prayers, and will not take kindly to you saying they can no longer use it. They would storm the church and snatch it away.'

'You are probably right,' said Michael. 'We shall have to devise another way to put an end to this madness. But I have seen enough. It is almost time for our evening meal.'

'If you are hungry, then do not go to Michaelhouse,' advised Redmeadow. 'We are so short of funds that Agatha is serving stale bread and pea pottage tonight. *We* are going to visit Deynman's brother at Maud's Hostel, where there will be roasted goose.'

'And I am dining at the Franciscan Friary,' said William. 'A man who has been working hard all day deserves more than mouldy bread and green paste. I intend to partake of fish soup and turnips.'

'I want meat,' said Michael, who did not feel he had eaten unless half a sheep was involved. He glanced down at the table. 'But nothing with bones in it.'

'I shall say a prayer for Chancellor Tynkell, and then I shall be finished here,' said Deynman, kneeling down. He looked up at William. 'He is a herbivore, you know.'

William's eyebrows went up, and he looked thoughtful. 'Perhaps that explains his peculiar aroma. A man who eats grass must surely smell differently from the rest of us.'

It was Deynman's turn to look bemused, but he put his hands together, closed his eyes and the conversation was mercifully at an end. William began to lock the Hand away while the two students prayed, and Bartholomew and Michael took the opportunity to leave.

'Lord!' said Michael, beginning to laugh as they walked into the evening sunlight. 'Deynman is a kindly boy, but he has the sense of a gnat! Tynkell is a herbivore indeed! Is that why he was asking after his health earlier? He believes the Chancellor has the digestive system of a cow?'

'He thinks Tynkell is a hermaphrodite, but could not remember the correct word. I will spare you the contorted logic he went through to reach this momentous conclusion.'

'His logic may be contorted,' said Michael, his laughter dissipating. 'But his conclusions are not. Tynkell is indeed a hermaphrodite, although I would rather keep this between ourselves. I do not want men like William claiming that a woman cannot hold the post of Chancellor. Tynkell is malleable, and does what I ask. I do not want him expelled, just because of an accident of birth.'

Bartholomew gaped at him. 'I do not believe you.'

'Have you not noticed that he never removes his clothes?' asked Michael. 'Or wondered why he refuses to let anyone see his body? Even *you* have not seen it, and you were his physician. Also, you must be aware that he does not bathe. That is because he cannot risk anyone intruding and viewing what he has sought to hide all these years.'

'No!' said Bartholomew in disbelief. 'You cannot be right!'

Michael shrugged. 'It is your prerogative to be sceptical. But look more closely at his shape when you next have the opportunity. You will notice swellings in the chest. And in the latrines—'

'But the condition is so rare,' interrupted Bartholomew, trying to recall what he had learned about a physiology he never thought he would see. 'I read about it, but I have never seen it manifest itself.'

'I imagine folk so afflicted do not make themselves available for general viewing. Most hide it, as Tynkell has done. It is safer, considering we live in a world populated by the intolerant and fanatical.'

'So Deynman's diagnosis was right?' Bartholomew narrowed his eyes. 'You are jesting with me!'

'Yes,' said Michael, convulsing with laughter.

'We are left with a mystery, Matt,' said Michael the next morning, as he and Bartholomew walked to St Michael's Church. Father William, ahead of them in the line of scholars that filed along the lane, turned to mutter about them setting a poor example to students by talking in the procession.

It was a pretty day, with a pale blue sky flecked by wispy clouds. The scent of spring was in the air, and bluebells and tiny white violets lined the grassy banks along the edge of the alley. Scruffy children were already gathering them to sell in the streets and at church doors. If they were lucky, they might earn enough to exchange for bread or an onion.

Despite the early hour, the town was busy. Traders gathered in the Market Square to sell their wares, and beggars were out in force, displaying sores and wounds, and raising piteous voices in an appeal for spare coins. Many gathered around the High Street churches, hoping to catch scholars in a pious frame of mind as they left their morning prayers.

'We still have no idea whether Deschalers killed Bottisham, then committed suicide, or the other way around,' Michael went on. 'Nor do we know why. We have established that Deschalers and Bottisham knew each other, and that they had quarrelled in the past. Warde told you Bottisham's antagonism had long since evaporated, but who knows whether that was really true? And, regarding the ancient dispute about the field, it is difficult to decide which of the two men was in the right.'

'What do you mean?' asked Bartholomew, surprised. 'Deschalers should not have been angry with Bottisham because he declined to break the law. I would say Bottisham was in the right.'

'And I would say Deschalers was. If Bottisham was squeamish about what needed to be done for his client, then he should not have agreed to represent him in the first place. But it does not matter what we think. What is important is what *they* thought. By all reports Deschalers was barely civil to Bottisham, so what led them to meet each other in such a curious place the night they died?'

'They must have agreed to go there,' said Bartholomew. 'The King's Mill is not somewhere you would happen upon by accident.'

'What do you mean?' asked Michael, ignoring William's black scowl.

'I might have suggested that Deschalers visited the mill to inspect the property he had invested in, and Bottisham spotted lights in a building usually locked at that time of night and went to investigate. But that is not possible: no one passes the mill by chance, because it is on a path that leads nowhere.'

'True. Then what about the possibility that one caught the other committing suicide, and ended up dead when he tried to stop him?' Michael shook his head and answered his own question. 'No. Neither was the kind to kill himself.'

'We know Deschalers intended to go to the mill, because he had the key with him,' mused Bartholomew. 'But why *he* was there is not really the question we need answered: we need to know why Bottisham was there with him.'

'We must come up with a solution soon, or people are going to start accusing the University of covering up a murder. It is one thing when someone lowly is killed by a scholar, but there will be a furious outcry about Bottisham killing a rich man like Deschalers.'

'It may have happened the other way around. In fact, if I were to wager on the outcome, that would be my choice: Deschalers was ruthless and inclined to be vicious, whereas Bottisham was more likely to wound with his tongue.'

'We will never prove either theory with the information we have now. I think—'

'If you must persist with this unseemly chattering, then leave the procession,' boomed William, finally driven to anger. Several students smirked at the sound of discord among the Fellows. 'I know you have murders to solve, but there is a time and a place for everything, and your investigations do not belong here.'

'He is jealous,' whispered Michael to Bartholomew, as William moved on. 'Now he is no longer my Junior Proctor, he feels left out when I am on a case.'

'Who will replace him? Do you have someone in mind?'

'I do not want a replacement.'

Bartholomew looked at him sharply. 'You did not use

238

the Junior Proctor's honorarium to pay for a Corpse Examiner, did you? I am effectively your subordinate, but with a different title?'

'Well, why not?' asked Michael, not bothering to deny that he had manipulated the situation. 'I know where I am with you. And better the devil . . .'

'And you certainly should not discuss the Devil while you process to mass!' screeched William. 'I am Keeper of the University Chest, and I will not stand by and see College rules shamelessly flaunted by Fellows who should know better.'

'And I am Senior Proctor, and outrank you,' snapped Michael.

'I am an important man,' argued William, although his voice dropped to a more reasonable level. He knew Michael was right. 'Particularly now the Hand of Valence Marie is in my care.'

Michael regarded him with cool, green eyes. 'And you must see how badly *that* will end. You have drawn attention to the fact that the University holds a relic that was discovered in the town's ditches. Note I say *town's* ditches, Father. It is only a matter of time before the burgesses claim we have taken something that is rightfully theirs.'

'I am doing what I think is ethical,' declared William hotly. 'The Chest is in *my* care, and *I* shall decide how to deal with its contents. I will not have *you* telling me what I can and cannot do.'

Michael continued to glare. 'Actually, you have no choice. I created the post of Keeper, and I can just as easily dispense with it. If you want to stay in power, then you will do as I say. You must devise a way to stop people coming to view the Hand without it resulting in ill feelings – or worse.'

'But I—' objected William.

Michael overrode him. 'This is not something for debate.

The Hand is dangerous, so you must ensure it is quietly forgotten. You have a week to devise a plan – or you will be Keeper no more.'

'Do not talk while we are processing to the sacred mass,' snapped William, unable to think of anything else to say. 'It creates a bad impression on the students.'

'Unless he puts an end to his little enterprise, creating bad impressions will be the least of our worries,' muttered Michael behind the friar's stiff, unbending back as they entered the church.

When the mass was over, Bartholomew went with his students to see Isnard. Unfortunately, the bargeman had appended his new wooden leg to the stump that was still healing, apparently anticipating that once he had made one or two trial circuits around his house, he would resume his previous life as though nothing had happened. He had not expected the pain of a reopened wound, nor had he known that walking with a false limb required more practise than twice around the hearth.

'I do not understand,' he cried when he saw Bartholomew. 'The bleeding had stopped, and you said it was better. I thought I would be back on my feet – my foot – in a few days.'

'I told you it would take longer,' said Bartholomew gently. 'You cannot bind a wooden leg to a raw wound and expect it not to chafe.'

'What do *you* two want?' demanded Isnard, as Quenhyth and Redmeadow sidled into the chamber with Deynman. 'You are not giving me another of them clysters. It did not ease my headache as you promised, and I do not like other men shoving pipes in my bowels. Well, who does?'

'Chancellor Tynkell enjoys—' began Deynman brightly.

Bartholomew cut him off, regarding the other two students uneasily. 'What did you do?'

'Isnard was unwell when we came to deliver his medicine last night.' Redmeadow's tone was defensive. 'So we persuaded him that a clyster would help. Quenhyth said—'

'How many times must we go over this?' asked Bartholomew quietly, fighting to control his anger. 'You must *not* prescribe medicines or treatments without my permission.'

'But we *did* have your permission,' objected Quenhyth, while Redmeadow hung his head. 'You said yesterday – after that nasty business with Rougham – that I was to examine him. I was acting on your orders.'

'But I did not tell you to start giving clysters,' said Bartholomew, exasperated. 'Bowels are delicate, and you need to be taught how to insert clyster pipes, so you do not rip them. You can cause a lot of harm if you do it badly.'

'It was not pleasant,' agreed Isnard. 'And I have never seen so much lard smothered on an implement in my life. I am sure half of it is still inside me.'

'We will talk about this later,' said Bartholomew, swallowing his ire and supposing that lard in the quantities Isnard described might have protected the unsuspecting bargeman to some extent. Perhaps his instructions had led Quenhyth to assume a freer hand than he had intended, but all the students knew the rules about what could and could not be done to patients unsupervised. There were no excuses for what they had done.

'You should not have removed the limb in the first place,' said Isnard to Bartholomew, rubbing the stump resentfully. 'It might have healed.'

'It would not,' said Bartholomew. 'You saw for yourself that it was smashed beyond repair. If we had left it, then you would be dead by now.'

'Perhaps that would have been a blessing,' said Isnard quietly. 'How can I work if I cannot walk? Now Bottisham

241

is dead I am running out of funds. I cannot stay here for ever, begging from friends.'

'I could ask Thomas Mortimer to give you some money,' offered Deynman. 'After all, it was *his* carelessness that brought you to this. He should be the one to support you.'

Isnard grimaced. 'I have already sent a message to Mortimer demanding funds, and he refused to acknowledge me. Redmeadow made his best writing, too.'

'I used large letters that are easy to decipher,' said Redmeadow proudly. 'Of course, Edward could have read it to his uncle, but I do not know how well they like each other these days.'

'What do you mean?' asked Bartholomew. 'Edward and Thomas work together at the mill, so they cannot dislike each other too much.'

'I heard them arguing when I went to deliver Isnard's note,' said Redmeadow. 'Edward called his uncle a drunken sot, not fit to have the care of a whipping top, let alone a mill. And Thomas called his nephew a cold-hearted killer, and said he would rot in Hell.'

'It is common knowledge that the Mortimer clan is fragmenting,' said Quenhyth, not to be outdone in gossip. 'And it is all Edward's doing. They no longer cleave together like treacle and feathers.'

'After Edward had finished yelling at his uncle, everyone else joined in,' continued Redmeadow. 'Cousins, uncles, aunts and brothers – all taking sides and squabbling. Constantine sat in the middle with his head in his·hands, and said he wished he had never bribed the King's officials. Edward took his knife from its scabbard and looked at him. I saw it, quite clearly, through the window.'

'Edward threatened his father with a dagger?' asked Bartholomew.

'He removed the weapon and fingered it, eyeing his father with this strange expression. It was not brazenly threatening, but it was a warning nonetheless. Constantine went white and left shortly afterwards. I caught him on his way out, and asked him to go back and deliver Isnard's message. He obliged – he feels bad about you, Isnard, even if his brother does not – and I watched him pass it to Thomas. Thomas read it, but then he threw it away.'

'You see?' said Isnard, disgusted. 'He did not even bother to reply.'

'You live dangerously,' said Bartholomew to Redmeadow, thinking the student should have knocked on the door with his missive, as most folk would have done. 'What would have happened if the Mortimers had caught you spying on them through their windows?'

'They would have slaughtered him,' said Quenhyth salaciously. 'Most folk believe the Mortimers killed Bosel the beggar, and they would have killed Redmeadow, too.'

'Quite,' said Bartholomew. 'So, I want you two to stay away from them from now on. You, too, Isnard. I had fourpence for examining a Peterhouse student who died from eating bad fish yesterday. You can have half.' He put the coins into Isnard's callused hand. 'That should keep you in bread for a day or two, and when it is gone we shall think of something else.'

Isnard's eyes filled with grateful tears. 'There is something else you can do for me, too. The fleas in my clothes are driving me to distraction, and I cannot rid myself of them lying here. You gave Una the whore a potion for her lice last year. Can I have something, too? They will kill me sooner than any rubbed stump!'

Since Isnard's clumsy attempts to attach his new leg had chafed the wound, Bartholomew decided he had better visit the apothecary, to purchase the ingredients he would need to make a healing poultice – along with the remedy for fleas. The students looked pleased: they were always

243

willing to visit Isobel and be on the receiving end of her alluring glances. They set off, aiming for Milne Street, where Lavenham's shop was located. At the door they met Paxtone. The King's Hall physician waved a phial at Bartholomew, and said he was going to conduct experiments on the efficacy of pear juice on a spotty complexion. He promised to share the results, since there were many adolescents in the Colleges and hostels who were in need of such a remedy. As he left he patted Quenhyth's shoulder.

'Do not let Rougham distress you with his insults.' He winked conspiratorially. 'No one should take any notice of a man who does not know his blackberries from his blackcurrants.'

Quenhyth grinned at him, and Bartholomew opened the door to enter Lavenham's house. It was a sturdy affair with thick, oaken window shutters and an immense door that protected the dangerous and valuable substances stored inside. It had two rooms on the ground floor – the shop, which was open to customers, and the apprentices' working area, which was not – and a larger chamber above that served as hall and sleeping quarters for the Lavenhams and their household.

The shop had a stone floor that could be easily cleaned. There was a bench along one wall, where clients waited for their orders to be assembled, while the other walls were filled with shelves holding bottles, boxes and casks. A long counter in the middle of the room served as a workbench for making up innocuous concoctions; stronger ones were mixed in the privacy (and safety) of the apprentices' area next door. Bartholomew loved the building's smell, which was rich with the scent of the herbs drying in the rafters, exotic powders known to have therapeutic values, and the honey and sugar used to make syrups.

Isobel was sitting behind the counter sewing, while her husband haggled with Robert Thorpe, the Master of

Valence Marie. Thorpe was a tall, slender man with a neat cap of silver hair. He looked tired, and Bartholomew wondered whether he lost sleep worrying about his son, or whether Warde's irritating cough still kept his colleagues from their rest.

'Why, hello,' said Isobel, standing to greet Bartholomew. She leaned across the counter in a way that was sure to reveal that her kirtle was unusually low cut. He heard a strangled gasp from Redmeadow, and was aware of the three students jostling for space behind him. Isobel rewarded them with one of her sultry looks, all fluttering lashes and smouldering eyes. She indicated the garment she had been making, and turned her gaze on Bartholomew. 'I have been sewing a tunic for Chancellor Tynkell and it is almost finished. Perhaps you could ask him to collect it, when you see him.'

'I seldom meet him,' replied Bartholomew. 'But one of my students—'

'I will take a message,' said Deynman, pushing forward, eager to offer his assistance.

'No, me,' said Redmeadow. Quenhyth looked as though he would dearly like to compete, too, but he preferred to retain a dignified aloofness in front of Isobel. He stood quietly as his classmates vied for her attention.

'You can both go,' said Isobel, favouring them with a wink that promised all sorts of favours when they returned. They darted from the shop to do her bidding, while Bartholomew glanced uneasily at her husband, hoping he had not noticed. He did not want it said that Michaelhouse students tried to ravish the wives of wealthy merchants, regardless of who had been seducing whom. But Lavenham's attention was on his customer, and Isobel was free to do as she pleased.

'It is an odd shape,' he said, nodding to the linen item Isobel shook out to fold.

'So is Tynkell,' she replied. 'But you probably have not noticed it under his academic robes. He says it is difficult to find clothes he likes, and regards me as something of a treasure, because I do not mind how he wants his undergarments sewn.'

'Have you seen him without them on?' Bartholomew asked, medical curiosity making him forget that it was an inappropriate question to ask a lady while her husband was in the room.

Even Isobel seemed taken aback by his candour. 'I have not!' she said, half shocked and half amused. 'He is a very private man, and disapproves of physical flaunting. That is what he told me. I do not know of anyone who has seen him *dishabille*.'

As she leaned across the counter, her bosom straining at its confines, Bartholomew knew exactly why the Chancellor had raised such a subject. Of all members of the University he was the one who could least afford to be seen breaking the rules regarding women, and the physician supposed Tynkell had been warning Isobel to keep her cleavage to herself. He wondered whether Tynkell's penchant for peculiarly moulded undergarments was evidence of the condition Deynman had ascribed to him, but knew it was equally likely that he was just a man who liked his clothes made in a certain way. Bartholomew empathised, since he preferred unfashionably loose leggings to the modern trend for tight hose.

'I need some *Pastilli Adronis*,' he said, changing the subject before they embarrassed each other further. 'I ordered it last week.'

'Here,' said Isobel, reaching for a package on a high shelf, careful to reveal a goodly portion of leg as she did so. 'It has been ready since yesterday, and I was beginning to think you did not want it.' She waggled her hips to indicate that he should have fetched it sooner.

'And resin of henbane,' added Bartholomew, tearing his eyes away. 'For Isnard's fleas.'

'An excellent solution,' said Isobel, disappearing into the back room. There was a jangle of keys and the sound of a cupboard being opened and closed. 'Fleas can drive men mad when they are confined to their beds. But henbane is a dangerous substance – especially ours, which is highly concentrated. You must tell him not to ingest it.'

'I will make a decoction for soaking his clothes. It will smell too bad for him to drink.'

'Isnard will drink anything,' said Isobel, truthfully enough. Bartholomew realised he might have to add something even more rankly aromatic to prevent the bargeman from testing whether the flea-killer had pleasant intoxicating effects.

'Doctor Bartholomew,' called Lavenham, spotting him and taking the trouble to court a man who, as a physician, was obliged to do a good deal of business with him. 'I hope you are well.' He looked pleased with himself and Bartholomew supposed he had been practising his English, since it was the first grammatically correct sentence he had heard the man utter.

Master Thorpe glanced up from his examination of a milky-red solution in a small pottery phial. He held it out for the physician to inspect. 'What do you think of this?'

'Watyr of Snayels,' said Bartholomew, reading the tiny letters on the label. 'Nasty.'

'Nasty, no!' exclaimed Lavenham, affronted. His English took a downward turn as he began to defend himself. 'He is purest quality, and he took my apprentice three day to made.'

'What is it for?' asked Bartholomew, aware that it was none of his affair. Water of Snails was an old-fashioned remedy that was seldom used, and he saw that Lavenham's concoction had not been properly filtered through sand, as Galen recommended, because it was murky. He thought swallowing such a tincture would probably do little good, and might even cause some harm.

'It is for Warde,' replied Master Thorpe. 'He cannot rid himself of his cough, and none of us have slept in days because of it.' He regarded the phial doubtfully. 'I do not know how I shall persuade him to drink this, though. I would not want snail juice washing around inside *me*.'

'Rougham recommended it,' said Isobel.

'What do you think?' asked Master Thorpe, still regarding the bottle with rank suspicion. 'Should I buy it? Or shall we persist with the syrups instead? Warde does not mind taking those.'

'Water of Snails has proven effective, if there is nothing else,' said Bartholomew ambiguously.

'But you would not swallow it yourself,' surmised Master Thorpe, reading Bartholomew's mind. He thrust the phial back into Lavenham's unwilling hands. 'Thank you, apothecary, but I think I will decline. What shall I have instead, Bartholomew?'

Bartholomew was uncomfortable; it was not good manners to recommend cures for other physicians' patients. 'You must ask Rougham. It is not for me to interfere.'

'Rubbish!' exclaimed Master Thorpe. 'He is always recommending alternative therapies to your patients, so I do not see why you should not do the same for his. He told Father William – he is yours – to drink fig juice to purge his bowels the other day, when he complained of a sore head.'

'Then try powdered angelica root,' suggested Bartholomew, wondering whether William was foolish enough to believe that purged bowels would cure a headache. 'Mix it with wine.'

'That sounds like something he would accept,' said

Master Thorpe with satisfaction, as Isobel went to the back room to fetch some. 'Thank you. I—'

What he was about to say was drowned by a low rumble, followed by a good deal of laughter from the apprentices. Isobel appeared with her hands on her hips and an angry expression.

'That pile of firewood you insist on gathering has collapsed,' she snapped to her husband. 'How much longer will it be before you stack it inside the shed? It will be no good for burning if it rains.'

'My apprentices too busy for woods,' replied Lavenham. 'It must await my intentions.' He watched her flounce out again.

'Had you heard news? I have been wrote by King himself. He give me a tusk.'

Bartholomew regarded him uncomprehendingly. 'Ivory?' he asked eventually, not sure what else to say, and feeling obliged to make some comment, since the apothecary was obviously expecting one. 'From the sea elephants of the north?'

It was Lavenham's turn to look blank. 'I refer to a great tusk set for me by King. He want me to examine matter of Mortimer's Mill.' He stood taller, clearly proud of himself.

'It is true,' said Master Thorpe. 'We heard this morning that the King has appointed four commissioners to examine the complaints about Mortimer diverting water from the King's Mill.'

'And I am first,' said Lavenham grandly. 'He want good and loyal Englishmen to do his work. He choose me, because he hear I am fine servant to His Royal Majesty.'

'Warde is another, and Miller Bernarde is the third,' added Master Thorpe.

'But Bernarde is the one who made the complaint,' said Bartholomew, startled. He looked at Lavenham. 'And *you*

249

are in the Millers' Society. It is an odd choice for an unbiased decision.'

'That is why it good *I* King's commissioner,' declared Lavenham. 'I will see justice done right, by destroy Mortimer.'

'See what I mean?' said Bartholomew to Master Thorpe.

He nodded. 'But Warde is a fair-minded man, and so, I hope, am I.'

'You are the fourth commissioner?' asked Bartholomew, thinking it was not a task he would have accepted for a kingdom. There were far too many ways to offend people and cause strife and, no matter what decision was made, it would make someone unhappy and resentful.

'I would not have chosen to do it,' confided Master Thorpe. 'But I am indebted to the King for reinstating me as Master of Valence Marie after my spell in York, and I am not in a position to refuse. But Warde is a fair man, as I said. Hopefully we shall reach a compromise that satisfies all parties. We intend to discuss it together this afternoon.'

'We soon have this mess resolve,' boasted Lavenham. 'We finish by dusk, and then we all go to King's Head for celebration ales.'

'We shall not,' said Master Thorpe firmly, accepting a pot of angelica root and handing some coins to Isobel. 'It is only a preliminary meeting, and we cannot hope to forge a solution so quickly. I anticipate we will be working on this for some time to come – hearing witnesses and the arguments of lawyers for both sides.'

'We see,' said Lavenham smugly.

The physician nodded his thanks to Lavenham, ignored the wink thrown in his direction by Isobel, and followed Master Thorpe outside. He was immediately aware of how the shuttered windows banished sounds, for it was noisy in the street. Carts clattered as their wooden wheels snapped across a section of the road that had recently been cobbled, and a cacophony of animal sounds emanated from the Market Square. A cow lowed, probably being led to Slaughterhouse Lane, and a group of pigs squealed in voices that were eerily human. People hollered back and forth, while a mangy yellow dog yapped at a group of boys who were pelting it with mud.

'I am sorry my son is here,' said Master Thorpe quietly, as they walked to the High Street with Quenhyth trailing behind them. Like Constantine Mortimer, the Master of Valence Marie had changed since his son's trial. He had lost his arrogance, and seemed kinder and more humble. 'I tried to persuade him to leave again, but he is no longer a boy, and he listens to nothing I say.'

'I doubt he listens to anyone,' said Bartholomew, sensing the man's distress. 'It is not your fault he turned bad.'

Thorpe swallowed hard. 'I hear Brother Michael is investigating the odd case of Deschalers and Bottisham in the King's Mill. My son is a . . . I am afraid . . .'

Bartholomew understood what he was trying to say. 'There is no evidence that your son had anything to do with it,' he said, but suspected he did not sound very convincing. 'Bernarde the miller would have seen him running away, had he been responsible.'

Thorpe was not so easily convinced. 'He is a cunning lad, Bartholomew, and fooling a miller would be no great challenge for him. He has killed before, and the murders of Deschalers and Bottisham have already set town and University against each other. Perhaps that is why he came back: to start a riot that will damage us all. He has always been spiteful, and his exile has made him worse.'

Bartholomew suspected that nothing he could say would allay Master Thorpe's fears. They ran deep, and there might even be something in them. Bartholomew had always thought it an odd coincidence that two dreadful murders

251

should have occurred just after Thorpe and Mortimer had reappeared. But could Bernarde's testimony be overlooked? And would the two young men really be so stupid as to kill as soon as they had been granted their royal pardons? He did not know the answers, but he did know that such a solution would exonerate Bottisham from the accusations that were beginning to circulate around the town. It was therefore an appealing one.

Master Thorpe said no more, and he, Bartholomew and Quenhyth walked in silence until they reached St Mary the Great. A small knot of people knelt outside the tower, eyes raised devoutly towards the chamber where the University Chest and its dubious contents were housed.

'I wish you had never found that Hand,' Bartholomew said fervently to Thorpe. 'Even though we proved it was not a real relic, there are still folk who insist on its authenticity.'

'I explained that phenomenon to you years ago,' said Master Thorpe, a little condescendingly. 'It does not matter whether it is authentic or not; what matters is what people believe. And people believe in the Hand. But you should not condemn folk for visiting it. Where lies the harm in giving them hope for hopeless causes?'

'Because it is not real,' said Bartholomew, wondering how many times he would need to say it. 'It is *not* the hand of a saint or a martyr. It is Peterkin Starre's.'

Master Thorpe sighed. 'You are still missing my point. Its authenticity *does not matter!* Do you really believe that the blood of Thomas à Becket can cure the blind? Or that St Etheldreda at Ely lies uncorrupted in her shrine? Of course not! We are men of science, who naturally question such claims. But *others* believe. And it is *they*, not the doubters, who are important here.'

'Are you saying the University should encourage people in this lie? Give them false hope?'

'I am saying the University should not keep the Hand from folk who think they need its comfort. Michael should make it available to everyone. There will be "cures" and "miracles", and the University should accept the gratitude of successful petitioners. And then there will be fewer prayers answered than requests made, and people will begin to lose faith. Gradually it will be forgotten, and *then* you can throw it in the river.'

'You mean we may be strengthening the cult by restricting access to the Hand?'

'Precisely. By keeping it secret, you merely tell people it is important. Once it is freely accessible, and people can see it, then it will lose its mysterious appeal. You should act on my advice, Doctor: it is the only way to deal with the Hand of Valence Marie.'

Bartholomew was on his way to take the poultice to Isnard when three familiar figures approached him. He was appalled when he saw that one was his brother-in-law, Oswald Stanmore. He had been under the impression that his family had intended to remain in Huntingdon for some weeks, and was horrified that they were home early now that young Thorpe was at large. Matilde was with Stanmore, on her way home from the Market Square, and two of Yolande de Blaston's children staggered under the weight of her purchases. The third familiar figure was Michael, who was rummaging in her baskets and brazenly helping himself to whatever edibles he could find. The children were far too sensible to try to deter the monk, while Matilde was so deeply engrossed in her discussion with Stanmore that she had not noticed what Michael was doing.

'Why are you here?' Bartholomew demanded of his brother-in-law when they drew level. 'You should be in Huntingdon. Where is my sister?'

'There is an affectionate greeting,' said Stanmore to

Matilde, his tone wry. 'I have not seen Matt for nigh on six weeks, and this is how he hails me.'

'Edith is still in Huntingdon,' replied Matilde, understanding the reason for Bartholomew's sharpness. 'She will not return for some weeks, so do not worry about her.'

'Good,' said Bartholomew fervently. 'But you should not be here either, Oswald, not with Thorpe stalking around. You should return to Huntingdon and stay there until he leaves.'

'I certainly shall not,' retorted Stanmore indignantly. 'This is my home, and no ex-apprentice will drive me from it. Besides, it is not *my* fault he committed murder and was caught. I do not see how he can hold me responsible for his downfall, just because he was living in my house when it happened.'

Bartholomew saw there was no point in arguing, although he was certain that was not how Thorpe viewed the situation. He looked at Matilde. 'How is Bess? Is she still with you, or have you found her somewhere else to sleep?'

Matilde frowned worriedly. 'She owns a huge hoard of coins. I cannot imagine where it came from. Not from a grateful customer – it is far more than the usual going rate for Frail Sisters in Cambridge – even the very good ones.'

Michael chuckled, his cheeks flecked with pastry as he investigated another of her parcels. 'Perhaps it came from Deschalers. I saw him towing her home at one point.'

'So did I,' said Bartholomew. 'It was last Saturday, the day before he died.' He saw Stanmore's thoughtful expression. 'But I do not think she is Deschalers's killer.'

Michael agreed. 'Especially if Bernarde is telling the truth about no one else being inside the mill.'

'I would be surprised if Bess is your culprit, too,' said Matilde. 'She is too addled, poor thing. I sewed a secret compartment in her cloak for her coins, but I doubt she

254

will keep them long, because she does not understand their value. She is staying with Una tonight.'

'What about Dame Pelagia?' asked Bartholomew. 'Has she gone, too?'

'She has. It is just me, Yolande, Robert and their ten children now,' said Matilde with a smile. 'My house feels almost empty!'

'Have you heard about the King's Commission?' asked Stanmore, who found town politics far more interesting than sleeping arrangements for madwomen.

Bartholomew nodded. 'Master Thorpe and Warde are good choices, but I do not think it was wise to have Bernarde and Lavenham on the committee, too.'

'Why not?' asked Stanmore. 'They will ensure the Millers' Society is properly represented.'

'But there is no one to put the Mortimers' side of the argument,' Bartholomew pointed out.

Stanmore waved a dismissive hand. 'That is unnecessary. They have no side worth presenting.'

Bartholomew was startled. 'Why are you against them?'

'The Mortimers full cloth at that mill, and it interferes with my business,' replied Stanmore grimly.

'But the next nearest fulling mill is in Ely,' said Bartholomew, puzzled. 'Surely Thomas Mortimer provides you a valuable service?'

'Not at the prices *he* charges,' said Stanmore stiffly. 'His brazen extortion is exactly the kind of sinful behaviour that will bring the pestilence back again.'

'I have never understood fulling,' said Michael, interrupting Bartholomew, who was about to argue that the price of cloth had nothing to do with whether the plague returned. 'What is it, exactly?'

'Only light cloths, like worsteds, are good without fulling,' said Stanmore, sounding pompous as he lectured on something he knew a lot about. 'But most materials these days are heavy broadcloths, and need to be felted. We do this by soaking them in an alkaline solution and pounding them. In the old days, this was done by men and women trampling the cloth with their feet, but we have moved on from primitive technology and use fulling mills now. These batter the cloth with wooden hammers that are driven by water. It is all very sophisticated. That is what happens at Mortimer's Mill.'

Michael rummaged in another of Matilde's baskets. 'Is that it? Cloth is soaked, then thumped with hammers?'

'Not at all,' said Stanmore crisply. 'That is only the beginning. After the pounding, the cloth is dried, then stretched on a device we call a "tenter". The nap is raised by rubbing with teasels, and then evened with shears. It is difficult and exacting work, and one wrong move can destroy hours of labour. Then it is dyed. That is where I come in.'

'That is a skilled process, too, I imagine,' said Matilde politely.

The clothier puffed himself up. 'It certainly is! I need to decide exactly how much of each dye will achieve the colour my customer wants, and I need to assess how long to leave a material soaking – too long may rot the cloth, too short will see it wash out. But it will not be long before Mortimer turns his hand to dyeing, too, and then where will I be? I have prayed to the Hand that he will lose his case, and that the King will order him to dismantle his mill before he does me harm.'

'But the Commission comprises two men who have a vested interest in finding against him,' said Bartholomew. 'Mortimer may decide to ignore its decision.'

'No one would dare go against the King,' said Stanmore. 'His word is law.'

'Until he changes his mind,' said Bartholomew bitterly. 'Look what happened with Thorpe and Edward and their royal pardons.'

Stanmore glanced around uneasily. 'You should watch what you say, Matt. It is not wise to criticise our monarch so openly. You do not know who might be listening. I admire Dame Pelagia, as you know, but she *is* the King's agent, and she may report you, if you are not careful.'

'She would not,' said Michael confidently, thrusting cake into his mouth. Matilde became aware that he was seriously depleting her supplies, and gestured for the children to move away. Michael sighed his annoyance, but still managed to secure some bread before they left.

'You would not know she was listening,' persisted Stanmore. 'She is like a shadow: here one moment and vanished the next. Still, I feel better knowing she has come here to help us.'

'She went to see Tynkell and Dick Tulyet today,' said Michael. 'Dick promised to lend her soldiers whenever she needed them. She says she plans to need them very soon.'

'God help us,' muttered Bartholomew. It was a bizarre situation indeed when men of power like the Chancellor and the Sheriff relied on an old lady to solve their problems.

'Constantine admits he made a mistake in buying a pardon for his son,' said Matilde. 'He all but killed the fatted calf when Edward returned, but Edward declines to have anything to do with him.'

'It is a pity Deschalers is dead,' said Stanmore. '*He* could control Edward, because the lad is his kin by marriage to Julianna – and obeyed him to be sure of inheriting his wealth. There are rumours that Edward had him killed, and that he hired Bottisham to do it.'

Bartholomew was horrified, thinking that while Edward might well have had a hand in Deschalers's death, Bottisham was unlikely to have been his willing tool. 'Surely you do not believe that?'

Stanmore shook his head. 'No, I do not. Edward and

Thorpe are far too clever to start killing as soon as they arrive back in the town. But . . .' He hesitated, and regarded Bartholomew uneasily.

'But what?' asked Bartholomew, with the sense that he was about to hear something he would not like.

'But Bottisham is a different matter,' said Stanmore. He held up a hand to quell the physician's objections. 'I know you liked him, Matt, but he and Deschalers had a history.'

'We know,' said Michael, throwing the bread to a hopeful dog. The discussion of the mill deaths had deprived him of his appetite. 'About the field and the funds for the chapel.'

Stanmore nodded. 'Deschalers's abrupt withdrawal made other benefactors rethink, too, and Gonville was left in a terrible mess. He once told me that he had managed the whole thing out of spite, to humiliate Bottisham. It would not surprise me to learn Bottisham was so angry that he lured Deschalers to the King's Mill and slew him. Then he killed himself when he realised he would hang.'

'People do not hang for murder these days,' said Matilde acidly. 'They spend a couple of years in France, then return to claim compensation for false conviction.'

'But Bottisham did not kill Deschalers, anyway,' said Bartholomew, finding the discussion distasteful. 'He would be more likely to use the law for vengeance.'

'Deschalers was very rich,' said Matilde thoughtfully. 'I should inspect his will, if I were you, to ascertain whether he intended to change or amend it. It would not be the first time a man expressed a desire to leave his wealth to someone different, and those about to be disinherited took matters into their own hands. You should not strike anyone from your list of suspects yet, and . . .'

She trailed off as she became aware of a commotion near St Mary the Great, where a large number of people had gathered, as usual. As they moved towards the massing crowd, one word could be heard spoken over and over again. Bartholomew's heart sank when he realised it was 'miracle'.

'Master Thorpe warned me about this,' he said to Matilde. 'He said there would be "miracles" if we continue to keep the Hand in a sealed room, and restrict access to it.'

'He is right,' replied Matilde. 'Folk are far more interested in things that are forbidden. Bring the Hand out and display it, and it will be forgotten in a few months.' She caught the arm of Una, who was hurrying away with her face set in a broad grin. 'What is it? What is going on?'

'A miracle,' declared Una. 'We knew it would only be a matter of time before one occurred, and we were right. This will be the first of many.'

'What kind of miracle?' asked Bartholomew warily.

'Isnard the bargeman,' said Una joyfully. 'His severed leg has just regrown!'

CHAPTER 7

'You are a heartless man,' said Michael approvingly, as he and Bartholomew walked home from Isnard the barge-man's house later that day. 'You dismayed half the town's population, embarrassed Isnard, and exposed Thomas Mortimer as a fraud, all within a few moments.'

'Mortimer is a selfish liar,' declared Bartholomew uncompromisingly. 'He informed everyone that Isnard's leg had grown back because *he* had petitioned the Hand of Valence Marie on Isnard's behalf. However, he knew it would not be long before someone noticed Isnard was still *sans* leg. When that happened, he planned to tell people that Isnard was so sinful, the cure had been withdrawn.'

'It was a daring plan. Had it worked, it would have seen him free of all the venomous mutterings over the cart incident.'

'He would have benefited enormously – at Isnard's expense. However, when Isnard eventually wakes up from his drunken slumbers, he will find himself in great pain. His wound has reopened, because he allowed Mortimer to affix the wooden leg and take him out on it too soon. He might even die, if it does not heal.'

'Isnard will do anything for a drink,' said Michael unhappily. 'Even sit in the company of the man who injured him. He allowed himself to be plied with ale, carried to St Mary the Great with his new leg, and paraded as though he was fully recovered.'

'And the astonishing thing is that people were prepared to believe it, even though Isnard could not stand and there was blood seeping from the injury.' Bartholomew was disgusted. 'That was partly Rougham's fault, for supporting Mortimer when he said Isnard's leg had reappeared. Was *he* drunk, do you think, to make such a stupid assertion?'

'He was sober,' replied Michael sombrely. 'And you have made yourself a greater enemy of him than ever, by pointing out his folly to the crowd. You should have seen his face when you removed the bandages to reveal a bloody stump and a wooden calf. If he had been a man for surgery, one of his knives would be embedded in you this very moment.'

'And he accuses my students of being dull-witted!' said Bartholomew angrily. 'He did not even bother to inspect Isnard before making his proclamations about complete cures.'

'How is Mistress Lenne?' asked Michael, interrupting what was about to become a diatribe against the man his friend seemed to detest more at every encounter. He hoped it would not continue to escalate, because Cambridge was too small a town for bitter disputes between men whose paths crossed with some frequency. It was the sort of situation that might end in a brawl between Gonville and Michaelhouse, as students demonstrated solidarity with their masters.

'She is dying,' replied Bartholomew shortly. 'The shock of losing her husband has made her listless and dull, and it will not be long before she joins him in his grave. I only hope her son will arrive from Thetford in time to say his farewells.'

'That is curious,' said Michael. Bartholomew followed his gaze and saw Wynewyk ducking into the small, dirty alley that ran down the side of St Botolph's Church. As the Michaelhouse lawyer disappeared from sight he glanced in his colleagues' direction, and grimaced when he realised he had been spotted. Bartholomew exchanged a puzzled look with Michael, then went to wait at the lane's entrance until he came out. Wynewyk was a relative newcomer to the town, and did not know many of Cambridge's seedier footpaths. But Bartholomew and Michael knew them well – and the one Wynewyk had chosen to dive down was a dead end.

'What is he doing?' asked Michael, bemused. 'His shoes will be filthy when he emerges.'

'He did not want us to see him,' said Bartholomew. 'Just as he does not want us to know he holds secret meetings with Paxtone.'

It was some time before Wynewyk's large nose eased through the lane's entrance, followed by his head and the rest of his body, like a rodent leaving its nest after a long winter. He almost leapt out of his skin when Michael spoke to him.

'You should not go down there alone. It is notorious as a daytime sleeping hole for those who prowl the streets at night for sinister purposes.'

'In that case, the Senior Proctor should ensure they are ousted,' said Wynewyk stiffly, trying to shake the muck from his shoes. 'But I saw no sleeping villains. The only person there now is that madwoman, who is playing with her gold coins and singing some dirge to herself.'

'Is she?' asked Bartholomew, peering into the gloom and wondering whether he should go to see her. But the lane was odorously sticky, rank with rubbish dumped there by those who could not be bothered to walk to the river, and it had been used as a latrine for months. He glanced down at what was a fairly new pair of boots and decided to leave Bess in peace.

'God alone knows where she got them from,' gabbled Wynewyk, transparently relieved to be discussing something other than his own reasons for frequenting such a place. 'Perhaps she has been plying her trade among the rich

262

merchants. I heard she serviced Deschalers the day before he died.'

'I do not see a fastidious man like Deschalers employing a creature like Bess,' said Michael, echoing what others had said. 'He preferred women of his own class, like Katherine Mortimer.'

'I doubt he had his money's worth on Saturday,' said Bartholomew, rather crudely. 'He was too ill, and Bess looked seriously uninterested. It would not have made for an energetic coupling.'

'I find such images nasty,' said Wynewyk primly. 'But I must be on my way. I have a lot to do.'

'Such as what?' asked Michael nosily.

Wynewyk gave a strained smile. 'The College is experiencing financial difficulties at the moment and there are people to see and arrangements to be made, if we are to eat next week.'

'In that case, continue,' said Michael, standing aside to let him pass. 'However, last night, I was fed chicken giblets and a pile of stale barley. Such victuals are unacceptable, and I sincerely hope you plan to do better in the future.'

'The food has only been poor over the last three weeks or so,' said Bartholomew. 'Before that, we all noticed a great improvement when you started to help Langelee with the accounts.'

Wynewyk smiled at him. 'Thank you, Matt. But we have had unforeseen expenses recently: we had to replace the guttering on the hall, then Bird got into the conclave and scratched the wax off all the writing tablets. And we have had to purchase new arrows.' His mouth hardened into a thin line.

'What for?' asked Bartholomew, startled. 'Who do you plan to shoot?'

'Thorpe and Mortimer,' replied Wynewyk. 'Or rather, Langelee does. An old lady came to inspect our weaponry this morning, and recommended we replace our old arrows, because they have become dangerously brittle. She seemed to know more about such things than most mercenaries.'

'Dame Pelagia,' said Bartholomew, not surprised that even an experienced warrior like Langelee should defer to her on issues of defence. 'If ever you are in a brawl, you could not do better than to have her at your side. I would even take her over Langelee.'

'I do not brawl,' said Wynewyk distastefully. 'But, as I said, I am busy, so you must excuse me.' He pushed past them, and was gone, walking briskly down the High Street with fussy little steps.

'That was odd,' said Bartholomew. 'Why was he trying to hide from us? Did you notice that he never did tell us what he was doing?'

'I doubt it was anything too mischievous,' said Michael dismissively. 'I am more concerned with Bottisham and Deschalers. We have learned that they disliked each other, but we still do not know who took a nail to whom. Or why their disagreement should erupt into violence now, after all these years. Perhaps it was exacerbated by the mill case: Deschalers on one side, Bottisham on the other. Or perhaps Deschalers decided that if he was to die, then Bottisham was going to go with him.'

'I am not sure about that. Perhaps Deschalers did draw vestiges of murderous strength from somewhere, as Rougham maintains – although I am not sure he is right – but is it likely? Deschalers was the kind of man whose idea of vengeance was to damage his enemy's finances.'

'As he did with his withdrawn donation for Gonville's chapel,' mused Michael. 'So we are back to the solution where we have Bottisham the killer, and Deschalers the victim. Damn!'

'I do not believe that,' insisted Bartholomew stubbornly. 'Not Bottisham.'

'I know how you feel,' said Michael with a sigh. 'I find it difficult to accept, too. But we cannot allow our liking for the man to blind us to the facts. Deschalers deserves justice, too, and if Bottisham killed him, then it is our moral duty to tell people what happened. However, while it is never good when a scholar kills a townsman, it is far worse when that townsman was a wealthy burgess.'

'Then we had better keep our theories to ourselves, until we are certain.'

Michael regarded him with raised eyebrows. 'Are you suggesting we prevaricate? That we warp the truth? I see I will make a University man of you yet!'

'That is not what I meant,' said Bartholomew tartly. 'I am not suggesting we stay quiet because I am politicking, but because I do not want unfounded speculations to cause rioting and mayhem – or to damage Bottisham's reputation prematurely.'

Michael rubbed his eyes and sighed again. 'And how do we do that? It has been four days since the murders, and we are no further on with our enquiries than when they first happened. Poor Bottisham! And poor Deschalers, too.'

They started to walk to Michaelhouse. Bartholomew kept his eyes on his feet as he stepped around the street's worst filth, only to collide with someone doing the same thing as he came from the opposite direction. It was Master Thorpe from Valence Marie, and in his wake were Warde, Lavenham and Bernarde the miller: the King's Commissioners.

Bartholomew had never seen a more unhappy group of men. Bernarde was so angry he was shaking, and his face was flushed a deep, dangerous red as he played with his keys. Bartholomew thought he needed to sit quietly and take some deep breaths before he gave himself a seizure. By contrast, Lavenham looked bewildered, as though he was still trying to understand what had transpired. Bernarde grabbed his arm and hauled him away, whispering into his ear in savage hisses. Meanwhile, Thorpe looked weary, while Warde coughed.

'I take it the first meeting of the King's Commissioners did not go smoothly?' asked Michael, amused. 'You have not resolved the dispute in an hour, as Lavenham predicted?'

Thorpe grimaced. 'I wish I were not involved in this. I see no solution that will please everyone, so someone must expect to be disappointed.' He spoke hoarsely, as if he had shouted a lot.

'*Everyone* will be disappointed,' said Warde. He cleared his throat, then spat. 'Both sides want nothing less than the dismantling of the other's mill. In a case like this, there *is* no mutually acceptable solution. In the interests of fairness, I am arguing for the Mortimers – since Lavenham and Bernarde are for the King's Mill; Thorpe is attempting to mediate. But it is worse than suing the French for peace. No wonder Bishop Bateman was never successful in Avignon! How can you reach an agreement with folk who will not even listen to you?'

'We appreciate there is a lot at stake,' said Thorpe tiredly. 'Both mills represent substantial incomes, plus there is the matter of employment. I do not want to hurt innocent labourers by closing down either mill. But it may come to that, if we cannot reach a compromise.'

Warde coughed again. 'Damn this wretched tickle! But that angelica is helping, Bartholomew. I must pay you for your advice.' He started to hunt for coins, but the physician stopped him.

'You can recompense me by not saying anything to Rougham. I do not want him to accuse me of poaching his patients.'

Thorpe was dismissive. 'Warde was your patient long before Rougham arrived. He poached from you, not the other way around.'

266

'I wish I had kept you, Bartholomew,' said Warde fervently. 'Did you know Rougham recommended Water of Snails for my malady? Does he imagine me to be a Frenchman, to suggest such a remedy? And that Hand is next to worthless! I have prayed to it three times now, and it has not seen fit to make me better.'

'I do not know what to do about the mill dispute,' said Thorpe, returning to the issue that clearly worried him. 'The Mortimers' case will be presented by the lawyers at Gonville Hall. Do you know why they agreed to become embroiled in this, Brother? It is because the Mortimers promised them a handsome donation for their chapel if they win! As I said, the stakes are high for all concerned.'

'They said nothing of this to me,' said Michael indignantly. 'And I asked Acting Master Pulham straight out whether Gonville had interests in the Mortimers' venture.'

Thorpe looked unhappy. 'Then he was lying to you.'

'We should visit the King's Mill again,' said Michael two days later, when Saturday morning's teaching was done and the Fellows were enjoying a cup of cheap wine and a plate of stale oatcakes in the conclave. The monk was depressed and worried – both about the lack of progress in his investigation, and about the continuing decline in College food. 'I need to see what it looks like when it is working, and I want to ask Bernarde more about what *he* knows of the two men who died so horribly among the grinding mechanisms he operates. He is my last hope – I cannot think of anything else to do that might throw light on this matter.'

'Did you ask Pulham about what Master Thorpe told us?' asked Bartholomew. 'About the Mortimers promising hefty donations, if Gonville can make the Commission find in their favour?'

'Not yet,' replied Michael shortly. 'The Bishop of Ely

summoned most of the Gonville Fellows to see him on Thursday afternoon – something about the deeds to a property Bateman did not properly transfer to them before he died. But I will catch them as soon as they return.'

'Bottisham deserves to have his name cleared of the unpleasant rumours that are circulating around the town – that he killed Deschalers,' said Father William, making Michael wince. It sounded like an accusation of incompetence. 'The townsfolk's anger against us is palpable when they come to visit the Hand. You should do all you can to prove him innocent, Brother.'

'He is working as hard as he can,' said Bartholomew sharply. 'I have never seen a case where there are so few clues, and he is doing his best. He has barely rested since this started.'

'I have barely eaten, either,' added the monk in a plaintive voice, obviously considering this far more serious. 'Will you come with me to the mill, Matt? Now?'

'You should not have discredited the Hand with such relish on Thursday, Bartholomew,' admonished Langelee, as the physician reached for his cloak. 'It might bring the University a great deal of money, and it does not look good when our own scholars scoff at its powers.'

'Hear, hear,' said William, pouring himself a third cup of wine, despite the fact that there was not much left and neither Kenyngham nor Wynewyk had yet had any. 'And you telling folk it is a fake does nothing for my status as Keeper of the University Chest, either.'

Bartholomew bit back a retort that told the sanctimonious friar exactly what he could do with his reputation. 'The Hand is *not* sacred. It came from Peterkin Starre, who drooled over his food, had the mind of a five-year old and was frightened of the dark.'

'Great wisdom often springs from the mouths of the simple,' preached Suttone piously. 'If we had listened to

Peterkin, then perhaps the Death would not have visited us in all its terrible glory.'

'If we had listened to Peterkin, then we would have been making mud pies in the gutters and singing our favourite lullabies when the plague came,' said Bartholomew caustically.

'But people say he was a saint – a prophet – who chose to deliver his message in the voice of a child,' argued Suttone. 'That is why his Hand can bring about miracles.'

'Adjusting the story to fit the facts.' Bartholomew shook his head in disgust. 'There is no reasoning with fanatics, is there? They fabricate answers to every question, and when something does not sit well with their beliefs they either ignore it or dismiss it. Such attitudes explain why men commit such shameful acts – like the vicious persecutions of the Albigensians and the Templars.'

'Those were perfectly justified,' declared William, who had taken part in some vicious persecutions of his own before his Order had placed him in the University, where they felt he was less likely to do any harm. Sometimes Bartholomew thought they were very wrong.

'I visited Albi once,' said Wynewyk conversationally. 'Albi was where the Albigensian persecutions took place – and where the heretical Cathars were finally eliminated. These days, it is a dirty place that smells of rotting olives, although its wine is very good.' He looked disparagingly at the brew William was imbibing with such relish.

'*I* do not accept the rubbish about the Hand's sanctity, either,' said Langelee to Bartholomew. 'But we must be pragmatic. Do not denounce it publicly and make Michaelhouse an enemy of the town. Dame Pelagia recommends that we keep silent on the matter – at least until she has found a way to rid us of Thorpe and Mortimer without too much bloodshed. After that, the Hand will be quietly forgotten.'

269

'I do not like the sound of "without too much bloodshed",' said the gentle Kenyngham in alarm. 'Dame Pelagia does not intend to practise her knife-throwing skills on them, does she?'

'I doubt it,' said Michael. 'If she had, she would have done it by now, and none of us would have been any the wiser. But the situation is delicate: that pair have the King's Pardon, and even she cannot slip daggers into men who have powerful friends. We do not want the King imposing enormous fines on us because we have murdered people under his protection. Do we?'

'No,' chorused the Fellows as one. It was a punishment too horrible to contemplate, and might interfere with the purchase of new books or – worse – the contents of the wine cellars.

'She needs to devise a solution that will see them safely removed – let us hope permanently – without it appearing that we had a hand in it,' Michael went on. 'It may take her a while, but she will not let us down, you can be sure of that.'

'I never doubted it,' said Langelee, pouring the remains of the wine into his goblet, then indicating with an apologetic shake of his head that Kenyngham was too late. 'She *is* Dame Pelagia, after all.'

'She put Rougham in his place the other day,' chortled William. 'We were all dining at the Franciscan Friary – my Prior likes to entertain – and Rougham advised me to take syrup of figs for a sore head on the grounds that it would cleanse my bowels. I informed him there is only one physician I allow near *my* bowels, and that is my esteemed colleague from Michaelhouse.'

'You said that?' asked Bartholomew, startled by the friar's loyalty.

'I did. Rougham then informed me that I would die if I took cures offered by you, and that I should listen to *his*

270

advice if I wanted to get better. But Dame Pelagia informed him that only fools muddled their heads with their bowels, and suggested he had better work out which was which before he dispensed any more of his remedies.' He guffawed furiously.

'Really?' asked Michael. He shook his head in fond admiration. 'She has a quick tongue. What did Rougham say?'

'There was little he could say. We all roared with laughter – jokes about bowels are popular in the friary – and no one heard what he mumbled in his defence. It was most gratifying. I do not like that man, especially since he has taken to slandering Matthew to anyone who will listen.'

'You must have upset him deeply, Matt,' said Wynewyk. 'Have you contradicted him, or offended him in some way? Stolen away one of his wealthy patients?'

'I do not know why he has taken against me so violently of late.'

'Then you had better find out,' advised William. 'His slanderous attacks are growing increasingly vicious, and you will have no patients left if you do not silence him.'

Bartholomew and Michael left the conclave, Bartholomew silently pondering the problem of Rougham, and walked to the King's Mill. It was working hard, and its great wheel creaked and thumped in a steady, endless rhythm as the strong current forced it round. The water downstream was frothy and brown, where silt and muck had been churned up. Bartholomew glanced upstream, to where Mortimer's Mill stood silent and still.

Michael knocked at the door of the King's Mill, but it was a pointless exercise given the thundering groans from the machinery inside. They entered and weaved around apprentices struggling under grain sacks, some being carried to storage bins for later milling and some for immediate grinding. The air was full of chaff and dust, and it caught in Bartholomew's throat. Michael began to sneeze.

The noise increased as they made their way closer to the wheel. Rye was being poured into a hopper with a tapering 'shoe' that allowed its contents to trickle on to the millstones, where it was ground into flour. Bartholomew had heard that the rod – which connected the shoe to the hopper and rattled to shake the grain on to the stones – was called a 'damsel', because it was never silent when the mill was working. It was certainly not silent now, and he resisted the urge to place his hands over his ears.

The mill was a different place from the night Bottisham and Deschalers had died in it. Light streamed through its open windows, and the engine chamber was a flurry of activity. The miller's boy stood sentinel by the hopper, monitoring the fall of the grain, while Bernarde himself flitted here and there as he gauged the running of this cog or that gear, making mental notes for later repairs or minute adjustments. Apprentices were everywhere, shouting orders or questions, and using expressions that were unfamiliar to Bartholomew, almost like a foreign language.

Bernarde saw his visitors and waved that he would be a moment, before turning his attention to a pinion with a wobble. The physician looked around him while they waited, and saw that the large pile of sacks, on which Michael had sat while he himself had inspected the corpses, had been dramatically reduced. Only three or four remained. An apprentice grinned cheerfully at him, as he squeezed around Michael to take one up in his burly arms.

'Another three and Peterhouse will be done,' he shouted over the racket.

Bartholomew watched him empty the sack into the hopper and come back for another. If he had not glanced down at the dust-covered floor as the man hefted the sack over his shoulder he would not have seen the object rolling from underneath it, heading towards a crack between the floorboards. He moved quickly, and managed to block the hole with his foot before the item disappeared.

'What is it?' yelled Michael.

'A medicine phial,' Bartholomew shouted back, leaning down to pick it up. 'I wonder whether it has anything to do with Bottisham and Deschalers, or whether it has been here for ages and has nothing to do with anything.'

'Is it empty?'

Bartholomew nodded. 'And the stopper is missing, so it is full of dust. I will never be able to tell you what it contained. However, I can tell you it was something powerful.'

'How?'

'Because apothecaries do not dispense weak or diluted potions in small pots like this. I wonder if it contained medicine prescribed by Rougham to help Deschalers with the pain of his illness.'

'Keep it,' Michael suggested. 'We can ask him later.'

'We cannot talk in here!' yelled Bernarde, brushing dust from his hands by rubbing them on a tunic that was so deeply ingrained with the stuff that its original colour was impossible to guess. 'And we are too busy to stop, even for a short while. It is unfortunate, because I am plagued with a sore head today, and even Lavenham's strongest medicine has not made it better.'

'What did he give you?' asked Bartholomew, thinking about the phial in his bag.

Bernarde shrugged carelessly. 'Something pink. I swallowed two doses of the stuff diluted in wine, but my head still aches. I should not have had so much ale in the King's Head last night.'

But the phial Bartholomew had found was dry and dust-filled, and had not contained medicine consumed that morning. It had been empty and discarded for longer than that – days or weeks, rather than hours. He and Michael followed the miller outside, where the swish and creak of the waterwheel was a welcome relief after the deafening rattle and clank of the building's inner workings. Bernarde led them a short distance upstream, stopping at a place where Mortimer's Mill was in clear view, its wheel hoisted out of the water while people moved over it with hammers and nails.

'A couple of their scoops broke this morning,' he said casually. 'Mortimer has been unable to work all day. I suppose they were damaged during that rain last night.'

'Were they, indeed?' mused Michael, his eyes glittering in amusement. 'I had no idea such sturdy structures could be harmed by the odd downpour.'

'Do most Colleges come to you with their grain?' asked Bartholomew, who had no idea where Michaelhouse's was milled. He tended to leave such matters to Langelee, who was paid to deal with them, or to Wynewyk, who enjoyed organising the everyday minutiae of College life.

'Yes,' said Bernarde. 'Not Gonville, though. And Valence Marie informed me today that they will purchase ready-ground flour from the market until the dispute with Mortimer is resolved.'

'Master Thorpe wants to be impartial,' surmised Bartholomew. 'That is wise. He is one of the King's Commissioners, so he *should* withdraw custom from both mills until this is over.'

'He should not be so moralistic,' countered Bernarde. 'I am not.'

'Really?' asked Michael silkily. 'In what way?'

'I do not allow mere scruples to shake *me* from a position I know is just. Both mills worked perfectly well together until Mortimer decided to convert to fulling. We might have resolved the problem amicably if it had not been for Edward. It was *his* idea to take our dispute to the King. I was all set to fire the . . .' His words trailed off, and he

274

regarded the scholars uneasily, waiting to see whether they had noticed his careless slip.

'I see,' said Michael. 'You planned to burn Mortimer's Mill as an easy way to dispense with an unwanted rival. Were the other members of the Millers' Society happy with this solution?'

'Deschalers was not,' said Bernarde bitterly, not bothering to deny the charge. 'But the rest saw reason, and agreed that a fire would be best for all concerned.'

'Not for the Mortimers,' said Michael. 'But this is interesting. Deschalers's was the only dissenting voice?'

'He said he did not want to commit such a grave sin when he was dying, but he would have come round to our way of thinking in time. Of course, Bottisham made an end of him before he could be persuaded.'

Michael shot Bartholomew a meaningful glance. Here was another motive for Deschalers's murder: he had balked at arson. And since Bernarde had not been honest about that sooner, what else had he concealed? Was it really true that no one had left the mill after he claimed he heard bodies hitting the wooden engines? Was he protecting the murderer? Or was he the culprit himself, and had concocted the story about the wheel's change in tempo, to throw them off the scent?

'Do you think Deschalers told anyone else about the plan to burn Mortimer's Mill?' asked Bartholomew. One of the Millers' Society – even Bernarde himself – might have murdered the grocer for revealing trade secrets.

'He told Edward Mortimer,' replied Bernard. He spat into the river. 'His new nephew by marriage.'

'You said it was Edward's idea to take the dispute to the King,' said Michael. 'Did he do that because you cannot burn his uncle's property if the King knows there is a quarrel between you? Obviously, you cannot fire your rival's mill now, without awkward questions being asked.'

Bernarde's expression was resentful. 'If that was his intention, then it has worked very well.'

'Was Deschalers reluctant to burn Mortimer's Mill because it belonged to his new family-by-marriage?' asked Bartholomew.

'I doubt Deschalers would have been swayed by something as foolish as in-law loyalty,' said Bernarde. 'But I must go. I have to finish grinding Peterhouse's flour.' Abruptly, he hurried away, and Bartholomew saw puffs of dust rising from his hair and clothes as he trotted along the path.

'That was revealing,' mused Michael. 'We can no longer take Bernarde's word that there was no third party in the mill now we know he is not a straightforward man. But I can tell you one thing for certain: *his* name has just been added to my list of suspects.'

'Mine, too,' said Bartholomew. 'Along with the other members of the Millers' Society – Cheney, Morice and the Lavenhams. And Edward's has been underlined.'

Bartholomew and Michael were silent as they took the river path back towards Michaelhouse, each engrossed in his own thoughts about the murders at the mill. The more Bartholomew considered the facts, the more likely it seemed that the Mortimers were somehow involved. Thomas had killed Lenne and maimed Isnard without remorse – and had probably had Bosel poisoned – while murder came naturally to Edward. Either one might have killed Bottisham and Deschalers.

He watched the river as he walked, seeing bubbles and eddies from the churning it had suffered at the King's Mill waterwheel. He wondered what the river was like when both mills were running at the same time. Even as he looked, a subtle change took place in the water. It became rougher and murkier, and he became aware that the groaning of wooden joints and cogs was louder. He glanced upriver, and saw that whatever Bernarde had done to Mortimer's Mill had not been too serious, because it was working again.

The water in the River Cam had never been clean, but Bartholomew saw a creeping stain float slowly but inexorably towards the town. It was a dirty, creamy-grey colour, residues from the 'fuller's earth' that was used to remove the grease from raw cloth. The discoloration kept pace with them all the way to St Michael's Lane, and Bartholomew was fascinated by the way it moved as it caught in tiny whirlpools. It reminded him of a thesis by Roger Bacon about the way liquids with different properties interacted with each other, and he forgot about the mill murders as he turned his mind to physics. However, his attention snapped back to more practical matters when he spotted Yolande de Blaston kneeling over one of the dilapidated piers with a pair of buckets in her hand.

'What is she going to do with those?' he wondered aloud. 'If she is taking them to Matilde's house, then I hope she does not plan on cooking with their contents. Not when the river is full of whatever Mortimer is pouring into it. Not to mention sewage and that dead duck.'

'Ask her,' suggested Michael wickedly, knowing the feisty Yolande would not appreciate such an enquiry.

'Matilde will not let me cook with river water, thanks to you,' replied Yolande, somewhat unpleasantly when the physician voiced his concerns. 'She makes me collect clean stuff from the well these days. I use this for laundry.' She drew herself up to her full height and spoke with pride. 'Did you know I am laundress of Gonville now? Matilde arranged it.'

'Congratulations,' said Bartholomew, pleased for her, despite the fact that he thought washing the scholars' clothes in river water would not render them much cleaner. 'That is good news.'

'It is,' agreed Yolande. 'Matilde says I should not ply my other trade now I am pregnant again, although being a laundress is far harder than life as a Frail Sister. However, I have kept one or two favourite clients, to make sure I do not lose my touch.'

'Like Horwood, who was mayor last year?' asked Michael nosily, always keen to hear gossip about prominent townsmen; such information sometimes came in useful.

'Him, of course,' said Yolande. 'We have met every Friday night for years now. And I have kept Apothecary Lavenham, because he makes me laugh with his funny English.'

'Lavenham hires you?' asked Michael in surprise. 'Does his wife not see to him?'

'Isobel goes out a lot,' replied Yolande ambiguously. 'And I entertain Bernarde when I am short of flour, and dear Master Thorpe of Valence Marie, now he is back from York.'

'Thorpe!' said Michael, his eyes glinting with mischief. 'I had no idea!'

'Few do. He says his evenings with me give him a proper perspective on life, which I imagine is a good thing. But there are some customers I was only too pleased to drop – such as Mayor Morice. I do not like his glittery eyes and pawing hands. And I told Chancellor Tynkell I did not want him, either. I am sorry if I offend you, Brother, but he smells. His hands are always sticky, and I do not like seeing the same dirty marks for weeks on end.'

'You have seen Tynkell undressed?' asked Bartholomew keenly. Michael started to laugh, knowing exactly what had prompted the enquiry.

'Not exactly,' said Yolande. 'He is one of those men who prefers to remain clothed. He usually wants the candles extinguished, too, so we cannot see what we are doing.'

'What do you do?' asked Bartholomew curiously.

Yolande regarded him coolly. 'I have heard about men

like you, who like to hear about the antics of others. But what I do with the Chancellor is none of your affair – although I can tell you that it is easy money for me. He does not like being touched, you see.'

Bartholomew decided he had better change the subject, before Yolande reported his interest to Matilde – and he did not want her, of all women, to think badly of him. He would have to learn more about Tynkell's intriguing physiology another way. 'What about the Mortimers? Do you entertain any of them?'

'I would not touch Edward,' said Yolande firmly. 'But I like Thomas, when he is sober. However, he is mostly drunk these days. It must be because he is frightened of his nephew.'

'Thomas cannot be frightened of Edward,' said Michael. 'He would not let Edward work at his mill if he were.'

'Edward said he would burn it to the ground if Thomas refused to employ him,' replied Yolande. 'And Thomas told me last night that he feared Edward might do it anyway, just for spite.'

'But why would he do that?' asked Michael. 'Then he would have nowhere to work.'

'He does not need it,' said Bartholomew. 'His wife has just inherited Deschalers's fortune.'

They had reached the end of St Michael's Lane, where their ways parted. To the right, Bartholomew could see the ever-present crowd milling in front of St Mary the Great. Some people knelt, while others stood with their heads bowed. Not everyone was there to pray: he saw several known pickpockets moving among the throng. Meanwhile, some of Constantine Mortimer's apprentices sold small, sweet loaves from trays balanced on their heads, while Cheney's men hawked tiny packets of cinnamon and pepper. The Hand represented a business opportunity, as well as a place to ask for divine favours.

279

'There is strife among the Mortimer clan,' said Yolande, shifting the brimming pails in her strong hands. 'A few weeks ago, you would never have seen one argue with another, but they fight all the time now. And Edward fans their disputes to make them burn more fiercely. But mention the Devil and he will appear.' She gestured down the High Street with her head. 'Edward and his rotten friend are coming this way, and I do not want to be anywhere near *them*, thank you very much!'

She hurried away, water slopping from her buckets as she went. Bartholomew was surprised at her reaction. Yolande was a hard, unbending woman whose dealings with some of the wealthiest and most influential men in the town meant she was normally afraid or in awe of no one. But she seemed afraid of Mortimer and Thorpe.

The two ruffians strutted confidently along the centre of the High Street, where the rubbish and ordure was piled less deep, and Bartholomew noticed that Yolande was not the only one who was reluctant to meet them. He saw the Lavenhams dive down a dirty alleyway they would not normally deign to use, and even the swaggering Morice shot back inside the tavern he had just vacated when he saw them coming.

'You have no right to keep the Hand of Justice in that tower,' said Thorpe to Michael as they approached. 'It does not belong to you.'

'The "Hand of Justice"?' echoed Michael in rank disdain. 'And what, pray, is that?'

'You know what it is,' said Thorpe. 'Some call it the Hand of Valence Marie, but we prefer the title "Hand of Justice", because of what it represents.'

'What does it represent?' asked Michael coolly.

'It represents justice,' replied Thorpe. He continued to speak before Bartholomew could point out that he had not really answered the monk's question. 'It does not belong to the University, to be shut away where honest folk cannot get at it.'

'I wish to God it belonged to no one,' said Michael fervently. 'I should have hurled it in the marshes when I had the chance.'

'Throwing it away would have been a terrible sin,' said Mortimer softly. 'Did you know that the Hand of Justice belonged to a great prophet, who came to Earth in the guise of a simpleton? He imparted much wisdom before he died, but folk did not listen. They are listening now.'

'Rubbish!' exclaimed Bartholomew, unable to help himself. 'Peterkin Starre was no prophet – anyone who remembers him will tell you that.'

'Folk are reassessing their memories,' said Thorpe, nodding at the pilgrims who knelt outside the tower. There was also a queue by the south door, and Bartholomew could see Father William bustling about importantly. He supposed the friar had chosen to disregard Michael's orders, and was still showing the Hand to people who asked. Or perhaps he was just not up to the task of solving the problem, so was simply continuing what he did well – making money for the University.

'Then they are wrong,' declared Michael, as dogmatic in his refusal to believe as others were in their desperation to accept. 'Who came up with this ridiculous title – the Hand of Justice – anyway?'

'We did,' said Mortimer coldly. 'It is amazing how quickly these things catch on once you mention them in one or two pertinent places. The Hand did right by us. We prayed to it after we were exiled – that justice would be done – and it did not let us down.'

'Then let us tell people that,' encouraged Michael innocently. 'They will see it as another miracle.'

'Later,' said Mortimer, seeing the implications of Michael's suggestion immediately. He was not stupid, and guessed few would thank the Hand for arranging that sort of 'justice'.

Thorpe looked around him in disdain. 'I do not like this town. I have no desire to endure hostile glares and snide comments in voices that are only just audible. But needs must.'

'What do you mean?' asked Bartholomew uneasily.

'My original plan was to ask the King if Valence Marie could have the Hand of Justice back,' said Thorpe. 'They were its first owners – because my father was the man who fished it out of the King's Ditch – and I feel it should reside with Valence Marie, not in the University Church. But my father says he does not want it. He is a fool, and I am disappointed in him.'

'Not nearly as disappointed as he is in you,' said Michael, intending to wound.

It worked, and Thorpe's eyes flashed with rage, although it was quickly suppressed. 'However, my colleagues at Gonville Hall are interested in having it instead. Rougham visits it regularly, and Ufford is devoted to it. Even Thompson, Pulham and Despenser have been to see it – although they claim they are not believers. Gonville can capitalise on the financial rewards it will bring, if Valence Marie is stupid enough to decline. Look at how many pilgrims are here already, and then imagine what it will be like when the Hand's fame has spread.'

'I see,' said Michael wearily. 'You intend to set College against College, and town against University by taking the Hand from one institution and passing it to another. That is why you came back. Really, boys! I expected something a little more imaginative from you when you staged your revenge.'

Thorpe shrugged, to indicate he did not care what the monk thought. 'All we want is for the Hand of Justice to be where it will do some good. The revenues raised from pilgrims will pay for Gonville's new chapel – and what better way to pay for a church than with money raised from a holy relic? Bishop Bateman would approve.'

Bartholomew watched them stride away, scattering folk before them as if they were feared invaders from a hostile land. He saw Sergeant Orwelle step to one side to avoid them, and was appalled to think that even the forces of law and order seemed to be intimidated.

'At least we now know what they plan to do,' said Michael. 'I should have guessed they had this sort of thing in mind. But I expected them to come up with something more original.'

Bartholomew was thoughtful. 'William may be a fool, but he is honest, and it would be very difficult for anyone to make off the Hand as long as it is in his care. However, it will be a lot easier to steal it from Gonville. *They* have no experience of looking after valuable and popular relics.'

'Especially if Thorpe is a member there,' mused Michael. 'With his own key. And, if the thing disappears, there will be a riot for certain – with the town furious at the University's incompetence.'

Bartholomew nodded. 'They are right about one thing, though. It will not be long before an attractive name like the "Hand of Justice" catches on – and then the damned thing will become more popular than ever.'

Later, Bartholomew visited Mistress Lenne, who lay wretchedly miserable as she awaited the arrival of her son from Thetford. Michael declined to enter the house with him, and slouched outside, his green eyes bleak and angry. When he emerged and saw the dangerous expression on the monk's face, Bartholomew tried to think of something that would take his friend's mind off the elderly woman's suffering.

'You said you were going to look at Deschalers's will. To see if he planned to change it.'

Michael nodded. 'I want to know if he threatened to disinherit Julianna. I doubt she has the intelligence to stage the cunning murder of an uncle, but her new husband certainly does.'

Bartholomew was thoughtful. '*Planned* to change his will. Father William said he heard something about a "plan" when Deschalers made his confession to the Hand. Do you think that is what Deschalers was talking about?'

Michael shrugged; even the prospect of solving a little part of the mystery did not take his mind off Mistress Lenne. 'It is possible, I suppose, although I would not class making a will as a "plan". However, Deschalers might have done, and we should bear it in mind. We should go and ask Julianna about it now.'

Bartholomew was unenthusiastic about the prospect of another encounter with Julianna, but since he had made the suggestion, he felt obliged to accompany the monk to Deschalers's house. They knocked on the door, and were shown into the ground-floor parlour by the elderly servant, who muttered something about fried cat before going to tell Julianna she had guests. While they waited for her to come, Michael sullenly devoured those dried fruits he had missed on the previous occasion.

The house was filled with voices, although none were lowered as a mark of respect to the recently dead. They did not seem to be especially friendly, either, and it sounded as though an argument was in progress. Bartholomew could hear Thomas, Constantine and Edward Mortimer among the clamour; Edward's tones were low and measured, in stark contrast to the bickering, savage tenor of his uncle and father.

'What are they saying?' whispered Michael, straining his ears.

'Something about who has the right to live where,' replied Bartholomew. 'This is a nice house, and I think Edward wants to stay here with Julianna, but Constantine has other ideas. It would be convenient for him: he lives next door, and could combine the two premises into an impressive mansion.'

'And something about death duties,' said Michael, cocking his head. 'Wills.'

'The King usually claims part of any large inheritance.' Bartholomew's hearing was sharper than Michael's. 'I think they are debating how much they should give him.'

'I cannot make out their words,' said Michael in frustration. He pressed his ear against the wall, but had not been in position for long when he became aware that someone was watching from the door.

'Brother Michael?' asked Julianna coolly. 'What are you doing?'

'Worms,' said Michael unabashed, although Bartholomew cringed with embarrassment on his behalf. 'I can hear them, chewing. You do not want those in your timbers, madam. I have seen houses collapse from the labours of their teeth.'

'Worms do not have teeth,' said Bartholomew, before he could stop himself.

'No,' agreed Edward, entering the chamber behind his wife, 'and neither do beetles, which is the nature of the creature that destroys wood.' The expression on his face was unreadable. 'We meet again, gentlemen. You seem to be everywhere today.'

Bartholomew glanced at the door, and saw that Edward and Julianna were not the only ones who had left the family squabble to see to their guests. Behind Edward, short and stocky in scarlet cote-hardie and matching hose, was Constantine. His face was flushed and he seemed out of sorts. Thomas was next to him, a goblet clasped in his hand. His red-rimmed eyes possessed a glazed, dull sheen that indicated he had been drinking most of the day. Bartholomew scowled at him: he had not forgotten what the man had done to Isnard. Raised voices continued to echo from the adjoining chamber, where uncles, aunts and cousins declined to allow the unannounced arrival of visitors to prevent them from finishing their quarrel.

'Quite a gathering,' said Michael. 'Are they here to see what Edward has inherited?'

'We have come to offer our condolences to Julianna,' said Constantine. 'And I have no need to assess Deschalers's property. We were neighbours for decades, and I know exactly what he owned.'

'Then who will inherit?' asked Michael bluntly. 'How many people will benefit from his will?'

'Two,' said Edward. 'He left a chest to his scribe, but, other than that, Julianna has everything – this house, two properties on Bridge Street, a shop near Holy Trinity, his business and all his money.'

'Of which there is a great deal,' slurred Thomas, leering at Julianna. 'Why do you ask?'

'No reason,' lied Michael. 'What is the name of this scribe? And why was he singled out for such a lordly prize, when none of the apprentices were remembered?'

'A box is scarcely a "lordly prize", Brother,' said Julianna. She looked the monk up and down. 'Well, it might be for someone like you, I suppose.'

'I could say that how Deschalers chose to dispose of his worldly goods is none of your affair,' said Edward, cutting across Michael's indignant response. 'And I would be within my rights to do so. However, we have nothing to hide, so we will answer you. Deschalers did not like his apprentices. He considered them lazy.'

'Then why did he keep them on?' asked Michael, glaring at Julianna. He was the son of a minor Norfolk nobleman, and considered himself a cut above merchants, so found her comments highly insulting. 'There are plenty of honest, hard-working lads who would relish an opportunity to train as grocers.'

'He did not want the bother of educating more,' said Constantine. 'And it has *not* been easy to find good workmen since the Death. They either died or became too expensive.'

'I own the business now,' said Edward, oblivious to the furious glance shot in his direction by Julianna. She clearly disagreed with the law that a wife's inheritance became the property of her husband. 'And Deschalers was right: they are lazy. I have dismissed most of them.'

'This scribe?' pressed Michael. 'Does he have a name?'

'Not one I remember,' said Julianna. She frowned. 'It is odd, actually, because Uncle did not like him any more than he did his apprentices, and I do not know why he was singled out for reward. Perhaps it was because he always came the moment he was summoned.'

'So Deschalers left this lucky man a chest,' said Michael. 'A chest of what?'

'Just a chest,' replied Julianna. She gestured to a substantial wooden affair under the window. 'There it is – just a piece of furniture. Uncle said he wanted the scribe to have it, so the fellow could lock away his possessions when he finally earns some.'

Bartholomew inspected the box without much interest. Plain and functional, it was not an attractive piece. The only noteworthy thing about it was its sturdy – and extremely greasy – lock, which comprised a complex system of iron rods. Julianna raised the lid, to show them it was empty. It went through Bartholomew's mind that selecting the clerk to be the recipient of such a reward might be Deschalers's way of insulting him.

'Uncle said it needed a thorough clean,' she said,

wrinkling her nose. Bartholomew knew what she meant: an unpleasant odour hung around the box, as though it had been used to store something nasty. 'He planned to do it himself, but died before he got around to it. Still, I am sure the scribe will not mind spending a few moments with a rag.'

'You seem very well acquainted with the contents of your uncle's will,' said Michael. 'I thought lawyers took their time over such matters, particularly when large sums of money are involved. After all, the King will want his share.'

Edward looked smug. 'Full inheritance of Deschalers's goods is part of my pardon. The King's clerks said it would serve as part-compensation for the suffering I endured in exile. They plan to reclaim death taxes from the town instead. So, Brother, *you* will be paying the King, not me.'

He began to laugh, and Bartholomew gaped at him, scarcely believing his ears. Not only was a killer walking free and unrepentant, but he was even making the town pay for the privilege.

'But it is not right, Edward,' said Constantine unhappily. 'My fellow burgesses will never agree to give the King what he should have had from Deschalers. It will cause all manner of strife. If you want to live here unmolested, you should do the honourable thing and pay it yourself. After all, you have plenty. Deschalers left Julianna a large fortune.'

'It will not be large once you have stolen my house,' snapped Edward.

'But that is my privilege,' objected Constantine. 'I am still out of pocket from buying your pardon.'

'That is not my problem,' snarled Edward. 'If you had been a proper father, I would not have been obliged to go to France in the first place. I owe you nothing.'

'One can never have enough money,' said Julianna comfortably, oblivious to the simmering emotions that

288

boiled around the Mortimers. She sauntered across to the dish of dried fruits and, finding it empty, began to look under the table, as if she imagined they might have fallen there. 'But we have been through this before, Constantine: the King absolved Edward from paying death taxes on Uncle's estate, and wants the town to pay instead. There is no more to be said on the matter.'

'But it is not wise to antagonise the other merchants,' pressed Constantine. He appealed to his brother. 'Tell him, Thomas! Do *you* want to pay the King on Edward's behalf?'

Thomas shrugged, and almost overbalanced. He took a gulp of wine to steady himself. 'I will have won the mill dispute by then, so will have funds to spare. Edward should keep the money and the other merchants be damned. After all, look what Bernarde, Lavenham and Cheney are doing to me. I hate the lot of them. They *should* pay.'

'But it will cause bitterness and resentment,' cried Constantine, becoming desperate. 'We cannot run a decent business if everyone is against us.'

'I disagree,' said Thomas, tottering to the table where a jug and matching goblets stood on a tray. He poured himself a generous dose. 'All the merchants are against *me*, and I am doing rather well.'

'Edward!' pleaded Constantine. 'This is not right, son.'

'Do not call me son,' hissed Edward. 'And do not expect me to believe that your motives were altruistic when you bought my pardon. It was not *my* name you wanted cleared, but that of Mortimer.'

'But I did—'

His words went unheard as Edward stamped out of the room, slamming the door behind him. The glass in the windows rattled, and the fire flared and guttered in the sudden draught. Michael watched, his eyes alight with interest, while Bartholomew merely felt uncomfortable at having witnessed a family spat that should have been held in private.

'Edward is very irritable these days,' said Julianna, who did not seem at all embarrassed. 'I cannot imagine why, when he has recently acquired me *and* a fortune. He has everything a man could possibly desire.'

'I agree,' said Thomas, patting her shoulder in a fatherly way. Bartholomew saw which side the miller favoured: Deschalers's fortune had made Edward and Julianna far richer than Constantine, and he intended to stick with them. He clenched his fists and experienced an uncharacteristic urge for violence. While Isnard lay at the mercy of benevolent donations, Mortimer's eyes were fixed on Julianna's massive fortune. He thought about the cruel plot to convince the bargeman that his leg had miraculously re-attached itself, and was hard pressed to control himself. Michael noticed, and rested a calming hand on his shoulder.

'You should have supported me, Thomas,' said Constantine resentfully. 'You know I am right. Edward will ruin us if he makes the town fund his taxes.'

'It is your own fault,' said Thomas nastily. 'I told you not to spend good money on a pardon, but you ignored me. Well, you have what you wanted, and now you must live with the consequences.'

'I wish to God I had let matter lie,' said Constantine bitterly. 'I have made a terrible mistake.'

'You certainly have,' agreed Michael.

Bartholomew and Michael left Deschalers's house with some relief, despite the fact that they still did not know whether the grocer had intended to change his will from the one that made Julianna virtually the sole beneficiary. In the yard, the apprentices were leaving. Packs of personal belongings lay in a pile, and a pony was being harnessed to a cart.

Men stood in a huddle, talking among themselves, and Bartholomew became aware that he and Michael were on the receiving end of some very hostile looks. It occurred to him that if there were rumours that a scholar had killed Deschalers, then the apprentices might well hold the University responsible for the loss of their livelihoods.

'That was revealing,' said Michael, as they walked briskly away from the festering resentment. 'Relations are not all they were in the Mortimer clan, and it seems more obvious than ever that Edward has some unpleasant plan in mind – other than giving the Hand to Gonville. If he is prepared to burn his bridges with the other merchants – Constantine was right about them not wanting to pay those taxes – then I would predict he does not intend to stay here long.'

Bartholomew agreed. 'And since he has benefited so handsomely from Deschalers's death, perhaps we should look no further than him for our killer. One possibility is this: Deschalers lured Bottisham to the mill with talk of a reconciliation. Edward followed Deschalers and killed him, then was obliged to kill Bottisham, too.'

'And engaged the engines and hurled the bodies into them to confuse us,' mused Michael. 'I suppose that makes sense – especially now we have learned that we should discount Bernarde's tale about no one being in the building but Bottisham and Deschalers. But this means that Bernarde lied to protect Edward. Why would he do that? The Mortimers are Bernarde's enemy.'

'Fear?' suggested Bartholomew. 'People are afraid of Edward.'

Michael considered. 'Bernarde did not seem afraid to me. Frightened people betray themselves by being brittle, hostile or overly willing to please. Bernarde was none of these. If he was lying, then it was not from fear.'

'But he was angry about bodies damaging his pinions. And you said you believed Bernarde's son when he told you his father dashed out the moment he heard the wheel's change in tempo. Are you sure we should dismiss Bernarde's testimony as untruthful?'

'No,' admitted Michael. 'But I am not sure about anything. I do not think I have ever been so confounded when trying to solve a case.'

They walked slowly, taking the long way back along the river bank, since it was still too early for the evening meal, and neither wanted to sit in the conclave while William boasted about the revenues he was amassing from the 'Hand of Justice'. Bartholomew heard several folk discussing the relic as they went, and was unsettled to hear its new name already in common usage. Edward was right: the epithet was one that people would readily adopt.

Early evening was a pleasant time in Cambridge, particularly when a blossom-scented breeze blew away the stench from the river and the manure-carpeted streets. The sun shone, giving an illusion of warmth, and seemed to cheer people as they wended their way home. Someone sang a popular song in a loud, toneless voice, and a small group of children, who had spent an exhausting day selling spring flowers, sprawled at the water's edge to chatter and laugh.

A barge had arrived from the Low Countries, bringing fine cloth for Stanmore, and his apprentices hurried to transfer the valuable cargo to his warehouses before daylight faded and the wharves became dangerous. Bartholomew was delighted to see that he and Michael were not the only ones taking an evening stroll. Matilde was also out, holding the hand of a reluctant Bess. As they closed the gap between them, he admired Matilde's slender body and the natural grace with which she moved. He hoped Yolande's husband would finish his house soon; he longed for the family to move out, so he could have her alone again. It had already been far too long.

'Your shadows are not with you tonight?' Matilde asked,

looking around as they met. 'Quenhyth, Redmeadow and Deynman?'

'Redmeadow and Deynman are at St Mary the Great,' replied Michael. 'Asking the Hand to tell them ways to discover whether Tynkell is afflicted with a certain rare physiology.'

'Redmeadow is a curious young man,' said Matilde. 'I saw him early last Monday morning covered in pale dust, so he looked like a ghost. He was brushing at it furiously, but the stuff was difficult to get off. He told me it was the result of a practical joke Deynman had played on him, but I am sure he was lying. I suspect he had been with a woman.'

Bartholomew recalled seeing a whitish powder ingrained on the student's sleeve, too, and supposed Redmeadow had used his teacher's convenient absence on Sunday night – while he investigated the bodies at the mill – to secure himself a lover. Some of the town's Frail Sisters used chalky substances on their faces, and Bartholomew knew such stains could be very difficult to remove.

'Quenhyth is studying,' said Michael, making it sound like the most dreadful of vices. 'He does nothing else, and is as tedious a young fellow as I have ever encountered. He will make an extremely dull physician one day, who will kill his patients by boring them to death.'

'He needs something to take his mind away from himself,' said Matilde. 'Also, he has the look of a young man who has been crossed in love.'

'Quenhyth?' asked Bartholomew, thinking of the student's prim manners. 'I do not think so!'

'You mark my words,' said Matilde. 'I am not saying he was involved in a physical affair, only that he loved someone who perhaps did not return his adoration. He is a passionate young man.'

Bartholomew supposed that was true. 'But all his passion is aimed at his studies.'

'For now,' said Matilde. 'But I would not like to be the woman – or the man – who attracts his devotion. He is very single-minded.'

'She does not look as if she wants to go with you,' said Michael, indicating Bess with a nod of his tonsured head. 'Where are you taking her?'

'To Una again,' said Matilde. 'I do not know what else to do with her. Nothing she says makes any sense. I wonder how long she has been looking for her man.'

'My man,' murmured Bess, looking as if she expected him to appear. 'Have you seen him?'

'What does he look like?' asked Bartholomew, thinking that if he asked often enough he might have an answer.

Bess smiled for the first time since he had met her. 'Beautiful and strong. Like a tree, with long limbs and smooth bark.'

'I have seen no one answering that description,' said Michael. 'Have you tried the forest?'

'My man does not visit woods,' replied Bess, unusually communicative. 'He prefers taverns.'

'Do you remember his name?' asked Bartholomew. 'And what makes you think he is here?'

'He might be here,' she agreed. 'His name was to have been "husband".'

'She had a lot of money two days ago, but there is not a penny left now,' said Matilde. She turned to the woman. 'Bess? Where is all that gold you had? Did someone take it?'

'He promised,' said Bess, her eyes filling with tears. 'He said he would tell me.'

'Someone promised to take you to your man if you gave him coins?' asked Bartholomew.

Bess nodded. 'But he did not know. I cannot find him. I have been looking since the snows fell.'

Matilde's face was a mask of fury. 'I *knew* some villain

294

would cheat her. Have people no shame? How could they take advantage of someone who is out of her wits?'

'Many felons will see her as fair game,' said Michael. 'I will ask my beadles to look for men spending gold they cannot explain, but I doubt we shall get it back for her.'

Bess went to stand at the edge of the river, gazing at the eddies created by the mills upstream.

Matilde watched her. 'I think her man is dead, and his demise damaged her mind. She could spend the rest of her life looking for someone who is already in his grave,' she said.

'She looks like Katherine Mortimer,' said Bartholomew. 'I see Katherine each time I meet Bess now.'

'But a very shabby and ill-conditioned Katherine Mortimer,' said Matilde. 'I wondered whether they might be related, too, and asked the Mortimers about it, but none admit to owning her as kin.'

'We have just been to Deschalers's house,' said Michael, bored with the subject of the madwoman. 'The Mortimers are squabbling over his estate like dogs with a carcass. It is not an edifying sight.'

'That does not surprise me,' said Matilde. 'Deschalers was wealthy, and there is a good deal to fight over. I heard they quarrel frequently now Edward is back, whereas before they were rather taciturn. The Frail Sisters do not enjoy visiting members of the Mortimer clan these days, although they enjoyed the rare occasions when Deschalers summoned them.'

'I did not know Deschalers regularly enjoyed whores,' said Michael baldly.

'He did not,' said Matilde shortly, not liking the crude reference to women she regarded as her friends. 'He liked an occasional female companion – but only after Katherine had ended their affair. He was also fond of Bernarde the miller's wife – before she died of the Death, obviously.'

'Bernarde's wife?' asked Bartholomew in surprise. He exchanged a glance with Michael. Here was another reason why the miller might have killed Deschalers. No man liked being a cuckold, and Bernarde's wife had been a pretty lady.

'It was a long time ago,' said Matilde. 'I do not know whether Bernarde was aware of it or not.'

'Would Deschalers have hired Bess?' asked Bartholomew, thinking about the day she had followed the merchant's horse, clearly bound for his home.

Matilde laughed. 'Of course not! He would never have gone with an unclean thing like her. He prided himself on his standards.'

'Then why was she with him on the High Street last Saturday?' asked Bartholomew.

'I have no idea,' said Matilde. 'Perhaps she was following him in the hope of information about her man.'

'Could Deschalers have known what happened to him?' asked Bartholomew.

'I doubt it,' replied Matilde. 'Unless he hired the fellow to guard his goods or some such thing. Unfortunately, with Deschalers dead, there is no one to ask. His apprentices are unlikely to co-operate, given their bitterness over being left nothing in his will and then dismissed by Edward, and Julianna will not know.'

'I do not suppose you have heard anything about Deschalers or Bottisham through the Frail Sisters?' asked Michael hopefully. A network of gossip was accumulated by the town's prostitutes and fed to Matilde, who was very good at making sense of disparate details and putting them into context.

'Not really,' said Matilde. 'I have asked them to listen for anything that may be important, but no one has said anything yet. Certainly no client has boasted of being the killer, or of knowing who the killer is. There is a lot of speculation, of course, but no evidence.'

'And what does this speculation say?' asked Michael, somewhat desperately.

'That Thorpe and Edward are responsible, so that the University will rise up and attack the town.'

'And what about Bosel the beggar?' asked Bartholomew. 'He has been all but forgotten.'

'Bess is alleged to have made an end of him,' said Matilde. 'It is said that Thomas Mortimer hired her, to prevent Bosel from speaking against him over the accident that killed Lenne. But you can see for yourself that she is incapable of carrying out even the most simple of tasks – and murder would be wholly beyond her.' She turned to Bartholomew. 'How is Mistress Lenne?'

'She is waiting for her son to arrive, but I think she will let herself die when he comes.'

'Should we take her to the Hand of Justice?' asked Matilde wickedly. 'It may answer an entreaty from her, since she has been the victim of a particularly dreadful miscarriage of justice.'

'Have you seen my man?' came Bess's pitiful voice from the river bank as she addressed someone who was passing.

Bartholomew turned just in time to see young Thorpe raise his hand to slap her so that she tumbled backwards on to the grass. Matilde gave a strangled cry and rushed to her side, while Bartholomew stepped forward and shoved Thorpe in the chest as hard as he could. He saw the young man's face run through a gamut of emotions before he lost his balance: satisfaction, followed by alarm, ending with shocked indignation. Then he hit the water with a tremendous splash.

Stanmore's apprentices released a great cheer when Thorpe disappeared under the sewage-dappled surface of the River Cam. The nearby bargemen started to laugh, and a number of children screeched their delight in high voices. Others flocked to join them, and soon a small but vocal crowd was watching the events that were unfolding on the river bank. It comprised scholars and townsmen, all united in a common purpose: when Thorpe emerged spluttering and spitting, they jeered at him with a single voice.

'I am not sure that was wise, Matt,' said Michael, watching with folded arms. 'No man likes to be made a fool of, and you have turned Thorpe into a spectacle for all to mock.'

'Help me!' cried Thorpe as he floundered. Bartholomew was not unduly alarmed. The river was deep at that point, but Thorpe was easily reachable. 'I cannot swim!'

'Let him drown!' called one of the apprentices. His sentiment was applauded by his fellows.

'Is she all right?' asked Bartholomew, kneeling next to Bess. There was a trickle of blood from a split lip, but she seemed more shocked than harmed. 'I do not like men who hit women.'

'Neither do I,' said Matilde furiously. 'And if you had not punched him, then I would have done so.'

'Help!' gasped Thorpe, his voice barely audible over the sound of splashing. 'Please!'

'Pull him out, Matt,' ordered Michael. 'Tempting though it is to leave him there, my monastic vocation does not allow me to stand by while men die. Give him your hand.'

'No,' said Bartholomew. 'He will drag me in with him.'

'Is this your idea of practising medicine?' came an angry voice at Bartholomew's shoulder. It was Rougham, and he wore a pained expression on his face. 'You stand gossiping while a man drowns?'

'I thought you were in Ely,' said Michael. 'With the other Gonville Fellows.'

Rougham looked smug. 'Someone needs to stay here and look after College business. I have been entrusted with

298

Gonville's safe keeping until Acting Master Pulham and the others return.'

'In that case,' said Michael, 'you can tell me why they all lied about the Mortimers' donation—'

Rougham brushed him aside. 'I will not answer questions put by the likes of you while a member of my own College perishes before my very eyes. *I* will save him!'

'He can swim,' said Bartholomew.

'He is dying,' countered Rougham firmly. He turned to the crowd. 'Bartholomew may be content to stand by and watch a man perish, but I, William Rougham of Gonville Hall, am not. Remember that when you next summon a physician.'

'Wait, Rougham,' began Bartholomew. 'He has—'

'We can discuss your refusal to save lives later,' said Rougham harshly.

He turned around, and made a great show of preparing himself. With much grunting and wincing, to demonstrate that what he did was not easy, he knelt on the river bank and offered an arm to the figure in the water. Thorpe flopped towards it, took the proffered hand and gave an almighty heave. Rougham went into the water head first, to emerge coughing and spluttering some distance away. There was another howl of delighted amusement from the onlookers.

'We *shall* remember you, William Rougham of Gonville Hall,' called Agatha the laundress, drawing more mocking laughter from the crowd. 'But I prefer my physicians dry, thank you!'

Thorpe hauled himself from the river with one easy, sinuous movement. He stalked over to Bartholomew, and, for an instant, the physician thought he might draw a knife or strike him with his balled fists. But Thorpe was not stupid, and was aware of Michael standing nearby, not to mention Agatha. Since harming Bartholomew and escaping unscathed was impossible – Michael had grabbed a stout stick, while Agatha was casually inspecting one of her cooking knives – Thorpe settled for a warning.

'I will not forget this, physician,' he hissed venomously. 'Your time will come.'

'Help me,' came an unsteady voice from the river.

'If you harm another woman,' said Bartholomew, in a quiet, calm voice that held far more menace than Thorpe's hiss, 'I will make sure you never feel safe again. That is not a threat, because threats are not always carried out.'

He shouldered Thorpe out of the way with more force than was necessary, and knelt on the bank to offer his arm to the floundering Rougham, hoping the Gonville physician did not also intend to drag his rescuer into the water. But Rougham was far too shaken to do anything of the kind. He grasped Bartholomew's hand with a grip that was painful, and allowed himself to be helped out, to lie on the grass gasping like a landed fish.

'He *could* swim,' he panted furiously. 'He said he could not. He deceived me!'

'My brother-in-law teaches all his apprentices to swim,' said Bartholomew, removing his cloak and offering it to his shivering colleague. 'It is an essential part of their training, because they unload barges at the quays, and they occasionally fall in. I tried to warn—'

Rougham snatched the shabby garment. '*You* deceived me, too,' he declared. 'You happily allowed me to fall foul of that trick. Thorpe is not the only one who will have his revenge.'

Michael sniggered at the sight of the portly physician waddling away up the towpath with water slopping from his boots. 'I did not think Rougham could despise you any more than he already does, Matt, but I see I was wrong. You have achieved the impossible!'

'It was his own fault for not listening to me.' Bartholomew

gave a sudden grin. 'But it was worth it! Who would have thought we would see Rougham *and* Thorpe take an unintentional swim? But it is cold here with no cloak. I am going home.'

They had barely reached the bottom of St Michael's Lane when they met Walter. The porter was wearing one of his rare smiles, and Bartholomew supposed he had been among those who had witnessed the lessons meted out at the riverside.

'You are needed at Valence Marie, Doctor,' he said. 'Urgent. Someone has been struck down and they want you to come. In fact, Master Thorpe said he would pay you double if you run.'

'You had better go to it, Matt,' said Michael. 'I shall return to Michaelhouse, and you can give me the grisly details later – but not while I am eating.'

'It is Warde,' elaborated Walter. 'He was eating his evening meal, when he began to cough. He is unable to stop and they think he will die.'

'You should come with me, Brother,' said Bartholomew, aware of a gnawing unease growing in the pit of his stomach. 'Warde has a tickling throat, not a disease of the lungs. He should not cough so much that his colleagues are in fear of his life.'

'What are you saying?' demanded Michael, alarmed. 'That someone has done something to him?'

'I think we should bear it in mind,' said Bartholomew, breaking into a run, not because of the promised double fee, but because he liked Warde. 'Do not forget that Warde is one of the King's Commissioners.'

CHAPTER 8

Because the Hall of Valence Marie enjoyed the patronage of the wealthy Countess of Pembroke, money was no object for the scholars who lived there, and a good deal of it had been lavished on their home. The floor of the main hall had recently been relaid with mature oak, so that rugs and rushes were not needed to hide it, like those in most other Cambridge buildings. Its planks shone, carefully polished to show off the fine grain of the wood. The walls were adorned with tapestries sewn in bright colours, and their quality was so outstanding that Bartholomew assumed they must have been made by the Countess's talented ladies-in-waiting.

At the far end of the hall was a new minstrels' gallery. It, too, was made from best-quality oak, and had been seasoned and oiled to ensure it would last. The roof was a complex hammerbeam design, and had been painted in bright reds, golds and greens, so that students bored with their lectures could tip their heads back and lose themselves in the intricate patterns that swirled and twined above. Bartholomew was grateful that Michaelhouse had no such tempting distractions.

'Quickly,' called Master Thorpe from the dais at the far end of the hall. On the raised platform stood a table, which was generally regarded as one of the finest pieces of furniture in Cambridge, even better than the one in St Mary's Guildhall, and was the envy of all the Colleges. Valence Marie Fellows had so much room, they were not obliged to sit sideways to make sure everyone had a place, and they had individual chairs rather than communal benches. Bartholomew ignored the brash luxury all around him, and strode to where Thorpe bent over someone who lay on the floor behind the table. Michael followed.

The Master of Valence Marie was white with shock, and his normally immaculate cap of silver hair was in disarray. His eyes were anguished as he watched Bartholomew approach. The other Fellows who clustered around him seemed equally appalled. Bartholomew recognised a man named Thomas Bingham among them; Bingham had stepped into Thorpe's shoes while he was in York, and had upset his colleagues with his poor table manners.

'We had just finished our evening meal, when Bingham began to wipe his teeth on the tablecloth again,' explained Thorpe unsteadily. He scowled at his Fellow. 'None of us like that, and Warde took issue with him. They argued and Warde started to cough. We took no notice at first, because he has been doing it for the last two weeks. You must have noticed him at the *Disputatio de quodlibet?*'

'I did,' said Michael. 'But most people thought he was doing it to create an atmosphere of suspense – he started just as he was about to announce the winner.'

'I am sorry,' said Bingham in a whisper. 'I would not have quarrelled with him if I thought it would lead to this. Look what has happened.' He gestured to the prostrate figure on the floor.

Bartholomew knelt to examine the stricken man. Warde's lips were pale, and he was having difficulty catching his breath. He gripped his throat with one hand, while the other clutched a crucifix.

'Help me,' he croaked, terror in his eyes. 'I cannot breathe. I am hot and my mind is spinning.'

'Lie still,' said Bartholomew. He spoke softly, knowing a calm voice often soothed a patient's anxiety, and helped to relax the constricting muscles that were part of the

303

problem. He ordered the circle of onlookers away, thinking it would be better for Warde to recover without an audience. He heard Michael questioning them about what had happened, but they had little to add to Thorpe's story. Warde had just consumed a broth of leeks and cabbage – from the bowl that had been shared by all – when he had argued with Bingham. After a few moments, he said he was short of breath. He then started to cough and fell to the floor, and Bartholomew had been summoned at Warde's own request.

'Bishop Bateman of Norwich habitually wiped his teeth on the tablecloth,' whispered Michael to Bingham. 'And look what happened to him.'

'You think Bateman's tablecloth was soaked in poison?' asked Bingham in horror, crossing himself vigorously. 'I shall never clean my teeth on communal materials again!'

'That is *my* patient,' came a loud voice from the far end of the hall. Bartholomew's heart sank when he saw Rougham striding towards them. The Gonville physician had changed his wet clothes, although he still wore Bartholomew's cloak. 'Stand back, if you please.'

Bartholomew could not argue. Warde *was* Rougham's client, and he did not want another fracas with the man. Many physicians guarded their wealthier patients jealously, and Rougham was one of them. He stood and backed away, but Warde snatched at his hand.

'No,' he croaked. 'Not Rougham. You.'

'Nonsense,' said Rougham, drawing up a chair and leaning over him. He was obviously not going to kneel, as Bartholomew had done. He smiled at the bewildered scholars who stood with Michael. 'Thank you for summoning me, Bingham. You may well have saved your colleague's life by ignoring his fevered demands for another *medicus*.'

Bingham looked sheepish when Thorpe raised questioning eyebrows. 'I sent word to both physicians, lest one should tarry or be unavailable,' he confessed. 'I am sorry, but I wanted to do all I could to help Warde.'

'What is the matter?' asked Rougham in a loud voice, as though his patient's choking had also rendered him deaf and stupid. 'Did you take the Water of Snails I prescribed? If you followed my recommendations I cannot imagine why you are in this state.'

'Angelica,' whispered Warde, clearly finding it difficult to talk. 'Please, I have a . . .'

'I did not hear you,' bawled Rougham. 'What about angelica?'

'Do not speak, Warde,' said Bartholomew. It was hard to stand by and see the man struggle to converse when it was obviously making his condition worse. 'Lie still and take deep breaths.'

'Angelica,' pronounced Rougham, eyeing Bartholomew coldly. 'That is something *I* would never prescribe, so it is doubtless one of your remedies. It is *your* fault Warde is in this state. If he had followed my advice, then he would not be lying here, on his deathbed.'

Warde's gagging grew more frenzied, and Bartholomew saw he had gripped the crucifix so tightly that it had cut his hand.

'Tell me,' demanded Rougham, taking Warde's arm and giving it a shake. 'Did you take angelica instead of the Water of Snails? Did you go against the express orders of your own physician in favour of a man whose methods are so dangerously irregular?'

Warde drew breath with difficulty, and Bartholomew felt anger rise inside him. 'Do not speak, Warde,' he said tightly, longing to push Rougham away from the ailing man. 'Just concentrate on breathing. We can talk later, when you are recovered.'

Rougham sneered. 'You are trying to silence him, so he

305

will go to his grave without incriminating you. You have killed him with your angelica, and you are trying to cover your tracks.'

The Valence Marie scholars listened with open-mouthed astonishment. Warde's breathing grew more laboured, as a result, Bartholomew thought, of Rougham agitating him by mentioning deathbeds and graves. He moved away, thinking that if he was out of Rougham's presence, the Gonville physician might not rant so. He would take him to task about his appalling bedside manners later, when there was no one to hear him tell the man he was a pompous fool.

'And now you are running away,' jeered Rougham. 'You are unable to watch a man die, knowing you are responsible.'

'Ignore him, Matt,' warned Michael, sensing his friend's growing anger. 'Angelica never did anyone any harm. My grandmother chews it all the time.'

'Warde was better after he took the angelica,' said Thorpe, joining the debate in a wary voice. 'His coughing eased, and he had a better night of sleep than he has enjoyed in a long time – we all did. We thought he was on the mend. Until now.'

'It is a delayed reaction,' pronounced Rougham author-itatively. 'With angelica you think you are well, but find you are suddenly worse.' He turned back to Warde again. 'I ordered you to pray to the Hand of Justice for a cure, too. Did you do it? I thought I saw you with the other petitioners.'

'Water of Snails!' rasped Warde, and everyone craned forward to hear him. 'I took it. Before the meal. Look on the table.' He coughed again, and Bartholomew itched to go to him, to ease him into a position where he could breathe easier. 'Not Bingham's fault.'

All eyes went to Warde's place at the high table, and

Bartholomew recognised the little phial containing the Water of Snails that Lavenham had prepared two days before. He wondered how Warde had come to have it, since Master Thorpe had said he would never persuade his colleague to drink such a potion, and had declined to purchase it for him.

'Oh,' said Rougham, knocked off his stride. He recovered quickly. 'But the harm was already done with the angelica, and my Water of Snails was taken too late to help.'

'It came from you,' wheezed Warde accusingly. 'You sent it. With a note. I took it. Because I was feeling better. But I wanted a quicker cure. The sermon.'

'He is due to give the public address at St Mary the Great tomorrow,' explained Thorpe. 'He has been worried that he will be unable to do it, because of the cough. I suppose he took the Water of Snails as a precaution. I can think of no other reason that would induce him to swallow the stuff.'

Warde's vigorous nodding showed his Master's assumptions were right. Bartholomew noticed there was a bluish tinge around his nose and mouth that had not been there before, and grew even more concerned. He saw students standing in a silent semicircle nearby, exchanging distraught glances. A kind, patient scholar like Warde would be sorely missed if anything were to happen to him.

'But I did not send you Water of Snails with any note,' said Rougham, puzzled. 'I gave a recipe for the concoction to Master Thorpe, who took it to Lavenham to be made up.'

'You sent it,' asserted Warde in a feeble voice. 'Today.' This time his coughing was so vigorous that he began to make gasping, retching sounds that were painful to hear.

'What are you saying?' demanded Rougham. 'Why would I send you such a thing, when I had already issued your Master with instructions and a list of ingredients?'

'Enough!' snapped Bartholomew, finally angered sufficiently to step forward and assert himself. Warde's breathing was becoming increasingly laboured, and he saw that unless Warde stopped trying to talk he would indeed die. 'Close your eyes and take deep, even breaths. Do not speak.'

Rougham drew breath to argue, but Bartholomew shot him a look so full of barely controlled rage that he closed his mouth with a snap audible at the other end of the hall.

'I saw the package and the letter,' said Bingham to Rougham. 'You sent Warde the phial, along with a message carrying instructions for him to swallow every drop.'

'But I did not send him anything!' insisted Rougham, becoming alarmed. 'I did not even know he had ignored my advice and taken angelica.' He almost spat the last word as he treated Bartholomew to a glare of his own.

Bingham crouched down and rummaged in Warde's scrip, producing a note scrawled on parchment: it was unquestionably Rougham's spidery hand. He handed it to Thorpe.

'"Drink all herein of *Aqua Limacum Magistr.* for purge of phlegm and consumptions of the lungs",' read Thorpe. He looked at Bartholomew. '*Aqua Limacum Magistr.*?'

'*Limacum Magistralis* is the Latin description for Water of Snails,' explained Bartholomew absently, more concerned by the patient's rapidly deteriorating condition. 'We can discuss this later. I want you all to leave, so Warde can lie quietly, and—'

'One of my students must have attached that message to the Water of Snails, and sent it to Warde by mistake,' interrupted Rougham. 'That is the only possible explanation. I prescribe *Aqua Limacum Magistralis* to lots of people. But enough of that. Warde must rouse himself and walk, so that exercise will clear his lungs of the phlegm that chokes them.'

'Leave him alone,' said Bartholomew quietly, as the

Gonville physician stepped towards Warde. He hauled the cloth from the table and bundled it under Warde's head, to make a pillow.

'Water of Snails,' whispered Warde weakly. 'Killed me.'

'You will not die,' said Bartholomew, although he was now not so sure. He struggled to hide his concern as he spoke gently to his patient, again hoping that a calm voice might work its own magic. 'Lie still, close your eyes and take a breath. And now release it slowly. And . . .'

He faltered, and the watching scholars strained forward to see why he had stopped speaking.

'What is it, Matt?' asked Michael quietly. 'What is wrong?'

Bartholomew sat back on his heels and looked accusingly at Rougham. 'He is dead.'

Rougham looked as shocked as Bartholomew felt. 'It was *you* who tended him as he breathed his last, not me. You are the one who killed him. You probably did it for the fourpence you will earn as Corpse Examiner. I always said it was not a good idea to appoint a man who needs the money.'

Warde had been a popular man, not just in the University, but in the town, too, and people were dismayed by his death. In Michaelhouse the following day, Suttone, the gloomy Carmelite, began to speculate about whether Warde's fatal cough meant that the plague had returned, pointing out that the pestilence had also carried folk away with horrifying speed. Bartholomew argued that it was not, but neither could convince the other, so they eventually fell silent by mutual consent, having thoroughly depressed anyone who had listened to them.

'No one believes Rougham's claim that you killed Warde, Matthew,' said Father William kindly, as the Fellows took their places at the high table for breakfast. It was a Sunday, and the sun was shining through the hall windows.

'He is saying that publicly?' asked Bartholomew, dismayed. 'Already? But Warde only died last night.'

'Rougham is an evil man,' declared Suttone. 'When the Death returns, he will be first to go.'

'You identify a good many people who will "go" the instant the pestilence appears,' observed Langelee, reaching for the ale jug and pouring himself a generous measure. 'Are we to assume that it will be of short duration, then? All the evildoers will be struck dead in the first few moments?'

'And the rest of you shortly thereafter,' replied Suttone, fixing him with a cool gaze. 'The wicked first, normal sinners second.'

'Who will be left?' asked Michael, snatching the bowl of egg-mess flavoured with lumps of mutton fat, just as Clippesby was reaching for it. 'You and which other saint?'

'Not Peterkin Starre, whose Hand lies in St Mary the Great, because he is dead already,' said Clippesby, who had brushed his hair with a teasel in honour of the Sabbath, and did not look quite as peculiar as usual. 'Walter's cockerel informs me that he was no saint anyway. Bird believes the whole business with the Hand of Justice is shameful, and says someone should put an end to such gross deception by telling the truth about it.'

'Does he, indeed?' asked William archly, not pleased that the enterprise he had created should be criticised from avian quarters. 'And what would Bird know of holy matters? He does not even know the correct time to crow. He woke up the entire College last night by braying at three o'clock in the morning. The scholars of Ovyng Hostel *and* Paxtone of King's Hall complained about him again today.'

'That thing is asking for its neck to be wrung,' agreed Langelee. 'Unfortunately, it is not easy to catch. I have tried, believe me, and so has Agatha.'

'Bird enjoys being chased,' said Clippesby, taking the bowl that had contained the egg-mess from Michael. He looked from the monk's heaped trencher to the empty vessel with narrowed eyes. 'I think you have taken my share there, as well as your own, Brother.'

'Have I?' asked Michael breezily. He rammed his knife into the eggs, and transferred a minuscule amount to Clippesby. 'There you are. The dish was half-empty this morning. I suppose it is just another example of Michaelhouse cutting costs.' He glared at Wynewyk.

'More,' said Clippesby, surveying the two unequal portions with dissatisfaction.

Michael sighed in annoyance, but did as he was told. Displeased about losing half his breakfast, the monk went on the offensive, determined to vent his temper on someone. 'When Matt and I were walking back from Valence Marie last night, after dealing with poor Warde, I saw someone lurking in the churchyard of St John Zachary. Now, what would an honest and law-abiding scholar be doing in such a place at such a time?'

Silence greeted his words, until it was broken by Langelee. 'None of us understands what you are talking about, Brother. Who do you mean?'

'Wynewyk,' said Michael, turning to fix steady eyes on the hapless lawyer. 'I saw him quite clearly, and he saw us – which was why he darted for cover, I imagine. He did not expect any of his colleagues to be abroad at such an hour.'

Bartholomew regarded Wynewyk in surprise. He had not seen anyone hiding behind bushes on his way home. However, he had not noticed very much, because his mind had been teeming with questions about Warde's death, and he had been furious about Rougham's accusations.

'It is not easy to stretch Michaelhouse's paltry income to cover all our needs,' replied Wynewyk stiffly. 'And, in order to make it go further, I am occasionally obliged to deal with men who make better offers than our regular suppliers. It sometimes requires the odd nocturnal assignation.'

'I do not like the sound of this,' said Suttone sanctimoniously. 'I do not want my College associated with shady deals that see me eating victuals that "fell off the back of a cart".'

'Nor do I,' agreed William. 'I have my reputation as Keeper of the University Chest to uphold. It would not look good for my College to be implicated in dishonest dealings.'

Bartholomew saw several students start to laugh, evidently thinking that the friar's conduct regarding the Hand of Justice was as dishonest as anything else happening in the town.

'It was nothing illegal,' protested Wynewyk, offended. 'I would never do anything to bring the College into disrepute. I am a respectable, God-fearing man. You will just have to trust me.'

'*I* trust you,' said Langelee. 'That is why I appointed you to help me in the first place. But time is passing and I want to visit the Hand of Justice. So, *benedictus benedicat*, and good day to you all.'

Fellows and students hastened to stand for the final grace, but most were still sitting when Langelee wiped his lips on his sleeve and strode from the hall, Wynewyk scurrying at his heels. Michael shook his head as they went, muttering that the lawyer was clearly engaged in something odd, and that it was only a matter of time before he learned what. Bartholomew preferred not to think about it, mostly because he felt he had enough to worry about with the mill murders and Warde's sudden death. He abandoned the high table and made for the stairs.

'I wonder whether all our concerns and problems are connected,' mused Michael, joining him in the yard.

'Thorpe and Mortimer return to Cambridge and begin to meddle in matters that they know will cause ill feeling between town and University. We have the "Hand of Justice" discussed on every street corner, and a brewing row about who should own it.'

'Then we have Deschalers and Bottisham dead in suspicious circumstances, and Deschalers bequeathing his fortune to his niece, who just happens to have married Edward Mortimer,' continued Bartholomew.

'But they were betrothed before his exile,' said Michael, turning his face towards the bright sun as he stretched his large limbs. 'They have only done what their families originally intended, and I do not see their wedding as anything significant.'

'I disagree. Originally, Julianna despised Edward so much that she considered Langelee a viable alternative.' Bartholomew gestured to the barrel-shaped Master, who was steaming towards the gate, wearing his best Sunday hat and swinging his beefy arms. 'Why did she change her mind?'

'Because Edward is no longer a gangling, awkward boy. He is a man who knows his mind and who has an air of danger about him. Julianna seems to like that sort of thing, and I am not surprised she fell for his "charms". But let us continue with our list of recent events and coincidences. We have Edward inheriting the murdered Deschalers's wealth. And we have the murdered Deschalers involved in a conflict between rival mills.'

'We should not forget the fact that Deschalers's house was burgled the night he died, either,' said Bartholomew. 'I saw someone there, and so did Una.'

'But what Una saw does not match your account,' said Michael dismissively. 'Her intruder left through the front door, while you chased yours through the back window. Una likes her wine, and we know she had some, because you treated her for a sore stomach the next day. But I do not think the burglary is important. The whole town was buzzing with the news of Deschalers's death – including the forty felons who are repairing the Great Bridge – and no self-respecting thief would have passed up such a golden opportunity.'

'Julianna would disagree. She believed the burglary *was* significant, because documents were rummaged through, even though nothing was stolen.'

'How could she tell whether anything was stolen?' argued Michael. 'She did not live with her uncle, and was not in a position to know what valuables he happened to leave lying around that night.'

Bartholomew wavered, not sure what to think. 'What about the possibility that Deschalers made another will? Laying claim to that sort of document would be a strong motive for breaking into his house the moment he died.'

'Edward and Julianna did not need to burgle Deschalers's home looking for a will that disinherited them. They could have gone any time, quite openly. She was his niece and only kin.'

'It would be useful to know the identity of Deschalers's scribe,' said Bartholomew. 'He must have written the document in the first place, and will know if there is more than one will in existence.'

'You are chasing clouds,' said Michael impatiently. 'Everyone knew – and expected – that Deschalers would leave all his money to Julianna. The deed was no surprise to anyone.'

Bartholomew supposed he was right, but thought it unwise to dismiss the burglary until they were certain it was irrelevant. He turned his mind back to their list of odd coincidences. 'Edward told Thomas to take the mill dispute to the King – on learning that the Millers' Society intended to burn Mortimer's Mill to the ground – and then they

314

secured the services of Gonville's lawyers to represent them. Bottisham was one of those clerks, but then he was murdered.'

'Or he committed suicide,' said Michael. 'The most likely explanation is still that Bottisham and Deschalers met, one killed the other and then took his own life in a fit of remorse. It was our original conclusion, if you recall.'

'But we deduced that when we trusted what Bernarde told us. Now we are not so sure, because we have caught him out in lies. We cannot discount the possibility that Bernarde killed the Mortimers' lawyer first, then murdered the man who is related to the Mortimers by marriage and who spoke out against burning his rival's mill.'

'True,' admitted Michael. 'Although I really did believe Bernarde's boy when he corroborated his father's story about the various thumps in the engines. But Bernarde is not our only suspect. We know Thomas Mortimer does not hesitate to kill – he dispatched Lenne with callous abandon. He is a drunkard, and it would not surprise me to learn that *he* had committed the murders in a fit of wine-fuelled rage.'

'Why? Even wine-fuelled rage needs something to set it off.'

'He may have slaughtered Deschalers and Bottisham without knowing what he was doing, so his family dumped the bodies in the King's Mill to throw us off the scent – to protect him.'

Bartholomew shook his head. 'I think Bottisham and Deschalers were killed where they were found. And a nail in the palate is not something that happens by chance. Both Deschalers and Bottisham were killed with ruthless efficiency, and I am not sure Thomas possesses the clarity of mind to carry out such a task. Besides, his involvement leaves your theory with an awkward question: why would he be in the King's Mill in the middle of the night?'

'We do not know what Bottisham and Deschalers were doing there, either,' Michael pointed out. He sighed heavily. 'We have answers to virtually none of our questions. However, I recommend keeping an open mind as far as *all* our suspects are concerned. And speaking of open minds, I have not discounted the possibility that Bess is involved, either.'

'I tried to catch her out once or twice, to see whether her rambling wits are carefully cultivated to fool us. But I have not succeeded.'

'That may mean she is just more clever than you,' said Michael bluntly. 'She is still the person most likely to have killed Bosel.'

Bartholomew was uncertain. 'She had a fortune in gold, but someone took it from her in exchange for information she never received. Do you really think a cunning manipulator would blithely hand over all her money, in return for nothing but vague promises and lies?'

'And finally, we have Warde,' said Michael, declining to acknowledge that the physician might have a point. 'One of the King's Commissioners. Rougham denies sending him the Water of Snails, but Warde received and drank it, and now the Commission is down to three members. Warde had taken it upon himself to put the Mortimers' side of the argument – since Bernarde and Lavenham were out to represent their own interests. That means one of the Millers' Society might have had him killed.'

'You think Warde was murdered?' asked Bartholomew, startled. 'But the claim of foul play was just Rougham being unpleasant towards me. There is no evidence to suggest he was wrongfully killed.'

'No evidence *yet*,' corrected Michael. 'But again, we shall keep open minds. I do not believe in sinister coincidences, and you said yourself that Warde's cough should not have killed him. But something did. You may be right, and

Warde's heart may have failed from the effort of continual hacking. Or perhaps he had a natural aversion to Water of Snails – which you tell me contains powerful herbs, as well as boiled garden pests.'

'Or Lavenham made a mistake with his ingredients, or Rougham in his instructions. There is no end to the possibilities, and I do not see how we will ever learn the truth.'

'Lavenham,' mused Michael, his eyes gleaming, so that he looked like a fatter, younger version of his grandmother. 'The apothecary who made up the potion, who is also a member of the Millers' Society, and who has a vested interest in ridding himself of a pro-Mortimer Commissioner.'

'Master Thorpe also refuses to accept the Millers' Society's side of the dispute without demur,' said Bartholomew tiredly. 'He agreed to remain neutral, while Warde put the Mortimers' case. If you are right about what happened to Warde, then you should warn Master Thorpe to be on his guard against mysterious potions sent from the apothecary.'

'I already have,' replied Michael. 'Not that he needed to be told. He knows that to be appointed a Commissioner in this particular case is a dangerous business.'

On a day of rest, when labour was forbidden at Michaelhouse, Bartholomew found himself at a loose end later that morning. Usually he would have worked on his treatise on fevers, with the window shutters closed so that the rigorist William could not see what he was doing. But such covert activities were difficult now he no longer had a chamber to himself. Redmeadow would have turned a blind eye, but the same could not be said for Quenhyth. When the student caught his teacher breaking the College's rules, his disapproving shuffles made concentration impossible, so Bartholomew was usually forced to abandon his writings.

Quenhyth and Redmeadow were at home that morning, and all Bartholomew's attempts to send them on errands or out for walks failed. Quenhyth sat on a bench with a religious tract on his knees – the only kind of reading allowed – and chattered about his family, his home in Chepe, and the new cloak his father had promised to send him. Redmeadow dozed on Bartholomew's bed.

'He has been stealing my ink again,' Quenhyth said to Bartholomew in a whisper, nodding his head at his room-mate. 'More than half of it had gone when I checked it this morning.'

'I did not,' said Redmeadow indignantly, showing he had not been asleep after all. 'You left the lid off, and it evaporates.'

'Not true!' cried Quenhyth.

'Are you calling me a liar?' demanded Redmeadow, coming off the bed in a lunge, and advancing menacingly. Quenhyth scampered away from him.

'Stop it,' ordered Bartholomew sharply. He had forgotten about Redmeadow's fiery temper. 'Sit down, both of you.'

'You need to do something about Rougham,' said Quenhyth, when Redmeadow was safely back on the bed. 'He is accusing you of killing Warde, when it is obvious that *he* is the culprit.'

'No one killed Warde,' said Bartholomew. 'He died from coughing.'

'But Warde should not have died,' pressed Quenhyth. 'You said so yourself. And Rougham was the man who prescribed the very last medicine Warde swallowed. You should investigate him.'

'You should,' agreed Redmeadow. 'He is not a nice man.'

He and Quenhyth began a venomous discussion, listing Rougham's various faults. Bartholomew tried to go back to his treatise, but it was no more possible to concentrate through their vicious character assassination than through Quenhyth's disapproving sighs, and it was not long before he gave up and left. He met Michael in the yard. The monk had crumbs on his jowls, and his lips were oily from the lard-coated oatcakes he had been devouring with Agatha by the kitchen fire.

'You have only just had breakfast,' the physician said accusingly. He glanced down, and saw the monk had secured a handful of the greasy treats for later, too. 'It is not good to eat all the time, Brother. You will create an imbalance of humours and give yourself stomach gripes, not to mention the fact that you are becoming corpulent. How will you chase errant students, when you cannot manage more than a waddle?'

'I am not corpulent,' said Michael, deeply offended. 'I have large bones, as I have told you before. And I do not waddle.'

'You have waddled since Christmas, and it is time to stop. You must adopt a more sensible dietary regime. Remember the seizure suffered by that fat monk in Ely last summer? Well, you will have one, too, if you continue as you are. I do not want you to die.'

'I am glad to hear it,' snapped Michael testily, grabbing one of Bartholomew's hands and slapping the oatcakes into it with such force that they crumbled into pieces. Walter's cockerel immediately darted forward, to take advantage of the unexpected feast showering to the ground. 'But do not pick on me because your students have driven you from your illicit labours.'

'I am sorry, Brother,' said Bartholomew, relenting. He knew the monk was right. 'These last few days have been difficult, what with Isnard, Mistress Lenne, Bottisham and now Warde.'

Michael accepted the apology with poor grace. 'Perhaps we should take a walk to visit friends – Matilde, perhaps,

319

or your brother-in-law. That may take my mind off my poor growling stomach.'

'We will just walk,' said Bartholomew, steering the monk towards the gate. It was customary to offer food and drink to visitors, and both Matilde and Stanmore kept well-stocked kitchens. The monk knew this perfectly well, just as he knew it would be discourteous to decline their hospitality.

They strolled slowly, stopping to exchange greetings with colleagues and acquaintances. Eventually, they reached the Mill Pool, where both mills stood silent, and where Isnard's neighbours had carried him to a bench outside his house, so he could watch the ducks quarrelling.

'These birds are like the Mortimers,' said the bargeman, as Bartholomew and Michael approached, not lifting his eyes from the feathered fracas in front of him. 'They only care about themselves. I heard the family arranged for poor Master Warde to die, too.'

'I doubt that was them,' said Michael, sitting next to him. 'The Millers' Society are the ones who will benefit from Warde's death, not the Mortimers. The Mortimers have just lost a Commissioner who was prepared to argue their point of view. Have you recovered from your foray to St Mary the Great with your new leg last Thursday?'

'No,' replied Isnard shortly. 'The Doctor says I damaged the wound so badly that I am forbidden to attach my new limb until at least the summer. I should never have allowed Thomas Mortimer inside my house. I thought he had come to make amends, but instead he used me for his own purposes. He did not even pay for the ale we drank together – he purchased it with the money the Doctor gave me.'

'Then what did you use to buy food and fuel?' asked Bartholomew.

'Paxtone gave me a penny. And so did Clippesby, although he claimed he delivered it on behalf of Bird, who was unable to come himself because of a "pressing appointment to discuss creation theology with the Master of Trinity Hall".' Isnard shook his head. 'Clippesby spins his tales with such an honest face that I do not know whether he is a lunatic or a saint.'

'A lunatic,' answered Michael. 'The Master of Trinity Hall knows nothing of creation theology.'

Isnard regarded Bartholomew sombrely. 'Are you sure about my leg? Only Mortimer said he *saw* it healed. If I went back to the Hand of Justice and asked it nicely, it might help me a second time . . .'

'Mortimer was lying,' said Bartholomew gently. 'Severed limbs do not regrow. He knew it would take little to intoxicate you in your weakened condition, and he deliberately set out to deceive you. He wanted to stem the tide of ill feeling over what he did to you and Lenne.'

'But Rougham said it was a miracle, too,' said Isnard miserably.

'Rougham is a fool,' said Bartholomew, no longer caring whether he offended his rival physician. Rougham had done nothing but criticise him, upset his students and make silly diagnoses for days, and he was heartily sick of it.

'Well, it made me happy for an hour,' said Isnard with a sniff. He glanced up. 'Here comes Master Lenne, old Lenne's son. He arrived late last night from Thetford.'

The younger Lenne had left Cambridge to become barber to the Cluniac monks at Thetford Priory some years before. He was a wiry man in his early forties, with thin hair and a perfect set of white teeth that looked as though they belonged in someone else's head.

'I owe you my thanks,' Lenne said to Bartholomew. 'You physicked my mother, but have not pestered her with demands for fees.' He regarded Bartholomew's shorn hair with a professional eye. 'Did my father do that? I heard he was losing his touch, but I did not know he had sunk that low.'

'It will grow,' said Bartholomew shortly.

'Eventually,' said Lenne. He handed Bartholomew a gold coin. 'This should be sufficient to see her through to the end. It cannot be long now.'

'It will not,' agreed Bartholomew bluntly. 'She only waited this long because you were coming.'

'Then I should go back to her,' replied Lenne. He hesitated, then addressed Michael. 'Isnard tells me Thomas Mortimer is not to be charged with my father's murder? Is this true?'

'Unfortunately, yes,' said Michael. 'There were no witnesses to the accident, and—'

'There was Bosel,' interrupted the bargeman bitterly. 'But Mortimer had him murdered, so he would not speak out. And there is me, but the lawyers say I do not count, because I am a victim. They claim they need independent witnesses to bring about a conviction.'

'That cannot be right,' said Lenne unhappily. 'There is no such thing as an independent witness in a place like Cambridge, where everyone is bound by allegiances, alliances and agendas. Even the beggar will have had his own reasons for stepping forward.'

'I am sure he did,' muttered Michael. 'And it would not surprise me to learn that he saw nothing of the accident. But I suspect it cost him his life nonetheless.'

'The law is unjust,' said Isnard softly. 'Thomas should pay me for my injury, and he should pay Lenne for the loss of his father. But the law disagrees. Meanwhile, Thorpe and Edward are claiming compensation because they were ordered to abjure the realm. They were guilty, and everyone knows it, but the law says the town is to pay them. I heard it this morning.'

'The King's Bench has reached a decision about that?' asked Michael. 'Already?'

Isnard nodded. 'A messenger arrived from Westminster

322

last night. The news is all over the town this morning, and people are furious – especially the merchants, who will be obliged to provide the lion's share. The King's clerks were quite clear about what was to happen.'

'Bribery,' said Lenne in a disgusted voice. 'I heard these clerks were *bribed* to issue the compensation order – with promises of a percentage of whatever was raised. Needless to say, the sum to be paid to Thorpe and Edward is a large one.'

'Are you sure about this?' asked Michael uncertainly. It did not sound likely, even for England's notoriously flexible legal system.

'Yes,' said Isnard bitterly. 'I have nothing to do but sit here and listen to gossip. Godric of Ovyng Hostel – he is a nice lad – came and told me all about the letter Sheriff Tulyet had from these greedy Westminster clerks.'

'I hope Tulyet orders Thomas Mortimer to pay most of it,' said Lenne in disgust. 'Justice!' He spat at the river, causing a flapping frenzy among the ducks, and stalked away. Bartholomew thought he had every right to be angry, and wondered if he might decide to dispense a little 'justice' of his own. He said as much.

'He will not,' said Isnard. 'He will rage and rail, then he will bury his mother and go back to Thetford. He is not stupid, and knows the law favours the rich. But perhaps he should ask his prior to petition the King, to tell him what is really happening here. His Majesty deserves to know what vile things are being done in his name.'

'Unfortunately, I suspect he already does,' said Bartholomew. He recalled what Tulyet had said about the law. 'But it is all that stands between us and chaos.'

'I suspect we will soon learn that it does not make a very good barrier,' said Isnard. 'There are rumblings of discontent in this town – about the ownership of the

Hand, about the mills, and about the compensation for Thorpe and Edward. It will not be long before we are in flames.'

Bartholomew felt even more restless after his encounter with Isnard, and did not know what to do to take his mind off the array of problems and questions that tumbled about his mind like demanding acrobats. When Michael would have strolled back towards Michaelhouse, Bartholomew steered him to the High Street instead, thinking they could walk as far as the Castle or beyond. The hill would be good exercise for Michael, and there was a sick woman in the derelict cottages opposite the fortress who might appreciate a visit from a physician and a monk.

As they approached the Church of All Saints in the Jewry, Bartholomew saw people begin to emerge after its Sunday service. Among them were Stanmore and Tulyet, who expressed their sadness over the death of Warde.

'What is this about the town paying Thorpe and Edward Mortimer for the costs of their exile?' demanded Michael, brushing their condolences aside. 'Surely it cannot be right?'

Tulyet's expression was disgusted. 'I had word from the King's Bench yesterday, and the sum we have been ordered to pay is enormous. It will cause all manner of strife, because the burgesses are already demanding that some of it should be paid by the University.'

'Why?' asked Michael indignantly. 'Neither Thorpe nor Mortimer were scholars when they committed their crimes. Why should the University contribute to compensation?'

'Because the merchants are already struggling to fund the repairs to the Great Bridge,' replied Tulyet tartly. 'Thorpe and Mortimer's demand has come at a very bad time.'

'The burgesses are right,' said Stanmore who, as one of

the town's wealthiest merchants, was likely to be asked to put up a significant amount. 'The University *should* help us with this.'

'Will you contest the decision?' asked Bartholomew of Tulyet. 'There must be something we can do to avoid rewarding criminals for their wrongdoings.'

'We have no case,' said Tulyet. 'The King's Bench has made a decision in His Majesty's name, and we cannot refuse to part with our gold because we think it is wrong. The King would respond by accusing us of rebellion. All we can do is pay the money, and hope Thorpe and Mortimer leave.'

'I will never pay a Mortimer,' vowed Cheney the spicer, overhearing their discussion as he walked past. He bustled forward to have his say. 'Not a penny! I hurl stones every time I see Edward swagger along the High Street, but I always miss.'

Cheney's Millers' Society colleagues were at his heels. They had evidently been using the service to engage in a little impromptu business, because all held documents, and Morice carried an abacus.

'We were sorry about Warde,' said Isobel, breaking off from an apparently intense discussion with Bernarde and her husband. 'He was a good man.'

'The King's Commission miss he,' said Lavenham gravely, when she pinched his arm to tell him to make a suitably sympathetic comment. 'He school-man with nose in book, but honest.'

'He was fair minded,' agreed Tulyet. 'I do not know how the King's Commission will fare without his calm voice and gentle reason.'

'Master Thorpe will be even-handed,' said Michael.

'So will I,' declared Bernarde, affronted. 'And Lavenham. We will give the King the verdict he wants.'

'Point proven,' muttered Bartholomew.

'I do not see your problem,' said Bernarde, genuinely puzzled. 'Surely you want the King happy?'

'Everyone wants the King happy,' said Stanmore, before his brother-in-law could incriminate himself by saying he did not much care. 'The King unhappy is always a bad thing, because it means increased taxes. None of us want that.'

There was a chorus of fervent agreement, with Cheney adding that it was especially true now everyone had to dig deep in his coffers to pay Edward and Thorpe's compensation – as well as financing the repairs to the bridge.

'Master Warde was not as unbiased as everyone believes,' said Bernarde, returning to the matter of the Commission. 'When we had our first meeting, he insisted on putting the Mortimers' point of view – and Master Thorpe actually listened to him.' He sounded as if he could scarcely credit their outrageous behaviour.

'Did he, by God?' said Cheney, pursing his lips in disapproval. 'I might have known *scholars* would support the wrong side. After all, the Mortimers did choose Gonville Hall to present their case at the formal hearing, and University men always stick together.'

'They cleaves with each other,' agreed Lavenham angrily. 'Like with Hand of Injustice, which belong to town. School-men claim belong to University.'

'The Hand of *Justice*, Lavenham,' corrected Bernarde. 'It does not do to confuse them.'

'Why not?' muttered Bartholomew. 'Everyone else does, including the King.' Michael gave him a hard elbow-jab that hurt enough to make him think twice about saying anything else.

'If the University is forced to help pay this compensation, they will definitely keep the Hand of Justice for themselves,' said Cheney angrily. 'They will continue to lock it in St Mary the Great, and it will cost us townsfolk dear each time we want to petition it.'

'But Father William has been charging scholars and townsfolk the same amount,' said Tulyet reasonably. 'There was a nasty argument this morning, because he refused Langelee a free viewing. They almost came to blows, and only the intervention of Dame Pelagia prevented a brawl.'

'That Hand will cause trouble wherever it goes,' said Michael. 'Young Thorpe has asked the King if Gonville can have it. But other Colleges are sure to be jealous. As far as I am concerned, the town can have the thing, and good riddance.'

'No, thank you,' said Tulyet hastily. 'I do not want to deal with the strife it will cause, either.'

'Warde's will is going to be read tomorrow morning,' said Stanmore, changing the subject to one all merchants loved: money. 'He was a wealthy man by University standards. I wonder what he will leave his College.'

'Books, I imagine,' said Cheney distastefully. 'It is what they all like. Did you hear about Deschalers's will? Julianna inherited the lot.'

'Except for a wooden chest,' said Stanmore. 'That went to some clerk, although I understand it is a paltry thing. The clerk admired it – he was probably being polite – and Deschalers took him at his word. I suspect the fellow is now wishing he had praised something a little more expensive.'

'I would be,' said Bernarde wistfully. 'A box is useful, but virtually worthless. Deschalers did not leave his apprentices a penny, you know. He was wrong to be so miserly. They served him for many years, and they deserved better.'

'And then Edward dismissed most of them,' added Cheney. 'It is almost as if he *wants* his business to fail. How will he run it without men who know what they are doing? He has neither the experience nor the knowledge to become a grocer.'

'I do not think he intends to stay long,' said Stanmore. 'A man intent on making a venture profitable does not rid

327

himself of those who can help him. I suspect he intends to reap what funds there are – from Julianna's inheritance and this wretched compensation – and then leave.'

'I hope so,' said Tulyet. 'He has done nothing criminal yet, but he has come close. He pesters the Frail Sisters, too. I doubt Julianna would approve, if she knew. Perhaps I should drop her a few hints. That would put an end to his philandering.'

'Be direct,' advised Stanmore. 'She is not a woman who understands hints.'

Tulyet balked. 'That would be a gentlemanly thing to do.'

Bartholomew listened to them with half an ear. He was looking towards the well in the Jewry, where the object of their discussion was lounging against a wall. Edward Mortimer, with Thorpe at his side, was watching the young women lining up to draw water. The girls soon became uneasy under their lecherous scrutiny. Mortimer moved close to one of the prettiest and whispered something in her ear, pushing himself against her. She dropped her bucket and fled, tears starting from her eyes, while the others edged closer together, their faces rigidly hostile.

Mortimer was unperturbed by their animosity. He merely selected another victim, and began to look her up and down as a housewife might examine a carcass at the butchers' stalls. Bartholomew took several steps towards him, intending to intervene if he made a nuisance of himself: he had meant what he had said to Thorpe on the river bank the previous day and, as far as he was concerned, the threat applied to Mortimer, too. He was just close enough to hear what was being said, when a familiar figure sidled up to the miscreants and the women used the distraction to scatter.

'I have been hoping to meet you, sir,' said Quenhyth with one of his ingratiating smiles.

'I have already told you that I do not want your services,' snapped Mortimer, angry to have lost his prey. 'I can write as well as, or better than, you, and I do not require a scribe.'

'But I need the money,' objected Quenhyth in a whine. 'How can I buy medicines for the patients I will soon have, if I have no funds? Every other student in the University makes ends meet by scribing for wealthy merchants, and I am the only one without a patron. Even Deynman writes for Stanmore on occasion.'

'Clear off!' growled Thorpe.

'But I have tried everyone else,' persisted Quenhyth. 'Redmeadow works for Cheney, and Ulfrid and Zebedee, the Franciscans, scribe for Bernarde and Lavenham. You are my last hope.'

'You are not the sort any decent man would hire,' said Thorpe nastily. 'You are opinionated and judgmental, and no one likes you.'

Bartholomew saw Quenhyth blanch, and felt sorry for him. He had forgotten Quenhyth was short of funds, and felt he must be desperate indeed if he was obliged to beg for work from Mortimer.

'I am liked,' said Quenhyth in a strangled voice. 'Deynman and Redmeadow are fond of me.'

'Deynman *tolerates* you,' said Mortimer unpleasantly. 'But Redmeadow *loathes* you. I heard him telling Cheney so the other day, when he was scribing for him in St Clement's Church. He says you spy on him all the time, so he cannot do what he wants.'

Bartholomew wondered what Redmeadow had meant, but then reflected that Quenhyth was a sanctimonious lad, who made no secret of the fact that he disapproved of rule-breaking. Redmeadow had probably learned that he could not drink in taverns, gamble, or flirt with the town's women as long as Quenhyth shared his room.

'We are busy,' snarled Mortimer at the hapless student. 'Do not bother us again.'

He strutted away, heading towards a tinker, who was flouting Sunday laws by sitting with his wares laid out on a dirty rug. The tinker reached out to attract his attention, and Bartholomew was astonished to see Mortimer kick him. The tinker reeled, but recovered to screech curses after the swaggering men. When they reached the edge of the Jewry, Mortimer turned and made an obscene gesture, which resulted in even more frenzied oaths. Thorpe immediately retraced his steps. Bartholomew could not hear what was said, but the tinker fell silent. He bowed his head as the two felons left.

Bartholomew watched with distaste. Folk who were obliged to peddle their wares from rugs on the ground were the poorest of traders, and could not be blamed if the occasional hand reached out to a potential customer. Bartholomew disliked being grabbed himself, but it was easy enough to pull away. Mortimer's kick had been vicious and unnecessary. Not for the first time the physician wondered what kind of men the King's clerks had set free with their casually granted pardons.

Michael was happy to continue gossiping with the merchants, but the incident with the tinker had unsettled Bartholomew. He followed Thorpe and Mortimer at a discreet distance until they entered a tavern on the High Street, open despite Sabbath restrictions. He peered through a window shutter and heard them demanding ale from a pot-boy. He supposed that as long as they were in an inn, the town's women would be safe enough – until the two men emerged fuelled for more mischief. He moved away as the first heavy drops of a spring shower started to fall, turning his thoughts back to whatever it was that Redmeadow wanted to do that Quenhyth's presence at

Michaelhouse made difficult. Was it more than a mere flouting of the University's rules? Had Cheney asked his scribe to do something to further the mill dispute, something Redmeadow was finding difficult because of his roommate's nosy presence?

Bartholomew retraced his steps up the High Street, passing the row of hovels opposite the Hospital of St John. The shacks had been an eyesore for years. Their roofs sagged, wall plaster dropped to the ground in clumps when it was too wet or too dry, and they stank of mould and decay. During the previous winter, snow had caused roofs to collapse, and some major restoration had been necessary – a task undertaken by the carpenter Robert de Blaston, on the understanding that one house would be his when it was completed. Matilde was looking forward to the day when the carpenter, his wife and their children moved into their own home, and so was Bartholomew. He longed to have her to himself again.

Since he was close, he walked to her house, and knocked on the door. The metal hinges gleamed like gold, and the wood had been polished so that he could all but see his face in it. He smiled. Blaston's brood were not taking Matilde for granted, and were doing small tasks to repay her for her hospitality.

Matilde was pleased to see Bartholomew, while Yolande immediately removed herself to the pantry at the back, where delicious smells indicated there was a meat stew simmering. She took one baby with her, and called to another to follow, but Bartholomew and Matilde were still accompanied by at least three children he could see, and a peculiar sensation at the back of his head made him suspect there were more hiding on the stairs. Within moments, they heard the sound of water splashing, and Matilde raised her eyes heavenward.

'Yolande has cleaned my pans at least three times today.

If she continues to scrub them so often, she will scour through their bases.'

'Would you like to go for a walk?' asked Bartholomew, unnerved by so many silent watchers.

'It is raining,' said Matilde with a laugh. 'But do not mind the children. They are always good when you are here. In fact, I am thinking of asking you to move in, too, because they are never so demure the rest of the time.' She ruffled the hair of the one who sat at her feet.

'We should introduce them to Dickon Tulyet,' said Bartholomew. 'He could learn from them how to behave when there are guests in the house.'

'Dickon is a reformed character,' said Matilde. 'He has met his match.'

'Did the Devil pay him a visit, then?'

'In a manner of speaking. Julianna Mortimer invited him to play with her daughter – the child that came from her marriage to Master Langelee – and Dickon has not misbehaved since. If he screams now, his mother only needs mention a visit to Julianna and he becomes as quiet as a lamb. I would not accept *her* as a patient, if I were you, Matthew. Leave her for Rougham.' Her expression was angry, and Bartholomew supposed she had heard the accusations Rougham had made about Warde. He did not want to discuss it, so said the first thing that came into his head.

'Michael appointed me as his Corpse Examiner last week,' he said, before realising that such a topic was hardly suitable for the ears of small children.

'I heard,' said Matilde. 'It is no more than you deserve, although I imagine you dislike being at his beck and call in an official capacity.'

'I need the money it pays. Most of my wealthy patients have gone to Rougham or Paxtone, and I cannot buy the medicines I need for the others without their fees.'

'You are a good man, Matthew,' said Matilde. 'I heard you gave your last penny to make a potion for Una, and you have not charged Isnard for your services. I would help you, but . . .' Her eyes strayed significantly to the child who had made itself comfortable on her feet. She changed the subject. 'I hear you earned another fourpence last night.'

'Warde from Valence Marie,' said Bartholomew. 'He died of coughing.'

'Is that natural?' asked Matilde. 'I have never heard of such a thing.'

'It is not impossible,' said Bartholomew. 'But I did not examine him properly when he was alive, so it is difficult to say what happened.'

'Rougham did not examine him properly, either,' said Matilde with distaste. 'He calculated a horoscope, but he did not put an ear to Warde's chest and listen to the sounds within, as you do.'

'How do you know?' asked Bartholomew curiously. 'Surely you were not present when Warde summoned Rougham for a consultation?'

'Neither was Rougham,' said Matilde. 'The whole thing was conducted through a messenger – young Alfred, here.' She nodded to a black-haired boy of nine years or so, who was sitting near the hearth, listening to the conversation with his chin resting on his cupped hands. 'Tell him, Alfred.'

'The scholars at Valence Marie often use me if they want messages delivered,' said Alfred proudly. 'They say I am honest and reliable. Master Warde paid me a penny for taking spoken missives to Doctor Rougham and carrying others back. I remember everything they said.'

'You do?' asked Bartholomew uncomfortably. He felt he was prying into Rougham's business, and had no wish to hear what had transpired between him and his patient, but Alfred was flattered to be asked for information and was already speaking.

333

'First, Rougham asked Warde whether he had pains in the chest. Warde replied there were none. Then Rougham asked whether coughing brought juices, and Warde replied that his flame was dry.'

'Phlegm,' corrected Bartholomew absently.

'Next, Rougham asked if Warde had a bleeding of the throat, and Warde said no. I was running between Valence Marie and Gonville for most of the afternoon.'

'He was exhausted when he came home,' confirmed Matilde. 'So, you see, Rougham no more examined Warde than you did. Perhaps you can counter his accusations against you by saying he was negligent, and that he should have taken the time to visit Warde.'

'But Warde's cough was not serious. I do not think Rougham did anything terribly wrong.'

'Would you question a patient about his symptoms by using a child to relay messages?'

'No, but—'

'Would you visit that person, or ask him to call on you?'

'Yes, and—'

'Well, there you are, then. You are the town's best physician, and if *you* would not act the way Rougham did, then your University logic leads me to conclude that *he* made a mistake.'

'Perhaps he did,' said Bartholomew. 'But this business will blow over soon, and I do not want to make a worse enemy of Rougham. We may have to work here together for a very long time, and we do not like each other as it is.'

'If Rougham's negligence killed Warde, then you should tell people,' insisted Matilde. 'It would be unethical not to. Folk will not want a physician who is careless, and they will use you instead.'

'That is precisely why I cannot say anything. Rougham would claim I was making accusations to poach his patients.'

334

'But he has been doing that to you,' objected Matilde. 'He regularly tells people that he considers your methods anathema. You must act to protect your reputation.'

'People can decide for themselves who they employ. I do not want to engage in verbal battles with him to see who is the more popular. I have neither the time nor the energy for that sort of thing.'

Her chin jutted out defiantly. 'He had better not say anything horrible about you in *my* hearing, or I shall tell him a few truths.'

Fortunately for Rougham, Bartholomew knew their paths were unlikely to cross, and so was not unduly worried about the possibility of an unseemly row between Gonville's Master of Medicine and the head of the Guild of Frail Sisters. He sighed, and stretched his legs towards the fire, feeling more relaxed than he had been for some time. A child immediately scrambled into his lap and curled against him like a cat. He hugged it to him, touched by its easy trust.

'So, how *did* Warde die?' pressed Matilde. 'The cough was minor – both you and Rougham agree on that. But he was a Commissioner. Do you think one of the interested parties killed him? By poison, perhaps?'

'Michael wondered that, but I do not see how Warde could have been poisoned. He ate and drank the same things as everyone else last night.'

'What about the Water of Snails?'

Bartholomew regarded her askance. 'Are you suggesting Rougham killed him? You sound like Quenhyth and Redmeadow, determined to have him indicted of some crime – any crime.'

'It was Quenhyth who started me thinking. We met on the High Street this morning, and he was beside himself with fury that Rougham should have accused you of killing Warde when he is such a poor physician himself.'

Bartholomew smiled indulgently. 'Quenhyth is young and sees matters in black and white.'

'But think about Rougham's behaviour, Matthew. I heard what happened from Yolande, who had it from Master Thorpe himself. Rougham sent Warde this Water of Snails, but when Master Thorpe confronted him, Rougham denied it. Yet the phial was there with the message – in Rougham's hand – for all to see.'

'I suppose he sent it and forgot what he had done.' He was about to add Rougham's own solution – that one of his students was responsible – when Matilde gave a sharp, derisive laugh.

'Do you really believe that? Is he a half-wit, then – dispensing cures, then forgetting about them? I do not think so! He either sent that note and the Water of Snails, and denies that he did so for sinister reasons. Or, he did not, and someone is trying to make him look guilty of murder.'

Bartholomew gazed at her. 'Now *you* are jumping to wild conclusions! There is no evidence to allow you to make those sorts of assumptions.'

'You are overly innocent,' declared Matilde. 'You will find that Rougham killed Warde.'

'Why?' asked Bartholomew. 'What reason could Rougham have for killing a wealthy patient? As far as he is concerned, Warde's death represents a sizeable loss of income.'

'Because he wanted to strike at the King's Commission. He is afraid they will find in favour of the King's Mill – against Mortimer. Since Gonville Hall has interests in Mortimer's Mill, Rougham cannot allow that to happen.'

Bartholomew was astounded. 'But Pulham told Michael that Gonville does *not* have interests in Mortimer's Mill.' He reconsidered, even as he spoke. Master Thorpe had mentioned that Gonville had been promised a handsome donation for their chapel if they won the Mortimers' case.

Michael had intended to ask him about it, but most of the Gonville Fellows were in Ely, summoned there by the Bishop in relation to some tedious issue about property rights.

'Pulham was lying,' said Matilde. 'Why do you think the Mortimers hired scholars from Gonville to represent them? It is not just because they are good with the law; it is because Gonville have a vested interest in seeing the Mortimers win, just as Lavenham and Bernarde have a vested interest in seeing the King's Mill win. It means Gonville will fight all the harder for their client's victory.'

'How is Bess?' asked Bartholomew, thinking he had better change the subject if he did not want to quarrel with her. Even if she was right, and Gonville did have a promise of handsome rewards, there was still no good reason – or one he could see, at least – for Rougham to kill Warde. Physicians simply did not dispatch their patients, and that was that. 'Have you discovered any more about her?'

'Not yet,' said Matilde shortly, aware that she was being steered on to safer ground. 'I have asked the Sisters to listen for rumours about her, but it appears she just arrived one morning and started to ask about her man. That is all anyone knows.'

'And what about her gold?' asked Bartholomew. 'Do you know how she came by that?'

'I know how she did *not* come by it. Even the most generous of clients would not give Bess more than a penny for her services. She carried her small fortune in a purse, but I do not think it is wise for lone women to have purses. They represent too obvious a target for robbers, so I sewed her gold into her cloak. It did not keep it safe, though, because someone still stole it from her.'

As she spoke, Alfred leapt to his feet and pulled something from a shelf over the hearth, which he handed to Bartholomew.

'Her money came in this?' asked Bartholomew, inspecting the small leather pouch. He recognised it at once, with its letter D inside a pot. 'It belonged to Deschalers. He dropped it on the High Street a few days ago, and I retrieved for him. *He* must have given Bess her gold.'

'I wonder why?' said Matilde, bemused. 'I told you he was fastidious about his women. He would never have taken Bess to his bed. And, furthermore, Yolande tells me his recent illness made him disinclined to see anyone, even his favourites.'

Bartholomew scratched his head. 'Deschalers was definitely leading Bess somewhere the day before he died. Perhaps he gave her the money then. The timing is about right. And this purse tells us for certain that he was her secret benefactor. Now we need to find out why.'

'We can hardly ask him,' said Matilde. 'And Julianna will be hopeless. She is only interested in things that affect her. She would not know and would not care why her uncle pressed gold on a beggar-woman the day before he died.'

Bartholomew sighed in frustration. 'Who is Bess? I am sure that if we knew, then much of this business would become clear, and we would understand exactly who killed Deschalers and Bottisham – and why.'

Bartholomew enjoyed teaching. He was good at it, and his students usually enjoyed the challenges he set them, with his streams of questions and unpredictable changes of subject. And he loved debating with them once they had mastered a text, cross-examining them and seeing whether they could use their knowledge to present alternative views set out in other commentaries. That Monday they were going to discuss the uses and virtues of grapes in the diet, as described by Galen. Although this was a basic subject, involving little controversy, Redmeadow had been arming himself for a good argument, while Quenhyth had been to the King's Hall library to see what Bacon had to say on the subject.

Deynman, meanwhile, who still had not mastered the knack of independent research, had visited several vineyards and amassed an array of different wines. Bartholomew helped him carry his wares to the hall, supposing he could use them to demonstrate Galen's contention that new, sweeter wines were processed into urine more quickly than sour or sharp ones. They had just reached the stairs when Deynman happened to glance across the courtyard.

'Oh, no!' the student cried in dismay. 'What is *he* doing here?'

Bartholomew was horrified to see Thorpe strolling towards them, looking quite at home and totally oblivious to the scowls and unwelcoming comments of Michaelhouse's scholars. Michael joined Bartholomew, and together they waited for Thorpe to reach them.

'What do you want?' demanded Michael coldly.

'I have come to hear Doctor Bartholomew lecture on Galen,' said Thorpe, an innocent expression on his face. 'I am recommended by Paxtone of King's Hall. I have his letter here.'

He produced a parchment from his scrip with a flourish. Michael snatched it away and scanned its contents, scratching his chin so that his fingernails rasped in the bristles.

'Very well,' he said, handing it back. 'But behave yourself. One hint of trouble and you are out.'

'Do not fear,' said Thorpe insolently. 'I have no intention of causing trouble here.'

Bartholomew glanced at him sharply, catching the implication that he intended to cause trouble elsewhere, but Thorpe merely smiled and pushed past them to the hall. Deynman promptly abandoned his wines and followed, muttering to Bartholomew that he would watch him like a hawk with a rabbit.

'Yes, but which is which?' said Michael, amused that a simple lad like Deynman should think he was a match for Thorpe.

'Why did you let him in?' asked Bartholomew. 'I do not want him in my lecture. I have students who are keen to learn, and I cannot have them distracted because they think he is going to set fire to the College or draw a crossbow from under his cloak.'

'The letter from Paxtone was genuine. He said Thorpe has expressed an interest in Galen's dietary regimes, and he knows you teach the subject on Mondays. He asked us to give him a chance, and allow him to sit quietly at the back of your class.'

'Very well,' said Bartholomew unhappily. 'But Thorpe will be disappointed if he thinks I am going to talk about how to kill people with grapes. My lecture is about how they can be used to improve health, not destroy it.'

'I will be watching him, too. Still, I doubt he will want to attend more than one of your diatribes on diet.' He rubbed his stomach ruefully, to indicate he was still hungry after being encouraged not to eat his fourth piece of bread at breakfast that morning.

Bartholomew entered the hall, where benches were arranged ready for teaching. He had about thirty students. Some were his own, but there were also those who had been sent by Paxtone and other masters. He too farmed out his students on occasion – there was no one as good as Paxtone for teaching basic Aristotelian physiology, while Lynton of Peterhouse gave solid instruction on the calculation of horoscopes.

It was not long before he forgot the smouldering presence at the rear of his class, enjoying the liveliness of his own students and their willingness to learn. Quenhyth grew

340

frantic as he struggled to write down every word his teacher spoke, while Redmeadow showed he had learned his texts well, asking questions and making astute observations.

Deynman's wine caused some amusement but, despite the levity, Bartholomew knew the scholars would remember the points he made about the different brews and their benefits or otherwise to the kidneys and bladder. It did not seem long before the bell rang to announce the end of lessons, and the students trooped out of the hall, clattering down the steps and talking in loud voices. When Bartholomew recalled that a killer had been in his class, he was obliged to run back up the stairs to ensure Thorpe had left, but the hall was empty and so was the conclave. Since there was nowhere else for Thorpe to be, the physician assumed he had slunk quietly away.

He felt the need for a few moments of peace before he returned to his room, so he headed for the orchard, pulling the scroll by Trotula from his bag as he went. He had been busy since Matilde had given it to him, and had not had the opportunity to inspect it properly. However, he had done no more than open the garden gate when he heard voices.

' . . . with Water of Snails,' one was saying. 'Or so he says.'

'Rougham often prescribes it, actually,' replied the second. 'Especially when there are extenuating circumstances. In this case, there definitely were, and . . .'

Bartholomew did not want to hear any more, and turned to leave. But as he did so, the latch clanked and the voices were immediately stilled. Then came the sound of running feet.

Thinking there was no need for flight if the meeting was innocent, Bartholomew set off in pursuit. He saw someone struggling with the gate that led to St Michael's Lane. It was hauled open, and there was another clatter of footsteps. Then silence. By the time he reached the door and shot into the lane, the pair were just turning into the High Street. He walked back to the garden, and replaced the bar. He had recognised Paxtone's lumbering gait immediately, and could only assume his fleeter-footed companion was Wynewyk. Troubled that they should feel the need to run from him, he tucked the Trotula under his arm and returned to his room, no longer in the mood for solitary reading.

'I assume Thorpe's presence was uneventful?' asked Michael, joining him there. 'I heard no quarrels or violent disputes – at least, none out of the ordinary. Your Monday lectures are always a little lively. I wish my theologians were as animated over their learning.'

'Theology is not a very interesting subject, Brother,' said Bartholomew carelessly, his mind still on Paxtone and Wynewyk. 'So you cannot expect tense excitement. But medicine—'

'A curious thing happened this morning,' interrupted Michael. 'I had a letter from Dick Tulyet, telling me he could not accept my invitation to the midday meal at Michaelhouse today.'

'Wise man. I saw Agatha picking nettles again this morning.'

'But I did not invite him,' said Michael, bemused. 'I would not – not the way our kitchens are at the moment. It is rather embarrassing. I suppose he must have received an invitation from someone else, and assumed it was me. Damn! Here come your wretched students. Do I have time to hide?'

'The rumours persist that Rougham accused you of killing Warde,' said Quenhyth without preamble, as he sat down next to Bartholomew. The physician noticed that the lad's nails had been bitten to the quick, and some had bled. 'But I have been telling anyone *I* meet that you are an honourable man, and would probably never murder anyone.'

342

'Thank you,' said Bartholomew dryly.

'You are welcome. However, I have also been pointing out that the same cannot be said for Rougham, and that I would sooner take physic from the Devil than from him.'

'I thought they were one and the same,' said Michael with a chuckle.

Bartholomew sighed. 'I know Rougham offended you the other day, Quenhyth, but abusing him will help no one. He will embarrass you publicly again, if you are not careful.'

'You stood up for me,' said Quenhyth warmly. 'You told that vile slug that he was wrong and that I was right. That is probably why he has been spreading nasty tales about you. But *he* is the one who kills for worldly goods, not you.'

'Kills for worldly goods?' echoed Bartholomew, puzzled. 'I do not recall either of us levelling that particular accusation at each other.'

'Have you not heard?' asked Redmeadow, his eyes round. 'Master Thorpe read Warde's will this morning, and Warde left his copy of Euclid's *Elementa* – books seven to ten – to you. It is a standard arithmetic text, dealing with the properties of numbers.'

'He knows what it is,' said Michael. 'He used it to teach you the Quadrivium, remember?'

Redmeadow grinned sheepishly. 'Of course. But now you have a copy of your own, and will not have to borrow Peterhouse's. You are doing well at the moment. First, Brother Michael gave you the Bacon, then Matilde bought you the scroll of Trotula's writings, and now you have Euclid.'

Although there was no harm in the lad's observations, they left Bartholomew with a sense of unease, as if Redmeadow perhaps entertained the notion that his teacher *had* killed Warde in order to secure the Euclid. He decided to decline Warde's bequest, or perhaps donate

343

it to the University, so others would not think the same thing, particularly with Rougham spreading his poisonous lies.

Michael touched his arm. 'That is good news, Matt, although I had no idea that you and Warde were such friends. Why did he go to Rougham for his physic, if he liked you so well?'

'He preferred Rougham's horoscopes to my suggestions for his diet,' said Bartholomew.

'I can understand that,' said Michael with feeling. 'Perhaps I should do likewise.'

'Only if you do not mind having medicines prescribed after an exchange of messages carried by children,' said Redmeadow superiorly. He nodded knowledgeably at Michael's surprise. 'Young Alfred de Blaston told me about Rougham's so-called consultation with Warde while we waited in Lavenham's shop together the other day. I was collecting supplies for Doctor Bartholomew, and he was waiting for a blackcurrant syrup for Warde.'

'You should be careful,' warned Bartholomew. 'Rougham will complain to the Chancellor if he learns you are collecting tales about him. And you do not want Tynkell to dismiss you.'

'Tynkell would not do that!' cried Redmeadow. He appealed to Michael. 'Would he?'

Michael nodded. 'Faced with a choice between keeping Rougham or you? Of course Tynkell will choose Rougham. We do not have so many masters of medicine that we can afford them to leave in sulky tantrums over students who are easily replaceable.' He patted Redmeadow's arm. 'But do not fret over Rougham. He is not worth the aggravation. Ignore him, and forget his insults. There will be ways to repay him in the future. I may even help you myself.'

'You will?' asked Quenhyth eagerly.

'Oh, yes. I shall not stand by and allow that arrogant

villain to insult my closest friend. It will irk Rougham deeply to learn that Warde left the Euclid to Matt, and not to his own physician – and we shall certainly make something of *that* small fact.'

'I have no idea why Warde did that,' said Bartholomew, disliking Michael teaching his students how to be subversive. It might prove a dangerous weapon in their inexperienced hands.

'I do,' said Redmeadow brightly. 'Warde explained it in his will, and I heard Master Thorpe telling his son about it in the High Street later.'

'You seem to be party to a large number of private conversations,' said Bartholomew, recalling how he had eavesdropped on the Mortimers, too. 'You are worse than Agatha for gossip.'

'She says I am her equal,' said Redmeadow with pride, although Bartholomew had not meant it to be a compliment.

'You heard Master Thorpe and his son talking?' asked Michael, not caring how Redmeadow had garnered his information, only that he shared it. 'I was under the impression that they barely acknowledge each other.'

'They were quarrelling,' said Redmeadow. 'Master Thorpe was telling Rob what was in Warde's will because he said he had done something similar.'

'I do not understand,' said Michael.

'Warde said in his will that Doctor Bartholomew is the only physician who will make proper use of the Euclid,' explained Redmeadow. 'He said Rougham, Lynton and Paxtone do not take arithmetic seriously, and he wanted his books to go where they would do some good.'

'He is right,' said Michael, recalling several lengthy discussions between Bartholomew and Warde on just this subject. 'Matt alone of the Cambridge physicians is interested in mathematics. But why did Master Thorpe tell his son this, when they can barely afford to be civil to each other?'

'It was part of the fight,' said Redmeadow, a little condescendingly. 'Rob asked Master Thorpe what *he* might expect to inherit when Master Thorpe himself died – he was being nasty, talking enthusiastically about his father's death.'

'Really,' said Michael drolly. 'He was being unkind? You do surprise me.'

Redmeadow flushed. 'I am sorry. I am so used to pointing out the obvious to Deynman that now I tend to do it for everyone. But, to continue with what I heard, Master Thorpe told Rob that all his property was willed to worthy causes – just as Warde's had been. The stuff about Warde's bequest to Doctor Bartholomew – about their mutual love of arithmetic – came out when Master Thorpe informed Rob that he was disinherited.'

Michael sighed. 'That was rash. Rob is a lad who might kill over that sort of thing.'

'But he is also the kind to kill for an inheritance,' said Bartholomew. 'Now he knows he does not have one, there is no point in making an end of his father. Master Thorpe probably knew exactly what he was doing.'

CHAPTER 9

Michael was intrigued by the fact that Paxtone and Wynewyk had fled the orchard when they thought they were about to be caught there together, but still declined to tackle either scholar until he had something more specific to ask them. But the more Bartholomew thought about their furtive, secret discussion concerning the Water of Snails and Rougham, the more worried he became. What if Rougham *was* innocent of giving the medicine to Warde, as he claimed, and Paxtone had been the one to send it, knowing it might aggravate Warde's cough to danger point? Bartholomew rubbed a hand through his hair. But Rougham's writing had been on the accompanying note. And why would Paxtone do such a thing to Warde, anyway?

Then he recalled another conversation he had overheard in the orchard – some five or six days ago now. Paxtone had been talking to Wynewyk about Rougham, and his words were still etched clearly in Bartholomew's mind: 'Rougham foils me at every turn, and is making a damned nuisance of himself. I may be forced to take some radical steps.' Had Paxtone taken 'radical steps' against Rougham, by dispensing remedies to unsuspecting patients in his name? And what business of Paxtone's had Rougham been foiling 'at every turn'?

From the outset, Bartholomew had remained firm in his belief that Warde's death had been due to natural causes – regardless of what his students and Matilde, and even Rougham, had claimed – but now doubts began to clamour at him. It was odd for an otherwise healthy man to die of a cough, and it was also odd that Warde's sudden and dramatic decline had occurred after swallowing Water of Snails. But Bartholomew's years as a physician had taught him that odd and inexplicable things happened to the human body all the time, so was he reading too much into the matter? However, Paxtone's words to Wynewyk in the orchard continued to nag at him.

'Paxtone knows about poisons, because he is a physician,' he said aloud. 'He could easily have slipped something toxic to Bosel and Warde – and even to Deschalers – by telling them it would improve their health. And while Rougham and I destroy each other with accusations, he will encourage all our bewildered and wary patients to employ him instead.'

'You think Paxtone is killing people in order to expand his practice?' asked Michael, startled. 'He does not seem the kind of man to stoop to those depths, Matt. I thought you liked him.'

'I do!' Bartholomew accepted that acquiring more patients was an unusual motive for murder – and that Paxtone was hardly likely to use someone like Wynewyk to help him to do it – but there was no other solution that he could see. 'How else can we explain his behaviour?'

Michael made no bones about the fact that he thought his friend was over-reacting. 'There is no point in confronting him – or Wynewyk,' he said practically. 'You heard them discussing Rougham and the Water of Snails together, but so what? Half the town is speculating about that this morning.'

'So we do nothing?'

'We watch and wait. They will reveal themselves eventually, and then we will have our answers. They do not know you are suspicious of them, so we have some advantage.'

'They *do* know, Brother – or Paxtone does. He said as

348

much when I overheard them last week.'

But Michael still refused to act, and even claimed that a member of his own College and a respected *medicus* would never engage in anything overtly untoward, and that although their behaviour was suspicious and odd, there was probably nothing illegal going on. Bartholomew gaped at him, knowing from experience that decent-seeming men often indulged themselves in all manner of heinous deeds, but he saw the monk would not be convinced otherwise, and there was no point in pressing the matter further. Unhappily, he tried to put it from his mind.

A while later, when the light of late afternoon began to fade into the gentler hues of early evening, he heard raised voices coming from the College's main gate. He abandoned his reading and went to look through the window to see what was happening. His students were in the room with him, but Redmeadow and Quenhyth were studying, and neither so much as glanced up at the commotion. Deynman, however, readily abandoned his Dioscorides and came to stand next to him.

Walter was hurrying across the yard towards them, his cockerel tucked under his arm. It did not look pleased when the porter broke into a trot and it found itself vigorously jarred, and Bartholomew did not think he had ever seen a more outraged expression on the face of a bird. Walter burst into the hallway and hammered on Bartholomew's door.

'Lenne's son has just been,' he said, clutching his pet firmly. 'He wants you to visit his mother's house. He says there is something seriously amiss, and asks if you will go at once. No, Bird!'

The chicken had wriggled out of his grasp and shot into Bartholomew's chamber. It fluttered straight under the bed, where it knew it would be difficult to oust. Bartholomew snatched up his medicine bag and headed for the door, content to let his students deal with the feathered intruder. Deynman had already grabbed a sword to encourage it out, and Walter was screeching his horror that a sharp implement might hurt it.

'I hope so,' muttered Deynman, poking furiously. 'It does not deserve to be in a College like Michaelhouse, with its dirty manners and unwelcome visitations. It should be at Valence Marie, where no one cares whether it wipes its teeth on the tablecloth.'

'Hens do not have teeth,' said Redmeadow, jumping forward to prevent the agitated Walter from hurling himself on to Deynman's back.

'Do not let it near my books,' warned Bartholomew as he left. He started to run across the yard, not surprised when he heard footsteps behind him and saw Quenhyth following. Redmeadow was not far behind, more than happy to let Deynman manage Bird and its angry owner alone.

'You might need us,' said Redmeadow breathlessly, trying to keep up with the rapid pace Bartholomew was setting. 'And I have been reading about diseases of the lungs all afternoon.'

They dashed up St Michael's Lane, then along the High Street and left into Shoemaker Row, where the cobblers were beginning to close their shops for the night. Awnings were lowered, windows shuttered, wares carried inside, and the familiar tap of hammers on leather was stilled.

The door was opened immediately and they were ushered inside. As usual, the room was hazy with smoke, and the remains of a simple meal – weak broth and a crust of bread – sat on a stone by the hearth. Mistress Lenne lay on her bed, the covers folded carefully around her. The room had been swept and dusted, and her few belongings arranged neatly on the shelves. Her son had not been idle, and had ensured she would not die in a house that was dirty or untidy.

'She is not breathing as she should,' said Lenne, gesturing to the pale, sunken-eyed figure. There was panic in his eyes. 'I do not know what to do.'

'You can summon a priest,' said Bartholomew, crouching next to the old woman and taking one of her bony wrists to feel a weak, thready pulse that beat erratically. 'You have made her comfortable and she is not in pain. There is no more either of us can do now.'

'Are you sure?' asked Lenne, aghast. 'So soon?'

'I am sorry,' said Bartholomew, standing. 'It will not be long now.'

'This is my fault,' whispered Lenne, stricken. 'I should not have done what she asked.'

'What?' asked Bartholomew, hoping he was not about to be burdened with the confession that Lenne had given her some potion prescribed by Rougham – or by Paxtone, for that matter.

'She asked me to carry her to St Mary the Great,' said Lenne tearfully. 'She wanted to visit the Hand of Justice. I told her I did not want to take her, but she begged me so pitifully.'

'You did the right thing,' said Bartholomew kindly. 'Perhaps the journey did hasten her end, but I doubt she would have lived beyond tomorrow anyway. You did what she asked, and I am sure she appreciates that.'

'I thought the Hand might save her,' whispered Lenne. 'I thought it might be moved by her suffering, and reach out to cure her. But I was wrong.'

'I do not think she wants a cure,' said Bartholomew, wondering what had induced the old woman to undertake a painful and exhausting journey in the last hours of her life. He was certain it was not to ask for her own recovery, since she had cared little about that after her husband's death. Perhaps it was to ask forgiveness for ancient sins – long forgotten by humans, but ones she feared would be remembered when her soul was weighed.

Lenne's eyes filled with tears. Quenhyth offered to fetch a priest, then slipped quietly out of the house when Lenne was unable to reply. Soon he returned with Father William, whom he had spotted leaving St Mary the Great after a hard day of supervising access to the Hand of Justice. William knelt next to Mistress Lenne, and began the final absolution. He spoke in a confident, booming voice that attracted a small group of neighbours, who removed hats and crossed themselves, and stood in a silent, deferential semicircle outside to wait for the end.

It was not long before William completed his business – his absolutions were almost as rapid as his masses, although people liked them because what they lacked in length they more than compensated for in volume. He promised to pray for her that night, then headed for the door, graciously declining Lenne's offer of a penny for his services. Before he left, he took Bartholomew's arm and pulled him to one side.

'Sheriff Tulyet took that poison business seriously,' he whispered in the physician's ear.

'What poison business?' asked Bartholomew, his attention still fixed on his patient. 'Bosel?'

William sighed in gusty exasperation. 'Where Rougham accused you of killing Warde with angelica, but then was caught delivering noxious potions himself. Rougham was taken to the Castle this afternoon, to answer questions about his Water of Snails.'

Bartholomew stared at him. 'Tulyet cannot do that. Rougham is a scholar, and is bound by the canon law of the Church. The University will riot for certain if it thinks the town is interrogating its clerks.'

'It was Rougham's own fault. He refused to acknowledge Brother Michael's authority. He said Michael is your friend,

352

and is therefore biased. Michael called his bluff, and turned the matter over to Tulyet. But Tulyet could not prove Rougham murdered Warde.'

'I am not surprised. There is no evidence to suggest Warde was poisoned.' But even as he spoke, he knew the doubt showed in his face.

'Are you sure about that?' demanded William, noticing it. 'Did you assess the *exact* nature of the substance in Rougham's so-called Water of Snails?'

'No, but—'

'The whole incident is highly suspicious,' William went on. 'You have a man with a minor ailment, who becomes disheartened when his own physician is unable to make him well. So, he hires a second physician. Meanwhile, the first physician sends him a potion, which the patient takes and promptly expires. The first physician denies sending the potion, and accuses the second physician of the crime *he* committed.'

'I am not sure it happened quite like that,' said Bartholomew. 'It was—'

'Most folk believe Rougham murdered Warde,' said Quenhyth confidently. 'He *is* the kind of fellow to kill, then watch an innocent colleague hanged for his crime.'

'I agree,' said William. He nodded towards Mistress Lenne. 'But you have work to do, Matthew. We can discuss this later, over a cup of mulled ale in the conclave.'

Bartholomew returned to the sickbed and put his head to his patient's chest to listen to her heartbeat. It was slow and weak, and he knew it would stop altogether in a matter of moments.

'Say your farewells,' he said softly to Lenne. 'She may still be able to hear you.'

'Now?' asked Lenne fearfully.

Bartholomew nodded, and moved away to give him some privacy. Quenhyth rubbed a sleeve across his eyes and sniffed as Lenne began to tell his mother that he loved her.

'I do not know how you do this,' Redmeadow whispered to Bartholomew in a strangled voice. 'How can you hear these things day after day, and still want to be a physician?'

'Being at a deathbed is part of the service you must provide for a patient. You need to ensure she is not in pain, and that she is comfortable. And then you must tell her kinsmen when she is finally dead, so they can prepare her for the grave. It is not unknown for them to start the process while she is still alive, unless a physician is on hand.'

'This is not right,' whispered Quenhyth unsteadily, as Lenne began to tell his mother in a broken voice how much he would miss her, and that his world would be a sad place without her smile. 'She should not be dying. This is Thomas Mortimer's fault, because of what he did to her husband.'

'Not now, Quenhyth,' said Bartholomew softly. 'And not here, either. I think she has gone. Go to her, and put this piece of polished pewter near her mouth. If she is breathing, it will mist over. Then listen to her chest, and see whether you can hear her heart beating.'

'Me?' asked Quenhyth in horror.

Bartholomew nodded. 'You will have to do it sooner or later, and this is as good a time as any. It is quiet, and you will find it easy to test for the signs of life.'

'No,' said Quenhyth, backing away. He swallowed hard. 'Redmeadow can do it, and I will take the next case.'

'All right,' agreed Redmeadow shakily. His face was white and, when he raised one trembling hand to smooth down his ginger hair in preparation for what he was about to do, Bartholomew noticed that the sleeve of his tunic was still peppered with the pale substance he had noticed before, and that Matilde had remarked upon.

Bartholomew took Lenne's arm and sat him at the table,

offering him a cup of strong wine in a vain attempt to calm some of his distraught sobs. Meanwhile, Redmeadow held the pewter at Mistress Lenne's mouth for so long that Bartholomew began to wonder whether he had forgotten what to do next, but eventually the student placed his tousled head against her chest and listened as hard as he could, eyes screwed tightly closed as he concentrated.

'She has gone,' he said, wincing when Lenne began to weep afresh. He tucked the blankets around the old lady's shoulders, as though she was being put to bed, then stood with his hands dangling helplessly at his side. 'We cannot do any more for her.'

Both Redmeadow and Quenhyth were unusually silent when they left the Lenne house a little later. Neighbours had come to help with the grim ritual of preparing the body for burial, and Bartholomew saw the distressed Lenne was in kind and competent hands. Redmeadow was generally full of chatter and questions after they had visited patients, sometimes to the point of aggravation, but he said nothing at all as they walked back to Michael-house. Quenhyth excused himself and virtually fled, tears pooling in his eyes. He made no attempt to disguise the fact that he intended to head straight for a tavern for a fortifying drink. Since he never broke the University's rules, Bartholomew saw the experience had shaken him badly.

Unfortunately, just as Bartholomew and Redmeadow were passing the Brazen George – both turning a blind eye as Quenhyth aimed for a discreet back entrance – Thomas Mortimer emerged through the front door. The miller was not drunk, but he was not sober, either, and had reached a point between the two states that rendered him dangerous, moody and unpredictable. Redmeadow stopped dead in his tracks and regarded him with considerable venom. Bartholomew grabbed his arm and tried to drag him on, not wanting a confrontation that might end in violence.

'No!' shouted Redmeadow, pulling away from his teacher. When he pointed at Mortimer, his finger shook with rage, and Bartholomew was reminded that the lad possessed a fiery temper to go with his flaming red hair. 'That man is a killer. He murdered Mistress Lenne.'

'I do not know the woman,' said Mortimer, beginning to walk away. It was the wrong thing to say.

'That is because you are a monster!' yelled Redmeadow, pushing Bartholomew away a second time. 'You are a devil, who kills the innocent and leaves behind him a trail of misery and sorrow. You are like the Death – and just as welcome.'

Mortimer took a threatening step towards him, but the student held his ground. Bartholomew saw that Redmeadow's face glistened wet with tears. Behind Mortimer, the inn door opened again and Edward stepped out with a couple of his cousins. He saw his uncle engaged in an altercation with a student, and his face broke into an amused grin.

'Come home,' said Bartholomew softly to Redmeadow. 'We cannot win this fight. Take your complaint to Sheriff Tulyet in the morning, and let him see justice done.'

'Justice!' sneered Redmeadow contemptuously. 'What do we know of justice in Cambridge?'

'*I* know about it,' said Thomas Mortimer, deliberately inflammatory. 'I prayed to the Hand that I would be free of accusations from the likes of Mistress Lenne, and look what has happened. Her malicious tongue saw her sicken – and I am told she will die.'

'She *is* dead,' said Redmeadow hotly. 'A short time ago, and *you* are responsible.'

'She brought it on herself,' said Mortimer. 'It was not

my fault her husband wandered under my wheels, and I was more than patient with her wicked allegations. But the saints in Heaven have taken pity on me. Mistress Lenne is dead, and will not sully my good name again.'

'You have no good name,' shouted Redmeadow furiously. 'None of your miserable family do. Edward was the first to bring you disgrace, but evil will out, and the rest of you are following him down the road of infamy and wickedness. It is—'

'You insolent dog!' snarled Mortimer, advancing on Redmeadow with fury etched on his purple-veined face. Bartholomew stepped forward to reason with him, but was almost knocked from his feet as Edward launched an attack of his own. Before the physician could say or do anything to prevent it, he was embroiled in a brawl – he and Redmeadow pitched against four Mortimers.

He saw the glint of steel in the fading light. Edward had drawn a dagger. Hastily he groped in his bag for one of his surgical knives, but Edward knew what he was doing and darted forward with the weapon flashing. Bartholomew only just managed to raise the bag in time to prevent himself from being run through. Edward tore it from his hands and tossed it away, advancing relentlessly with the encouraging howls of his cousins ringing in his ears. Bartholomew recalled what both Redmeadow and Ufford had said about Edward: that during his exile he had learned fighting skills that made him a formidable opponent. And Bartholomew had allowed himself to be manoeuvred into a position where he was facing him alone, without so much as a stick to defend himself.

'It is just you and me, physician,' taunted Edward, beckoning him forward with one hand while he waved the dagger with the other. Bartholomew cursed Redmeadow for his hot temper. 'You have insulted and denigrated me ever since I returned, and it is time you paid for your insolence.'

He leapt forward again, and Bartholomew managed to grab his wrist, trying to shake the weapon from his grasp. Edward used his free hand to seize the physician by the throat. As the younger man's fingers started to tighten, Bartholomew used his greater size and strength to force him back against the wall. They crashed against it hard enough to make Edward grunt in pain. But it did not stop him for long – he tipped back his head, then brought it forward sharply, intending to break Bartholomew's nose with his forehead. Unfortunately for Edward, Bartholomew had seen this particular move before. He twisted away, turning Edward as he did so, and heard the man's head crack against the wall with considerable force. While Edward staggered, dazed, Bartholomew knocked the dagger from his hand.

But the Mortimer cousins were not willing to stand by and see one of their own defeated. They moved in quickly and Bartholomew saw they both carried knives. He wondered how many moments he would have on Earth before one of them speared him.

'If you kill him, you will have to kill me, too,' came a calm voice from the other side of the street. 'I will be a witness to your crime, and I will certainly testify against you. I will see you hang.' It was Master Thorpe of Valence Marie, who had been attending a mass in nearby St Mary the Great.

'You!' sneered Edward, turning on him with an eagerness that was frightening. Master Thorpe did not flinch. 'I will happily kill you as well, you traitorous pig!'

'But then you will have to kill me,' said Thomas Bingham, stepping out of the shadows and standing shoulder to shoulder with the Master of his College.

'And me,' said Pulham of Gonville Hall, swallowing hard. He lacked the calm courage of the Valence Marie men, and his eyes showed that he was terrified, but he stood firm nonetheless.

'And then you can *try* to kill me, but I run fast and will reach Michaelhouse and tell the Senior Proctor what you have done long before you complete your slaughter,' added Ufford, joining them. He still limped from his last encounter with Edward, so Bartholomew doubted he was telling the truth about his speed.

Other scholars began to move forward, too, none armed and all senior members of the University. There was Tynkell – standing apart, because even in a tense situation, no one wanted to be too close to him – and Paxtone from King's Hall. Michaelhouse was also represented, and Wynewyk, Kenyngham and Clippesby hurried to wait at Bartholomew's side. Bartholomew felt a sudden guilt for his suspicious thoughts about Wynewyk and Paxtone, who were prepared to risk their lives to save him.

There was a slight flicker in the shadows nearby. Bartholomew spotted Dame Pelagia, watching the scene with her bright, thoughtful eyes. He saw something glint in her hand, and supposed she held one of her famous throwing knives, ready to hurl it with deadly precision should the incident not end as she wanted. He sincerely hoped she was not a secret supporter of the Mortimer clan.

'Put up your weapons and go home before anyone is hurt,' said Kenyngham, ever the peace-maker. 'All of you.'

The Mortimers knew they were beaten. Rubbing his wrist and looking more dangerous than Bartholomew had ever seen him, Edward stalked away. Nervously, as though anticipating a sly attack from behind, his cousins followed. Thomas hurried after them, flinging Redmeadow away from him as he went. The student scrambled to his feet, and Clippesby was obliged to grab his arm to prevent him from running after the miller to fight him again. Kenyngham murmured softly in his ear until the lad's rage began to subside. When Bartholomew glanced into the shadows again, Dame Pelagia was nowhere to be seen.

'You are lucky we happened to pass when we did,' said Wynewyk, looking Bartholomew up and down to ensure he was unhurt. 'Master Thorpe heard the commotion, and suggested we investigate.'

Master Thorpe was white-faced, his bravado turning to shock now the danger had passed. 'You must not fight the Mortimers or my son, Bartholomew. You will not win against them.'

'But I did win,' objected Bartholomew, thinking he had comported himself rather well against a man whom everyone seemed to hold in such fear. 'But then his cousins joined in.'

'The Mortimers always fight as a pack,' said Bingham. 'Our students often complain about it.'

Tynkell fixed the physician with a stern stare. 'Cambridge teeters on the brink of serious civil unrest, and I had hoped my senior masters would know better than to add to the turmoil by brawling in a public place like the High Street.'

'I am sorry,' said Bartholomew, knowing it would be churlish to point out that the quarrel was none of his making.

'Good,' said Tynkell with a faint smile. 'That is what dark alleys are for.'

'It is not what *I* use them for,' said Wynewyk, leaving the other scholars very curious as to what the lawyer did do in the shady lanes to which the Chancellor referred. Bartholomew longed to ask, especially since Paxtone was there, but it did not seem appropriate after what they had just done for him.

'I owe you an apology, Matt,' said Paxtone, raising both hands in the air, as if in surrender. Bartholomew felt an immediate uneasiness. 'I should have asked you first, but he seemed so keen to learn about Galen that I felt it unprofessional not to help. On reflection, I think I was unwise.'

'Rob Thorpe?' asked Bartholomew, a little disappointed that that was all. 'And your letter recommending him? It did not matter. He sat at the back and I forgot he was there.'

'Perhaps my first impressions were right, then,' said Paxtone, relieved. 'He really did want to learn about Galen. After I had written it, I began to wonder whether I had done the right thing. Still, I shall not do it again. I do not think it is a good idea for us to let killers visit any College they fancy.'

Bartholomew wholly agreed with him. 'Do *you* often come to Michaelhouse?'

Paxtone seemed surprised by the question, then laughed, although Bartholomew was sure he caught a glitter of alarm in the man's eyes. 'That is a nice association of sentiments, Matt! I talk of killers in our Colleges and you ask me whether I frequent your own! But you know I do not. You are the only one I know from Michaelhouse, and you say you will not invite me to dine until the food improves.'

Bartholomew did not know what to make of his answer, but did not like the fact that Paxtone was lying to him. He grabbed Redmeadow by the scruff of his neck and hauled him away, leaving his colleagues proudly discussing their outwitting of the Mortimers.

'I am sorry, sir,' said Redmeadow sheepishly. 'I was upset about Mistress Lenne. I did not mean to drag you into a fight.'

'Well, do not do it again,' said Bartholomew shortly. 'We might not be so lucky next time.'

'I gave that murdering bastard a good punch in the eye, though,' added Redmeadow, with the shadow of a smile. 'And I saw blood. Perhaps I have done him more harm than he knows. Especially if he goes to Rougham for a cure.'

'I would not take Rougham's accusations too seriously,

Matt,' said Michael, as he and Bartholomew sat in the conclave the following morning after breakfast. 'Dick Tulyet saw them for what they are: feeble and transparent attempts to shift the blame for Warde's death on to someone else.'

'It is not Dick I am worried about,' said Bartholomew, stretching muscles that were stiff after the fracas of the previous evening. 'I am concerned about folk who do not know me so well, and who might believe Rougham is telling the truth. He has not stopped talking about me since Warde died on Saturday night – and it is now Tuesday. There is hardly a soul in Cambridge who has not heard that I killed Warde with angelica in order to inherit a book.'

'People are not stupid, Matt. They can see Rougham is a pompous, blustering fool. You are right not to respond in kind, because each new outbreak of accusations merely serves to underline the fact that he is a graceless, un-dignified oaf.'

'I do not understand why he has taken against me so rabidly. We have never been friends, but we have tolerated each other politely enough until just recently. What has changed?'

'He does not like your students, particularly Redmeadow and Quenhyth,' said Michael. 'But it is hard to condemn him for that – I do not like Quenhyth myself, while Redmeadow is a hot-headed brawler. He was also furious when you were made Corpse Examiner, because he wanted the post for himself. He says he needs the fees to help pay for Gonville's chapel.'

'But these are hardly good reasons to declare war on me.'

'Envy is a powerful emotion,' preached Michael. 'I told you before: he is jealous of your success.'

'And his claim that I caused Warde's death is unfair,' Bartholomew went on, barely hearing him. 'If *he* had not forced Warde to speak, then perhaps he might not have died.'

Michael's eyes were round. 'Are you accusing *him* of murder now? I thought you had Paxtone in mind for that particular crime.'

'I did . . . do. Well, perhaps.' Bartholomew rubbed his eyes tiredly. 'I do not know.'

Michael was thoughtful. 'You have not mentioned your suspicions about Rougham before. Perhaps I should ignore his refusal to acknowledge the authority of the Senior Proctor and arrest him anyway. Who knows? He may confess to killing Bottisham and Deschalers, too. After all, they were both his patients.'

'I doubt he killed them deliberately,' said Bartholomew wearily.

'A nail through the roof of the mouth is not deliberate?' asked Michael. 'What was he doing, then? Practising some obscure method of cautery, to effect a cure for Deschalers's canker?'

'I mean I do not think Rougham is their murderer. I would *like* him to be – to be rid of him and to solve the mystery at the same time – but he is so averse to surgery that taking a nail to someone would be anathema to him.' He smiled. 'Matilde is certain he killed Warde.'

'And his motive?' Michael answered his own question. 'To attack the King's Commission – partly because Gonville men are the Mortimers' lawyers, and partly because Gonville has been promised Mortimer money for their chapel if they win against the Millers' Society.'

'That is what she thinks. But there is no evidence that Warde was murdered. He just choked.'

'But you just said Rougham's actions brought about Warde's death. Make up your mind, Matt. Which is it: did Rougham kill Warde with his ministrations, or did he not?'

'Not on purpose. I think he genuinely believed he was

363

helping, although even Deynman would have known not to make a gagging man speak – and not to mention deathbeds and graves.'

'Then what about the Water of Snails?' asked Michael. 'Could that have killed him?'

'You mean did it poison him? *Aqua Limacum Magistralis* is not a pleasant concoction, but it is basically harmless. However, Matilde said we only have Rougham's word that it contained Water of Snails and not something else.'

'She has a point,' said Michael. He shuddered. 'I would never drink anything with a name like "Water of Snails". I would sooner eat cabbage – and that should tell you something!' He rummaged in his scrip. 'But I have the phial here, as it happens. I took the precaution of securing it when you examined Warde, for no reason other than that it was to hand. Will you test it now?'

Bartholomew took the tiny pottery container, and removed the stopper to inspect its contents. Warde had not obeyed Rougham's instructions to swallow it all: about half was still left. It was a milky reddish colour, and Bartholomew recalled thinking in Lavenham's shop that the apothecary had not taken as much care with its preparation as he should have done, because the potion had not been filtered through sand, to clear it.

'I want to know *exactly* what is in that,' Michael went on. 'The note Rougham sent Warde urged him to drink its contents in their entirety. Now, I am no physician, but I have never heard *you* encouraging a patient to swallow an entire phial's worth of a remedy.'

Bartholomew stared at him. 'You are right. Small pots, like this one, usually hold powerful medicines that are given only in minute quantities. I would never tell a patient to down the whole thing.' He sniffed carefully at the contents. 'That is odd.'

'What?' demanded Michael. 'Do not tell me you really

have discovered poison? I thought we were just devising ways to expose Rougham as dangerously incompetent.'

'I can detect ingredients here that I would expect – such as coltsfoot for loosening phlegm – but it should also contain powered liquorice root. Liquorice root has a strong scent, and tends to mask other aromas. But it seems to have been left out.'

'Perhaps Lavenham forgot it,' suggested Michael. He regarded his friend intently. 'What is the matter? You have noticed something suspicious – I can tell from your face. What is it?'

Bartholomew looked at the phial. 'There is something nasty in this – a strongly scented herb that I cannot identify.'

'Oh,' said Michael, disappointed. 'I suppose we shall have to look elsewhere for ways to discredit Rougham, then, if you cannot be more specific.'

'I have not started yet,' said Bartholomew indignantly. His scientific method for analysing complex compounds comprised more than a few arbitrary sniffs and the conclusion that one ingredient smelled vile. And he had not been entirely honest when he said he was not able to identify the strong herb in the concoction, either. He had a notion that it might be henbane – a powerful poison that might well have caused the sweating and breathlessness Warde had experienced before his death – but he wanted to conduct proper experiments before he shared his concerns.

He left the conclave and went to the storeroom where he kept his medicines. Michael followed, intrigued to know what he planned to do. In the bedchamber next door, Quenhyth and Redmeadow were studying. Redmeadow was none the worse for his skirmish the previous evening, although he had expressed a reluctance to leave the College that day.

'What are you doing?' he asked, when both students came to see why their teacher and Michael were crammed into the small room.

'I am going to test this phial, to see whether it contains poison,' explained Bartholomew.

'Why?' asked Quenhyth. 'The label says it is Water of Snails. Used sometimes for coughs,' he added triumphantly, pleased to show he had remembered his lessons.

'It was the only thing Warde drank that his colleagues did not on the night of his death,' said Michael. 'So, we need to determine what is in it.'

'It is a good idea to test it,' said Quenhyth approvingly. 'It came from Rougham, and we all know what kind of man *he* is. He may well have murdered Warde with "medicine" that he claimed would make him better.' His eyes gleamed, and Bartholomew saw he was delighted with the notion that the hated Rougham might be unveiled as a villain. 'I will assess it for you. It will not take a moment.'

'How?' asked Bartholomew curiously, wanting to know why he seemed so confident of success in so short a time.

'I will feed it to the College cat. If the cat dies, then we shall know Rougham fed Warde poison. If the cat lives, then Rougham is innocent.'

'And what about the cat?' asked Bartholomew, who was fond of the burly tabby that prowled the kitchens in search of rats. 'What has it done to deserve being used in such a manner?'

'Its life is unimportant in the advancement of science,' declared Quenhyth grandly. 'But you seem to believe that Rougham is guilty, or you would not be worried about it.'

'I do not think any such thing,' said Bartholomew, afraid Quenhyth might start another dangerous rumour. 'But leave the cat alone. If I find out you have harmed it, I shall see you are expelled.'

'And I will run you through with Deynman's sword,' added Redmeadow. His voice was hard and cold, and

Bartholomew was certain he meant what he said.

Quenhyth ignored him. 'I am only offering to do what you have taught me: experiment and explore the evidence with an open mind. And besides, it is only a cat.'

'I like cats,' said Bartholomew firmly. 'Especially that one. So keep your hands off it.'

'Very well,' said Quenhyth sulkily. 'But how else will you prove Rougham is a killer?'

'I am not trying to prove Rougham is a killer,' said Bartholomew, becoming exasperated. 'I am trying to determine whether this Water of Snails contains an ingredient that might have hastened Warde's demise. That is a different thing altogether.' He did not explain that finding poison in the Water of Snails would not leave Rougham as the sole suspect for murder: there was Paxtone, too.

'Rougham *is* a killer, though,' said Quenhyth matter-of-factly. 'And he is stupid. He told Redmeadow he believes in the existence of the *secretum secretorum*. Can you credit such nonsense?'

'A *secretum secretorum* would come in very useful,' said Redmeadow, who clearly did not share his room-mate's scepticism about the fabled cure-all. 'I would like to own one myself, but not nearly as much as Rougham would. He is desperate for one.'

'Then he will remain desperate,' said Bartholomew shortly. 'Because such a thing does not exist.'

'It does!' objected Redmeadow. 'Bacon says so. I read it myself.'

'You cannot believe all you read in books, Redmeadow,' said Michael tartly. 'Not even Bacon's.'

'Did you notice signs of poisoning as Warde died, sir?' asked Quenhyth, changing the subject. 'I do not think you did, or you would have denounced Rougham immediately – or he would have used the opportunity to denounce you.'

'Not all poisons have obvious symptoms,' said Bartholomew. 'That is why they are popular with killers who want to conceal a murder.'

Bartholomew stood on a bench to retrieve a piece of equipment from the top shelf in his medicines room. It was a small metal stand with a shallow dish on top, and there was room underneath it to light a candle. He made sure the dish was clean by wiping it on his sleeve, then poured half the phial's remaining liquid into it. His first task was to strengthen the solution by evaporation. Then he would use the concentrate to test for specific ingredients.

Because the candle provided a very gentle heat, it would be some time before the excess liquid boiled away, and Bartholomew accepted Quenhyth's offer to monitor its progress. He and Michael went to wait in his bedchamber, where Redmeadow started to read aloud from the new copy of Bacon's *De erroribus medicorum*.

It was not long before a discussion began about the nature of the continuum, and whether or not it consisted of indivisible mathematical parts that could be finite or infinite in number. Redmeadow held his own for a while, but then just listened as the Fellows put their points with impeccable logic. Bartholomew enjoyed the debate, feeling that he and Michael were fairly evenly matched, while Michael grew positively animated. They were both so preoccupied that it was several moments before they became aware of Quenhyth standing in the doorway, holding a limp bundle of feathers.

'Rougham *did* poison Warde,' he said triumphantly. 'While I was waiting for your experiment to work, I performed one of my own. I took the rest of the potion from the phial and fed it to Bird. He is quite dead.' He gave the feathers a vigorous shake, but there was no response.

Bartholomew gazed at him in horror. 'You have killed Walter's pet? How could you do such a thing? You know it is the only thing he loves.'

'But nobody else does,' said Quenhyth, unrepentant. 'We all complain about Bird – even you – because he crows all night, and damages books and belongings. Look what he did to your Trotula.'

He pointed to the shelf above the window, where Bartholomew saw that part of his newly acquired scroll had peck marks all along one edge. An avian deposit had also been left on it.

'We were going to tell you about that,' said Redmeadow uncomfortably. 'Bird got at it before we could stop him. We were leaving it to dry, so we could scrape off the lumpy bits without making too much of a mess.' He brightened. 'But he did not eat any parts with words on, so it is still legible.'

'We all hate Bird for destroying our most precious possessions,' Quenhyth went on, capitalising on his teacher's dismay as he inspected the ravaged document. 'And none of us will miss him. Agatha can put him in the stew tonight, and Walter will think he has flown away.'

'His wings are clipped,' said Bartholomew. 'He cannot fly.'

'A fox, then,' said Quenhyth, waving a hand to indicate that such details were unimportant. 'But are you not pleased? You had long and tedious experiments in mind, and I have given you your answer instantly. Bird died almost at once. He fought for breath for a few moments, but then just perished, as I heard Warde did.'

Bartholomew rubbed his eyes, then looked at the pathetic bundle under Quenhyth's arm. Doubtless most College members would indeed be glad to be rid of the chicken that had plagued their sleep for years, but he did not know how he was going to tell Walter what had happened. He decided to let Quenhyth do it. Perhaps, when the student was forced to witness Walter's distress, it might make him think twice about sacrificing animals in the future.

'Where is the cat?' demanded Redmeadow, looking around him suddenly. He came to his feet with a murderous expression in his face. 'You did not—?'

'No,' said Quenhyth coolly. 'You told me not to.'

'Bird's death is not enough to convict Rougham,' said Bartholomew, inspecting the ball of feathers closely in the hope that Quenhyth's diagnosis had been premature and that there might be something he could do to revive it. There was not: the cockerel was quite dead. 'For all we know, chickens might have an aversion to one of the ingredients in Water of Snails, and Bird's demise might mean nothing as far as humans are concerned. There are other tests we need to conduct. Has the water boiled yet?'

Quenhyth blanched and dived quickly into the store-room. Bartholomew followed, knowing exactly what he would find. He was not mistaken.

'Oh, no!' cried Quenhyth, running to where a small fire danced merrily on the bench top. 'I only left it for a moment.'

'But, unfortunately, it was a moment too long,' said Bartholomew, throwing a cloth over the flames. 'And now we have none of the mixture left. You fed half to Bird, and you allowed the rest to burn away.'

Quenhyth's face was a mask of shame. 'I was only trying to help. I did not mean to cause a disaster.'

'It is not a disaster,' said Michael, less fussy about empirical experimentation than Bartholomew. 'I am a practical man, and believe what my eyes tell me. Bird died when he was fed Water of Snails from that pot, and that is good enough for me. We *can* conclude that Warde was poisoned.'

'Not necessarily,' argued Bartholomew. 'Nor do we know what kind of poison was used.'

'Why does that matter?' asked Quenhyth. 'Poison is poison, and its type makes no difference to Rougham's guilt.'

'You can always make up a name, if someone asks,' suggested Redmeadow helpfully. 'Quenhyth is right: poison is poison, and trying to identify a particular kind is irrelevant to what was done with it.'

Bartholomew ignored them both, and continued to address Michael. 'Nor do we know for certain that Rougham gave it to Warde. He says he did not. Someone else may have sent it in his name – Paxtone for example.'

Quenhyth was outraged. 'That is a terrible thing to say! Besides, I heard Paxtone say in a lecture once that he has no use for Water of Snails, because it brings about excessive wind. He would never prescribe such an old-fashioned remedy.'

Redmeadow agreed. 'I attended that lecture, too. Rougham is the guilty culprit here, not Paxtone. Paxtone does not go around poisoning his patients. I do not think the same can be said for Rougham.'

'But we cannot *prove* that Rougham sent Warde the poison,' insisted Bartholomew.

'Well, Warde said he did, and so do Master Thorpe *and* Bingham,' said Michael, exchanging a triumphant glance with the students. 'Things are not looking good for Rougham at all.'

Bartholomew was not happy with Michael's conclusions, and felt the 'evidence' was too open to alternative explanations for Rougham to be charged with Warde's murder. He insisted they should investigate further before openly accusing the Gonville physician, and decided they would begin by visiting Lavenham the apothecary, to ask whether he recognised the phial and then to question him about the possibility of a mistake with ingredients. These were not questions he wanted to put to a man who supplied most of his medicines, but, he felt he had no choice.

'Do you think Warde's death is related to the murders in the mill?' asked Michael, as they waited outside the porters' lodge for Quenhyth to emerge. Bartholomew had forced him to confess immediately, and did not want to leave the College until he was sure the lad had done his duty. 'That if Rougham killed Warde, then he also dispatched Bottisham and Deschalers? We did find that other phial in the King's Mill. Remember?'

Bartholomew shrugged, most of his thoughts on Walter. 'It is possible that Rougham murdered Deschalers using whatever was in the pot we found, then was obliged to kill Bottisham because he inadvertently witnessed the crime – and that he used the nails to disguise what had really happened. It is a simple enough solution, but, again, it is not one we can prove – especially given Rougham's aversion to surgery and sharp implements. And we must remember Bernarde's testimony: he did not see Rougham or anyone else escaping after the two men died.'

'Ignore Bernarde's story for now,' said Michael. 'Do you find Rougham a plausible suspect?'

Bartholomew considered the question for a long time. 'I would not be surprised to learn he eased a patient into an early grave to benefit himself in some way. That is what he has been saying about me, so such things have obviously occurred to him. But I do not see him sneaking around dark mills armed with nails.'

'You claimed originally that Bottisham and Deschalers *both* died from wounds to the mouth. Are you now saying that one might have been poisoned – and that only one actually died from stabbing?'

'It is possible. Many poisons are impossible to detect,

and we did find that phial: someone obviously swallowed some strong substance in the King's Mill. However, if you recall, that pot was full of dust. It may have been dropped there the night Bottisham and Deschalers died. But, equally, it may have been there for a good deal longer and have nothing to do with their deaths.'

'Do you still have it?' asked Michael.

Bartholomew handed it to him, and the monk held it up, next to the one from Warde. They were identical.

'That does not mean anything, Brother,' warned Bartholomew, seeing the monk's eyes light up with glee. 'All apothecaries use phials like that for powerful potions. We will never prove it contained something lethal; just that it once held something strong.'

'Water of Snails?' asked Michael hopefully.

'Yes, perhaps. Along with a host of other things.'

'I excelled myself in tact and cunning at Julianna's house yesterday,' said Michael, mulling over the information for a moment, and then addressing a different issue. 'Acting on your suspicions, I mooted the possibility that Deschalers might have planned to change his will, but she did not put her hand in the air and admit to killing him before he could send for his clerk.'

'I imagine not.'

'Then I had a pry in his office, while the entire house-hold was preoccupied with a tantrum thrown by Julianna's daughter – she is a feisty brat, just like Dickon. However, I found no stray wills. I think Deschalers really did leave everything to her, and did not change his mind at the last moment.'

'She and her new husband would hardly leave a second will lying around for you to discover,' Bartholomew pointed out. 'Edward can read, and neither is stupid. If Deschalers did change his mind about heirs, then you will never find evidence of it just by rummaging through his possessions.'

'Here comes Quenhyth,' said Michael, not deigning to acknowledge that his friend was right. 'Crying like Julianna's baby. Poor Walter. How will he manage without Bird?'

Bartholomew and Michael left Michaelhouse and its weeping inhabitants, and made their way to Lavenham's premises on Milne Street. It was mid-morning and the town was busy, with folk flocking to and from the Market Square and barges arriving to deliver goods to the merchants' warehouses. Milne Street was more congested than usual, because of the presence of a small group of men wearing dirty black gowns. They lay in the filth of the road with their arms outstretched in the pose of the penitent, while their leader informed anyone who would listen that unless some fervent repentance took place, the Death would return. Bartholomew saw Suttone nod heartfelt agreement, although he did not deign to soil his own robes by joining the zealots in the ordure.

When the leader rang a bell, his followers clambered to their feet. He handed them long, white candles, and they formed a line, chanting a psalm in unnaturally deep voices. Their tidings and singing were funereal, and they were allowed to go on their way without any of the jeering and ridicule such people usually attracted. When they had gone, and their sepulchral notes had faded among the clatter of hoofs and feet, people went about their business in a more sombre frame of mind, recalling loved ones lost the last time the plague had visited the town.

'I hope *they* do not stay here long,' said Stanmore disapprovingly, spotting his brother-in-law and coming to speak to him. The physician saw two mercenaries hovering nearby, hands on the hilts of their swords as they scanned passers-by for signs of evil intent. Stanmore was taking no chances while his ex-apprentice was free to roam. 'We would all rather forget the Death, and it does no one any good to dwell on it. I am sorry I could not dine with you yesterday, Matt. However, you should know better than to invite me on a Monday, when I am always busy with new deliveries.'

'I did not invite you to dine,' said Bartholomew, startled. 'We are experiencing some financial difficulties at the moment and I would not ask anyone who does not have a penchant for nettles and mouldy bread.'

'You did,' said Stanmore indignantly. 'You sent me a letter, but I forgot to reply.'

'Tulyet had an invitation, too – allegedly from me,' said Michael. He shook his head, amused. 'Ignore it, Oswald. It is one of the students, thinking that rich townsfolk will take pity on us and make a donation once they see what we are obliged to eat.'

'There is always a meal for you in my home,' said Stanmore to Bartholomew. 'You are welcome any time.'

'We will come tonight, then,' said Michael immediately, ever the opportunist. 'But let us visit this apothecary first, and see what he has to say for himself.'

Lavenham's shop was a hive of activity. The apprentices were in the back room, furiously mixing and boiling remedies for delivery later that day; Lavenham wielded a pestle and mortar, grinding something to within an inch of its life with powerful, vigorous strokes; and Isobel greeted customers. She leaned across the counter in her low-cut dress and gave Michael a smile that indicated she knew perfectly well he would rather admire her cleavage than purchase tonics or remedies. Meanwhile, a small, neat figure hovered silent and unobtrusive in the shadows thrown by the shelves. Bartholomew watched the unmistakable silhouette of Dame Pelagia uneasily, wondering what she was doing in a place where poisons could be bought.

'Come and look at my leeches, Brother,' invited Isobel, when she saw she might lose the monk's attention to his

375

grandmother. 'They are best-quality creatures from France, and arrived this morning.'

'Nothing that comes from France is of the best quality,' Dame Pelagia muttered.

Bartholomew supposed a lifetime of spying in an enemy state might well result in that sort of opinion. 'They look like English ones to me,' he said, inspecting them with the eye of a professional.

'But more expensive,' said Isobel. 'Foreign goods are always more costly than common English wares. Is that not so, husband?'

'It true,' said Lavenham, not looking up from his labours. 'But I always say English best. The King English, and choose me for Commissioner. He know fine Englishman when he see one.'

Dame Pelagia turned a snort into a cough, and diverted her attention to a row of plants that were being dried against the wall.

'We found a phial of Water of Snails in Warde's possession when he died,' said Michael. 'How did he come by it?'

'I not know,' said Lavenham, sounding surprised that he should be asked such a question. 'I not sell *Aqua Limacum Magistralis* to Warde. Doctor Bartholomew recommend angelica, and I sell he instead. I keep *Aqua Limacum Magistralis* for other occasion.'

'Where is it, then?' asked Michael. 'Show it to me.'

Lavenham sighed and abandoned his pestle. He went to a wall cupboard in the main part of the shop, which he unlocked with a key – or which he pretended to unlock with a key. Bartholomew saw it was actually open, and the fact that the apothecary was ready to pretend otherwise indicated it was not the first time he or his household had been careless with security. Lavenham pointed to a row of identical phials on the bottom shelf.

'He one of these,' he said vaguely. 'But I not know which one. I sell several in month.'

'We do sell Water of Snails occasionally,' agreed Isobel, adjusting her clothes so that an even more enticing expanse of bosom was on display. Bartholomew saw the monk's attention begin to waver again. Dame Pelagia gave another cough, and her grandson's eyes snapped back to Isobel's face.

'What do you put in it?' asked Bartholomew.

'The usual ingredients,' replied Isobel, moving around the counter so she could rub past the monk, who did nothing to make her passage any less cramped. 'Ground ivy, coltsfoot, scabious, lungwort, plantain and betony, all mixed with a touch of hog blood and white wine.'

'What about snails?' asked Bartholomew archly.

'Well, snails of course,' she replied irritably, straightening up and depriving Michael of his entertainment. She was wary now, and less inclined for fun.

'Henbane?' asked Bartholomew. Dame Pelagia turned sharply. He had surprised her.

'Of course not henbane,' snapped Lavenham. 'He poison.'

'Liquorice root, then?' asked Bartholomew. Dame Pelagia was now giving the exchange her full attention. 'It is one of the most important ingredients in *Aqua Limacum Magistralis*.'

'Not always,' countered Isobel furtively.

'Always,' stated Bartholomew authoritatively.

'Perhaps in country that fashioned-old,' argued Lavenham. 'But not in country that have modern approach to disease. England can learn much from other country. Like Norway.'

'You just said English goods were best,' said Dame Pelagia softly. 'Now you say we should be following examples set in Norway.'

Lavenham was confused. He glanced from Bartholomew

to Pelagia, and his mouth worked soundlessly as he fought to come up with an answer.

'Be honest, Lavenham,' said Bartholomew. 'You did not add liquorice to the Water of Snails in the phial I saw, and, if I were to look at your remaining bottles, I would find them similarly lacking.'

'No!' cried Lavenham, backing up against his cupboard and protecting it with outstretched arms. 'You leave alone! Liquorice expensive, because he not grow in England, and I have not much. It cannot be taste in Water of Snails anyway. It better to keep for other potions.'

'I see,' said Bartholomew. 'And I suppose these "other potions" are ones you make for wealthy clients?' Lavenham's shifty eyes answered his question. 'That is disgraceful!'

'It is fraudulent, too,' said Dame Pelagia. 'The King would not approve of such activities, especially in one of his Commissioners. I cannot imagine what he will say when he finds out.'

'You tell him?' whispered Lavenham, aghast.

'I might,' said Dame Pelagia. 'It depends on how helpful you are. The good doctor here wants to know what you put in your Water of Snails. I suggest you answer him truthfully.'

'Just what we said,' said Isobel, reaching under the counter to produce a book. She flicked through its thick pages, then pointed to an entry. Bartholomew read it quickly, and saw that Lavenham's recipe for *Aqua Limacum Magistralis* was much the same as any other apothecary's, or would have been, had he included a healthy dose of liquorice root to disguise what was probably a foul taste. Bartholomew was not surprised Warde had only swallowed half of it.

'Who has bought Water of Snails in the last month?' he asked, although since Lavenham was careless with his cupboard it really did not matter: anyone could have stolen a pot.

'Rougham buy some,' replied Lavenham.

'Paxtone?' asked Bartholomew casually. His heart beat slightly faster as he waited for the reply.

'Paxtone will not use *Aqua Limacum Magistralis*,' said Isobel. 'He claims it causes wind,'

'Lynton buy none, neither, because he say potion smell bad without liquorice.' Lavenham shot Bartholomew a stricken look when he realised he had just admitted that other physicians had complained about the missing ingredient, too. He hurried on, as if he hoped his slip would not be noticed. 'And Cheney and Bernarde, for pains in head. And Morice to soothe sore tail.'

'For an aching lower back,' translated Isobel quickly, before they could assume the Mayor had demonic physical attributes.

'Cheney, Morice and Bernarde,' mused Michael. 'All members of the Millers' Society. That is interesting.'

Bartholomew thought it would be more so, if Lavenham could guarantee that no other pots had been stolen. He knew the apothecary kept a record of who bought what – in order to help him predict what remedies might be needed at specific times of the year – and asked to see it. The entry under Water of Snails showed that ten phials had been sold: Rougham had purchased four at the end of February, while Morice, Cheney and Bernarde had each bought two the previous Tuesday. There were no other entries.

'And you are sure you added no henbane?' he pressed. 'By accident?'

'Of course not,' said Isobel. 'Henbane is poisonous – especially ours, which is concentrated. We would never use it in a potion that was to be swallowed. We always mix swallowing remedies on a different bench to the ones for external use, so mistakes such as the one you suggest cannot be made.'

'Why do you ask about henbane?' asked Dame Pelagia, taking Bartholomew's arm and leading him outside. They left behind an apothecary who was more than a little alarmed by the encounter. Michael followed, first making an elegant bow to Isobel, although she was far too disconcerted to flirt with him. 'Was it in the potion Warde drank before he died?'

'Possibly,' said Bartholomew. 'But I cannot be sure, and now Quenhyth has destroyed what remained of it, I never will be.'

'Pity,' said Pelagia. 'I, too, have reached the conclusion that Warde was murdered, and have been assessing the possibility that someone poisoned him. He was a King's Commissioner and, in my experience, when such men meet untimely ends it is always wise to investigate them with care. You would be surprised how often they transpire to be sinister.'

'I assure you I would not,' said Bartholomew, who had plenty of experience with such matters himself although, he suspected, nowhere near as much as Dame Pelagia.

She smiled. 'What have you learned so far?'

'That Lavenham will lie to protect himself, and that it would be very easy to steal medicines from the cupboards in his shop. However, what I *do not* know is whether he put the henbane in Warde's Water of Snails himself, or whether someone else added it after it had been sold.'

Dame Pelagia nodded. 'I am in complete agreement with your conclusions. We shall both have to probe a little deeper into these unsavoury affairs.'

Dame Pelagia disappeared on business of her own after their meeting outside Lavenham's shop, and Bartholomew had the distinct impression that the old lady was already several steps ahead of them. He went to St Botolph's Church, where he inspected Warde's body again, but there was little to see. The signs of henbane poisoning were impossible to spot after death and, apart from a faint rash on Warde's face, the examination told him nothing. Then he attended Warde's requiem, and returned to Michaelhouse. He felt dispirited and guilty, as though he had let the Valence Marie scholar down. When he met Michael in the conclave, the monk looked equally disheartened.

'The Gonville scholars are back from Ely, and I asked them about this claim that they stand to gain the Mortimers as benefactors if they win the mill dispute. They denied the charge – and Rougham threatened to make an official complaint to the Bishop if I mentioned it again.'

'Do you believe them?' asked Bartholomew. 'About the Mortimers' alleged promise?'

Michael shrugged. 'Then I questioned Rougham about what happened on Saturday with Warde. Pulham forced him to co-operate, but he was not happy about being interrogated by the "Murderer's Familiar", as he called me. He denies sending the potion to Warde, and claims the writing on the accompanying note is nothing like his own. I compared it with something else he had scribed, and, while the two were very similar, there were enough inconsistencies to make me hesitate. The upshot is that I do not know whether Rougham sent Warde the potion and the letter telling him to drink it.'

'Who else might have done it?'

'Not Paxtone,' said Michael, reading his friend's thoughts. 'But perhaps someone from the Millers' Society. Or someone from Valence Marie for reasons we do not yet understand. We admired Warde, but that does not mean his colleagues felt the same way.'

'They did, Brother. He was honest and kind, and even townsfolk liked him. But at least we are clear on one thing:

Warde was definitely murdered. I was inclined to believe so when Quenhyth fed the contents of the phial to Bird, but your grandmother has dispelled any lingering doubts.'

'You say – and Rougham certainly agrees – that we do not have sufficient evidence to prove *he* did it, though,' said Michael.

'No, we do not. However, we have plenty of clues that *may* help us identify the culprit. It is just a matter of understanding what they mean and how they fit together. I think your original suggestion was right: we will find our solution to these deaths – Bottisham's, Deschalers's and now Warde's – in the mill dispute.'

'I am not so sure about that any more.' Michael rubbed his eyes. 'I am beginning to think we shall never have our answers.'

'Your grandmother will,' said Bartholomew. 'The killer had better hope we catch him first, because then he will just be exiled and can apply for a pardon. If Dame Pelagia wins the race, she may use some of the poison she stole from Lavenham's shop today – and that will be the end of him.'

Michael gaped at him. 'You saw her steal poison?'

Bartholomew nodded. 'She made sure of it. I think she was trying to demonstrate how easily it can be done.'

'We had better put our wits to work, then,' said Michael, taking a deep breath to fortify himself and steering Bartholomew out of the conclave – William had arrived and looked ready for one of his dogmatic diatribes – and towards the orchard. Bartholomew was amused to note that Michael's apathy had vanished like mist under the summer sun, and the notion that his grandmother might solve the case first was enough to spur him into action. The monk was so determined to prove his worth to his formidable forebear that he did not even bother to stop *en route* to see what edible treats might be worth pilfering.

Or perhaps he had already conducted one kitchen raid that day, and already knew there was nothing worth having.

When they arrived at the apple tree they found Wynewyk there, legs stretched in front of him and a book open on his knees. He was fast asleep. Bartholomew wondered whether he was expecting another visit from Paxtone, and looked around to see if his fellow physician might be lurking among the trees.

'Gratian's *Decretia*,' said Michael, lunging forward to catch the tome before it dropped from Wynewyk's lap – the lawyer had awoken with a violent start. There was another book beneath it, but when he tried to read the title of that one, too, Wynewyk gathered it up hastily, so he could not see.

'I am teaching Gratian next week,' gabbled Wynewyk, fussing with his tomes in a way that made Bartholomew certain he wanted to hide something. 'My students are studying that and *De simonia* this year. I must have fallen asleep; it is warm when the sun is out. Well, back to work.'

He began to read, and it was obvious he was not going to explain his peculiar behaviour, nor was it possible for Bartholomew and Michael to talk there as long as he remained. It occurred to Bartholomew that Wynewyk now behaved oddly – suspiciously, even – virtually every time they met. From the troubled expression on the monk's face, Bartholomew saw he was also worried, and that he had finally accepted that the Michaelhouse lawyer might be embroiled in something untoward.

'I have so many questions that my head is spinning,' Michael said, as they left the orchard. 'We should discuss what we know in the comfort of an inn, with a few edibles to fuel our questing minds.'

They had scarcely stepped across the threshold of the Brazen George when the landlord was scurrying forward to greet them, asking after the good brother's health and ousting a pair of disgruntled merchants from a secluded back parlour so that the Senior Proctor could conduct his business in private. The chamber was a pleasant one, with a blazing fire and a stone floor covered in thick woollen rugs. Michael gazed expectantly at the landlord, who began to list the various dishes on offer that day.

'I do not think I shall have the pike in gelatine,' said Michael with great solemnity. The ordering of food was a serious business and required his complete and undivided attention. 'Pike are dirty creatures, and I do not like the look of their teeth. I shall have the chicken roasted with grapes and garlic, some salted pork and a bit of fat beef. And bread, of course. No meal would be complete without bread. And perhaps a pear pastry. And—'

'Enough, Brother!' exclaimed Bartholomew, laughing. 'No more "ands"! There are only two of us here, not you and the King's army.'

'You want some of it, too?' asked Michael in alarm. 'I was ordering for myself, and thought to let you choose what you wanted separately.'

'You can always ask for more later, if you find you are still hungry,' said the landlord, although Bartholomew doubted that would be the case. The Brazen George was noted for its ample portions, which was one of the reasons Michael liked it. 'You need to keep your strength up if you want to solve these nasty murders – Bottisham, Deschalers, Bosel and now poor Master Warde – to say nothing of making sure Thomas Mortimer has his comeuppance for Lenne and Isnard.'

'It is a daunting task,' agreed Michael, fixing Bartholomew with a glare to indicate that the victuals ordered were wholly inadequate to fuel such monumental labours.

'And you have to combat Rougham,' added the landlord. 'He was vocal in his denunciation of Doctor Bartholomew again this morning , and accused him of killing Warde with angelica. My wife uses angelica for cooking, and *she* has never poisoned anyone. I told Rougham to take his wicked tongue elsewhere. But I have just been told that *he* was the one who poisoned Warde all along!'

'Told by whom?' asked Bartholomew warily.

The landlord scratched his head. 'I cannot recall where I first heard it, but the news is circulating the town like a fire in a hayloft.'

He went to fetch Michael's monstrous meal, leaving Bartholomew uneasy that lies and rumours seemed to spread with such ease. Although he was not particularly worried about what folk thought of Rougham, he was concerned about what they might think of him. He had very few wealthy patients left, and could not afford to lose the last of them because of Rougham's slanderous lies. And what of his less wealthy patients, who might be so alarmed by Rougham's claims that they did not summon him when they should? How many people would die before the spat ran its course?

'I did not think my grandmother would listen to Rougham's yarns without striking back,' said Michael comfortably, guessing the source of the tales about the Gonville physician. 'She likes you.'

'Which part of the case shall we discuss first?' Bartholomew asked, suspecting that the old lady's ploy had not made the situation any better. All she had done was add fuel to an already raging fire. He eyed with some trepidation the food that was beginning to pile up on the table. 'God's teeth, Brother! How much meat do you think we can eat? We are not wolves, you know.'

'Meat is better for you than vegetables,' declared Michael authoritatively. 'I owe my sleek and healthy appearance to the amount of meat in my diet. If I confined myself to women's foods, like cabbages, I would not be the same person at all.'

'Women's foods?' asked Bartholomew, who had never heard vegetables so described before.

'They are green, and so increase the phlegm in the spleen. They are something all women should eat because they make them more phlegmatic – less excitable. Men, on the other hand, should eat red foods – meat – which increase the blood and make them choleric. It is obvious.'

'Is it, indeed?' asked Bartholomew, startled that the normally sharp-witted monk should invent such outlandish notions. But then, Michael was not a rational man where food was concerned.

The monk ripped the leg off a chicken. 'Those peas are all yours, by the way. Peas are a waste of stomach space.'

'We should discuss these murders,' said Bartholomew, watching Michael feed with weary resignation. The monk's restricted diet had lasted a mere two days. 'Where shall we start?'

'At the beginning: with Deschalers and Bottisham.' Michael took a knife from his scrip and began to hack chunks of pork from a bone. 'They did not die naturally, but we do not know whether we have two murders, or a suicide and a murder. If the latter is true, we do not know which of the pair killed the other or why. We know they disliked each other, and we know Deschalers played cruel tricks on Bottisham. Each had a motive to kill.'

'Deschalers *may* have used the last of his strength to stab Bottisham, but I am not convinced. I still think he was too ill.'

'In which case we have Bottisham killing Deschalers, then himself. If he slew Deschalers by accident – although it is hard to imagine how he "accidentally" slipped a nail into his rival's palate – then I suppose he may have decided that suicide was the only way to escape from his predicament without shaming his College. Still I find it hard to imagine anyone killing himself by driving a nail into his mouth. It cannot have been easy.'

'No,' said Bartholomew thoughtfully. 'Neither man had been dead long before the bodies were discovered, and Bottisham was not the kind of man to make such a momentous decision without careful consideration. Besides, I still cannot believe that Bottisham would kill anyone, even an ancient enemy like Deschalers. I liked him, Brother. He was a good man.'

'I know,' said Michael, his mouth full of meat. 'But we cannot afford to let sympathy cloud our judgement. However, do not forget the phial you found at the King's Mill. It is possible there was something in that which lent Deschalers the strength to commit murder – or something that turned gentle Bottisham into a killer.'

'Perhaps,' acknowledged Bartholomew.

'Bernarde,' mused Michael. 'What about him as the culprit?'

'I can see him dispatching Bottisham, who was due to argue against him in the mill dispute. But not Deschalers, who was on his side.'

'But Deschalers was not on his side,' said Michael, spearing a slab of beef. 'He refused to burn Mortimer's Mill when the rest of Millers' Society thought it was a good idea. And do not forget that he had recently become Edward Mortimer's kin by marriage.'

'I am more inclined to look elsewhere for our culprits – towards two men who we *know* have a liking for violent death.'

'Thorpe and Edward,' said Michael. 'They arrive in the town, and within days two men are dead in odd circumstances. It *is* suspicious. But neither is stupid. Why would they indulge in a killing spree as soon as they return to the place that has charged them with such crimes before?'

'Because Edward has gained a good deal from Deschalers's death? He is now a wealthy man.'

'But he will not reap the benefits of what has been a thriving business,' said Michael, chewing thoughtfully. 'He dismissed the trained apprentices, and it is only a matter of time before the enterprise Deschalers crafted so lovingly withers away.'

'Do you think Edward is damaging it intentionally, to spite the town? Deschalers was a good grocer, and the loss of his services will be a serious blow to his customers.'

'Possibly. Where else will we purchase fruit, onions, cheese and dried beans? But perhaps he just does not care about what might happen tomorrow. He is a young man, and they are often prone to live for the moment, with no thought for the future.'

'But why kill Bottisham? Bottisham had never harmed either him or Thorpe.'

'Perhaps Bottisham was in the wrong place at the wrong time,' suggested Michael. 'Or perhaps Thorpe and Edward did the killing together. It would make sense. It could not have been easy to murder two men one after the other – one would have tried to escape. If Edward and Thorpe acted together, they could have dispatched both victims simultaneously. However, this assumes Bernarde and his boy are lying: that there *were* other people in the mill when they say it was empty.'

'We must not forget Rougham, either,' said Bartholomew. 'There was henbane in the Water of Snails he is alleged to have sent one man. Gonville wants to make a great deal of money from the Mortimers, so we can conclude that Rougham did not care for their enemy Deschalers, despite the fact that he was a patient. He may well have poisoned Deschalers.'

'You may be right about that, but he *liked* Bottisham – who was going to defend Mortimer's Mill to the Commission, and who was a respected member of his own College. I doubt very much whether Rougham killed *him*.'

But Bartholomew was not so sure. 'This chapel is important to Rougham, and I believe he will do virtually anything to see it built. Do you recall why Deschalers hated Bottisham? Because Bottisham refused to resort to bribery to win a case. It is possible that Rougham prefers his lawyers corruptible, too, so he can be certain Gonville will win for the Mortimers – and secure a handsome donation for the chapel into the bargain.'

Michael's eyes were bright. 'You argue this very strongly. It was not many hours ago that you were telling me the evidence against Rougham was thin.'

'That was before we knew for a fact that Warde was murdered,' replied Bartholomew tersely. Paxtone flashed into his mind, but he kept the thought to himself. 'Also, we must not neglect Lavenham. He mixed Warde's potion.'

Michael rubbed his chin. 'And he might have added a fatal dose of henbane to it.'

Bartholomew nodded. 'Either because he made a terrible and careless mistake. Or because Warde intended to represent the Mortimers' arguments to the Commission.'

Michael was thoughtful. 'The Water of Snails arrived with the note, and Bingham took both to Warde. But who knows what happened to the phial while it was in Warde's room? Any of his colleagues might have got to it. Last time I mentioned this, you told me they have no motive, but it may be that we just have not discovered one yet.'

Bartholomew sighed. 'So, our suspects for Deschalers's murder are the Mortimers, Thorpe, Rougham and Bottisham. Our suspects for Bottisham's death are the Mortimers, Thorpe, Rougham, Deschalers and the Millers' Society. And our suspects for Warde's death include Rougham, Lavenham and the scholars of Valence Marie.'

'*And* the Millers' Society. Do not forget who else bought Water of Snails, besides Rougham – Cheney, Morice and Bernarde.'

Bartholomew was disheartened. 'So, we have a wealth of potential culprits, a few patchy motives, but not much else. We do not know what Deschalers and Bottisham were doing in the mill together. Nor do we know whether we can believe Bernarde's testimony that they were alone when they died.'

'But there is a common thread: Bernarde's name crops up more often than it should. However, I have pushed him as far as I can without actually accusing him of lying. We shall just have to wait.'

'Wait for what?'

'To see if our felon leaves us any better clues the next time he claims a victim.'

CHAPTER 10

After leaving the Brazen George, Bartholomew and Michael saw a tabarded figure huddled in a nearby doorway with a large book under his arm. They watched Wynewyk nod quickly to someone, as though concluding a discussion, then glance around quickly before leaving. Wynewyk was not very good at conducting secret business without being seen, for he did not notice that Michael was observing his antics intently. But compared to Paxtone, who left their hiding place openly, as though there was nothing odd about two grown men crushed into a small place and muttering together, he was a veritable master of discretion.

While Paxtone headed for the Trumpington Gate, Wynewyk went north, but balked when he saw his Michael-house colleagues. He crossed the High Street so their paths would not meet. Michael's eyes narrowed as he, too, cut across the road, ignoring the angry yell from a carter whose horse reared at the sudden movement. Wynewyk held his ground until the very last moment, when he shot back across the street. He was not pleased when he found Bartholomew blocking his way.

'Going somewhere?' asked the physician. His eyes strayed to the book under Wynewyk's arm. A chain was attached to it, one end secured to the spine and the other hanging free. There were marks, where someone had taken a file and hewn through the links, releasing the tome from its secure place in a hall or a library. The damage looked new, and he recalled Wynewyk touting a book with a broken chain on a previous occasion.

'Please,' said Wynewyk, trying to nudge his way past. 'I do not want to stop here.'

Bartholomew glanced across the road, and saw Michael pause to give Rob Thorpe a long, hard stare as they met. Thorpe glared back, his expression loaded with malice, but Michael was used to dealing with rowdy and occasionally violent undergraduates, and the ruffian found himself unable to intimidate the monk as he had many others in the town. Michael continued to glower until Thorpe was forced to look away and move on.

'I am late,' said Wynewyk, trying to push Bartholomew out of his way. The physician declined to let him. He was growing tired of Wynewyk's suspicious behaviour, and wanted some answers.

'You see a lot of Paxtone these days,' he said.

'Who?' demanded Wynewyk testily. 'I know no one of that name.'

Bartholomew regarded him uncertainly, thrown off guard by such flagrant lying. He saw Wynewyk's shifty eyes and uncomfortable manner, and was about to demand the truth when Michael arrived. The monk snatched up the severed book chain and gazed accusingly at Wynewyk.

'You could have borrowed a key to unlock this. You did not have to destroy the chain to get at it – they are expensive, you know.'

'I *do* know,' snapped Wynewyk. 'I am in charge of the College accounts, remember? It is my duty to purchase chains, and I assure you that I am aware of exactly how much they cost. And I can also tell you we can ill afford to replace this one.'

Michael prevented Wynewyk from walking away. 'What are you doing out with Michaelhouse's much-prized copy of John Dumbleton's *Summa logicae et philosophiae naturalis*?'

'Someone has sawn halfway through its moorings,' replied Wynewyk coldly. He waved the jagged end in

Michael's face. 'So, I completed the task, and I am taking it to the smith for repairs. What would you have me do? Leave it for the would-be thief to steal when he finds time to complete his work? It is not the first time it has happened, either. Now, if you will excuse me—'

'You should have reported it,' said Michael, stopping him again. 'Then I would not have assumed *you* were the thief.'

When it dawned on him that Michael had him marked down for a very grave crime, Wynewyk's expression was one of open-mouthed horror. 'You jump too readily to the wrong conclusions, Brother! Why would I want Dumbleton? I am a lawyer, not a philosopher. And why would I steal from my own College when, as you pointed out, I can borrow a key any time I like?'

'That is the only copy of the *Summa logicae* in Cambridge,' said Bartholomew, not bothering to point out that while Dumbleton's text did indeed deal with philosophical issues, it was better known for its application to the study of logic. And logic was the basis of any academic discipline. 'It deals with the intention and remission of certitude and doubt, and is very valuable.'

'What are you implying?' asked Wynewyk, red with indignation. 'That I intend to sell it?'

Michael answered with a meaningful silence.

Wynewyk sighed and glanced behind him again. 'I see what you are thinking. You imagine I was avoiding *you* when I crossed the road. Well, you are wrong. It was *him*.'

He pointed down the High Street at Thorpe who, as if he knew he was being discussed, stopped suddenly and turned to give them an insolent wave. Wynewyk took a gulp of breath, then released it in a gust of relief when Thorpe walked on.

'Thank God you were here, or he would have had this tome away from me in an instant,' he said. 'He is at Gonville, and they are teaching him well – he would guess it is worth a lot of money.'

'How do you know him?' asked Michael curiously. 'You are a newcomer to the town, and you were not here when he committed his first spate of crimes.'

'I had the misfortune to find myself in his company when I went to visit the Hand of Justice three weeks ago – Thorpe *and* his horrible friend Edward Mortimer. I had heard about the Hand, and I wanted to see it for myself. Actually, that is not true – I went to ask whether it might intercede on our behalf in the *Disputatio de quodlibet*. I had a feeling we would not do well, and I so wanted to win.'

Michael raised his eyebrows. 'But you had me and Matt to argue by your side.'

'Yes,' agreed Wynewyk. 'And you are the best Michaelhouse has to offer. However' – here the drop in his voice indicated he thought Michaelhouse's best was somewhat below par – 'Matt's logic is sometimes flawed, while your mind is too often on your other duties, Brother.'

'I see,' said Michael coldly. 'Pray continue. You asked the false relic to help you, because you believed Matt and I were not up to the task.'

'I was right,' retorted Wynewyk haughtily, refusing to be intimidated. 'We lost, did we not?'

'Then you must conclude that the Hand did you no good, either,' Bartholomew pointed out.

'I do not think the Hand is as holy as folk say,' said Wynewyk. 'I have seen many relics – in Albi among other places – and our Hand does not possess the proper aura of sanctity. Father William touches it for a start, and you do not toss real relics around as though they are pomanders. However, all this is irrelevant. I was trying to tell you how I met Thorpe and Mortimer.'

'Then do so,' suggested Michael, as the lawyer paused to gather his thoughts – or his lies.

'The day I decided to visit the Hand was the one they happened to choose, too. William took the three of us to see it together. We went into the tower and knelt, but when William went to an upper chamber to fetch the Hand, Thorpe demanded my purse. I could not believe my ears! They were robbing me, not only in the sacred confines of a church, but within spitting distance of a holy relic. I was disgusted with myself for being terrified of them, and even more disgusted when I handed my purse over without a word. Unfortunately, it contained Michaelhouse's monthly food allowance.'

Michael gazed at him. 'Is *that* why we have been living like peasants recently?'

Wynewyk nodded miserably. 'I probably should not have relinquished it quite so easily, but I am not a man for fighting. However, it is easy to be wise – and brave – about events once they are over. That is what Master Langelee said, when I told him what had happened.'

Bartholomew thought back to his first encounter with Thorpe – in St Michael's Lane on the day of the *Disputatio*. Wynewyk had been with him, and he recalled the lawyer raising his hood to hide his face. He had assumed Wynewyk had not wanted a man with such a violent reputation to see and remember him, but it had been because Wynewyk had been afraid that Thorpe would recognise a man who had already fallen prey to his intimidation.

'What else did Langelee say?' asked Michael angrily. 'And why did you not tell me?'

'He said their pardons make them untouchable – even by you. He did not want you to demand our money back, and have them complain about you to His Majesty. He also believes the town will tolerate their vile behaviour for a while, but that they will soon vanish, never to be seen again anyway.'

Bartholomew was sure the Master had reached this conclusion when Dame Pelagia had arrived. She had a way of making people disappear quietly, and Langelee greatly admired her for it.

'The sooner the better,' said Michael fervently. 'But you should have confided in me, man. I do not stand by while my colleagues are robbed in broad daylight.'

'Please do not tackle them about it,' begged Wynewyk. 'I do not want them coming after me for getting them into trouble.'

'You should know me better than that. Besides, they would deny the incident if I approached them directly. But I *shall* repay them for what they did.'

'So, who tried to take the book?' asked Bartholomew, pointing to the tome under Wynewyk's arm. It crossed his mind that the lawyer might plan to exchange it for groceries. There were plenty of scholars in Cambridge who would love to acquire a copy of *Summa logicae*.

'I have my suspicions,' said Wynewyk, looking down the street to where Thorpe was still a figure in the distance. '*He* was in our hall recently, after all.'

'He did sit near the books,' recalled Bartholomew. 'I did not notice him sawing, though.'

'Obviously, or you would have told him to stop,' said Wynewyk, who evidently thought the physician should have been ready to confront Thorpe, even though he had failed to do so himself. He turned to Michael. 'How is your investigation, Brother?'

Wynewyk had relaxed now that Thorpe had disappeared from sight. He shifted the book under his arm, and Bartholomew watched unhappily, not convinced by his explanations. Something told him that Wynewyk was lying, which unsettled him. He did not want the lawyer to be embroiled in something that would see him dismissed from his Fellowship – or worse.

'Not well,' replied Michael. 'In fact, it is essentially at a standstill.'

'I dined at Gonville a few nights before Bottisham died,' said Wynewyk, eager to be helpful now he felt he was off the hook. 'I am friendly with their lawyers. Bottisham talked about Deschalers and how the grocer wanted an end to their feud. But he was suspicious.'

'You think Deschalers summoned Bottisham to discuss a pact, and then killed him?'

Wynewyk nodded. 'That would be my conclusion. Deschalers had wanted to meet Bottisham fairly soon, and this was a few days before they died. It seems to me that Bottisham allowed himself to be convinced that Deschalers meant well, and was murdered for his trust.'

'Why did you not mention this before?' asked Michael irritably.

'I thought Rougham would tell you,' said Wynewyk defensively. 'He heard the conversation as well as I did, and it was *his* colleague who was killed, not mine.'

'Well, he did not,' said Michael shortly. 'And you must have heard that Rougham is not enamoured of Michaelhouse at the moment?'

'He is not enamoured of Matt, but I have not heard him criticising the rest of us.'

'So, why did Bottisham and Deschalers meet at the King's Mill?' asked Michael, stifling a sigh. 'Why not at Deschalers's house, where there are plenty of refreshments to hand, and where he could show his reluctant guest some sumptuous hospitality?'

'Probably because Bottisham declined to enter the lion's lair, so they agreed to meet on neutral territory,' suggested Wynewyk. 'Would you go to the house of a man who hated you, where he could slide a dagger into your ribs and bury you in his garden with no one the wiser?'

'But surely Bottisham would consider a deserted mill at midnight equally dangerous,' said Bartholomew. 'Your reasoning makes no sense.'

'It does,' insisted Wynewyk. 'Deschaler's house would be full of his retainers and apprentices – he could hardly be expected to oust them from their beds just because Bottisham was soon to arrive. But the mill was different: Bottisham could have watched it for hours to ensure no one was there but Deschalers. I certainly know which venue *I* would choose, if I had been Bottisham.'

'You may be right,' admitted Bartholomew. 'We know Deschalers had a key to the mill, and where better for a quiet discussion? Deschalers knew it would be closed for the night, and that they would not be interrupted.'

'He must have rammed the nail through Bottisham's palate, taking him by surprise, then engaged the wheel and tossed him in its gears to disguise the injury,' surmised Michael. 'But it did not work as well as he had hoped, because the stones did not grind his victim up. Instead, the sudden noise attracted the attention of the miller. And then what?'

'We found the phial of medicine, remember?' said Bartholomew. 'It was in the type of pot used for very strong potions – such as that prescribed for painful conditions like a canker in the bowels. Deschalers took it to dull his senses, then drove a second nail into his own mouth, making sure that he, too, would fall into the moving machinery.'

'I do not know about this,' said Wynewyk unhappily. 'It sounds rather contrived. Why would Deschalers bother to hide his crime when he was going to die anyway? And he must have killed himself very quickly after dropping Bottisham into the wheel, if Bernarde is to be believed.'

'Quite,' said Michael grimly. '"If Bernarde is to be believed." We have wondered about that from the start. We shall have to have more words with our friend the miller, and find out whether he helped Deschalers with his suicide and its attempted disguise.'

*　　*　　*

398

While Michael went to see Chancellor Tynkell, to explain his tentative suspicions and conclusions, Bartholomew reflected on the audacity of a man who had dared to sit in the hall of another College and file away the chains that secured its valuable books. He accompanied Wynewyk to the blacksmith's forge, aware that the lawyer was nervous and ill at ease in his company. When they finished, and the smith had agreed to have the chain repaired by the end of the following day, Wynewyk escaped gratefully, claiming he had private business elsewhere.

For want of anything better to do, and because he was nearby, Bartholomew went to visit Paxtone at King's Hall. He longed to hear that his medical colleague's odd meetings with Wynewyk were harmless, and knew the matter would prey on his mind until it was resolved, no matter how hard he tried to ignore it. He hoped Paxtone would mention in passing some perfectly reasonable explanation for his strange behaviour, and obviate the need for an unpleasant interrogation. But he knew he was deluding himself. Whatever Paxtone and Wynewyk were up to involved secret meetings that necessitated lies, and Bartholomew knew their antics were unlikely to be innocent.

Paxtone was reading Philaretus's *De pulsibus* to his students, and was behind with his timetable; Bartholomew had finished Philaretus and his commentaries weeks before. Paxtone was a thorough teacher and his lectures were well organised, but he made dull work of explaining what was an exciting text. Most of his class was bored, and some were even asleep.

While he waited for Paxtone to finish, Bartholomew found a roaring fire and a pile of spiced oatcakes at the back of the hall. He ate four, then wished he had stopped at three, but the cakes contained cinnamon and sugar, both of which were a rare treat, and it was difficult to resist anything that smelled so delicious. He ate a fifth and began to feel queasy.

'Rougham has finished Philaretus and is on Galen's *Aphorismi,*' said Paxtone gloomily, when his students had clattered out at the end of the lesson. 'I do not know how he manages it.'

'But how well do his students know the material?' asked Bartholomew, declining to mention that he had finished the *Aphorismi,* too. 'Still, I suppose we shall find out at their disputations.'

'If you fail anyone from Gonville, Rougham will claim it is revenge for this business with Warde,' warned Paxtone. 'I know you are not the kind of man to strike at Rougham through his students, but that will not stop him from making accusations. He is a fool. It will not be long before Michael unearths proof that his Water of Snails was responsible for Warde's death – whether Rougham killed him deliberately or not.'

'His Water of Snails contained henbane,' said Bartholomew, watching Paxtone's jaw drop in horror. He knew he should have said nothing, since the rumours about Warde's death were escalating out of control, but decided to press on regardless, to see whether his revelations induced any meaningful reactions in a man whose own behaviour was also suspect. 'We do not know whether Rougham added it himself, whether Lavenham made a mistake, or whether someone else decided to dispatch one of the King's Commissioners.'

'My God!' breathed Paxtone. 'Henbane? Are you sure? I understand it can be deadly when swallowed in large amounts.'

Bartholomew nodded. 'We found a similar phial in the King's Mill, after Deschalers and Bottisham died. Do you know what Rougham prescribed for Deschalers's sickness?'

'Nothing in a phial. We argued about it, actually, because I said Deschalers needed something more than barley water.'

'Rougham prescribed *barley* for a debilitating and painful disease?' asked Bartholomew, shocked. 'But that is tantamount to giving him nothing at all! Deschalers would have needed a powerful pain-reliever. In fact, he must have been getting one from somewhere, or he would not have been able to leave his house, let alone ride about the streets of Cambridge.'

'*I* did not prescribe him one,' said Paxtone. 'But Lynton may have done. He was also appalled by Rougham's refusal to give Deschalers what we felt he needed.'

'But why did Rougham do such a thing? Was it revenge for the time when he withdrew the funds offered for Gonville's chapel?'

'He said Deschalers's ailment was incurable,' said Paxtone with some disgust. 'And he believes there is no point in giving medicine to a man who cannot be made well again. He says such practices are a criminal waste of the patient's money.'

'He said that? Did he imagine Deschalers would want to save his treasure for the future, then?'

'I would have recommended henbane seeped in hot mud, had Deschalers asked for my advice,' said Paxtone. 'Not taken internally, of course, because henbane causes warts, but applied as a plaister to the skin of the stomach.'

'I see,' said Bartholomew, thinking Deschalers had had a narrow escape from Paxtone's ministrations, too. He only hoped Lynton had had the sense to give the poor grocer a sense-dulling potion, since the other two physicians had failed him.

'Was there henbane in the phial you found in the King's Mill?' asked Paxtone. 'As well as the one that did away with Master Warde?'

'It was empty, so I could not tell. But, if it did, then I do not think Deschalers could have killed Bottisham. The henbane would have made that impossible.'

401

'Then perhaps it did not include any such thing,' suggested Paxtone. 'Perhaps it just contained some strong decoction of poppy, which is what Lynton – and you, no doubt – would have recommended for Deschalers. If that were the case, then Deschalers might have swallowed it to dull the ache in his innards before he killed Bottisham. I *knew* Bottisham was no killer.' He gave a grim smile of satisfaction.

Bartholomew supposed it was possible – just. But, even without the agonising pain of his sickness to contend with, he was not sure whether Deschalers could have mustered the strength to overpower Bottisham with nails. Paxtone seemed eager for Deschalers to bear the blame. Was it because he, like Bartholomew himself, had been fond of the gentle Bottisham? Was it because the town would have no excuse to attack the University if it was found that a townsman had killed a scholar and not the other way around? Or did he have his own reasons for wanting such a solution accepted?

'But do not look to me for answers about Deschalers, Matt,' Paxtone went on, when the physician did not reply. 'I do not interfere with Rougham's patients, no matter how wrong I think his treatments are. Have you considered the possibility that Deschalers *stole* the phial from him, in desperation?'

'Or perhaps Rougham misled you, and he did prescribe something strong.' Bartholomew sighed; every fact he uncovered seemed to raise more questions than ever.

'Bishop Bateman was poisoned, too,' observed Paxtone philosophically. 'At Avignon. That papal court sounds a dangerous and disagreeable place – full of Frenchmen. But speaking of disagreeable, I attended a stabbing today. A debate spiralled out of control at Gonville, and knives were drawn.'

'Gonville? Then why was Rougham not called? It is his College.'

'He could not be found, and they needed someone quickly. Ufford came looking for you or me. He found me first.'

'I assume Thorpe was the culprit?'

Paxtone nodded. 'He had inflicted a shallow wound that bled a lot and frightened everyone.'

'Who did he stab?' asked Bartholomew. 'Not Rougham if he was away, more is the pity.'

'The priest, Thompson. By all accounts, Thompson was trying to prevent the fight, and received a blade in the arm for his pains. Young Despenser was the real object of Thorpe's ire. They were quarrelling over the Hand of Justice, apparently.'

'Oh, that,' said Bartholomew in disgust.

'It is gaining in popularity. I know what you think about it, but you are in a dwindling minority. I petitioned it myself recently, and confess I felt better afterwards. God invests power in unusual things, so who is to say the hand of your pauper cannot inspire miracles?'

'There have been no miracles. Isnard's severed leg did not regrow. Una is still suffering from bile in the stomach. Old Master Lenne is still dead.'

'But Thomas Mortimer claims the Hand has absolved him of responsibility in that death – and folk believe him. The furious whispers against him have abated.'

'Lenne's son's have not, and neither did his wife's.'

'Two dissenting voices in a host of believers,' said Paxtone. '*I* prayed that Michaelhouse's cock would desist from waking me with its crowing in the middle of the night. That was answered.'

'Quenhyth killed Bird,' said Bartholomew, thinking it an unkind petition to have made. 'Damn! If folk believe the Hand can achieve that sort of thing, there will be no end to the trouble it will cause. As you said, there are already quarrels in Gonville about it.'

'Thorpe offered to ask the King if Gonville can have the Hand – to raise funds for their chapel,' Paxtone went on. 'But Despenser told him they have no right to it, and is afraid it will lead to Gonville being attacked by jealous townsfolk. That is why they fought. Acting Master Pulham told Thorpe that if he tries to win an argument with knives again he will be expelled – Hand or no. Of course, Pulham's heart was not really in the reprimand.'

'Of course,' said Bartholomew. 'That would mean the loss of the Hand, as well as a student.'

Stanmore had taken pity on his brother-in-law's starving colleagues, and had asked Kenyngham, Clippesby and Langelee to dine with him that evening, as well as Michael and Bartholomew. Wynewyk, William and Suttone were pointedly excluded from the gathering, on the grounds that the merchant did not like William's fanaticism, Suttone's obsession with the Death, or Wynewyk's habit of diving in and out of seedy alleys. Dame Pelagia was also present, although, judging by Stanmore's stammering surprise when she was shown in, the merchant had evidently not expected her. The food was excellent, the fires burned warmly in the hearth, and plenty of wine flowed, but it was a gloomy party nonetheless.

The scholars were weighed down by their concerns regarding the possibility of a riot over whether Bottisham had killed Deschalers – except Clippesby, who was more worried that the continued cold weather might make life difficult for hibernating dormice – while the clothier fretted about the state of commerce in the Fen-edge town. He railed to the uninterested Fellows that Edward Mortimer had encouraged his uncle to raise fulling prices to a ridiculous level, and had already all but destroyed Deschalers's empire. The repercussions were expected to be enormous, and the burgesses had suspended their payments for the repair of the Great Bridge until the matter was resolved. The last statement grabbed their attention, and all five scholars regarded him uneasily.

'But the carpenters have dismantled parts of it,' Bartholomew pointed out. 'It cannot be left as it is. It is dangerous – and people are still using it.'

'It will remain that way until we know where we are with our finances,' replied Stanmore firmly. 'But, hopefully, the King's Commission will find against the Mortimers, and business will return to normal. Once we are comfortable with the situation again, the repairs can be restarted.'

'But there are broken spars and bits of half-built scaffolding everywhere,' objected Bartholomew. 'Sergeant Orwelle bruised his ankle there yesterday, and one of Yolande de Blaston's children suffered a badly cut hand on a carelessly placed nail. It cannot stay as it is.'

'The cat from the Hospital of St John said the same,' agreed Clippesby. 'A duck was killed by falling masonry, and Robin of Grantchester's pig had a splinter in her tail. She is very angry about it.'

'A duck is dead?' asked the gentle Kenyngham, reaching out to touch the Dominican's hand in a gesture of sympathy. Clippesby's eyes filled with tears, and he looked away.

Michael looked down at his platter uneasily. 'Is this duck?'

'Cockerel,' replied Stanmore.

Clippesby jumped up in horror. 'Not Bird!'

'No,' said Langelee. 'We are having him tomorrow – if we have not been burned in our beds by angry townsmen by then. Dame Pelagia, do you think we should write to the King, and ask whether he will rescind the pardons granted to Thorpe and Edward? I am sure most of our problems would evaporate if they left our town.'

'I would not try it, unless you intend to accompany the letter with a handsome sum of money,' advised Dame

Pelagia. 'King's Pardons tend to be the last word in such cases, and it costs a good deal to have them overturned.'

'What about the compensation we are ordered to pay?' asked Stanmore. 'What if we offered these corrupt clerks *that* money, instead of giving it to Thorpe and Mortimer?'

'It would not be nearly enough,' replied Dame Pelagia. 'Royal justice does not come cheap, you know. I am not surprised Constantine Mortimer wants Deschalers's house to help defray the original costs of the pardons. If it were not for the additional money earned from his brother's fulling mill, he could never have afforded to buy his son's release.'

'Damn them all!' muttered Stanmore venomously. 'I went to the Hand of Justice yesterday, and asked it to do something about the situation. Since I do not believe in the sanctity of the thing, and since I know perfectly well that it came from poor Peterkin Starre, you can see the depths to which I am prepared to sink to rid my town of these louts.'

'I am not one of its followers, either,' said Langelee. 'But I must admit that William's treatment of it is very clever. He has it in a splendid reliquary – which always impresses the poor – and he makes sure that pretty blue-green ring can always be seen when he gets it out.'

'A tawdry bauble,' said Dame Pelagia dismissively. 'But unusual enough to catch the eye and draw the penitent's attention away from the pins that hold the thing together. You should not have allowed this cult to gain such momentum, Michael. It is dangerous, and will certainly end in trouble.'

Michael flushed at the reprimand, and Bartholomew did not think he had ever seen the monk so discomfited.

'Sheriff Tulyet still has not discovered the identity of that poor corpse,' said Kenyngham in the silence that followed. 'It is a shame, because I like a name when I pray for a soul.'

'The duck's name was Clement,' said Clippesby in a small voice. 'He hailed from Chesterton.'

'Actually, I meant the man in the snow bank outside Bene't,' said Kenyngham. 'I found him a few weeks ago if you recal.'

'Oh, him,' said Langelee, not very interested. 'Bartholomew had a look at his body, but there were no wounds, and it was concluded that he had been standing under the roof when the snow sloughed off it. It was a case of a fellow being in the wrong place at the wrong time.'

'But the Sheriff wants to find out who he was, nonetheless,' said Kenyngham. 'His clothes were decent, so he was not a beggar. He was not from the town or the nearby villages, and we think he was probably a messenger.'

'A messenger?' asked Dame Pelagia curiously. 'What makes you draw that conclusion?'

'Because he carried a letter from a London merchant to a Cambridge friar. The Sheriff said it was professionally written, and that this man's boots were worn in a way that suggested he spent a lot of time travelling. Unfortunately, the friar to whom the missive was addressed – Godric of Ovyng Hostel's predecessor – is dead, so we cannot ask him about it.'

Michael stared crossly at him. 'And where is this message now?'

Kenyngham raised apologetic hands. 'I lost it.'

Michael was unimpressed. 'You should have given it to me. First, it might have helped us identify this messenger, and second, it may have contained information important to one of my investigations.'

'It did not,' replied Kenyngham. 'I cannot recall exactly what it said, but it was only something about a visit by a man to his kin – a visit that probably did not happen, given that all the roads were blocked by snow back then. I meant to pass it to you but I forgot, and then I lost it.

But it contained nothing important, I am sure of that.'

Bartholomew sat forward and stared into the wine in his cup. 'There is someone in Cambridge who has been desperately hunting a man who went missing in the winter snows.'

'Bess?' asked Langelee. He looked thoughtful. 'I suppose this corpse might have been her beau.'

Bartholomew tried not to be angry with Kenyngham. 'You say the message he carried was from a London merchant? Bess told Quenhyth *she* was from London.'

Kenyngham smiled beatifically. 'Then she will know his name. What was it?'

'She has not told anyone,' snapped Michael, still peeved at the elderly friar's incompetence.

'Poor Bess,' said Bartholomew softly. 'What shall we do? The only way to know for certain is to show her his body, but he has been in the ground too long now.'

'Tulyet kept the hat he wore,' said Kenyngham. 'I shall ask him to take her that – first thing tomorrow morning. It would be unkind to leave it any longer.'

The news that the man Bess had longed to find might be dead cast an even darker shadow of gloom over Stanmore and his guests, and they were all grateful when Langelee declared that his scholars had an early start and suggested they all return to Michaelhouse.

Bartholomew slept poorly until the early hours, when he was summoned to tend a patient near the Castle. He did not finish the consultation until dawn, when he walked slowly along the High Street towards Michaelhouse. He met Paxtone, who guessed from his weary and dishevelled appearance that he had been up for a good part of the night, and invited him to breakfast in King's Hall. For the second time in less than twelve hours, Bartholomew ate a large and sumptuous meal.

Paxtone was full of ideas and questions about the text by Lanfrank of Milan he had been reading, which

408

Bartholomew would normally have relished. But he was tired and worried about what Paxtone might have done, and could not summon the energy to debate with him. Paxtone sensed his lack of enthusiasm but put it down to fatigue. He insisted on prescribing a tonic, and nagged until Bartholomew agreed to accompany him to Lavenham the apothecary to collect it. Bartholomew had no intention of swallowing anything from Paxtone or Lavenham, and determined to throw the cure in the river as soon as neither was looking.

They walked through the handsome grounds of King's Hall, and up King's Childer Lane to Milne Street. The black-robed prophets of doom were out, railing at anyone who might have petitioned the Hand of Justice and warning them that it would take more than relics to save them from eternal damnation. Suttone was among them, informing Deschalers's ex-apprentices that laziness and sloth were deadly sins and that they needed to find gainful employment before the Devil seized their idle souls. Cheney and Mayor Morice agreed, pointing out that there were no dried peas to be had now the apprentices had stopped working. The apprentices retorted bitterly that it was not their fault, and that Edward Mortimer was responsible for the problem.

The two physicians edged around the small crowd that had gathered to listen to the altercation, and had not gone much farther when they saw a second knot of people standing around someone who lay on the ground. Bartholomew saw Sheriff Tulyet among the onlookers, as well as Matilde. Quenhyth and Redmeadow stood shoulder to shoulder, while Bernarde and the Lavenhams watched from a distance, where they would not be obliged to rub elbows with peasants.

When Matilde saw Bartholomew she rushed forward to grab his arm. 'Come quickly, Matt! Bess has swooned, and none of us can bring her round. Your students tried to help, but they are too inexperienced to know what to do.'

Bartholomew knelt next to the huddled shape, and saw there was a very good reason why Bess was not responding to the appeals made by well-meaning passers-by. She was dead. Her face had a peaceful look, as though she had finally been relieved of a great burden. It seemed Bess's search was finally over, and in her pale, thin hands, she clasped what had once been a hat.

'The last time I saw this poor lass,' said Paxtone, leaning over Bess's crumpled form with a sad expression, 'was when Bernarde the miller led her off to some dark corner. Late last night, when I was returning home after matins and lauds.'

Everyone turned to look at Bernarde, who blushed and began to deny the charge in an angry voice, waving his keys as if they were a weapon. Isobel giggled in the kind of way that suggested she knew better, and Bernarde's outrage convinced no one. Lavenham glanced from one to the other looking baffled, while Tulyet simply shook his head in disgust at them all.

'I showed her the hat, as Master Kenyngham suggested,' the Sheriff said to Bartholomew. 'The man in the snow bank *was* her man – I could see the recognition in her eyes when she took the cap. She wandered off alone, but I did not know learning the truth would make her ill.'

'There is nothing I can do,' said Bartholomew. He gestured towards the doom-mongers, among whom Suttone was still visible. 'Will you fetch Suttone, Redmeadow? She needs a priest.'

'A priest?' echoed Matilde, appalled. 'But she was talking to me not long ago.'

'About what?' asked Bartholomew. 'The death of her man?'

'No, she asked whether I had seen him recently,' said Matilde. She gave Tulyet a weak smile. 'I suspect she had already forgotten what you told her about the body in the snowdrift.'

'How did she seem?' asked Bartholomew.

'Unwell,' admitted Matilde. 'But you know how odd she is, and I did not think anything of it. She said she was hot and that her mind was spinning – but I think it span most of the time. And she was short of breath, as if she had been running.'

'Someone should carry her to a church,' said Bartholomew. 'Does she have any of her gold left, or perhaps something from Bernarde? Or will the town bury her?'

'I did not pay her,' snapped Bernarde angrily. He reddened again when he realised it sounded as though he had used her and declined to settle the debt. 'Well, I gave her a penny, but it was only because I felt sorry for her.'

'Well, she does not have a penny now,' said Tulyet, deftly searching the woman's rags. 'An informant told me Rob Thorpe offered her information about her man a few days ago, but said it would cost. The poor woman handed over her coins, only to receive a lot of lies in return. I imagine the penny went the same way this morning. She was incapable of learning from her mistakes and would do anything for news of her lover, no matter how unreliable the source.'

'I might have known it was Thorpe,' said Matilde bitterly. 'How can you let him get away with this?'

'Because my informant is too frightened to give evidence against him publicly,' replied Tulyet. 'And now Bess is dead we have no case – no complainant.'

'Then the law is wrong!' declared Matilde coldly. 'If it cannot protect the weak and the gullible from such low tricks, then there is something seriously amiss with it. You *must* do something.'

'My hands are tied. If I charge him with cheating a woman

who is now dead – and who could never have brought her case in person, anyway – Thorpe will tell the King that we are harassing him. We cannot afford to pay more royal fines. We are struggling to pay this compensation as it is.'

'Your laws have nothing to do with justice,' said Matilde, tears of outrage sparkling in her eyes. 'They protect criminals, but leave the innocent to fend for themselves. It is a wicked system!'

Bartholomew agreed, but the street was not the right place for a debate with the Sheriff on the King's Peace. Tulyet tried to apply the law fairly, and it was not his fault that Westminster clerks did not do likewise.

'The loss of her gold makes no difference to Bess now,' he said. 'She is finally at peace.'

'With her man,' said Tulyet softly. 'Although she never did tell me his name.'

Once the excitement was over, and the swooning woman had become just another corpse, people began to wander towards the plague prophets, who were engaged in a strident argument with Father William about the Devil's role in the Death. Bernarde was among the first to slink away, unwilling to admit to what had transpired between him and Bess the previous night. The Lavenhams were next, heading for the Market Square. Bartholomew saw Rougham skirt around the edge of the crowd, his eyes darting here and there in an attempt to see what was happening without becoming involved. Tulyet left to fetch stretcher-bearers, and asked Bartholomew to wait with Bess until he returned, while Matilde went to see why Redmeadow was taking so long to bring Suttone. Eventually, Bartholomew and Paxtone were alone. Paxtone began to cover the dead woman with her cloak, but stopped when something fell out of it. It was a phial.

Bartholomew picked it up, noting it was like the one that had contained Warde's Water of Snails and the one he had

412

found at the King's Mill. He studied it carefully, but Lavenham probably had dozens of identical containers for potions that were powerful or that were required in small amounts. Its similarity to the others meant nothing. He removed the stopper and squinted down the neck to assess its contents. Inside, the mixture was a murky red-white, and looked uncannily like the substance that had killed Bird.

'Be careful,' warned Paxtone, watching. 'Those little pots usually contain something to be treated with caution – and it is not always medicine. I have purchased viper venom in one of them before now.'

'What did you want that for?' asked Bartholomew uneasily.

'Another time,' replied Paxtone enigmatically, in a way that made Bartholomew's senses jangle all manner of warnings. 'What is in it? Can you tell?'

Bartholomew sniffed its contents gingerly. He shook his head. 'It smells the same as the *Aqua Limacum Magistralis* that killed Warde. I can detect coltsfoot quite strongly, but no liquorice. And there is something bitter and nasty underlying its other scents.'

Paxtone took it. 'You are right. But if there is no liquorice, then perhaps it is not Water of Snails. Liquorice is one of its essential components.'

'Lavenham omits expensive ingredients from his recipes, if he feels he can get away with it.'

'Does he indeed?' asked Paxtone, round eyed. He turned his attention back to the phial. 'This dirty scent is familiar. It smells rank.'

'Could it be henbane, do you think?' suggested Bartholomew casually, watching him intently.

'It could,' said Paxtone, nodding vigorously. 'But I have never heard of it used in a medicine to be swallowed before. I only ever add it to plaisters for *external* use.'

'Unfortunately, since Quenhyth destroyed Warde's

mixture in a misguided effort to be helpful, we have no way of knowing whether Bess's phial and Warde's pot contained the same things.'

'We also do not know if she drank it or that it killed her,' Paxtone pointed out reasonably. 'She may have found an abandoned bottle and picked it up because it was pretty – but did not sample the contents. Do not forget she was not in her right mind. And is henbane really that deadly when swallowed? I have never come across a case of ingestion before.'

Bartholomew pointed. 'There is a pink trail on her chin, where it dribbled from her mouth, and, like Warde, she died feverish, dizzy and gasping for breath. These are all symptoms of henbane poisoning, and mean that she *did* swallow the stuff.'

Paxtone shook the phial gently. 'You are more knowledgeable than me, Matt. I did not know how to recognise the signs of henbane ingestion. I think I shall take this pot to King's Hall and perform a few experiments. You do not want Quenhyth "helping" you a second time. He may use your College cat now the cockerel is unavailable, and I like that animal.'

Bartholomew did not think it was a good idea to allow Paxtone to make off with the potion, when his own role in the grisly business was far from clear, but did not know how to stop him – at least, not without showing that he did not trust him. He watched Paxtone tuck the phial away and wondered whether he would ever see it again – or whether it would make its next appearance when another victim was claimed.

'What do you think this means?' he asked, trying to hide his misgivings. 'That Bess purchased poison intending to take her own life? Or did someone give it to her?'

'I do not see why anyone would want to kill her. She had lost her wits.'

'Perhaps someone was afraid she might regain them.' Bartholomew regarded Bess's body thoughtfully. 'Deschalers gave her a purse of gold. He was not a generous man, so he must have had some reason for providing her with such a large sum. Perhaps there are others who felt obliged to pay her, but they decided to kill her instead, in a bid to save their money.'

'You make everything so complex,' said Paxtone accusingly. 'You have been too long in the company of Brother Michael, and you see plots and connivance wherever you look. Bess was a poor wench, who either intended to die or who mistook poison for something pleasant. She could not have blackmailed Deschalers, because she did not have the wits. And remember he was dying, Matt. Dying men are apt to be charitable. He gave Bosel new clothes, too.'

'So he did,' said Bartholomew, recalling that Bess had said as much to Redmeadow. 'That means two recipients of his uncharacteristic generosity are now dead.'

Paxtone sighed in exasperation. 'And a good many others are doubtless still living. It is dangerous to be poor in Cambridge, you know that. Beggars are often killed by those who think it is good sport to attack the defenceless. Bess's death has nothing to do with your other cases.'

Bartholomew was not so sure. He considered the people he had recognised in the crowd that had gathered to watch her die, and who were connected to the other deaths. There was Rougham, hovering in the background – Bartholomew's prime suspect in the poisoning of Warde. There was Bernarde, whose stories about discovering the bodies of Bottisham and Deschalers made no sense, and who had frolicked with Bess hours before her death. There were the Lavenhams, who dispensed Water of Snails from their shop, and who admitted to varying their recipes. Two other members of the Millers' Society were close by: Cheney and Morice, who bought Water of Snails from Lavenham,

415

and might know what an added dash of henbane would do. Bartholomew suspected Thorpe and Edward Mortimer would not be too far away, either. And, of course, there was Paxtone himself.

'She had just learned about the death of her lover,' said Paxtone, seeing his colleague was not convinced. 'She was distraught – just look at the way she clings to his hat, even in death.'

'But she had forgotten what Tulyet had told her by the time she met Matilde. She did not take her own life. In fact, I am willing to wager a jug of ale in the Brazen George that when we discover the truth behind her death, we will also know more about these other murders.'

'I do not drink in taverns,' said Paxtone primly, standing up and moving away as Suttone arrived. 'But you can bring it to me in my quarters. It is a long time since I won a wager of ale – and I *will* win, because what you are suggesting is nonsense. The demise of a beggar-woman will not be connected to the death of rich merchants and respected scholars.'

'We shall see,' replied Bartholomew stubbornly.

When Tulyet eventually arrived with the stretcher-bearers, Bartholomew told him what he had reasoned about Bess's sudden death. The Sheriff rubbed his nose between thumb and forefinger, and asked how many more murders would be committed before they had worked out what was happening.

'We do not know they are all connected,' said Bartholomew. 'Paxtone thinks not.'

'Of course they are connected! How could they not be? You found those little phials with Deschalers and Bottisham, then Warde, and now Bess. Paxtone is trying to mislead you.'

'But if Bottisham and Deschalers died in the same way

416

– with a nail in the palate – as we first surmised, then the flask at the King's Mill is irrelevant. We *think* Deschalers took it there, to ease his pain – or perhaps to subdue Bottisham – but we have no evidence to support such a theory.'

'This town is falling to pieces,' muttered Tulyet. 'And there seems to be nothing I can do to save it. Thorpe and Mortimer are having their revenge indeed. There is nothing like a few unexplained murders of townsmen *and* scholars to produce panic and discord.'

Bartholomew walked back to Michaelhouse, mulling over the new facts he had uncovered. When he arrived, Quenhyth and Redmeadow were sitting quietly, both engrossed in their studies. Bartholomew walked into the room, then tripped over a chest that had been placed at the foot of his bed. It had not been there before.

'What is this?' he asked irritably, rubbing his skinned shin. It was not a nice box – it smelled and its large lock bespoke functionality rather than aesthetics. He decided it would not remain there for long. But, even as he glared at it, he realised he had seen it before.

'That is Quenhyth's inheritance,' explained Redmeadow disapprovingly. 'Deschalers left it to him, and Edward and Julianna wanted it out of their house today, because they think it is nasty.'

'*Quenhyth* is the clerk Deschalers remembered in his will?' asked Bartholomew in surprise. He recalled Julianna saying that her uncle had appreciated the fact that his scribe was always punctual – and punctuality was one of Quenhyth's strongest virtues. Bartholomew remembered something else, too, and realised he should have made the connection sooner: Quenhyth had recently been petitioning merchants for scribing work, telling them that he was anxious for funds. That had been because he had lost his regular employer when Deschalers had died.

417

'Deschalers liked me,' said Quenhyth, although Bartholomew recalled Julianna stating quite categorically that he had not; the grocer had just appreciated Quenhyth's timeliness. 'He promised to leave me a chest, but I did not think he would remember. I am flattered he did. It is not as fine as the furniture in my father's home, but it will do until I can afford better. It has a strong *lock*.' He glared at Redmeadow.

'Redmeadow and I will not touch your possessions,' said Bartholomew, suspecting it would be difficult to persuade Quenhyth to get rid of the thing. 'And no one else comes in here.'

'Brother Michael does,' said Redmeadow meaningfully.

Bartholomew wondered what he imagined Quenhyth owned that would tempt a man of taste and culture, like Michael. Then it occurred to him that Quenhyth might want to protect his private food supplies when the monk came raiding – in which case, a lock would be very useful indeed.

Quenhyth smiled. 'We all need additional victuals now Michaelhouse is failing to feed us properly. And I can secure other things in it, too – such as my pens and inks.'

'We are not interested in *those*,' said Redmeadow scornfully.

Quenhyth regarded him balefully. 'You are! And it is very annoying to come home and find my writing supplies mysteriously depleted.'

'You can sell the chest,' suggested Redmeadow, ignoring the accusation with a blitheness that made Bartholomew wonder whether it was justified. 'But I do not think you will get much for it.'

'I cannot – not yet,' said Quenhyth. 'That was one of the conditions of my accepting it. Deschalers said I can only sell it when I have owned it for a year and a day.'

'What a curious stipulation,' said Bartholomew. He knew

Quenhyth would follow the instruction to the letter, and suspected Deschalers knew it, too. Perhaps Deschalers was trying to inconvenience the lad by bequeathing him such an unwieldy object, and it was his idea of repaying him for being so annoyingly meticulous. It would be just like the laconic grocer to devise such a plan.

'You did not tell me you were Deschalers's scribe,' said Bartholomew, somewhat accusingly. The student should have mentioned it sooner, since they had been investigating the grocer's murder.

Quenhyth shrugged. 'I was not. Not really. I saw him once a week – if that – for the occasional bit of writing. I offered to do more, but he preferred to keep most of his business in his head.'

'Did you write his will?' asked Bartholomew.

Quenhyth nodded, then gave a rueful grin. 'It was one of the briefest I have ever seen: the chest for me and everything else to his niece.'

'Did he make another at any point? Or talk about doing so?'

'Not with me. There was an older will from years ago, in which he left a house on Bridge Street to his apprentices. But, he always said they were lazy, and I am not surprised he changed his mind.'

'When did he make the new will?' asked Bartholomew. 'How recently?'

'A month or so ago,' replied Quenhyth. 'Julianna will show it to you, if you ask her. You will see it is beautifully crafted. I have the best handwriting in Michaelhouse – Wynewyk says so.'

'What did you make of the death of that whore?' asked Redmeadow conversationally, bored with Quenhyth's boasting; his own writing was far from tidy. 'She was hale and hearty one moment, and dead the next. Quenhyth and I could do nothing to rouse her once she had fallen down.'

419

'And we tried,' said Quenhyth, keen as always to secure Bartholomew's favourable opinion. 'I know you felt sorry for her, so we did our best to revive her.'

'She was not a whore,' said Bartholomew to Redmeadow sharply.

'Frail Sister, then,' said Redmeadow impatiently, obviously considering that there was not much in a name, and a whore was a whore at the end of the day. 'But what did you think? She was fit in body, even if her wits were mashed, and it was odd to see her die so abruptly.'

'You two can attend her requiem mass,' said Bartholomew, knowing they would find it a chore, but thinking it was about time they both learned to be more tolerant. He did not like Redmeadow's salacious interest in Bess's death and was not sure that he wanted to answer the lad's questions. 'She was a patient, and we owe her that respect.'

'But I do not want to go,' objected Quenhyth. 'I have my studies to think of.'

'Too bad,' said Bartholomew. 'This is part of your training.'

'No,' said Quenhyth firmly. 'I do not like requiem masses. They upset me.'

'Even more reason to go to this one, then,' argued Bartholomew. 'You did not know Bess well, so her passing will not be overly distressing to you. It will inure you to the many such occasions you will attend in the future, if you become a physician.'

'But I do not intend to lose as many patients as you do,' said Quenhyth, somewhat rudely. 'I intend to be good.' He glowered as Redmeadow released a sharp giggle of embarrassment.

'Then perhaps this will be your last,' said Bartholomew, unmoved. 'But you will both be there.'

'Very well,' conceded Quenhyth reluctantly. 'I shall see what I can do.'

'Me, too,' added Redmeadow with a long-suffering sigh. 'Especially if you can explain to us why she died so suddenly.'

'Poison,' said Bartholomew bluntly, deciding to give Redmeadow his answers, since he was so intent on having them. He saw the shocked expression on their faces. 'I suspect someone added henbane to the Water of Snails she swallowed.'

'Why would she take Water of Snails?' asked Redmeadow. 'Did someone give it to her? Or did she buy it herself? I suppose you can ask Lavenham, but what apothecary would admit to selling a potion that had killed a customer? It would be devastating for his business.'

'Or he might just lie,' said Quenhyth.

Bartholomew thought his students right to be suspicious of any answers given by Lavenham, and knew he would be wise to regard anything the apothecary or his wife said with a healthy scepticism.

Michael banged his hand on the windowsill in Bartholomew's room to vent his frustration later that morning. 'We can arrest no one for these murders, because we have no solid evidence, and I do not know what to do next. I went to visit Bernarde at the King's Mill earlier, but it was closed.'

'Closed?' asked Bartholomew. 'During the day, when they have grain from King's Hall to grind?' He frowned thoughtfully. 'There is a connection for you, Brother. Just when business was looking bad for the Millers' Society – with the Mortimers diverting water and bodies in the millstones – they secure a lucrative contract from no less a place than King's Hall.'

'And King's Hall boasts the patronage of the King. And the King enjoys a share in the profits from the King's Mill. It is all rather incestuous, is it not?'

Bartholomew nodded. 'I cannot help but wonder how far your grandmother is involved. She has an eye for the King's interests, and I would not put it past her to tell the Warden of King's Hall to send grain to Bernarde in his time of need.'

'My grandmother would not demean herself by meddling with matters so far beneath her,' said Michael loftily. 'But I have the feeling her investigation is proceeding a lot faster than ours, and I do not want her to think I am an incompetent in my own domain. However, I can tell you that Bernarde has closed his mill because he is at a meeting of the King's Commissioners in Lavenham's shop. We should pay them a visit, to see what transpired at this momentous event.'

He threw Bartholomew his cloak and set off. On their way they saw Stanmore, who was standing outside Trinity Hall with Cheney and Mayor Morice. Their voices were lowered and they were evidently talking about matters they considered of some importance, if the solemn, intense expressions on their faces were anything to go by. Morice was uneasy, and kept glancing this way and that, as though anticipating some kind of attack. Bartholomew wondered whether he had cheated anyone recently and was afraid of their revenge.

He was about to walk past them when he glimpsed a black tabard out of the corner of his eye, and saw Wynewyk ducking down Water Lane. It looked as if he had been travelling along Milne Street to return to Michaelhouse, but had decided to take a diversion in order to avoid his colleagues. There was a flash of blue, too, and Bartholomew recognised the distinct colouring of a cloak from King's Hall. He did not need to see its owner to know it belonged to Paxtone, and that the physician was as keen as Wynewyk not to be seen.

'Matt,' called Stanmore, when he spotted Bartholomew.

The physician noticed that his brother-in-law was still taking no chances with his safety, and the tough-looking mercenaries loitered nearby, armed to the teeth. 'We were talking about the Mortimers – trying to devise a plan to have Edward banished from Cambridge. It is all very well for the King to pardon him, but His Majesty does not have to live with his bad behaviour day in and day out.'

'But that would still leave us with Thorpe,' said Bartholomew. 'And he was once your apprentice and a far greater danger to you than Edward.'

'But *Edward* is damaging the town's commercial activities,' growled Cheney. 'He has already destroyed Deschalers's business, and he has only been in charge a few days! The fall of that empire affects us all – the sale of spices, flour *and* cloth, not to mention our investments and speculations. The whole affair is vexing, and I have been obliged to take two doses of strong medicine to calm my aching head.'

'And me,' said Morice, keen for everyone to know that the Mayor was also distressed about the town's disintegrating financial situation. 'My back always smarts when I am upset.' He put both hands to his waist and flexed himself, wincing dramatically to illustrate the pain.

'Most of us are more concerned that he might kill someone,' said Bartholomew dryly.

'He took so much water for fulling yesterday that Bernarde was forced to operate at half speed *all day*, and Ovyng Hostel took their grain elsewhere,' said Morice, ignoring him. 'This cannot continue.'

'We must ensure he does not intimidate the Commissioners,' added Cheney. 'He has already hired Rougham to murder Warde, and we do not want Lavenham and Bernarde to feel vulnerable.'

'Or Master Thorpe,' said Michael, noting they were only concerned with the safety of the men who would further their own interests, not with the one who was neutral. 'But this is a serious allegation – that Edward hired Rougham to kill Warde. Do you have evidence?' He did not sound hopeful.

Cheney made an impatient gesture. 'Why do you need evidence when you have common sense? You scholars are all the same, unwilling to recognise the guilty without a mountain of proof. That is why none of you will ever succeed in the world of commerce.'

'They are meeting now,' said Morice, jerking his head towards Lavenham's shop. 'The three surviving Commissioners. They are going to discuss what can be done to confound Mortimer and his evil ways. We are waiting to see what they have decided.'

'Lavenham closed his shop for the occasion,' added Cheney. 'And Bernarde shut down his mill. So you can see how seriously *they* are taking this matter. No trader wants to inconvenience his customers, which is exactly what happens when you cease trading for an hour without prior warning.'

'I want words with Bernarde,' said Michael. 'I intend to find out why Bess died after he availed himself of her services. Also, she had a phial in her possession similar to the one we found in *his* mill after the deaths of Deschalers and Bottisham.'

The merchants gazed at him in surprise. 'I do not think Bernarde is your killer, Brother,' said Stanmore eventually. 'He is a miller.'

'What does that have to do with anything?' asked Michael, bemused. 'He had good reason for wanting Bottisham dead: Bottisham was about to represent his rival in a court of law.'

'Very well; we accept that,' said Cheney, after a moment of thought. 'But he had no reason to harm *Deschalers*. And I imagine not Bess, either. He was not alone in taking her

424

for a tumble. Even Deschalers escorted her to his home once, and he was ill. And there were others.'

'Who?' demanded Michael.

'She offered herself to me,' said Morice, indicating to Bartholomew that the poor woman must have been desperate. 'But I declined, because my wife does not approve of whores in the house.

'She came to me, too,' said Cheney. 'She offered to do whatever I liked in return for information about her man. But I had nothing to tell her, so I decided against taking her up on her suggestion.'

'Very noble,' muttered Michael. 'But what about Deschalers? Did he have information for her?'

'None he shared with us,' said Stanmore. 'But you cannot seriously think Mad Bess is involved in this, Brother? Perhaps she just found this phial and drank its contents because she was too addled to know that consuming things you find in the street is unwise.'

Bartholomew was about to point out that henbane was expensive and Bess was unlikely to have discovered some by chance, when Paxtone hurried up to them. His face was bright with excitement as he took Bartholomew and Michael by the arms and dragged them away from the merchants. Bartholomew smiled warily, uncertain how to react to a man who had so recently darted down an alley to avoid meeting him. Paxtone did not seem to notice his distrust.

'I analysed that phial you found, Matt. You are right: it did contain poison! As far as I can tell the compound is indeed Water of Snails – it contains blood and shell, not to mention part of a leaf that is definitely scabious. But I found something else too: henbane, just as you predicted. I believe it was boiled down to form a very concentrated poison, which explains why Bess sweated, was dizzy and complained of not being able to breathe – all symptoms of swallowing henbane, as you said. I sent one of my students to look it up in Gonville's library. They have volumes on that sort of thing.'

'You did not go yourself?' asked Bartholomew, wondering whether he would admit to being seen with Wynewyk just a few moments before.

Paxtone looked puzzled. 'No, why?'

'You have been in King's Hall since we last met?' pressed Bartholomew. 'The whole time?'

This time Paxtone's expression was more difficult to read. 'I was afraid one of my students would tamper if I left the experiment unsupervised. You know what these young men are like. God knows, Deynman, Redmeadow and Quenhyth are meddlesome enough.'

Bartholomew agreed, trying not to show that he found Paxtone's prevarication deeply disturbing. Could he trust Paxtone's analysis of the poison, when it was possible he had administered or created it himself. But, if that were the case, then why was he so willing to share his 'findings'? Surely, the safest thing would be to deny it contained poison at all? Bartholomew exchanged a glance with Michael, and saw the monk was as confounded as he was.

'Thank you,' said Michael, aware that the King's Hall physician was waiting for his discoveries to be acknowledged. 'This will help us greatly. However, we still do not know the answer to one basic question: did Bess knowingly obtain and swallow this potion; was she given it, because she had uncovered something she should not have done in her quest to locate her man; or did she simply find it, then take it because she was addled?'

'We will have to question Lavenham again,' said Bartholomew. He glanced at the apothecary's shop and saw Isobel loitering outside, passing the time by waggling her hips at anyone who looked in her direction. 'Bess's phial probably came from his shop, and the one that killed Warde

426

certainly did. We should ask him how many more of the things are loose in the town.'

'You have already interrogated Lavenham,' said Cheney. Bartholomew jumped in alarm; he had not noticed the silent approach of the merchants behind him, keen to hear what was being said.

'And he did not like it, either,' added Morice, his blue eyes darting here and there so that Bartholomew began to ask himself if there was anyone in the town who could hold a conversation without behaving as though he had just committed the most heinous of crimes. 'He was upset, and claimed you hinted that he had poisoned Warde, Deschalers and Bottisham. It is all nonsense, of course. Deschalers is no good to any of us dead. We needed him alive.'

'You cannot interrupt the Commissioners' meeting,' said Cheney, catching Michael's arm as the monk started determinedly towards Lavenham's shop. 'We want them to decide whether there is enough evidence to warrant a formal hearing – and if you disturb them now, they may never make up their minds. Lavenham and Bernarde are fighting for us, but Master Thorpe is annoyingly neutral.'

'Look at the Mortimers,' said Paxtone, pointing to where Thomas, Constantine and various nephews milled about. Thorpe was with them. 'They are as keen to know the verdict as you are.'

'Of course,' said Stanmore, watching as Thomas reeled against one of his clan, who struggled to hold him upright. The miller tugged a wineskin from his belt, and Bartholomew saw he was fortifying himself in anticipation of grim news to come. 'There is a lot of money at stake.'

'Look!' exclaimed Bartholomew, gazing at the shop. 'Is that smoke?'

'It *is* smoke,' said Stanmore, hurrying towards it. 'And

there are flames. Lavenham's shop is afire! Fetch water! Sound the alarm!'

In a town where many buildings were made of wood and had thatched roofs, and lots of houses were crammed into a relatively small area, fire was something all citizens feared. To some, it was even more frightening than the plague, and there was nothing like the stench of burning to throw the Fen-edge community into a panic. Humans were not the only ones terrified. Bartholomew could hear horses whinnying in alarm, kicking their iron-shod hoofs against stable doors with a rhythmic drumming sound. He hoped someone would let them out in time.

Stanmore's frantic cries had not brought people running with buckets of water to douse the flames. Instead they had caused havoc, with folk running here and there, desperate to return to their own properties and protect them before the fire could spread. Stanmore himself was among them. His house was not far from Lavenham's shop and, although he was wealthy enough to have purchased a building without immediate neighbours, there was always the danger that his wooden storage sheds would be ignited by the orange sparks that were dancing ever higher in the sky.

Bartholomew knew he should organise a chain of people with pails and other utensils, from the well in the Market Square to Lavenham's house. He also knew there would be burns, or injuries caused when folk fell in their haste to escape. But Matilde was at home that day, and his first thoughts were for the safety of his friend. So like all the others, he ran to see to his own interests, rather than trying to control the flames while there was still a chance.

Matilde was sitting quietly with Dame Pelagia when Bartholomew burst in on her. She listened to his garbled explanation, then climbed the steps to her bedroom to throw open the window shutters and see what was

428

happening. Bartholomew followed, and saw that across the tiled and thatched rooftops smoke rose in a thick black pall, lit here and there by orange embers that zigzagged into the grey sky like wild spirits. He and Matilde watched as the reed roof of Trinity Hall began to smoulder. Scholars scrambled across it, flapping with blankets and rugs.

'Young Alfred told me he saw Bess leaving Lavenham's shop moments before she died,' Matilde said quietly. 'I was just telling Dame Pelagia about it. I blame Lavenham for Bess's death. He sold her a dangerous potion knowing she was unstable in her mind. I think it was wrong of him.'

'You do not know he sold her anything,' said Bartholomew reasonably. 'He may have refused her, and she found the phial somewhere else. Apothecaries are careful with dangerous potions for exactly this reason: it is easy to blame them for accidents. For all his faults, Lavenham is not a fool.'

'But he is not careful, either. He will sell anyone anything, as long as they can pay. Alfred said Bess had something in her hand – probably the phial. But you should go, Matt. The wind is from the north, and the fire will not affect me. See what you can do to help others, while I round up Yolande's children. She will be beside herself if she comes home and finds they are not all here.' She stood on tiptoe and kissed him. 'Be careful, and come back when this is over.'

Bartholomew hurried down the stairs and raced through the parlour, noting it was already empty. Dame Pelagia had gone, but he was sure she did not intend to use her wiry strength for hauling buckets of water from the town's wells – she was more likely to use the chaos as a diversion to carry out some mission of her own. He ran to Michaelhouse, where Langelee had students gathering every available utensil that could hold water. They had already saturated the stable roof; sodden thatch made for poor kindling. The Master had the situation well under control, so the physician went to Stanmore's house on Milne Street, which was a good deal closer to Lavenham's shop, to see whether his brother-in-law needed an extra pair of hands.

The sheds on Stanmore's premises contained large quantities of valuable cloth, and the merchant stood in the centre of his yard with his hands on his hips, bawling orders to an army of scurrying apprentices. Every surface was to be drenched. The ground was already flooded, and apprentices were still hauling water-filled containers from the clothier's private well.

'Put that sheet over there!' he yelled. 'We will go up like Lavenham otherwise. Hurry, lads!'

The activity grew even more frenzied, and Bartholomew could hear leather buckets scraping against the well's stone sides as they were hauled up and down. Feet slapped in puddles as apprentices tore here and there, and the swish and drip of cascading water soon added to the cacophony. Bartholomew coughed. Smoke was swirling in thick, gagging clouds, and the town reeked of the acrid stench of burning. He could taste it in his mouth, and it seared the back of his throat.

He left the organised chaos of Stanmore's yard and went to the very disorganised chaos of the area around Lavenham's shop. The fire had taken hold completely and the roof was a sheet of blazing yellow that sent sparks far into the sky and released a column of thick, poisonous smoke. Paler billows poured through the windows, and the houses on either side were beginning to catch, despite desperate attempts by their owners to save them. Already they were a lost cause. Wynewyk and Paxtone were among the folk who gaped open-mouthed at the destruction. Paxtone was soot-stained, as if he had been closer to the blaze than was wise. They saw Bartholomew looking at them and immediately moved apart, as though trying to show that their proximity to each other was coincidence.

But there were more pressing matters than Wynewyk and Paxtone. Across Milne Street was Trinity Hall, which Bartholomew could see was too close for comfort to the blaze, and Clare College was not much safer. Students were everywhere, struggling to lay heavy, sodden blankets across the roofs. On a darker note, apprentices of masters whose homes were not at risk began to mass, and Bartholomew thought some of them might decide it was a good time for a fight. He heard one or two mutter that the Hand of Justice did not belong in the University's church.

'I have just been to the Hand of Justice,' said Morice, who was watching Lavenham's house burn without making any effort to prevent it. Cheney was with him. 'I asked it to make the wind blow a little more to the east, so that sparks do not come too close to my own property.'

'Where is Lavenham?' asked Bartholomew, looking at the apothecary's house and sure no one inside it would still be alive. The building was a flame-engulfed shell, and loud pops from within indicated that potions and bottles were exploding in the intense heat.

'I have not seen him,' said Morice. 'Nor Thorpe or Bernarde. Damn! It would be unfortunate to lose more Commissioners, after what happened to Warde. The King will wonder what we have been doing with them.' His foxy face assumed an expression of alarm. 'He might even raise our taxes, to warn us to be more careful in the future! That will not make me popular as Mayor.'

'You will not have to worry about your popularity soon,' said Bartholomew sharply. 'Because you may not have a town to rule. You should organise people with buckets, so the fire does not spread.'

'Mayors do not deal with buckets!' said Morice haughtily. 'And there is nothing I can do to prevent this disaster, so I may as well stand here and have a good view of it. At

431

least I will be able to tell the deceased's next-of-kin exactly what happened to their loved ones.'

Bartholomew gaped, astounded that Morice was not prepared even to try to save the town that had elected him. He was relieved when he heard a clatter of hoofs and saw Sheriff Tulyet cantering towards them on his grey mare.

'We will lose the whole town if we do not douse those flames,' Tulyet shouted to Morice, flinging himself out of his saddle. He was sweaty and breathless, as though he had ridden hard. 'I was returning from Trumpington when I saw the sparks. They knew the name of that man.'

'What man?' asked Bartholomew, bemused by the Sheriff's disjointed babble.

'Bess's lover,' said Tulyet impatiently. 'The villagers remembered a London messenger passing through just as the snows started. His name was Josse. Poor Josse. He has been all but forgotten, because of Bottisham, Deschalers, Bosel, Lenne, Isnard and now Warde. God's blood, Matt! This is a violent little town. Is Oxford as bad as this?'

'Your list of deaths and injuries will be even longer if you do not bring this blaze under control.'

Tulyet took a deep breath and turned to Morice. 'Right. What has been done so far?'

'Why are you asking me?' demanded Morice, startled.

Tulyet's face was a mask of disbelief. 'Because you are Mayor, man! It is your responsibility to take charge in situations like this.'

'Brother Michael and his beadles are collecting vessels that hold water,' said Cheney helpfully. 'And the scholars of Trinity Hall are on their roofs, flapping out flames.'

'Other than that, there is little we can do,' finished Morice carelessly. 'Fires are always devastating when they occur in confined areas. However, I asked the Hand of Justice to turn the wind away from my home. I once gave

Peterkin Starre a penny, so his bones should remember me kindly.'

Tulyet regarded him with furious disdain. 'Sweet Jesus! You cannot stand here and chatter like an elderly widow while the town ignites around your ears! What is wrong with you?'

'The wind is shifting to the east!' cried Morice, unperturbed by the Sheriff's reprimands. 'My prayers to the Hand have been answered! My house is saved! It is a miracle!'

'Not for the scholars of Gonville,' said Bartholomew in horror. 'They are now directly in the fire's path. Their hall will start to smoulder in moments!'

'Go and warn them,' ordered Tulyet. He glared at Morice and Cheney, then leapt into his saddle, controlling the horse tightly when it pranced, frightened by the showers of sparks that rained around it and by the explosions still emanating from Lavenham's shop. He cantered away in search of soldiers, while Bartholomew ran the short distance from Lavenham's inferno to Gonville Hall.

Everyone from Gonville, Fellows and students alike, had gathered in their yard, voices raised and expressions of anger and agitation creasing their faces. Bartholomew immediately sensed something was amiss that had nothing to do with the blaze. Three horses were tethered near the gate, laden down with saddlebags. Someone was leaving.

Pulham walked up to Bartholomew when the physician arrived hot and breathless. 'I know what you are thinking, and I am afraid you are wrong. It is not Thorpe who is going, more is the pity.'

'The wind has shifted,' said Bartholomew, thinking they could discuss Gonville's changing membership later. 'You need to take action now, or your roof will catch.'

'Do not presume to direct us in our own College!'

snapped Rougham. 'You, who cannot prescribe the correct potion for a man with a tickling cough.'

'The fire is being blown in this direction,' insisted Bartholomew, pointing to the smoke that was beginning to drift across the sky above their heads. 'I am trying to help.'

'We saw what your "help" did for Warde, and we want none of it here,' said Rougham nastily. 'We have enough problems without you interfering: Ufford, Despenser and Thompson are leaving.'

Bartholomew looked behind him, and saw the three scholars bowing to their other colleagues as they made their farewells. They were dressed for riding, with thick cloaks and boots with spurs. They completed their leave-taking, and walked towards Pulham and Rougham.

'We are sorry, Pulham,' said Thompson. Bartholomew saw that his arm was bandaged, and recalled he had been stabbed during the fight Paxtone had talked about. 'But we cannot stay here as long as Thorpe is a student.'

'Or as long as you intend to have the Hand of Justice installed,' added Despenser. 'I want no part of any institution that houses that fraudulent thing.'

'You will have nowhere to house anything if you do not act,' said Bartholomew urgently.

Rougham regarded him coldly. 'Are you still here? I thought I told you to leave.'

'I was mistaken when I prayed to it so fervently,' said Ufford, ignoring Rougham and addressing Pulham. 'I thought it was a holy relic, but now I see it is nothing of the kind. The sore on my mouth healed naturally, just as Bartholomew said it would.'

'What made you change your mind?' asked Pulham curiously, blithely oblivious of the danger his College was in. 'You, of all of us, were its most fervent adherent.'

'Thorpe,' said Ufford with a grimace. 'The very fact that *he* has taken an interest in it is enough to make me doubt

434

its authenticity. I was a fool, too eager to accept it without question. But I question it now, and Despenser is right: I want no part of Gonville as long as either Thorpe or the Hand is associated with it.'

'But the Hand will allow us to build our chapel,' Rougham protested. 'You know we are short of funds – indeed, we are in debt already and have been obliged to sell our books – so you cannot blame us for seizing an opportunity like this.'

Listening to them, Bartholomew suddenly understood exactly why Rougham had been so willing to spread the rumour that Isnard's leg had regrown. If the Hand were to be housed in Gonville, then it made sense that he should want it connected to as many miracles as possible. It was not just blind stupidity that had made Rougham claim Isnard was cured, but greed, too.

'We can and we do,' said Despenser quietly. 'That Hand will bring nothing but trouble. What do you imagine the other Colleges – or the town – will say when Thorpe asks the King to give it to Gonville? They will not sit back and allow it to happen, and I do not want to be part of the turmoil that will surely follow. I have my reputation to think about.'

'So do I,' said Ufford. 'I intend to do well at Court, and the King will not promote me if I am implicated in a riot. Besides, I have had enough of Thorpe. Where is he, by the way?'

'Probably somewhere near the fire,' said Despenser disapprovingly. 'It was probably him who started it. Ufford is right: Gonville will soon fall from grace if he is allowed to stay here.'

'The fire is spreading,' said Bartholomew, glancing at the sky again, and wondering why they persisted in having their debate now, of all times. He jumped back as Rougham came at him with a murderous scowl, and for a moment thought he intended to use his fists. He tensed, but Rougham was not the kind of man to engage in brawls he could not win – and he was wise enough to recognise that Bartholomew was bigger, fitter, and likely to hit back. Meanwhile, the students saw the danger of fire, even if the Fellows did not, and were pointing at the smoke and muttering uneasily. One or two, with more sense than their colleagues, started to run for buckets.

'But we cannot rid ourselves of Thorpe!' said Pulham, appealing to his three departing Fellows. 'He paid a term's fees in advance and we have spent the money on building materials. Also, we need the Hand of Justice, and he is our only chance of gaining it. And what about the fine altar cloths he will sew for our chapel? Do we let those go, too?'

'Have you seen him put a stitch to them?' asked Ufford. He saw the expression on Pulham's face. 'No, I thought not. He attacked me without provocation, and now he has stabbed Thompson. We will not stay here while he murders us all.'

'The fire!' shouted Bartholomew again. 'You *must* fetch water, or you will lose more than fees.' More students began to rush away from the Fellows, to collect pails.

'I told you to mind your own business,' snarled Rougham furiously. 'Get out! You are not welcome here.'

Bartholomew considered doing as he suggested, but Michaelhouse was not far away, and his own College would be in danger if Gonville burned. He could not leave until something was done to prevent the inferno from spreading.

'I am sure we can come to some arrangement that pleases us all,' pleaded Pulham, sounding almost tearful as Ufford started towards his horse. He looked up at the sky, and Bartholomew saw he was torn between the need to prevent his three richest Fellows from leaving and the urgency posed by the flames. 'Perhaps we *should* rid ourselves of Thorpe, and you may be right about the Hand.'

Ufford paused with his foot in the stirrup. 'If you mean what you say, then perhaps we can reconsider our position.' His colleagues gave nods of agreement. 'We shall reside in the Brazen George for the next few days, and discuss this further,' he said, then swung himself into his saddle and was gone, the sound of hoofs on cobbles all but drowning out the snap of sparks.

Rougham glared at Pulham. 'What did you say that for? You know we cannot afford to lose either the Hand of Justice or Thorpe. We have been forced to sell our books, and soon we shall be obliged to cut back on our feasts, too. We cannot squander an opportunity to earn more money such as the Hand presents. To do so would be a dereliction of our duty as Fellows.'

'They have a point,' said Pulham stubbornly. 'Thorpe is violent and unpleasant, and I do not blame them for not wanting him here. I do not enjoy his company myself. And they are also right about what will happen if the King gives us the Hand of Justice. There is no point building a fine chapel if it is to be burned to the ground in the next riot by irate townsmen.'

'You do not have to wait for the next riot,' said Bartholomew, breaking into their discussion and pointing to their roof. 'Your College is ablaze now!'

CHAPTER 11

For a moment, no one did anything, and then pandemonium erupted. A spark had fallen on to one of the College's roofs, and had quietly smouldered while the scholars had argued. It burst into flames with a low roar, and greedily consumed the rotten reeds and straw that comprised the thatch. White smoke swirled this way and that, as the flames were fanned by the wind.

'We are doomed!' cried Pulham, raising his hands in despair. 'What shall we do?'

'Fetch ladders, buckets and water,' ordered Bartholomew. He saw the scholars look at Rougham to see if they should do as his rival had ordered, and lost his temper with them. 'Hurry!'

'No! Rescue the silver and the hutches containing our money,' shouted Rougham, setting no store by Bartholomew's fire-fighting skills. 'And then see what furniture you can salvage. We shall lose the buildings for certain, so do not waste time on them.'

'Do you need help, Matt?' called Michael breathlessly, charging through the gate. His beadles were behind him, smoke-stained and dishevelled. Bartholomew nodded in relief, having anticipated that the scholars of Gonville planned to let him combat the fire alone.

While the scholars hauled their belongings to the yard – where they posed a formidable obstacle to those trying to contain the blaze – Bartholomew, Michael and the beadles set about attempting to rescue the buildings. Bartholomew climbed a ladder and laid wet blankets across

438

the smouldering thatch, while Beadle Meadowman climbed to its apex and poured bucket after bucket of water on to it. The damp straw hissed, spat and smoked horribly, stinging Bartholomew's eyes, but at last water won the contest with flames. Just as Rougham had supervised the evacuation of Gonville's last bench, Bartholomew announced that the fire was out and that the roof was too soggy for it to rekindle.

'Are you sure?' asked Pulham. Exhausted, he flopped into a handsome wooden chair. 'We have saved our College?'

'*We* have saved your College,' corrected Michael crisply. 'Matt, my beadles and I. *You* spent your time uselessly ferrying objects here and there. Well, you can carry it all back inside again now.'

'The fire is truly out?' asked Rougham, staring at the building as though he hoped it was not, just so he would not be proven wrong.

'It is,' said Michael. 'You will have to abandon your chapel in order to repair your roof, but you are lucky you still have walls. You were foolish not to have listened to Matt.'

'But I was right,' objected Rougham. 'Our first duty was to save what we could from indoors—'

'You were wrong,' interrupted Pulham angrily. It appeared he had had enough of Rougham and his opinions. 'You were wrong about that, and you are wrong about Thorpe and the Hand of Justice, too. I would rather have Thompson, Ufford and Despenser, than Thorpe and a false relic.'

'Now, you listen to me—' began Rougham sternly.

'No, *you* listen to *me*!' shouted Pulham. 'I am Acting Master here, and it is for me to decide what to do. So, Thorpe will leave, and I shall write to Colton in Avignon and see what *he* wants to do about the Hand.'

'Very well,' said Rougham stiffly. He gave Bartholomew

a hostile glower, and ordered the students to carry the furniture inside again. They groaned and complained bitterly, but the first splatters of a spring shower began to fall, and Michael called gleefully that they would have to look lively if they did not want their fine wood spotted with raindrops. They began to hurry, and had soon forgotten about Bartholomew, Michael and the beadles.

Bartholomew slumped against a wall, exhausted by the physical effort of scaling ladders and struggling with blankets made heavy with water. He flexed his shoulders, knowing they were going to be stiff the next morning, and took a deep breath of smoke-tainted air. Gonville might be safe, but there were other buildings still battling with flames.

'They did not even have the courtesy to offer us a drink to slake our thirst,' said Michael, aggrieved. His face was black with soot, and his normally immaculate gown was filthy with burned thatching. His hair was lank and oily, and sweat had given him a streaked appearance, like tigers and other mythical beasts Bartholomew had read about in the writings from the East. He suspected he did not look much different himself.

'You must forgive our manners,' said Pulham, emerging on cue with two goblets of claret. 'In all the confusion, we did not thank you.'

'Rougham never will,' said Bartholomew, drinking some, then pointedly passing the cup to Beadle Meadowman, who had worked as hard as anyone.

Pulham pulled a disagreeable face as he watched his best silver goblets pass between the rough hands of the University's beadles. 'Rougham means no harm. It is just his way.'

'He *does* mean harm,' said Michael, trying not to laugh as his beadles amused themselves by aping manners they thought might be employed by scholars at the high table

– cocked fingers and grotesquely puckered lips – as they sipped from vessels that would cost them a year's pay. 'He has accused Matt of killing Warde, when it was the medicine *he* prescribed that did the harm.'

'I am sorry he has been abusive. But you know what medical men are like. They are obliged to be arrogant and overbearing, because that is the only way to make their patients take the unpleasant potions they prescribe. They are all the same.'

'Are we?' asked Bartholomew, thinking that Pulham was probably right, generally speaking. A patient was far more likely to swallow something horrible if his physician bullied him into doing it.

'I did not come to argue,' said Pulham wearily. 'I came to thank you. I shall write to Colton, and *he* can decide whether we accept the Hand of Justice. It is too momentous an issue for me. Meanwhile, we are lucky the Mortimers have hired our legal skills, or we would be destitute. I do not suppose you know the Commissioners' verdict – about whether there will be a formal hearing?'

'The meeting was still in progress when the fire broke out,' said Michael. 'We do not know if everyone escaped, and the Commissioners' decision – if they reached one – seems unimportant now.'

'It will certainly be unimportant to Lavenham,' said Bartholomew. 'He has lost his house, his property and his livelihood.'

'Only if he is lucky,' said Michael. 'Let us hope he has not lost his life, too. But we should see what is happening elsewhere, and leave these scholars to quarrel about where to put their furniture.'

Pulham was dazed and unhappy as he escorted Bartholomew and Michael to the gate. His hands were unsteady, and the physician wondered whether he was up to the task of running a College in his Master's absence. Rougham was dismissive of him, and might well stage some sort of coup.

'Thank you, again,' he said, opening the door to let them out. 'If I can reciprocate in any way, then you must let me know. I am in your debt, and, if you make a request of me that is within my power to grant, I shall try my best to oblige you.'

'Then abandon the business with the Hand,' said Michael immediately, turning to face him. 'You must see it is more trouble than it is worth.'

'I know,' said Pulham wearily. 'But Rougham's voice is a powerful one, and he will also write to Colton and put his views. You may have asked for something beyond my capabilities to give.'

'Then tell me something about Bottisham that may help me solve his murder,' suggested Michael. 'I know there are things I have not been told because you want to preserve Gonville's integrity.'

'There are not—' began Pulham, glancing uneasily behind him.

Michael overrode him. 'There are. One small detail you neglected to pass on concerns the Mortimers – that they promised a handsome donation for your chapel if you took their case against the King's Mill. Master Thorpe mentioned it to me. Since Bottisham was to be one of the lawyers for this event, the offer of a large amount of money is surely pertinent information for a Senior Proctor investigating his murder? But I asked you about it twice, and you denied it.'

Pulham sighed in resignation. 'The donation was supposed to have been kept quiet until the dispute had been resolved, so we would not be accused of improper practices. Besides, there is always the possibility that we will lose, in which case the Mortimers will give us nothing.'

'Nothing stays secret for long in a place like Cambridge,' said Michael. 'But the time for games is over, Pulham. I want to know *anything* that might have a bearing on Bottisham's murder.'

Pulham rubbed his hands over his face, smearing it with soot. 'Very well. Deschalers sent messages offering Bottisham a truce, but Bottisham had fallen foul of that trick once, and was not about to let it happen again. You see, Deschalers had once offered to help pay for our chapel, claiming it would mark an end to the enmity between them, but then he withdrew with devastating effect.'

'We know that,' said Michael. 'It is common gossip in the town.'

Pulham nodded. 'Deschalers made no secret of the fact that he had made a fool of Bottisham. But about a month ago, he tried it again – he kept sending messages, begging Bottisham to parley with him. He even followed him to matins and lauds one night, and encouraged him to slip away from his devotions and speak to him in St Michael's graveyard! Bottisham refused his "hand of friendship", but Deschalers was persistent. In fact, Bottisham received a letter from him the morning before they died. He wanted to meet that very day, to discuss the terms of a truce.'

'We know this, too,' said Bartholomew. 'But why would Bottisham entertain meeting such a bitter enemy in a place like the King's Mill – and in the dark?'

Pulham frowned. 'But that is the odd thing. The letter did not suggest the King's Mill at night. It recommended the Brazen George at noon – in one of those private chambers at the back that the landlord keeps for sinister assignations.'

'Did Bottisham go?' asked Michael, not mentioning the fact that he used one of those chambers himself on a regular basis.

'I advised against it. But when he showed me Deschalers's letters, I felt they had a note of genuine contrition, and we knew he was mortally ill. It seemed churlish not to see what he wanted, so I offered to go in Bottisham's place.'

'So you went to the Brazen George at noon on the day they died,' surmised Michael, trying to keep his temper under control about the fact that Pulham had not been more honest earlier. 'Then what? Was Deschalers peeved that you arrived instead of Bottisham? Did he refuse to speak to you?'

'He understood why Bottisham declined to meet him. He was disappointed, but not surprised. Then he said he was thinking of changing his will in a way that would see a princely sum come Bottisham's way – for our chapel.'

'I see,' said Michael flatly. 'And did you believe him?'

'Yes. I think he was sincere this time.'

Michael could contain himself no longer. 'Then why did you not tell me all this sooner?' he exploded. 'Surely you must see it has a bearing on the case?'

Pulham was defensive. 'But I really do not believe Deschalers's will had anything to do with Bottisham's death – and *that* is why I did not mention my meeting to you. I did not want to lead you astray with information that was irrelevant and confusing.'

Michael was angry. 'That is for *me* to decide. Do you think me a fool, unable to distinguish between what is important and what is not?'

Bartholomew could see Pulham regretted having spoken to Michael, and that the monk's ire was likely to make him wary of confiding anything else. He laid a warning hand on Michael's shoulder. 'What else can you tell us, Master Pulham?' he asked gently.

Pulham took a deep breath. 'When we were at the Brazen George, Deschalers showed me his new will. This had been signed, but not sealed. It was quite simple. Bottisham was to have a house on Bridge Street, and Julianna was to have the rest. Two beneficiaries. He said it was to atone for years of bitterness and anger that should have been avoided.

But he said he would not seal it – so it would not be legal – unless Bottisham came to him in person.'

'The will was made out?' asked Bartholomew, angry in his turn. 'Here is something Quenhyth neglected to mention.'

'I doubt Quenhyth wrote this,' said Pulham. 'That boy has neat, rather lovely writing. This one was scribbled, as though it was jotted down in great haste. Deschalers told me it was his third will. The first made a bequest to his apprentices, but he had decided against doing that a month ago. The second left everything, except a chest, to Julianna. And the third was to have benefited Bottisham.'

'I see,' asked Michael tightly. 'And *then* what happened?'

'I do not know. I returned to Gonville, and told Bottisham what had transpired, but it was the last conversation we ever had. I do not know whether he believed Deschalers's sincerity, and I do not know whether he contacted Deschalers and asked to meet.'

'This is all very intriguing,' said Michael icily. 'But Deschalers's will was *not* changed. Julianna inherited everything except Quenhyth's box – and Bottisham died before he could acquire this Bridge Street house anyway.'

Pulham nodded. 'So you see why I said nothing about this earlier. And yet . . .' He trailed off.

Michael regarded him with beady eyes. 'And yet what?'

Pulham closed his eyes, and seemed to be undergoing some sort of inner battle. Bartholomew watched in fascination. He had never seen so many emotions – worry, doubt, fear and unhappiness – so clearly etched on the face of a man. Eventually, Pulham opened his eyes and began to fiddle with the purse he carried at his waist. Wordlessly, he handed Michael a document. The monk scanned it, then passed it to Bartholomew. It was a deed, badly written and bearing a mark that the physician recognised as Deschalers's 'signature' – a crude letter D.

'It is Deschalers's new will,' he said, returning the parchment to Michael. It amounted to powerful evidence, and he did not think Pulham should have it back. 'It gives Bottisham the Bridge Street house and Julianna the rest of his property.'

Pulham nodded miserably. 'It is the one Deschalers showed me in the Brazen George – signed, but not sealed.'

'Deschalers gave you this?' asked Bartholomew, slightly puzzled. Pulham shook his head, and several facts came together in the physician's mind. 'It was *you* who burgled Deschalers's house the night he died? I almost caught you, and you escaped by climbing down the back of the house.'

Pulham looked startled. 'I assure you I did not! Do you imagine me capable of that sort of agility? I was hiding under the bed, waiting for you to leave.'

'But you emerged to stop me from falling through the window,' said Bartholomew. 'I *knew* that old servant did not have the strength to haul me to safety! It was you.'

Pulham flushed bashfully. 'I only just managed to reach you in time. I escaped when the servant came and started burbling about crow pie – I just walked down the stairs and left through the front door. However, the window shutters opened in Cheney's house as I left, and I think he saw me.'

'His prostitute did,' said Bartholomew. He turned to the monk. 'When Una claimed she saw someone leave through Deschalers's front door, we assumed she was either mistaken about the time, or drunk. But she was right, she did see a burglar: Pulham.'

'Why did you do it?' asked Michael, regarding Pulham with rank disapproval. 'You are Acting Master of a highly respected College. Theft should not be something you enjoy.'

'I did not *enjoy* it,' cried Pulham, distressed. He made an attempt to calm himself. 'When I heard Bottisham and

446

Deschalers had died in peculiar circumstances within hours of Deschalers making his new will, I knew what people would say. Bottisham was a good man, and I did not want his reputation besmirched by scandals and rumours.'

'You thought folk would assume he had killed Deschalers for the Bridge Street house,' surmised Michael. 'But what did you intend to do with the new will, once the fuss had died down? Contest Julianna's inheritance?'

'I could not, even if I wanted to. I am a lawyer and I know about this kind of thing. This will is signed, but it bears no seal. As far as the courts go, it is not worth the parchment it is written on. But can you imagine what folk would have made of such a thing anyway?'

'People do not care about legal niceties,' agreed Bartholomew. 'They would only see the fact that Deschalers changed his will in Bottisham's favour – and died suddenly in Bottisham's company.'

'Quite. They would have claimed Bottisham had tried to murder him, and the two engaged in a fatal struggle. I took the will to protect them both. I probably should have destroyed it.'

'I am glad you did not,' said Michael. 'It is evidence. Is there anything else you want to tell me?'

'Just one thing,' said Pulham. 'I was not the only one raiding Deschalers's house that night. Someone else was there, too, creeping around in the dark. He gave me quite a fright, I can tell you.'

'Who?' asked Michael.

'I have no idea. I thought it might be Julianna, Edward Mortimer or young Thorpe. Or even a merchant, looking for incriminating documents about past unsavoury business deals. But I did not see his face, so I cannot tell you who he – or she – was. Just that he slithered out of the back window.'

'And you cannot identify him, can you, Matt?' asked

Michael accusingly, as though the physician was deliberately trying to thwart him.

'I have already told you it was too dark,' said Bartholomew patiently. 'It could have been anyone – man, woman, scholar, townsman. But at least we know why Una's account conflicted with mine.'

'Yes, but it does not help,' said Michael crossly. 'It is only yet another loose end to clear up.'

Bartholomew and Michael walked the short distance from Gonville to Lavenham's shop. The entire town seemed to have been affected by the blaze, even though the damage had been mostly confined to the houses immediately adjacent to Lavenham's home. People darted here and there, calling loudly to each other in excitement, and pools of water from slopped buckets lay in every pothole and dip in the road. A greasy veneer of soot coated many buildings, and the streets were even more littered with rubbish than usual.

Lavenham's home had been reduced to a black skeleton, punctuated by jagged, charred pieces of fallen timber. The houses next door had fared little better; one still had its roof, but neither would be safe for human habitation again. The air around them was rank with the stench of burning, and Bartholomew detected something rotten and unsettling underneath, where potions that should not have been heated or mixed had combined to deadly effect.

'Have you discovered what happened?' asked Michael when he saw Tulyet, who looked as weary as Bartholomew felt. The Sheriff's clothes were stained and sodden, indicating that he had been in the thick of the action. Morice and Cheney, who still hovered near the seat of the fire, were relatively pristine, suggesting their role had been confined to spectating. This had not gone unnoticed, and they were being given a wide berth and plenty of dark looks

448

by townsfolk and scholars alike. Neither seemed to care.

'The fire started in Lavenham's shop,' said Tulyet. 'We do not know how yet, but an apothecary is always boiling some potion or other, so it is not surprising something was forgotten and caught alight. Accidents happen, even in the most careful of households.'

'An accident?' asked Michael cautiously. 'But the King's Commissioners were inside at the time.'

'So?' asked Tulyet. He caught the glance exchanged between monk and physician. 'You think the fire was started deliberately, to interfere with the Commissioners' business?'

'Or worse,' said Michael. 'Do not forget that Warde has already been murdered.'

'God help us,' muttered Tulyet. 'So, who do you suspect of committing such a heinous act? Whoever it was deserves to hang, because the entire town might have been lost.'

'I saw the Mortimer clan – including Edward and Thorpe – lurking around just before the alarm was raised,' said Michael. 'Not to mention two merchants who have a financial interest in the case – Morice and Cheney.'

'And Paxtone and Wynewyk,' said Bartholomew to himself. 'I hope to God their suspicious behaviour has not extended to arson.'

'So, you have no idea who might have started this mischief?' said Tulyet. 'Your suspects for the fire are essentially the same as your suspects for the murders of Warde, Deschalers and Bottisham?'

Michael nodded. 'Our culprit is a clever man – or a lucky one – and left little in the way of clues.'

'Poor Lavenham,' said Tulyet, gazing at the mess of spars and hot, crumbling plaster that still smoked gently. 'But I thought we were going to lose Gonville Hall, too, when the wind shifted. It was selfish of Morice to ask the Hand of Justice to do that, just to save his own property.'

449

He glared at the Mayor, who had sent a servant to fetch his wineskin and was enjoying a little liquid refreshment while he gawked at the destruction around him.

'I do not think Morice had anything to do with the wind changing direction,' said Michael, puzzled that Tulyet should think it should. 'It happens all the time, quite naturally.'

'But not usually at so opportune a moment,' argued Tulyet. 'I shall reserve judgement on the matter, personally. Many folk heard him praying, and his favour with the Hand is the talk of the town. How else do you think he stands unmolested, when so many folk are furious with him for not helping to quench the fire? They are afraid that if they attack him, the Hand will strike them down.'

'Where are Lavenham and the other Commissioners?' asked Bartholomew, changing the subject before the Michael and the Sheriff could begin a debate over the matter. He could see the monk was itching to tell Tulyet exactly what he thought of folk who believed the relic was responsible for events that had a perfectly rational explanation. 'They escaped the inferno, I hope?'

'I have not seen them,' replied Tulyet. 'But then *I* have not had time to stand around and look for people. *I* have been busy.' He cast another venomous glower at Morice.

'We all have,' said Michael soothingly. 'And tonight you must come to Michaelhouse, so we can exchange information about this case. I have a few things to tell you.'

'I have very little to tell you,' said Tulyet gloomily.

'Arrive early,' Michael went on. 'We are having blood pudding and pig-brain pottage, followed by fried gooseberries – saved from last year, so they are a little sour and we have no sugar. Ensure you are punctual, because you will not want to miss it.'

'Come to me instead,' said Tulyet, trying to hide his revulsion. 'My wife plans roasted lamb with rosemary and carrots for today. And I can ask her to make Lombard slices,' he added, a little desperately, when Michael hesitated.

'Very well,' said Michael, sounding as though he was doing him a favour by accepting. Relieved by his narrow escape from a Michaelhouse repast, the Sheriff strode away to supervise the dumping of yet more water on the smouldering remains of Lavenham's house. Fires had a nasty habit of rekindling, and Tulyet had no intention of allowing a second blaze to start.

Bartholomew started to laugh. 'Agatha is cooking fish soup with cabbage this evening.'

'I know,' said Michael comfortably. 'But I do not like cabbage, and Tulyet's wife keeps a good table. Her Lombard slices are among the best in Cambridge. She says her secret is that she fries them in butter, rather than lard, and that she soaks her almonds overnight in wine.'

'I see,' said Bartholomew, not very interested in recipes that had no known medical application. 'But I am worried about the Commissioners – especially Master Thorpe. I would not like to think of him roasted in the fire with Lavenham and Bernarde.'

They watched the apothecary's apprentices pick their way through the steaming, hissing rubble, hopping lightly so they did not burn their feet. One stood on an unstable timber, and it started to tilt. Bartholomew tensed, anticipating that he would bring the whole fragile structure down on top of him, but the fellow leapt away with impressive agility, and no harm was done.

'Where is Lavenham?' Bartholomew called to him, after a scan of the onlookers who fringed the ruins told him the apothecary was still not among them. 'And Isobel?'

'We have not seen them since that meeting started,' replied the apprentice. He grimaced. 'You would think they would be here, would you not? Trying to salvage what they can, and not leaving the dirty work to us.'

'Yes,' said Bartholomew softly. 'You would.'

'What will happen to us now?' grumbled another lad, lifting a plank to look underneath. 'How are we supposed to work with the premises gone? Does Lavenham have enough funds invested to buy another house, so we can start again? Or do we have to seek alternative employment?'

'Let us hope not,' said Bartholomew soberly.

Bartholomew wanted to go home to Michaelhouse, to wash the smoke and grime from his clothes and hair, but a nagging concern for Master Thorpe, Bernarde and Lavenham kept him on Milne Street and he became one of a small crowd that simply could not bring themselves to leave. He kept anticipating that sooner or later an apprentice would pick up a piece of 'wood' that was harder, denser and oilier than the others, and they would then know exactly what had happened to the Commissioners. Michael lost interest and wandered away. He had not been gone long before he returned.

'Look who I found in St Mary the Great,' he said, smiling as he indicated a soot-stained Master Thorpe. 'Giving thanks for his deliverance.'

'To God,' said Thorpe firmly. 'Not to the so-called Hand of Justice.'

'I am glad to see you,' said Bartholomew warmly, taking Thorpe's hand. 'I was worried you might have been trapped inside when the fire took hold.'

Thorpe smiled his pleasure that he should care. 'I escaped by climbing through a window on an upper floor and jumping to safety. I shouted to Bernarde and Lavenham to follow, but the smoke was swirling around so thickly that I could not see whether they did. It is a grim business when a son hates his father so. Perhaps I was wrong to disown him when he returned with his King's Pardon.'

Bartholomew raised his eyebrows. 'You think your son set the fire?'

'I saw him with Edward Mortimer, watching Bernarde and me as we entered Lavenham's shop. Who else would want to harm us? Lavenham has no enemies, and neither does Bernarde.'

'They do,' said Bartholomew vehemently. 'The Mortimer clan, for a start.'

'And who leads the Mortimer clan these days?' asked Thorpe archly. 'It is not Thomas or Constantine. It is Edward. And Edward is my son's friend.'

'So, they thought they would strike two birds with one stone,' mused Michael. 'A hated father, and two Commissioners who were sure to argue against Mortimer's Mill. How did the meeting go, or should I not ask?'

'We had not reached a decision,' said Thorpe wearily. 'I wanted to set a date for a formal hearing, but Lavenham and Bernarde said the evidence was so clear cut that further enquiries were unnecessary. They wanted a verdict against Mortimer issued there and then.'

'This is what happens when you appoint Commissioners who have a vested interest in the outcome,' said Michael. 'Any discussion is limited to repeated statements of "fact".'

'Since we were unable to agree, I said we should ask the King to appoint new Commissioners. Bernarde and Lavenham opposed that, of course.'

'And then the fire started?' asked Bartholomew.

Thorpe nodded. 'The apprentices and Isobel had been sent away for the afternoon so that they would not disturb us. The blaze was *not* a result of their carelessness, as Tulyet thinks. There were no workmen around, and there were no potions bubbling in the workshop. Our meeting took place in the solar upstairs, and I am sure the fire started directly below us.'

They all looked around when there was a shriek from

one of the apprentices. Expecting that he had picked up timber that was too hot to hold, or had twisted an ankle in the shifting rubble, Bartholomew dashed towards him, hopping from foot to foot as the heat penetrated the soles of his boots. But pain had not caused the young man to scream. He pointed an unsteady finger into the wreckage, and the physician bent to inspect what he had found.

'Well,' he muttered, moving a piece of charred wood. 'Someone did not escape the inferno.'

'Who?' asked Michael, leaning forward, but backing away hurriedly when he saw the misshapen figure huddled up with clenched fists and hairless head. 'Is it Lavenham?'

'It must be,' said Thorpe grimly. 'He must have lingered, to see whether he could save his shop. Now the crime is more serious than arson, Brother. It is murder. Even my slippery son will find himself unable to wriggle free from *that* charge again, and I shall see he does not – even if I have to ride to Westminster and petition the King myself.'

'I think we can prove the fire was started deliberately,' said Bartholomew, clambering over more scaly-black timbers to reach what had been Lavenham's yard. 'There was a huge pile of kindling here. I heard Isobel complaining about it when I visited their shop last week. Some of it has gone, and I am willing to wager it was used to light the fire.'

'Would Thorpe and Edward have known about convenient sources of combustible material in Lavenham's yard?' asked Michael doubtfully. 'Or are we jumping to unfounded conclusions?'

'Perhaps Isobel and Lavenham argued about it in front of other customers, too,' said Bartholomew, making his way back to the corpse again. 'It was not a secret.'

'Is there any way to prove that is Lavenham, Matt?' asked Michael, still hanging back. 'I know there is not much to go on – no clothes, no hair, no face, and not much in the way of anything else – but you have a way with these things, and we cannot ask Isobel to do it.'

'It is not Lavenham,' said Bartholomew, pulling the charred corpse to one side with great care, not liking the way bits flaked off and landed on his feet. He pointed at something near the body's waist. 'There is a lot of metal here – melted, but metal nonetheless. And who do you know who carries a good deal of metal on his belt?'

'Keys?' asked Michael. 'Your melted metal is a bunch of keys? That means our corpse belongs to Bernarde, who was always jangling the things.'

'Then where is Lavenham?' asked Master Thorpe.

'I do not know,' said Bartholomew. 'But not here, I think. We must search elsewhere for him.'

Bartholomew headed for the newly constructed lavatorium as soon as he reached Michaelhouse. Hurling his smoke-spoiled clothes into one corner, he scrubbed his bare skin with icy water. Michael joined him, but washed only those parts that were not covered by clothes. He declined to wet his hair, too, maintaining that it might bring on an ague. Instead he rubbed chalk powder into it, which he claimed would counteract the darkening effects of soot. He donned a fresh habit and handed the dirty one to Agatha, who said it needed no more than a good brushing and a day or two of airing in the latrines. Michael was pleased it did not need laundering, because there was always a danger the wool would shrink, and he claimed tight habits made him look fat.

Bartholomew felt better when he had changed into a tunic and leggings that did not stink of smoke. He scrubbed at his damp hair with a rag, while Michael doused himself liberally with rosewater in an attempt to mask the stench of burning that his careless ablutions had done little to remedy. The lavatorium began to smell like a brothel, and

Bartholomew left, complaining that Michael's perfumes were worse than the odour of cinders and ash.

'Now what?' asked Michael, making his way to his room to collect his spare cloak. 'Shall we search for Lavenham ourselves, or shall we leave it to Dick Tulyet? It is suspicious that he should disappear quite so soon after a devastating fire destroyed his home and killed Bernarde. Should we be concerned for Isobel, do you think? Or will she be the mastermind behind this nasty business?'

'She might,' said Bartholomew tiredly. 'She seems more intelligent than her husband, and might well conceive of a plan to ensure the Commission found in favour of the mill she had invested in. But their house, their livelihood and Bernarde's life seems a high price to pay for it.'

'I have always been suspicious of Lavenham,' said Michael. 'He acts as though he understands very little of what goes on, but I am sure he knows more than we think. He had good reason to kill Bottisham – he was about to represent his rivals in the mill dispute. Meanwhile, Warde was a Commissioner prepared to listen to the Mortimers' side of the quarrel. Lavenham might well be our killer.'

'And Deschalers? Why would Lavenham kill him?'

'Deschalers's death was incidental. Lavenham followed Bottisham one night, intending to murder him. Bottisham went to the King's Mill. When Deschalers, arriving to meet Bottisham, caught Lavenham red-handed, he was obliged to kill him, too.'

'There is a flaw in your reasoning, Brother. Deschalers had the key to the mill, so he must have arrived at this meeting first, not Bottisham. Deschalers would not have stood by and watched Bottisham murdered without doing something.'

'He was mortally ill,' argued Michael. 'Weak. He might have been too feeble to help Bottisham. But you are quibbling. The point is that this case has taken a new turn, and

Lavenham is mysteriously missing. We should at least ask him why. Will you come with me to St Mary the Great?'

'What for?' asked Bartholomew, who longed to lie down and rest. He was desperately tired, physically and mentally, and wanted time to allow the weariness to drain from his muscles.

'For two reasons,' replied Michael. 'First, Redmeadow is in your room and is waving at you in a way that suggests he wants some text or other explained. You will have no peace there. And second, I want to ensure the Hand of Justice has not attracted some large and hostile post-fire crowd that might cause mischief when darkness falls.'

Reluctantly, Bartholomew followed the monk up St Michael's Lane and on to the High Street. The sweet aroma of roses wafted around them as they walked, almost, but not quite, masking the stench of sewage from a blocked drain and the sickly-sweet reek of a dead cat that had been tossed on top of a roof, possibly by the cart that had killed it. Bartholomew started to think about Thomas Mortimer and his reckless driving, and wondered whether Lenne had returned to Thetford now that his mother had been buried.

The town had an atmosphere of unease that was so apparent, it was almost physical. People looked around warily, and the yelling that had accompanied the fire, had dropped to whispers and low voices. The High Street was unusually quiet, with only the rattle of carts and the thump of horses' hoofs on compressed manure breaking the silence.

'I do not like this,' muttered Michael, unnerved. 'It feels as if something is about to happen.'

'It is odd,' agreed Bartholomew. 'But there are no apprentices or students massing on street corners, so it does not seem that folk are spoiling for a fight.'

'But there is an aura,' declared Michael, gazing around him.

'Meaning what?' asked Bartholomew sceptically.

'Meaning that I shall have every one of my beadles on duty tonight, and that any scholar seen on the streets after dusk can expect to be detained in my cells until morning. I shall recommend that Dick takes similar steps with the townsfolk.'

'Do you think it is something to do with the Hand of Justice?' asked Bartholomew. 'I do not mean literally, since we both know it is no more holy than that rosewater you hurled all over yourself. I mean do you think people might be waiting for it to do something?'

'Such as what? Sprout wings and wend its way to Heaven in front of our sinful eyes? Burst free from the tower in a spray of stone and mortar, and slap anyone who has committed a crime? It will have its work cut out for it, if it intends to do that. It will be busy from now until dawn.'

'Jest if you will, Brother, but what *we* think is irrelevant. It is what its followers believe that is important now.'

The small crowd that was usually present outside the University Church had swelled to a gathering of impressive size, just as Michael had predicted. Most folk were kneeling or standing quietly with bowed heads, and the mood was more reverent than threatening. Michael tended to disapprove of any large assembly when the sun was about to go down, but there was little he could do about this one – people had a right to pray where they liked, and no one was actually doing anything wrong. Even the pickpockets had ceased trading for the day, and were sitting harmlessly in the churchyard.

The two scholars eased through them, careful not to jostle anyone who might take offence, and entered the church's shady interior. This, too, was full, and a number of people knelt on the flagstones or leaned against the sturdy pillars of the nave. A mass was in progress, led by Chancellor Tynkell, and the High Altar was bathed in a golden light from dozens of candles. The aroma of cheap incense that wafted along the aisles competed valiantly with the stink of Michael's rosewater. William, who had been near the back of the nave, spotted the monk and hurried to join him, religious devotions forgotten.

'Have you heard?' he asked without preamble. 'Thomas Mortimer is dead.'

'Dead?' asked Bartholomew, shocked as he listened to the Franciscan friar's bald pronouncement. 'But I saw him not long ago, loitering in Milne Street while the Commissioners met.'

'Well, he is in the Lady Chapel now. Come and see for yourself.'

He headed towards the sumptuously decorated chapel before either of his colleagues could ask further questions. A couple of Mortimer cousins loitered at the entrance, but they stood aside and allowed the three scholars to enter. Bartholomew was surprised to find the oratory full. Virtually all the Mortimer clan and their womenfolk were present; only those with small children had been left at home. At the front, Constantine was kneeling before a hastily erected bier on which lay a body. The pendulous ale-drinker's gut rising under the covering sheet could be no one's but Thomas's.

Lurking by the window was Edward, his face expressionless, while Julianna perched on a stool, looking bored and restless. Thorpe lounged against a nearby pillar, and his face creased into a sneer when he saw Bartholomew and Michael. Both he and Edward wore clothes that were dishevelled and soot-stained, although Bartholomew suspected they had done little to help quench any flames.

'This was Mistress Lenne's doing,' said Constantine, when he heard footsteps behind him. He turned to face the scholars, and Bartholomew was shocked by the change in the man. He seemed small and cowed, and his bristling confidence had been replaced by a crushing grief.

'She is dead,' said Bartholomew, thinking the man must be out of his wits. 'Whatever happened to Thomas was not her fault.'

'It was!' cried Constantine, so loudly that his voice echoed all around the church. Tynkell faltered at the High Altar mass, and the baker struggled to regain control of himself and explain. 'She cursed Thomas with the Hand of Justice. She asked her son to carry her to it the day she died.'

'She did,' said Bartholomew to Michael. 'The journey hastened her end by several hours. I wondered why she had insisted on going to the Hand, when it was clear she did not want to live. I assumed she was making an act of contrition for some ancient sin that plagued her conscience.'

'She met Thomas there,' continued Constantine in a whisper. 'She looked him in the eye, pointed her finger at him, and declared he would die horribly for what he had done to her husband.'

'We assumed the Hand of Justice had seen his side of the story when he was not struck down immediately,' added Edward, who did not sound at all sorry that his uncle was dead. Bartholomew wondered if he stood to benefit in some way – perhaps he had urged his drunken kinsman to sign a document that would see him inherit the mill to the exclusion of more deserving heirs. 'I see we were wrong.'

'Mistress Lenne brought about my brother's death,' wept Constantine. 'Poor innocent Thomas!'

'He was hardly that!' remarked Julianna from her stool. 'Your brother *did* kill Mistress Lenne's husband, Constantine. We all know that was no accident. I saw it with my own eyes.'

Bartholomew stared at her. 'You did? But why did you not tell the Sheriff?'

Julianna raised her eyebrows in cynical amusement. 'You think I should have told Tulyet that I saw my uncle-by-marriage so deep in his cups that his eyes were closed – I am sure he was asleep – when he drove his cart into that old man? Have you not heard of family loyalty, Bartholomew?' Her voice took on a mocking quality, and she glared at Constantine, as if she had heard these words rather too often since her wedding.

'Shut up, woman!' snapped Edward.

'Why?' flashed Julianna. 'Thomas is dead now – cursed by an old woman whose piteous voice was heard by the Hand of Justice. What difference does it make whether I speak out? Will you kill me, as you murdered Bosel?'

'You must protect the Mortimer name – your name – now,' said Constantine in a low, shocked voice. 'You are our kin. And we did not kill Bosel. I have no idea who did that.'

'Marriages can be annulled,' said Julianna sulkily. 'I know men who can arrange it, and I do not want Edward any more. He is disappointing as a lover now he has secured the Deschalers fortune. He prefers the company of his man-friend to that of his wife.' She made an obscene gesture in Thorpe's direction, lest anyone be in any doubt as to what she meant.

'No, I am just weary of *you*,' said Edward unpleasantly. 'Other women in the town can attest to my manliness, so do not think to tarnish me with that brush.'

'I do not care about your family obligations,' said Michael sternly to Julianna. 'You should have told the truth about what you saw.'

'I know,' said Julianna bitterly. 'I should have denounced the old sot and seen him hanged.'

'So what stopped you?' demanded William.

'This lot,' said Julianna, waving a hand at her assembled in-laws. 'They kept droning on and on about kinship and

461

loyalty, and they nagged me so much that I did as they asked, just to shut them up. But justice prevailed in the end. The Hand and Mistress Lenne saw to that.'

'You are *still* under an obligation to put your new family first, Julianna,' said Constantine hoarsely. 'Thomas's death does not change the fact that you are married to my son.'

'Perhaps,' replied Julianna enigmatically, causing Constantine to look sharply at her, although Edward did not deign to respond. He smiled, rather unpleasantly, as though he knew something she did not. Bartholomew guessed what it was: Julianna was clearly under the impression that she could have her marriage dissolved, just as she had done with Master Langelee, but she would be in for a shock. Marriages were not often annulled, especially not if the husband objected. Julianna's inheritance represented a fortune, and Edward was not going to let any part of it slip through his fingers. Poor Julianna was stuck with him, no matter what she thought.

'What happened to Thomas?' asked Michael, looking down at the shrouded figure.

Edward stepped forward and whisked the sheet away so that Bartholomew and Michael could see the extent of the injuries Thomas had suffered before his death. His clothes were drenched in blood, his face was crushed almost beyond recognition, and his limbs and chest were unnatural shapes where bones had broken. But if Edward had wanted to shock the scholars, he was disappointed. Bartholomew had an academic interest in such matters, while Michael, although he disliked the more grisly aspects of his post, had sufficient self-control not to flinch. Even William had seen enough violent death to be dispassionate.

'A horse bolted from Lavenham's stables during the fire,' said Constantine, sounding as if he was going to cry again. 'It collided with Thomas, and he was trampled.'

'He was drunk when the fire raged,' said Bartholomew,

462

recalling how the miller had reeled and slobbered from his wineskin just before the inferno had started. He edged past Michael to inspect the body properly, and frowned. The injuries did not fit with the story he had been told. 'But there are no hoof marks here. Just signs that he was crushed.'

'Rubbish,' said Edward. 'There are hoof marks everywhere and we shall use them as proof.'

'Proof of what?'

'Proof that will allow us to sue Lavenham,' said Edward, casually inspecting his fingernails. 'He was negligent in the way he stabled his nags. If he had tethered them properly, they would not have escaped and Thomas would still be alive.' He exchanged a grin with Thorpe.

Bartholomew gazed at him, uncertain whether he was making a jest in poor taste, but he seemed perfectly serious. Julianna saw the physician's bemusement.

'He means it,' she said. 'He really does intend to make Lavenham pay for the death of Thomas.'

'After what *you* have just said?' asked Michael, astounded. 'That Thomas killed Lenne and injured Isnard because he fell asleep at the reins? Does it not occur to you that suing Lavenham would be a gross injustice?'

Thorpe did his best to be nonchalant, but he was enjoying himself too much to succeed. His smile was triumphant when he saw the scholars' shock. 'We know our rights. The town did not care about justice when Edward and I were ordered to abjure the realm, so why should we care about it now?'

'Well, you might take a lesson from Thomas,' suggested Michael. 'He thought he could evade punishment for his sins, and look what happened to him.'

Thorpe had the grace to look uneasy, but Edward did not react. 'That is different,' he said.

'Why?' asked William.

'Because *we* have not been cursed by Mistress Lenne.'

463

'No,' agreed Thorpe, regaining his confidence. 'Nor did we crush any old men with carts. The folk *we* killed two years ago deserved to die.'

Some of Edward's family looked distinctly uncomfortable with this claim, and one of them collected his wife and aimed for the door. Two or three others followed, and Bartholomew saw there were fractures in the clan that had not been there before. A month ago, they would have stuck together no matter what, but Edward's outrageous behaviour seemed too much, even for them. Constantine watched the dissenters leave with a troubled expression.

'The Hand of Justice will never allow mischief to befall *us*,' Thorpe continued, ignoring the small exodus. 'It knows how we have suffered – exiled to places like Albi and Calais.'

'But even if Lavenham survived the fire, he will be penniless,' reasoned Michael. 'The fire deprived him of all he owns. He will not be able to pay you anything – negligently tethered horses or no.'

'That is not our problem,' said Thorpe loftily. 'The town will pay – as it will pay the compensation owed to me and Edward for our unjust banishment. After all, it is only fair.'

Neither Bartholomew nor Michael could think of much to say as they walked to Tulyet's house on Bridge Street that evening. They were appalled by Edward's plan to sue Lavenham and, while they hoped the law would be sufficiently sane to see the claim for the outrage it was, their recent experience with England's eccentric legal system and its dishonest clerks did not fill them with confidence.

'I cannot believe this,' said Michael, as they passed the outskirts of the Jewry. A miasma of rosewater still encased him, and Bartholomew tried to keep his distance. 'If the Mortimers gain a single penny over Thomas's death I shall join those restless peasants who are urging rebellion, and overthrow the King myself.'

464

'Michael!' exclaimed Bartholomew, glancing around him uneasily. The monk's voice had been loud, and there were plenty of people close enough to have heard. 'You are always warning me about making treasonous remarks, but I have never made that sort of proclamation on the High Street.'

'Well, I am angry,' pouted Michael. 'And disillusioned. I have been upholding University laws for five years now, and I thought right was on my side. But, in the last two weeks I have seen murderers pardoned; I have seen them awarded money for their "suffering"; I have seen a drunken merchant crush folk under his cart with no reprisals; I have seen Deschalers, Warde and Bottisham dead by foul means and I do not know why; and I have seen Bosel callously dispatched to protect Thomas's precious reputation. And now Edward plans to sue the destitute Lavenham.'

'We do not know Lavenham is destitute,' said Bartholomew. 'He may have a fortune secreted away – he certainly still has his share of the King's Mill. And he may be dead and therefore beyond the Mortimers' clutches. We do not know Bosel was killed to protect Thomas, either. Constantine says not. And finally you know as well as I do that "right" and "justice" have nothing to do with the law, so you cannot be disillusioned.'

At Tulyet's house, Michael rapped on the door, becoming impatient when it was not answered immediately. He had missed a number of snacks that day, so was hungry and wanted to get at Mistress Tulyet's lamb and Lombard slices as soon as possible.

'Summer must be closer than I thought,' said Tulyet, ushering them inside. 'I can smell blossom. Rather strongly, actually. Or perhaps one of the Frail Sisters passed this way, and her scent lingers.'

'Weeds,' said Tulyet's wife, coming to greet them and also detecting something aromatic. 'Like lily of the valley or some such plant. No. It is less pleasant than that. Henbane. I believe that reeks at this time of year.' She inspected the bushes that grew along the front of her house.

'Henbane killed Warde,' said Michael, making his way to Tulyet's solar and oblivious to the mortified expression on the faces of his hosts as they identified the origin of the stench. 'It is not hard to believe that something so foul-smelling contains such a virulent poison.'

'And Bess,' said Bartholomew, not wanting her to be forgotten. He entered the solar behind Michael and was surprised to see Stanmore there, sipping warmed wine by the hearth. The clothier winked at Bartholomew and told him that it was more pleasant to inveigle invitations from friends than to dine alone while his wife was away.

'God's angels!' exclaimed Michael suddenly. 'What is that?'

He pointed to an object that lay on its side in one corner of the room, all wooden legs and frayed fur, like a Trojan horse that had seen some terrible wars. Its face was unscathed, however, and Bartholomew immediately recognised the beady, malevolent eyes and grinning, tooth-filled mouth of the toy Quenhyth had crafted.

'We have young Quenhyth to thank for that,' said Tulyet with a fond smile. 'He gave it to Dickon when he hurt himself, and it has become his favourite toy. I offered to return it, since it was originally intended for Quenhyth's brother, but the kind lad said we could keep it.'

Bartholomew imagined that Quenhyth's generosity had nothing to do with kindness. He knew he was likely to be asked to help tend Dickon in the future so would not want to accept the toy back and run the risk of being speared by Dickon's wooden sword when their paths next crossed.

'What is it?' asked Michael dubiously, picking up the object by one of its legs. It had suffered during its few days in the Tulyet house. One of its feet had broken, there were bald patches where its fur had come off, and it was missing its tail.

'It is a rat,' came the piping, childish voice of Dickon from behind them, where he had been eating the sugared cherries off the tops of all the Lombard slices. 'You stink! I am a Saracen!'

With a wild whoop and little warning, Dickon produced the dreaded sword and rushed at Michael, brandishing it to show he meant serious harm. Bartholomew had never seen the monk move so fast, and Dickon's weapon succeeded only in cleaving thin air. Aggrieved to be deprived of his target, the brat looked around furiously, and drew breath for another attack.

'Dickon!' shouted Tulyet. 'What have I told you about assaulting guests?'

Dickon's dark eyes settled rebelliously on his father, and then with calm deliberation he issued another ear-piercing war-shriek and aimed for Michael a second time. This time the monk was ready. He gripped the rat in both hands and used it to block the sword's hacking blow. The toy disintegrated in his hands, the head skittering off to land in the fire and the body falling in two unequal pieces to the floor. Michael was left holding a hind leg that ended in some vicious-looking splinters. Dickon gaped at the shattered ruins in disbelief, and his little sword dangled at his side.

'Oh, dear,' said Michael flatly. 'Now look what you have done.'

Slowly it dawned on Dickon that his rat was irreparably damaged. He opened his mouth and roared his fury at the world – and at Michael in particular – with all the power his lungs could muster. Bartholomew winced, certain it was not normal for a small child to generate such volume.

'You will hurt your throat,' he warned, although whether

467

Dickon heard him was a matter of conjecture. He considered repeating the message, then decided that a sore throat might actually benefit Dickon's parents. He should not deprive them of a quiet week by attempting to soothe the brat.

'I will take him to the garden,' shouted his mother. 'You said you wanted to talk, and you will not be able to do so with him here. Do not forget to bar the door. He will not stay outside for long.'

'Do hurry back,' said Michael to Dickon, with what Bartholomew thought was raw menace. 'I would like to play with you again.'

Dickon's howls stopped, and he regarded Michael with a coolly assessing eye. Bartholomew watched him reach the understanding that Michael was not someone who would be easily bested. Dickon was the first to look away. He continued his bawling, although not quite as loudly, as his mother led him away by the hand.

'Are you sure he is yours, Dick?' asked Michael, following Tulyet into the chamber he used as an office and watching him secure the door in a way that would have probably deterred several real Saracens. 'Only I have heard that the Devil occasionally sires a child.'

Tulyet was not amused. 'Matt says he will grow out of his tantrums soon. We probably should not indulge him so, but my wife still has not forgotten the time when ruthless men stole him from us.'

'I would like to see them try now,' said Bartholomew, thinking that anyone who deliberately sought out the company of Dickon deserved everything he got. Stanmore added a nod of heartfelt agreement.

'He is a dear child,' said Tulyet. 'But I can barely remember what it is like to have a peaceful home. Still, he will soon be old enough to play with other children, and that may calm him.'

'Julianna's daughter?' suggested Stanmore. 'She is a brat who knows her own mind. You should betroth them. It would be an excellent marriage for both children.'

'An excellent marriage for their parents, perhaps,' said Bartholomew. 'But they would probably kill each other on their wedding night.' He thought he heard Stanmore mutter 'quite'.

Tulyet poked the fire in the hearth until there was a merry blaze. Shadows flickered across the walls, making the murals seem alive, with leaves moving in a breeze and strange beasts lurking among the foliage. Tulyet gave a hearty sigh when Dickon gave his most almighty screech yet, and made a comment about how difficult it was going to be to get him to sleep that night, after the excitement of the day.

'He shouted "fire",' said Bartholomew, going to the window and throwing the shutter open. So far, Dickon's parents had kept him away from flames, but the physician knew it was only a matter of time before the hellion learned it was a usefully destructive force. He did not want to be sipping wine in Tulyet's sealed office while the house burned, and end up like Bernarde.

'He saw the blaze this afternoon,' said Tulyet. 'He is just playing.'

'No!' said Bartholomew, leaning out of the window. 'There *is* a fire. I can smell it.'

He followed Tulyet out of the office and along a corridor to the pantries. A pile of kindling stood in the middle of the floor, and the room was full of thick, white smoke. Bartholomew snatched up a pan of water and dashed it over the flames, while Tulyet, Stanmore and Michael kicked the thing apart and stamped out the cinders. There was a rich stench of burning fat, and Bartholomew realised someone had added fuel to the sticks, to ensure the fire would catch.

'How odd,' said Stanmore, regarding it with a puzzled expression. 'Which of your servants would light a fire on the floor, when there is a perfectly good hearth for that kind of thing?'

'This is not the work of a servant,' said Bartholomew. 'Someone lit it with the express purpose of burning Dick's house to the ground. The oil was added to make it burn more quickly. Besides, no retainer is foolish enough to set a blaze in the middle of a room, then leave it unattended.'

'You mean someone wanted Dick to go the same way as Bernarde?' asked Stanmore, aghast.

'Bang!' came Dickon's strident voice from the garden. 'Pow!'

'Is anyone with him?' asked Tulyet, watching as his wife and most of their household crowded into the pantry to inspect the mess. 'It is getting dark, and I do not want him to let the chickens out.'

'I will go,' said Bartholomew, relieved to be away from the smoke, because his throat was still raw from inhaling so much of it earlier that day. He entered the cool garden and took a deep breath of spring-scented air before beginning to look for Dickon. It was not difficult to locate him. He was screaming happily as he whirled his wooden sword around his head.

'Yah!' he screeched, stabbing some bushes. Suddenly, there was a rustle and someone broke free and raced across the garden towards a wall at the rear. Dickon was after him in a trice, whooping his delight at the prospect of live quarry. His victim reached the wall and began to scale it, driven to a new level of acrobatic achievement by the sword. Dickon jabbed hard at the leg that dangled so tantalisingly in front of him, and there was a shriek of agony. The boy's face creased into a satisfied grin, and the intruder disappeared over the top. There was a thud, a grunt of pain and then uneven footsteps as the would-be arsonist limped away.

'Pow,' said Dickon, pleased with himself. 'He dead.'

* * *

470

'Are you sure you did not see who it was?' asked Tulyet, as they sat in his office – barred again against juvenile invasion – and poured more wine to wash the smoke from their throats. 'It would be good to know the identity of the man who just tried to incinerate me and my family.'

'He was just a shadow and he ran too fast for me to see,' said Bartholomew. 'It was unfortunate for him that he did not run faster still, because then Dickon would not have tried to sever his leg.'

'It serves him right,' said Tulyet unsympathetically. 'Damn the fellow! Now I shall have to organise guards to protect my house, and I do not have men to spare. I need them all in the town. It felt very uneasy earlier tonight, as though we are on the brink of another riot.'

'But who would want to kill you?' asked Stanmore. '*And* damage the King's Commission, since two arson attacks in a day are more than coincidence.'

'Well, it was not Bernarde,' said Tulyet. He had closed the window shutters, but the racket made by Dickon as he screeched his way around the herb beds was still very audible. 'It was definitely his body we found in the ruins of Lavenham's house. There were things other than his keys that allowed us to identify him – the buckles on his shoes, his mouth of crowded teeth, and a ring.'

'So, if we assume that whoever killed Deschalers and Bottisham also set Lavenham's fire, then Bernarde is in the clear,' said Stanmore.

'Actually, he is not,' said Bartholomew. 'How do you know he did not set the blaze, then get caught in it accidentally?'

'That is unlikely,' said Michael. 'Only a fool would allow himself to be ensnared in the inferno he had created, and our killer is not a fool. However, I think Bernarde *was* innocent of all these crimes – although I cannot say the same for Lavenham and Isobel. They have disappeared, and if that is not a sign of guilt, then I do not know what is. We have a witness who saw Bess in their shop moments before she was poisoned, and they will know we want to interview them about it.'

'We need look no further than Thorpe and Edward Mortimer for all this chaos,' said Tulyet firmly. 'They are the obvious culprits. Perhaps one of them attacked my house, too. Could the intruder have been either of them, Matt?'

'I could not tell,' repeated Bartholomew. 'Dickon had him on the run too soon. It could have been anyone – Rougham, for example. His College is deeply involved with the Mortimers, and we cannot discount the possibility that he poisoned Warde with Water of Snails. Also, he is so keen to claim the Hand of Justice for Gonville that I think he would stop at nothing to get it.'

'No,' said Stanmore. 'Young Thorpe and Edward will be behind this. You mark my words.'

'Or Cheney and Morice,' said Bartholomew. 'They are desperate for the King's Mill to win its case, *and* they bought Water of Snails from Lavenham. We have that in black and white – or we would have done, had the fire not destroyed Lavenham's record books.'

'So, we all believe in different suspects,' said Tulyet. 'Matt thinks Rougham, Cheney or Morice are to blame; Michael has Lavenham in his sights; and Oswald and I think our culprits are Thorpe and Mortimer. Some of us must be wrong – either that or we must concoct a solution that has all of them acting together. And I cannot see how that could be.'

'There are simply too many victims,' said Stanmore. 'Deschalers, Bottisham, Warde, Bosel, Bess and now Bernarde. A grocer, two scholars, a beggar, a madwoman and a miller. How are we supposed to identify the connections between these people?'

'Perhaps there are none,' said Tulyet. 'At least, not between all of them.'

'Their deaths *are* related to each other,' said Michael firmly. 'Deschalers and Bottisham died in Bernarde's mill, and Bess, Bosel and Warde were poisoned. Paxtone did some tests this morning, and he is certain Bess died from ingesting henbane, just like Warde.'

'Paxtone,' mused Stanmore. 'He and Wynewyk have been acting very oddly lately. They are constantly scurrying in and out of dingy alleys together. It is most unbecoming in senior scholars.'

'There is nothing to suggest Paxtone had anything against these victims,' Bartholomew pointed out, still reluctant to see the pleasant King's Hall physician implicated in such horrible murders, despite the evidence that was mounting against him.

'You defend him because you like him,' said Stanmore. 'But you know as well as I do that murderers can be the most charming of folk.'

'I cannot vouch for Paxtone, but I do not believe Wynewyk is our killer,' said Michael, holding out his cup to be refilled. 'He has no motive.'

'None that we know about,' corrected Stanmore. 'He told me not long ago that he has been to France. Perhaps he met Thorpe and Mortimer there.'

As he spoke, fragments of information began to melt together in Bartholomew's mind, and he frowned as he concentrated. Then the answer was there, in a flash. 'Albi! Wynewyk said he was in Albi, in southern France.'

'That town has a reputation for violence,' mused Tulyet. 'I recall being told about a vicious inquisition that once took place there, with hangings and burnings aplenty.'

Bartholomew turned to him. 'Quite. And where better to learn the secrets of soldiery and killing? However, I also know that Albi was where Edward Mortimer became a

473

man, because Julianna told me. Thorpe also mentioned Albi as somewhere *he* visited during his banishment – he did so just this afternoon, when we were inspecting Thomas Mortimer's body in St Mary the Great.'

'You think Wynewyk met them in Albi?' asked Michael. 'It must have been well before we knew Wynewyk, since he took up his Fellowship months after they had been exiled. You think they might be in this nasty business together?'

'I do not know,' said Bartholomew. 'Wynewyk says he is terrified of them, and claims they stole his purse while they were waiting to pray to the Hand. That might mean they are not allies, but enemies – and Wynewyk *wants* them accused of these crimes.'

'Are you saying Wynewyk killed six people with the express purpose of having Thorpe and Mortimer blamed for it?' asked Stanmore uncertainly.

'I do not know about this, Matt,' said Michael, also doubtful. 'Why kill innocent men to strike at your enemies? Why not just kill your enemies? It would be simpler and probably a lot more satisfying.'

Tulyet cleared his throat and looked unhappy. 'There is something I have not told you. I did not know whether it was important, and I was afraid of leading your investigation astray with speculation, so, I kept it to myself. But . . .'

'What?' asked Michael warily, not liking the tone of the Sheriff's voice. He suspected he was about to hear something he would not like. He was not mistaken.

'I rode hard from Trumpington when I saw smoke in the sky above Cambridge, but just as I reached the Gate I saw something odd. *Everyone* was rushing towards Lavenham's house – to help or to watch. Except one person. He was running – very fast – in the opposite direction.'

'Who?' demanded Michael. 'Who was fleeing the scene of his crime?'

'You cannot assume he was doing that—' began Bartholomew, ready to point out that the two events might be unrelated. Michael waved him to be quiet, so Tulyet could speak.

'I do not know who it was,' said Tulyet. 'But he was wearing a scholar's tabard.'

Bartholomew and Michael were silent as they walked home from Tulyet's house. They had discussed the case until their heads span, but were no closer to any answers. Bartholomew fretted about Paxtone and Wynewyk's odd behaviour, while Michael confessed that he felt his lack of progress was an insult to the memories of Bottisham and Warde. Stanmore mourned the loss of Deschalers, while Tulyet was distressed because Dickon was tearful over the destruction of his beloved toy. He offered an enormous sum to encourage Quenhyth to make a new one, and Bartholomew contemplated abandoning medicine to enter the toy-making business instead, since it was a good deal more than he had ever earned for treating a patient.

It was a dark evening, with any light from stars or moon shielded by a thick layer of cloud. Rain was in the air, which smelled of damp earth, the marshes to the north and the scent of spring. There was also Michael's rosewater. Shadows flitted back and forth, lurking in doorways and slipping down black, sinister alleys when they recognised the portly frame of the University's Senior Proctor. No felon wanted a set-to with a man of Michael's reputation.

'Thomas Mortimer,' said Michael out of the blue. 'I am not sorry to see him dead, and I cannot think of a more appropriate way for him to perish, given what he did to Lenne and Isnard. But I am not happy about it.'

Neither was Bartholomew. 'The horses *were* terrified by the smoke. We both heard them screaming, and it was obvious that when they had kicked their way out of the stable they were going to bolt. But I have seen men trampled to death before, and Thomas did not have the right marks on his body. He looked crushed, but not by hoofs.'

Michael was thoughtful. 'I certainly do not believe Mistress Lenne caused his death by an appeal to the Hand of Justice. There may well be a hand of justice working here, but it is not a divine one.'

'Lenne's son?' asked Bartholomew. 'He seems the obvious suspect to batter Thomas to death and blame it on fleeing nags.'

'Unfortunately not – unfortunately for us, that is, because it would have made for a neat ending to this unsavoury incident. But Lenne's son had already left Cambridge when the fire started. Sergeant Orwelle rode with him as far as Drayton, way up in the Fens, so I know it is true.'

Bartholomew took a deep breath, and thought about Mistress Lenne's lonely death and Isnard's pain and anguish. 'Perhaps you should not look too closely into the details of Thomas's death, Brother. You may not like what you find.'

Michael shot him an unreadable glance. 'You did not kill him, did you?'

'I did not!' said Bartholomew, offended that the monk should ask. He regarded his friend askance. 'Why? Did you?'

Michael did not deign to reply. 'I wonder if my grand-mother . . . Her sense of justice is strong . . .'

He let the thought trail away, and Bartholomew did not feel like passing comment on it. Dame Pelagia had a sense of justice all right, but it was not always one that corres-ponded with his own. They were about to leave the High Street and turn down St Michael's Lane, more than ready for sleep after the trials of the day, when Michael stopped dead in his tracks and peered down the shady road. The sturdy huddle of St Michael's was to their left, while Gonville lay to their right. Further along was the bigger, blacker mass of St Mary the Great, silhouetted faintly against the sky.

'Why is there a light in the tower?' asked Michael, straining his eyes in the gloom. 'No one should be there now. The church should be locked, and William will be tucked up in his bed.'

'We should ignore that, too,' advised Bartholomew. 'It may be someone in the process of stealing the Hand, and I would not be sorry to see that thing go!'

'There are other valuable items in the University Chest besides the Hand,' said Michael urgently. 'There are property deeds, charters and all manner of documents, not to mention all those payments William has collected from displaying that vile relic. We cannot ignore it.'

'Come on, then,' said Bartholomew reluctantly, heading for the University Church. He drew a knife from his medicine bag, and pushed his cloak back over his shoulder, so his arm would not become entangled in the cloth if there was a fight. He glanced up at the tower as they made for the door, and saw a shadow cross the window in the chamber where the Hand was stored. Someone was definitely there. Michael produced a key, and Bartholomew winced as sharp metallic clinks echoed around the silent churchyard. He wondered whether they would be audible to the thieves inside.

'This is interesting,' whispered Michael, indicating that the gate had been locked. 'This is the only door not barred from the inside – it is always secured with a key.'

'Who has keys?' asked Bartholomew.

'William, who will be asleep by now. Chancellor Tynkell, who I happen to know is dining with my grandmother and Mayor Morice this evening. And me. Therefore, only one conclusion can be drawn: whoever is in the tower must have hidden in the church before it was secured for the night.'

'In that case, I have two questions,' said Bartholomew. 'The first is why are the premises not checked before they are locked, to prevent this sort of thing? And the second is why do we not summon the beadles to help us confront whoever is here?'

'They *are* checked,' snapped Michael. 'So, I imagine we are dealing with someone who is extremely good at hiding himself.' He stepped into the dark interior.

'The beadles, Brother,' said Bartholomew firmly, stretching out a hand to stop him. 'I do not want to tackle these intruders alone.'

'I will be with you,' said Michael, as if that were enough. 'And I do not want to wait for reinforcements if there are felons after the University Chest. It is far too valuable.'

Bartholomew was unhappy, but the monk dismissed his concerns as he made his way to the tower. In the dead silence of the church Bartholomew could hear the monk's soft breathing, and the way his leather boots creaked as he walked. With infinite care, Michael opened the tower door and began to ascend the spiral staircase. They passed the document-storage room, and continued to the second floor, where the Chest was kept.

Bartholomew heard voices as they climbed, and his misgivings increased when he realised there was not one intruder in the tower, but two or three. He wondered how he and Michael would be able to contain them, using only a surgical knife and a pewter candlestick Michael had grabbed from the nave. When they reached the door, Michael threw it open with such force that the crash made Bartholomew's teeth rattle. The monk leapt into the chamber with a challenging shriek, candlestick held ready to brain anyone who tried to pass him.

'William!' exclaimed Bartholomew, entering a little less dramatically.

'Lavenham!' said Michael, eyeing the terrified apothecary with cold, angry eyes. 'And Isobel! What are you doing here?'

CHAPTER 12

'This is not as it looks,' said William nervously, moving forward with what Bartholomew felt was a good deal of agitated menace.

'No?' asked Michael mildly, indicating with a nod that Bartholomew was to remain by the door and prevent a bid for escape – by any of the room's occupants.

'It looks as though I am supervising the theft of the Hand of Justice,' said William unhappily. The Lavenhams sat side by side on the window bench, and said nothing. 'But I am not. I cannot.'

'And why is that, pray?' asked Michael coolly.

'Because it is not here,' said William with a strangled cry. He picked up the handsome reliquary and lobbed it across the room. 'See?'

Michael almost dropped the box, and the candlestick he had been holding clattered to the ground. 'God's blood, man, have a care! You do not toss these things around as though they were juggling balls! I know I have been sceptical of the Hand of Justice, but I do not want to risk the wrath of an irked saint by treating the thing with brazen disrespect.'

'Open it,' suggested William.

'Do not,' advised Bartholomew. 'Men have been struck down for tampering with holy relics. Remember William's sermon about the man who touched the Ark of the Covenant?'

'But you do not believe this particular relic *is* holy,' William pointed out with impeccable logic. 'Neither of you do. So open the box, Brother.'

Reluctantly, Michael complied, while Bartholomew held his breath, half anticipating that the room would fill with a blinding light that would incinerate them all. Michael pulled out the satin parcel and unwrapped it, looking like a man who expected to discover something terrible inside.

'It is a glove' said Michael in surprise, shaking the object out on to the table. 'A glove stuffed with old wool, or some such thing.'

Bartholomew inspected it carefully, noting the rough stitches and the way its creator had used odds and ends to assemble something that might fool a busy friar at a pinch – it was the same shape and size as the original Hand, and would pass for the real thing as long as it was inside the satin. The glove used was old and cheap, and might have been discarded by just about anyone, now that winter was over.

'My relic has been a glove for the past five days!' wailed William, flopping on to the University Chest and rubbing his eyes. 'At least, that was when I first became aware that the original Hand had gone – last Friday. God only knows when it really disappeared.'

'But you have continued to accept money from folk who want to pray to it,' said Bartholomew accusingly.

'Well, why not?' snapped William. 'Their prayers are still being answered, even though the Hand is not here. Mistress Lenne appealed to it on Monday – three days after I noticed it was missing – and Thomas Mortimer died, just as she requested.'

'Never mind the Hand,' said Michael, looking at Lavenham and his wife. 'What is going on here? You are right to be defensive, William. This situation does indeed look suspicious. This pair are needed to answer questions, and they appear just when you confess that your relic has been stolen.'

'It might not have been stolen,' procrastinated William. 'It might have gone of its own volition.'

'Leaving a stuffed glove behind it?' asked Michael archly. He turned his attention back to the Lavenhams, who looked apprehensive. There was a small box on the bench next to them; its lid was open, and it was so full of gold that it was overflowing. 'What do you have to say for yourselves?'

'They went to the Chancellor after the fire, in fear of their lives,' said William, speaking for them. 'Tynkell asked for my help, so I brought them here. It is only for a night. They will be away at dawn tomorrow, back to Lavenham.'

'So, no one was hiding in the church when it was locked up for the night,' said Bartholomew to Michael. 'Both William and Tynkell have keys.'

'We cannot go *back* to Lavenham, Father,' said Isobel pedantically. 'We have never been there. I am from Peterborough, and my husband is from Norway.'

'Hah!' exclaimed Michael. 'I always thought there was something strange about you.'

Bartholomew did not think hailing from Peterborough or Norway implied strangeness, although it certainly suggested a degree of deception. But it was a minor one, and lying about one's antecedents was not a particularly suspicious thing to have done. He said so.

'You are right,' said Isobel. She made an effort to pull herself together, and managed to give Michael a flash of her cleavage. The monk's glare did not waver, and Bartholomew admired his self-restraint. Isobel's expression turned sulky. 'We have done nothing wrong, so do not glower so! When someone set our house alight, we decided this town was too dangerous for us, and made up our minds to leave. We do good business here, but it is not worth dying for.'

'Someone deliberately fired your shop,' said Barthol-

482

omew. 'We assumed it was to harm the Commissioners. Were we wrong?'

Isobel exchanged a glance with her husband. 'We do not know who was responsible. But when we saw what happened to Thomas Mortimer, we decided to leave before his kinsmen blamed us for his death – even though it was not our fault.'

'He was trampled,' said Michael. 'Did you see someone drive a panicked horse in his direction?'

Isobel grimaced. 'If only we had! Human violence is something I can understand, but this was something else altogether. Just after the alarm was raised, he entered our yard and started stuffing things into his bag.' She shook her head, as though she could scarcely credit such behaviour. 'It was brazen theft, but at least he had the grace to blush when he saw us. He turned to run away – loaded down with our possessions, I might add – when a beam fell from an upper floor and crushed him.'

'But he was not found in your yard,' Bartholomew pointed out. 'He was found in the street.'

'The Mortimers are always trying to make money from others' misfortunes,' said Isobel. 'I am disgusted by the compensation the town is forced to pay Thorpe and Edward, and I did not want Thomas's corpse found on our property: I did not want them blaming us for his death.'

Bartholomew could see her point. 'You moved him?'

She nodded. 'I do not know who started the rumour that our horses killed him, but it is not true. He died from falling timber – and because he was so drunk that he could not move quickly enough to save himself when the roof started to collapse.'

Bartholomew believed her, and supposed blaming the horses had been the Mortimers' idea. It would be easier to claim compensation from the owner of a stampeding nag than from the owner of a burning house that Thomas had been busy looting.

Isobel continued. 'But, on reflection, we decided not to stay here anyway. We salvaged our gold from what is left of our home, and we will leave Cambridge at first light tomorrow.'

'Chancellor find us hide in cemetery,' added Lavenham. 'He help us good.'

'Why should Tynkell help you?' asked Bartholomew curiously.

'I know things,' replied Isobel vaguely.

'It would not be about the Chancellor's unusual medical condition, would it?' asked Bartholomew, recalling that she sewed his undergarments.

'Do not press me to betray his trust,' said Isobel softly. 'He has been kind to us.'

'Bess,' said Bartholomew, trying another line of enquiry. 'Did you sell her poison?'

'Of course not!' said Isobel crossly. 'She was witless and would have swallowed it. She came to our shop asking about her man, and I could see she was not well, so I gave her a comfit to suck. I heard she died shortly afterwards, but it had nothing to do with us.'

'Is that what Alfred de Blaston saw in her hand?' asked Bartholomew. 'A comfit?'

Isobel nodded. 'I expect so. I saw her toss it away as soon as she was outside.'

'How do we know you are telling the truth?' asked Michael. 'How do we know you did not set the fire, kill Thomas and even steal William's relic?'

'I can answer that,' said Bartholomew, sitting next to Isobel. 'I should have pieced this together sooner. Master Thorpe said the fire broke out while the three Commissioners – including Lavenham – were arguing in the solar, which means Lavenham could not have lit it himself.

484

And I saw Isobel in the street when the arsonist would have been at work. They are innocent of that charge.'

'And Thomas Mortimer's death?' asked Michael.

'I would say they are telling the truth about that, too: his injuries suggest crushing, not trampling. And they did not steal the relic, either. You can see their worldly goods in that box of gold, and the Hand is not in it.'

Isobel smiled at Bartholomew, underlining her appreciation with a flash of bosom. 'Thank you, Doctor. You have absolved us of these vile accusations.'

'Not all of them,' said Bartholomew. 'I still have questions about the potion that killed Warde and Bess. Did you add henbane to your Water of Snails? Accidentally?'

Lavenham bristled indignantly. 'I not! I make Baker Dozen – thirteen phial. You see entry in my book, and know how many I sell. Two of Cheney, two of Bernarde and two of Morice in first batch. In second, four of Rougham and three spare. Bernarde, Cheney and Morice drank and still alive.'

'Bernarde is not,' said Bartholomew, although he did not think Water of Snails was responsible.

'Rougham gave three of his phials to his Gonville colleagues, and they are not dead,' said Isobel. 'So, you cannot accuse *us* of adding henbane to the one he prescribed for Warde. Warde and Bess must have died from something else.'

'Rougham,' mused Bartholomew thoughtfully. 'We are back to him. I do not suppose he has purchased other toxic substances from you recently, has he?'

'He is a physician, and is obliged to use plants like henbane occasionally,' said Isobel. 'You also purchased some – for Isnard's lice. And Paxtone bought a little for his Warden's gout.'

'Rougham bought henbane?' pounced Bartholomew, ignoring Paxtone for a more promising villain. 'What for?'

'We did not ask,' said Isobel indignantly. 'It is not our business to question our customers. He bought a lot of it about a month ago, but he did not tell me why.'

'Isobel has given me a gold noble for my help tonight,' said William, becoming bored with murder. 'For the University Chest, of course. Perhaps I can use it to purchase another Hand . . .'

'No!' said Michael quickly. 'We have had enough of those, thank you very much.'

'I suppose someone stole it when I was out of the chamber,' said William, frowning as he tried to identify a culprit. 'I occasionally leave trusted individuals alone, so they can make their petitions in private. I do not want to be party to too many guilty secrets and hidden desires.'

'You told us you always keep the reliquary locked,' said Bartholomew, suspecting that trust and bribes went hand in hand with William. 'So, how did it come to be stolen?'

'I have been busy,' said William in a whine. 'I may have forgotten to secure it once or twice. So many people came to appeal to the Hand . . .'

'Who?' demanded Michael.

'Bernarde for one,' replied William. His jaw dropped. 'You do not think *he* took it, and that is why he was burned to a cinder in the inferno? The Hand of Justice repaid him for his audacity?'

'There is no proof of that,' said Michael firmly. 'Who else?'

'I left Edward and young Thorpe unattended, because Wynewyk was with them, and I assumed he would prevent any mischief. But he now tells me they robbed him.'

'That is why we have been dining on nettles and stale bread for the past three weeks. Who else?'

William began reeling off names. 'Mayor Morice would be my first suspect, but he took nothing with him because I would have seen it bulging under his tight-fitting tunic.

486

Stanmore came, but he is an honest man. Quenhyth prayed briefly. Paxtone visited, but Pulham was with him, and I do not think they are close enough to trust each other with theft. Thomas and Constantine Mortimer popped in, bringing their servants. Cheney was in company with Langelee and Redmeadow. Clippesby and Kenyngham. Rougham came several times . . .'

'Rougham,' said Bartholomew. 'He is determined to have the Hand for Gonville. He took it!'

'My money is on Thorpe and Mortimer,' said Michael. 'But since the thing is a fraud anyway, I do not think we need waste any more time on it.' He gazed at the Lavenhams. 'I appreciate why you are keen to leave, but you must remain here a little longer, in case we have more questions.'

'Very well,' said Isobel reluctantly. 'We will stay tomorrow – if we are permitted to hide in this chamber. But we go at dawn on Friday, whether you have questions or not.'

'Rougham,' said Bartholomew, as they walked home from mass the following morning, 'I *knew* he was involved. We should confront him with what we know, before he has the same idea as Lavenham and slips away with his ill-gotten gains.'

Michael did not think Rougham's visits to the Hand necessarily implied that he had stolen it, but agreed that another trip to Gonville was in order. Rougham had not been honest about the fact that he had purchased four phials of Water of Snails from Lavenham, and the monk felt he needed to explain why he had lied and what he had done with them.

There were only two Gonville Fellows left, following the death of Bottisham and the flight of Ufford, Despenser and Thompson. Rougham and Pulham were in the conclave finishing breakfast together and, judging by the pleasure with which Pulham greeted the Senior Proctor and his Corpse Examiner, he considered the interruption a timely one. Rougham sat morosely silent, and his face turned sour with disapproval when the Acting Master waved the guests in.

'Have some claret,' said Pulham, ignoring Rougham's angry sigh. 'Bishop Bateman brought it the last time he visited. We shall miss him in more ways than you can imagine.'

'What do you two want here?' demanded Rougham. 'I have already said you are not welcome.'

'You have questions to answer,' said Bartholomew sharply, not liking his tone.

'I do not answer questions put by you,' retorted Rougham, his voice dripping with contempt.

Bartholomew's patience finally broke. 'What is the matter with you? Why are you acting in this way? What have I done to offend you?'

Rougham looked as though he would not deign to reply, but Pulham joined the affray. 'He is right, Rougham. Your manners are worse than those of a ploughboy when he appears. It is unlike you to be discourteous.'

'What would you have me do?' Rougham shouted, appealing to his colleague. 'The man is healing patients under false pretences, and using his successes to belittle me.'

Bartholomew was astounded by the charge. 'What do you think I have done?'

'The *secretum secretorum*,' hissed Rougham angrily. 'The thing Bacon described, which turns lead to gold, and an old person to youth again. You have one.' He glared at Bartholomew.

Bartholomew stared back, wondering whether the man had lost his wits. 'But it does not exist.'

'You have made one,' said Rougham accusingly. 'That

488

is why you read so many foreign books, and why you were so determined to buy our Bacon. I would never have sold it, had I known it was going to you. You outwitted me shamelessly by asking the Chancellor to purchase it on your behalf.'

'I did not—' objected Bartholomew.

But Rougham was in his stride now. 'You scoured Arab texts for the secret, and you learned it. *That* is why you have no need to petition the Hand of Justice for cures, like the rest of us.'

'And how did you reach this conclusion?' asked Bartholomew, more convinced than ever that the man's mind had become impaired. He recalled the argument they had had about Bacon earlier, when Rougham had professed himself to be a believer in the *secretum secretorum.*

'Redmeadow told me. He said you can heal *all* ailments, and that you will teach him how to do the same. He confessed to it when I berated him over that confusion between catmint and calamint.'

'You drove him to anger when you embarrassed him, and he spoke out of spite,' said Bartholomew. He could see that Pulham and Michael also thought Rougham was addled. 'Redmeadow has a fiery temper and is always blurting things he does not mean in the heat of the moment.'

'Then why do your patients live when you conduct surgery? And how do you heal old women and peasants, who are in poor health to start with?'

'By using all the means at my disposal – the techniques my Arab master taught me, as well as those learned from books. There is no magic.'

'Then what about Bishop Bateman?' demanded Rougham, still on the offensive. 'The Chancellor said you poisoned him.'

'What?' gasped Michael, astonished. 'But Matt was not in Avignon when Bateman died.'

Bartholomew thought back to the discussion in St Mary the Great on the day of the *Disputatio de quodlibet*, when Tynkell had asked odd questions about poisons and Rougham had been present. He recalled the shocked expression on Rougham's face and cursed the Chancellor for his insensitivity.

'You do not need to be *with* your victim when he dies of poison,' said Rougham sulkily.

'Tynkell does *not* think Matt killed Bishop Bateman,' said Michael firmly. 'I have never heard a more ludicrous suggestion. The Chancellor has griping stomach pains – you tend them yourself on occasion – and it crossed his mind that poison might be the cause. But it was not.'

'No one would bother to poison Tynkell,' said Pulham to Rougham with calm reason. 'It would be a waste of time, because he has so little real authority. And, although there are rumours that Bateman died from foul means, there is no proof of that, either. These tales are inevitable when important men die in foreign places. You are wrong to accuse Bartholomew.'

'And *this* is why you have been so hostile lately?' asked Bartholomew, unsure whether to be angry or amused. 'You believe I dabble in sorcery, and think I am capable of poisoning bishops hundreds of miles distant?'

'You did nothing to dissuade me from my beliefs,' said Rougham coldly. 'It is *your* fault our rivalry grew so bitter.'

Bartholomew did not bother to point out that he could hardly correct Rougham's misapprehensions when he did not know what they were. He only wanted to ask his questions about the murders and leave, hoping that the next time they met, Rougham would at least be civil to him.

Rougham was still seething with resentment when a servant arrived with platters of breakfast food. There were eggs, salted herrings, fresh bread and pickled walnuts to eat, and Bartholomew thought it was not surprising that the College was running short of funds if its Fellows regularly devoured such sumptuous victuals. He ate little, because it was hard to raise an appetite with Rougham scowling so furiously at him, although Michael did not seem to notice and attacked the meal with gusto.

'You bought four phials of Water of Snails from Lavenham,' said Bartholomew, wanting the uncomfortable meal to end, so he could leave. 'You used one for Warde. Where are the others?'

Rougham shook his head in exasperation. 'I did *not* give Water of Snails to Warde! How many more times must I tell you that? I gave one each to Ufford, Despenser and Thompson.' He reached into his scrip and produced a familiar little pot. 'And I have the fourth here. I doctored them, but it did not work.'

'Doctored?' asked Bartholomew warily, laying down his knife. 'In what way?'

'I added laudanum,' snapped Rougham. 'It is said to make people more amenable.'

'I see,' said Bartholomew, disgusted. 'You hoped this potion would make your three colleagues see the "wisdom" of your plans to have Thorpe and the Hand of Justice at Gonville.'

'You dosed them with strong physic in an attempt to make them stay?' asked Pulham, aghast.

Rougham rounded on him. 'We *need* Thorpe and we *need* the Hand. And we need Ufford, Despenser and Thompson, too, if we are ever to finish our chapel. Once we have the Hand, we can claim the bones of the sainted Bateman, too. He was poisoned and is therefore a martyr. Then we shall have plenty of relics to attract pilgrims, and our College will prosper.'

'So, that is it,' said Michael. 'You want to establish Gonville as a shrine. But Bateman was not a saint – he was a good man, but not a holy one – and murder is not necessarily grounds for a beatification anyway. Which is just as well, considering how many we have around here.'

'We could never claim Bateman's bones regardless,' said Pulham, addressing his colleague and looking as though he was seeing him for the first time. 'Dame Pelagia told me he asked to be buried before the High Altar at Avignon.'

'Lies!' cried Rougham. 'He wanted to be here, with his friends.'

'Not if he thought we intended to profit from his death,' said Pulham firmly. 'He was not that kind of man, and no one here will allow you to defile his memory in so despicable a manner.'

'Giving folk potions to make them open to your ideas is hardly ethical, either,' said Bartholomew, more concerned with the way Rougham practised medicine than with his penchant for relics. 'You might have harmed someone.'

'Well, I did not,' snapped Rougham. 'Ufford, Despenser and Thompson swallowed their potions – which I told them would cleanse their bowels and make them better able to learn – but they were not rendered pliable at all.' He appealed to Pulham. 'You must see I did it for our chapel! I cannot allow it to remain foundations in the grass for the next hundred years.'

'Then we will *pray* for help,' said Pulham sternly. 'We will not resort to using illicit medicines on our friends – or demanding the bones of our founders when they want to be left in peace.'

'Water of Snails was not all you bought from Lavenham recently,' said Bartholomew. 'He says you also purchased a large amount of henbane.'

'You did not . . . Warde . . . ?' stammered Pulham, eyeing Rougham uneasily.

'No! I did not poison anyone. I did buy henbane, but it was for Deschalers.'

'You poisoned Deschalers?' Pulham was appalled.

'Of course not!' cried Rougham, becoming agitated. 'He did not want it for himself.'

'Paxtone said you refused to prescribe strong medicine for Deschalers's sickness,' said Bartholomew, wondering whether the grocer had believed the toxin might help him with his pain. 'You argued about it with him and Lynton.'

'Deschalers was beyond any potion I could give him,' said Rougham. 'So I decided not to waste his money on "cures" that would not work. But I did not purchase the henbane for his sickness. He asked me to make him a poison for the rats in his house. He paid me sixpence for it.'

'Rats?' asked Bartholomew. Perhaps Deschalers's role in the murders needed further assessment after all, he thought. 'Do you mean human ones?'

'Do not be ridiculous,' snapped Rougham. 'I mean rodents. Being a grocer, with plenty of food on his premises, he had problems with them. He showed me one he had caught – and it was the size of a cat. I made him a poison that would be fatal to any rat coming within an arm's length of it.'

'How?' asked Bartholomew sceptically.

'I mixed the henbane with hog grease and cat urine to ensure it stank. One sniff will kill the most robust of pests. Deschalers contacted me a day later and said it was working.'

'I see,' said Bartholomew, not sure Deschalers had been entirely honest with Rougham. Had the grocer murdered Bottisham after all, then killed himself to hide the fact? 'We should go,' he said, heading abruptly for the door. He was aware of the others' startled faces, but he did not stop. 'Thank you for your time.'

'Is that it?' hissed Michael, trying to slow the physician's rapid progress across Gonville's yard. 'Rougham has just confessed to buying and dispensing poisons. Who knows what more he might have said had we probed deeper?'

'He would have said nothing,' said Bartholomew, 'because he is not our killer. I was wrong. I have been wrong about a number of things. We initially assumed Deschalers and Bottisham died in an identical manner, because of the nails. But that is not what happened. Bottisham probably died from being stabbed in the palate, but I think Deschalers was poisoned first.'

'Wait,' said Michael, grabbing his arm. He steered the physician into the cemetery surrounding St Michael's Church, where he sat on a tomb with his arms folded, waiting for an explanation. 'Well?'

'Rougham does not know how to use henbane,' said Bartholomew, pacing back and forth.

'How do you know that?' Michael was unconvinced.

'Because he thinks the smell alone will kill rats. It will not – it needs to be ingested.'

'But our only other suspect for the henbane killings is Paxtone,' said Michael unhappily.

'He is not guilty, either. Paxtone and I also discussed henbane, and he has no more idea about how to use it effectively than does Rougham. In fact, he had to send a student to a library to look up the symptoms of henbane poisoning after Bess died.'

'Then what about the Water of Snails?' asked Michael. 'We know the phials Rougham gave Ufford, Despenser and Thompson contained no henbane – or they would be dead – but the ones swallowed by Bess and Warde did.'

'Rougham had four phials and they are all accounted for – we can ask Ufford, Despenser and Thompson, but I am sure they will confirm his story. He was telling the truth.'

'Then we must look at the three men who bought the other six between them: Morice, Cheney and Bernarde. You have always been suspicious of them.'

'I have. But I do not think their Water of Snails was the culprit, either. When we visited Bernarde at his mill once, he confessed to being plagued with a sore head and told us two doses of Lavenham's strong medicine had not eased his pain. I suspect he took what he bought himself. Meanwhile, Cheney and Morice said much the same. They claimed to have aching heads and backs induced by worry over Edward Mortimer's foray into commerce, and they also said they took Lavenham's medicine to cure themselves.'

'Then we are out of suspects – unless the Water of Snails is irrelevant, and has led us astray.'

Bartholomew gazed up at the sky, and thought about all they had learned. Whoever killed Bess and Warde had probably used the remaining phials from Lavenham's batch of thirteen. But because the apothecary's shop was a pile of smouldering rubble, they would never be able to prove the last three phials were missing – stolen from the cupboard the man was careless about locking. He thought about people who might know about henbane and its effects. The killer was not only someone with a knowledge of herbs and cures, but someone who was ambitious and greedy. Then he wondered whether that ambition and greed had led him to steal the Hand, too.

He started to think about the stuffed glove, which the thief had wrapped in satin in the hope that William would not notice the real one was missing. The item had been stuffed with fur. Bartholomew recalled Dickon's fur-covered rat, and smiled at the memory of the boy's outrage when it had been destroyed. Then his amusement faded. The skills used to fashion a toy from an old cloak and sticks, and to make a glove look like a relic, were very similar.

'We are not out of suspects,' he said in a low, quiet voice. 'We have just overlooked him.'

'Who?' asked Michael, who could think of no one.

'Quenhyth. He is our killer.'

'Quenhyth?' asked Michael in astonishment, gazing at the physician in disbelief. 'How did he come to be in your equations?'

'It is falling into place,' said Bartholomew as he paced back and forth. 'I see it now. Quenhyth knows about poisons like henbane, because I have taught him about them.'

'But you teach all your students the same things,' objected Michael. 'It could be any of them – Deynman, Redmeadow, and any of the thirty or so others. Poor Quenhyth. He is not a killer.'

'I talked about henbane with Quenhyth, but no one else,' said Bartholomew, remembering the discussion the two of them had had on their way to Isnard's house the previous week while Redmeadow and Deynman lagged behind. 'It was also Quenhyth who "helped" me test Warde's Water of Snails – and he destroyed it all in the process. I see now that was no accident or carelessness. He poisoned Warde, and then he destroyed the evidence that might have led back to him.'

'No,' said Michael with calm reason. 'He had no reason to kill Warde.'

'He wanted Rougham blamed for a suspicious death,' said Bartholomew, rubbing a hand through his hair as more became clear to him. 'The day after Warde's death, he suggested that we should examine the medicine Rougham prescribed. He did not overtly tell me to analyse it – he is not stupid, and that might have led to awkward questions – but he certainly put the idea into my mind. And Matilde's. He told her his "suspicions" too.'

'And he knows you listen to her,' mused Michael. 'Clever.'

'Quenhyth hates Rougham because Rougham humiliated him in the High Street over blackcurrants. He is a proud young man, and does not take such things in his stride. It will have festered. He wrote a note purporting to be from Rougham and sent it with the poisoned phial to Warde. He writes beautifully, and mimicking Rougham's script would not be difficult for him. You said yourself there were differences between the note Warde received and Rougham's own hand.'

'But this still does not make sense, Matt,' warned Michael. 'If he wanted Rougham blamed for Warde's murder, then why did he destroy the potion he pretended Rougham had sent? Why not keep the phial and its contents, to let you prove beyond the shadow of a doubt that it was poison?'

'Because he used *henbane*, and he was afraid I might remember that he had asked me about it. He was just being cautious, hoping that I would not care which poison was used – just that the medicine was toxic. He basically said as much after he had destroyed it.'

'All right,' said Michael. 'I accept that Quenhyth killed Warde in order to have Rougham discredited, but what about the others? If he killed Warde, then he must also have killed Bess.'

'The answers to some of our questions lie with Deschalers's chest,' Bartholomew went on. 'Quenhyth knew it was going to be bequeathed to him – and indeed it was. It is in my room as we speak. But that was only true of the will Deschalers made *a month* ago. He made a later one, in which there were two beneficiaries – Julianna and Bottisham. No mention was made of a scribe inheriting a chest in the later document. We know this, because we have read it.'

'But how could Quenhyth know what was in these deeds?' demanded Michael. 'No one saw the later will, because Pulham stole it the night Deschalers died.'

Bartholomew sighed. 'Quenhyth *wrote* it – he wrote both

of them. He was Deschalers's scribe, remember? He killed Deschalers, so the later document could never be legal – Deschalers died before it was sealed and, as Pulham told us, it is worthless in a court of law. Quenhyth knew it would never be legal, and that is why he wrote it in a scribble, not in his usual careful hand.'

'Quenhyth murdered Deschalers because he wanted a box?' Michael sounded dubious.

'He is a lad who puts great store by possessions, and who is short of funds at the moment. Also, he has a resentful temper, and would be furious to learn he had been disinherited, no matter how small the bequest. Think about the burglary the night Deschalers died.'

'The night Pulham made off with the unsealed will?'

Bartholomew nodded. 'Pulham said there was a second burglar in the house, and Una's story confirms that. She saw Pulham leave through the front door, and it was Quenhyth who escaped with great agility out of the back window. We know exactly why he was there: Quenhyth wanted the later will, too, because it deprived him of his chest.'

Michael rubbed his chin. 'This cannot be right, Matt. Quenhyth may be temporarily impoverished, but he is scarcely a pauper.'

'He likes the notion of locking his belongings away,' pressed Bartholomew. 'He is always accusing Redmeadow of stealing.'

'He may have known that Deschalers planned to meet Bottisham in the King's Mill, too,' said Michael thoughtfully, slowly coming around to Bartholomew's point of view. 'As scribe, he probably penned the note from Deschalers to Bottisham, suggesting a time and place. So, what do you think happened? Quenhyth followed Deschalers to the mill, aware that if Bottisham made up with Deschalers, he would lose his chest? Then what?'

'I suspect he gave Deschalers the same poison he later used on Warde and Bess. We found an empty phial beneath the mill's sacks. Three phials were in that insecure cupboard in Lavenham's shop and we have three cases of poison: Deschalers, Warde and Bess.'

'So, did Quenhyth hide the phial we found in the King's Mill? He buried it under the sacks?' Michael answered his own question. 'No. If he had wanted to hide it, then he would have thrown it in the river. He either forgot about it, or it rolled away during the confusion. So, we can conclude that he poisoned Deschalers. How?'

'Deschalers was in agony with his illness, and Rougham would not prescribe proper pain-killing medicines. I imagine Deschalers was only too grateful when a medical student arrived and proffered a substance he claimed would help. Quenhyth is a studious, precise sort of lad, and Deschalers would have no reason to doubt his competence.'

'So,' said Michael, 'Deschalers lay dead, and suddenly Bottisham arrived. Quenhyth stabbed him with a nail – his medical knowledge would tell him such a wound would be fatal. Then he pierced Deschalers's corpse with another nail to confuse us. You trained him well, Matt: it worked perfectly.'

'Then he engaged the waterwheel and threw the bodies into the machinery to muddy the waters even further. But how did he escape without being seen by Bernarde? Or do you think Bernarde did see him, but declined to mention the fact? We will never know, now he is dead.'

'But we know *why* he is dead,' said Michael. 'Quenhyth burned him to ensure he never told. It had nothing to do with the meeting of the King's Commissioners, as everyone has assumed.'

'The fire allowed him to kill Bernarde *and* prevent us from proving that three phials of Water of Snails and some henbane were stolen from Lavenham's shop,' said

Bartholomew. 'I doubt Quenhyth *bought* them, because Lavenham would have mentioned it last night. Besides, Quenhyth has no money.'

'And we must not forget what Dick Tulyet told us, either,' said Michael. 'After the fire started, only one person was running in the opposite direction – someone in a scholar's tabard.'

'I thought he meant Wynewyk or Paxtone,' said Bartholomew. 'But it was Quenhyth. We know the fire was started using wood that Lavenham had been collecting. Quenhyth was with me the day I heard Isobel complaining about it, so he knew there was convenient kindling to hand. And, of course he killed Bess.'

'Why? She was a lunatic.'

'But she was a lunatic who had some connection to Quenhyth. I should have seen this days ago.'

'How?'

'Because of his reluctance to attend her requiem mass, for a start. And the way he did not want me to go near her, and kept drawing attention to the fact that she spoke nonsense – so I would not believe anything she said. When I pulled her away from the Great Bridge once, she addressed her questions to him, not to me. I thought she was simply deranged. But she was speaking to a man she thought might give her answers. He must have murdered Bosel, too.'

'Because Bosel haunted the same places as Bess?' suggested Michael. 'She confided her story to him, and he threatened to tell? We know Bosel enjoyed blackmailing folk when he could.'

'It was good luck for Quenhyth that Bosel was a witness to Lenne's accident. We all assumed Thomas Mortimer had killed him. But Thomas had nothing to do with it, just as Constantine said.'

'We have been pondering and floundering for days, and

500

yet, within a few moments, we have many of our questions answered,' said Michael wonderingly. 'How has that come about?'

'Because of an act of kindness to a child,' said Bartholomew. 'The rat Quenhyth made Dickon was covered in old fur, similar to that used to fill the glove masquerading as the Hand. It suggested to me that Quenhyth stole the relic. And the rest just . . . came together.'

'Let us hope you are right this time,' said Michael, standing up and preparing for a confrontation. 'We do not want to accuse *everyone* of these crimes before we snare our culprit.'

Knowing that the Lavenhams did not intend to linger in Cambridge long, and sensing they might make a bid for escape sooner than they had promised, Bartholomew and Michael left the churchyard and headed straight for St Mary the Great. Father William was with Chancellor Tynkell in the room below, and waved to indicate they were to climb to the upper room without him. Lavenham and Isobel were still there, but they wore riding cloaks and brimmed hats that would hide their faces, and their saddlebags were packed. They were leaving.

'It is not just the loss of your shop and the vengeful Mortimers driving you away, is it?' asked Michael, leaning against the door jamb and presenting a formidable obstacle to their departure. 'You have been careless, and you are afraid you will be held accountable for the consequences. Warde, Bosel and Bess are dead of poison, and that poison came from you.'

'No!' cried Lavenham. 'We always careful in keys and locks.'

'But you are not,' said Bartholomew coldly. 'I saw you pretend to unlock a cupboard that had been left open myself. You are not as cautious with dangerous substances

501

as you should be.' He recalled Dame Pelagia making off with something, too, to demonstrate how easily it might be done. It had not taken the old lady long to identify Lavenham's laxness.

'It is my fault,' said Isobel in a tight, strangled voice. 'But he seemed a nice fellow, and I have a soft spot for pretty young men.'

'Quenhyth,' said Bartholomew flatly. 'What happened?'

'He was interested in our work and, since he was going to be a physician, I showed him our workshop. It was only later that we missed a quantity of henbane and some concentrated poppy juice. At first I thought I was mistaken, and put the matter from my mind, but then I heard about Warde and I guessed what had happened.'

'Then why did you not tell me?' demanded Michael angrily.

'We was feared,' said Lavenham hoarsely, while Isobel started to cry. 'We feared still. Quenhyth steal henbane. He use it in Water of Snails which he also steal. He care nothing that Isobel blamed.'

'Why did he poison Bess?' asked Michael, sounding disgusted. 'Did she see him doing something to Deschalers, and was murdered for her silence?'

'She was killed too long after Deschalers's murder for that,' said Bartholomew. 'We have already said her death may hold the key to the mystery. I still think it does.'

'Quenhyth knew her,' said Isobel tearfully. 'From home.'

'Quenhyth comes from Chepe,' said Bartholomew, 'and Bess came from London, of which Chepe is a part. Were they lovers once? Matilde said she thought Quenhyth had been crossed in love.'

'Then why did he kill her?' asked Michael. 'That is no way to deal with old flames.'

'He always acted oddly around her,' said Bartholomew, frowning. 'And I would say, with the benefit of hindsight,

502

that there was a vague recognition in her behaviour towards him. But it does not tell us why he might have killed her.'

'We shall have to ask him ourselves,' said Michael grimly.

They walked to Michaelhouse, with Michael urging Bartholomew to hurry so they could question Quenhyth before anyone else died, but the physician dragged his heels, loath to learn for a fact that he had harboured a killer. When they arrived at the College, Redmeadow was strolling in the yard with the Franciscan students, Ulfrid and Zebedee. Michael asked whether they had seen Quenhyth, but the three exchanged looks of disgust and said they would not willingly spend free time in *his* company, when all he did was accuse folk of stealing.

Redmeadow was not wearing his tabard, and his tunic was exposed. Bartholomew saw yet again the ingrained white substance on it, and recalled Matilde telling him that Redmeadow had appeared white and ghostly the morning after the murders in the mills. The student had told her the mess was the result of a practical joke. Then Bartholomew remembered how much flour dust had been caught in his own clothes when he had searched the mill for clues, and felt a sudden lurching sickness. Whoever killed Deschalers and Bottisham would also have been covered in dust. He pointed to the stains.

'How did that happen?' he asked flatly, wondering if all his reasoning had been wrong, and Quenhyth was innocent after all.

Ulfrid answered before Redmeadow could speak. 'Do not start him off, Doctor. We heard nothing but gripes about the ruin of his favourite tunic all last week. He was furious that Quenhyth borrowed it without asking, and then returned it in such a state.'

'Two Sundays ago,' added Redmeadow angrily. 'Agatha has been able to do nothing with it, and Quenhyth will not even admit that he was to blame! I cannot imagine what he did to it. Lady Matilde saw me in it the next day, so I fabricated a story blaming a practical joke – she caught me by surprise with her blunt question, so I said the first thing that came to my mind. I could see she did not believe me, and I felt a proper fool.'

Bartholomew supposed that Quenhyth had anticipated dust as he embarked on his killing spree, and had prepared himself by wearing his friend's clothes. 'Why did you not tell me?' he asked.

Redmeadow was surprised. 'Because you are far too busy to bother with something stupid like this.'

'How do you know it was Quenhyth who dirtied the tunic?' asked Bartholomew unhappily.

'Because only he and you have access to our room.' Redmeadow regarded his teacher uneasily. 'Do not tell me it was you! You *were* at the King's Mill that night – where there is flour dust.'

'It would be too small for me,' said Bartholomew, pushing past him to reach his room.

He opened the door with Michael behind him, dreading the confrontation that was about to occur. But when he stepped inside, Quenhyth was on the floor. The student's face was sheened with sweat and his breathing was laboured. It did not take a physician to see there was something badly wrong.

'Help me!' Quenhyth wheezed. 'I have been poisoned!'

Bartholomew rushed to Quenhyth's side and began to measure the speed of his pulse, while his mind raced in confusion. Had he been wrong? Was the killer Redmeadow after all, with his incriminating tunic and fiery temper?

'How did this happen?' asked Michael, bemused.

'I do not know,' said Quenhyth weakly. 'But my mouth and fingers burn, and I cannot move.'

Michael went to the window to pour a goblet of wine for the lad. He rolled his eyes, to indicate he thought Quenhyth was exaggerating the seriousness of his condition, but Bartholomew pushed the cup away. 'Do not give him wine.'

Michael regarded him askance. 'You mean he really is poisoned?'

'Very definitely. By Deschalers, I suspect.'

'Deschalers is dead,' said Michael, bewildered.

'But the chest he gave his scribe is still here – the scribe he *admired* for his punctuality, but whom Julianna told us he did not *like*. And I think I know why. Deschalers was not being generous with his benefaction: he had a score to settle – something to do with Bess.'

'Bess,' mused Michael, watching Bartholomew soak a rag in water and wipe the student's face. 'We know Deschalers gave her money, despite the fact that he had no use for prostitutes. He was not paying her for her services, but for some other reason. What was it, Quenhyth?'

'Never mind her,' groaned the student. 'She was nothing but a faithless whore who deserved to die. Help me. I am still alive. Close the window, the light hurts my eyes.'

'Rougham made a henbane-based substance for Deschalers's rats,' said Bartholomew. 'He added pig grease and cat urine, and claimed it would slaughter any rodent that so much as sniffed it. There is plenty of oil on the chest you inherited from Deschalers, and we have all noticed how it stinks. He wanted his henbane to kill more than rats.'

He leaned close to the lock and sniffed it cautiously. It reeked of urine and rancid fat, overlain with the now-familiar odour of henbane. He remembered the odd clause Deschalers had put in his will – that Quenhyth was to keep the box for a year and a day before selling it. Now it was obvious why he had stipulated such a thing:

he had wanted to ensure the poison had plenty of time to act.

'But Quenhyth does not open the chest with his teeth,' reasoned Michael. 'And you said henbane needs to be ingested to do its work. How did the poison go from the lock to his innards?'

Bartholomew gestured to Quenhyth's hands. 'He bites his nails. The poison went from the chest to his hand, then into his mouth when he chewed his fingers. You can see the stains on them now. *And* he has started to store his personal food supplies in the box – to keep them safe from you.'

Quenhyth was beginning to shake, although his skin was burning. 'I have been feeling unwell since Julianna first insisted I took the box from her, but I became far worse after I tried to clean the excess oil from the lock. How will you save me? Will you give me charcoal, to counteract the acidity? Or will a purge expel the sickness from within? Give me a clyster! That heals most ills.'

His pulse was dangerously fast, and he was rapidly losing control of his muscles. Bartholomew knew no clyster, purge or medicine could help now that the poison had worked so deeply into his body. He lifted him from the floor and placed him on the bed, making him comfortable with cushions and blankets.

'Drink this,' he said, mixing wine with laudanum and chalk for want of anything else to do. 'It will ease the burning in your mouth.'

'But it will not cure me?' asked Quenhyth in an appalled, breathless voice. His face was shiny with sweat, and deadly pale. 'I will die?'

'Yes,' said Bartholomew, who was never good at lying. 'The wine will only ease your passing.'

'You have committed grave crimes,' said Michael, pulling chrism and holy water from his scrip, ready to give last rites. 'You murdered Deschalers, Bottisham, Bosel, Warde, Bess and Bernarde.'

'I did not mean to kill Bernarde,' said Quenhyth tearfully. 'When I set the fire I wanted Lavenham to die and his shop to be destroyed, so no one would associate me with the missing Water of Snails and henbane. Tulyet saw me as I ran away, but I know he did not recognise me.'

'And Warde?'

'Because I wanted Rougham to suffer. Everyone knew Warde was ill with his cough, and that Rougham was his physician. It was too good an opportunity to overlook and Rougham deserved it. He should not have embarrassed me and Redmeadow in public. Nor should he have slandered you.'

'What about Bosel?' asked Bartholomew.

'Blackmail,' whispered Quenhyth. 'He heard Bess's tale and threatened to tell, unless I paid him lots of money. But I do not have lots of money. I offered him a skin of wine as down-payment.'

'And it contained quicklime or some such thing?' asked Bartholomew.

'It was horrible,' breathed Quenhyth, tears coursing down his face. 'And noisy. I decided not to use such a substance again. But you keep your poisons locked away, so I had to go to Isobel instead.'

'You hurt Bess in some way, and it made Deschalers angry. He asked Rougham to prepare something for his "rats", but he had a change of heart as he became more ill, and decided to reprieve you. Julianna said he intended to clean the chest, presumably to remove the poison. But you murdered him before he could do so, and brought about your own death in the process.'

'So, what did Bess tell him?' asked Michael. 'That you and she were lovers?'

'We *should* have been lovers,' said Quenhyth feebly. 'I

507

adored her for years. But she met a messenger called Josse, and fell in love. Josse came to Cambridge to deliver some missive and never returned, so she came to look for him. But grief had turned her wits.'

'Josse,' said Michael thoughtfully. 'The man under the snowdrift.'

'What happened to him?' asked Bartholomew. But he had already guessed. 'I suppose you were arguing when the snow dropped on him? And then you walked away, leaving him to suffocate?'

Quenhyth swallowed with difficulty. 'It was an act of God, nothing to do with me. Besides, there was the danger of another fall. I did not want be buried as well.'

Bartholomew looked away, not caring to imagine what Josse must have gone through as he had died, knowing the only man who could help him was Quenhyth – and Quenhyth bore a grudge. 'I suppose Bess recognised you, and drew her own conclusions. What did she do? Confront you in front of Deschalers?'

Quenhyth nodded. 'I thought he did not believe her, because he gave her money and sent her on her way – and he dictated the deed leaving me the chest the same night. But he was a changed man in the days before he died – making another will to help Bottisham, giving more coins to Bess and being generous to the poor.'

'Dying can do that to a man,' remarked Michael. He glanced at Quenhyth. 'To some men.'

'She was comely once,' said Quenhyth with the ghost of a smile. 'I did not love her as you knew her – filthy, addled and full of lice. Deschalers said she reminded him of someone called Katherine.'

'But you did not kill Bess until two days ago,' said Bartholomew. 'Why wait so long, when she had already told Bosel and Deschalers her story, and might have confided in others?'

508

'I did not *want* to hurt her. I am not a bad man, and she became less inclined to·gabble after her first couple of days here. I hoped she would just move on, but then Sheriff Tulyet showed her Josse's hat, and she came after me again. I *had* to kill her then.'

'Tell me about Deschalers,' said Michael. 'You followed him to the King's Mill and found him in agony, waiting for Bottisham to arrive. Then what?'

Quenhyth closed his eyes. 'I had given him pain-dulling potions before – because that bastard Rougham would not. I stole some from Isobel.'

'I thought someone had taken pity on him,' said Bartholomew. 'He could not have ridden his horse that Saturday if someone had not stepped in to do what Rougham should have done.'

'He was so grateful for my sudden appearance in the mill that night that he did not even ask why I happened to be there. He died within moments.'

'And Bottisham caught you with the body, I suppose?' asked Bartholomew.

'He came early and started to screech. I did not know what to do, so I grabbed a nail from the floor and jerked it upwards as I came to my feet. He was leaning over me, and I ended up stabbing him in the mouth. I did not mean to hit him there, but it was effective.'

'Then you stabbed Deschalers, to make the deaths appear identical. You did not want us to know he had been poisoned, lest we connect you with what had been stolen from Isobel. You dropped both bodies into the machinery, in the hope that the resulting mess would confound us. But there is one thing I do not understand: how did you escape from the mill without Bernarde seeing?'

Quenhyth looked at Michael. 'I need absolution. Will you hear my confession?'

Michael nodded, and indicated that Bartholomew

509

should leave. The monk was busy for a long time, and the physician began to wonder what other crimes Quenhyth had on his conscience. He went to the fallen tree in the orchard and sat, waiting for Michael to come and tell him it was all over.

He thought about the people who had died, and why. Bottisham had perished because he was willing to extend the hand of peace to a dying enemy. Bess had died because she guessed her man had been left to freeze in the winter snows, and Bosel because he had attempted to blackmail a killer. Deschalers had been murdered because he had rescinded on a promise to give Quenhyth a chest and because Bess had confided her secret to him – and because a madwoman had borne such a close resemblance to the lady he had loved that he had been prepared to listen to her. Warde had been dispatched because Quenhyth intended to teach Rougham a lesson. And Bernarde had been incinerated because Quenhyth wanted Lavenham and his workshop destroyed.

None of the deaths were connected to the King's Commission or the mill dispute, and Rougham, the Mortimers and Thorpe were innocent of everything except offensive behaviour. Thomas was gone, too, killed because he was too drunk to understand the dangers of looting burning houses. And Paxtone and Wynewyk were guilty only of curious meetings and perhaps the theft of a book or two – although Bartholomew was careful not to think about Paxtone's confession to Wynewyk that Rougham 'foiled' him at every turn. He did not want to know what the two men were plotting against the unpleasant Gonville physician.

'He is dead,' said Michael, coming to sit next to his friend at last. He sighed wearily as he leaned forward and rested his head on his hands. 'His confession chilled me, Matt. His selfish righteousness will haunt my dreams for a long time.'

'But it is over,' said Bartholomew. 'He cannot harm anyone else now.'

Bartholomew woke the next morning with an uneasy feeling in the pit of his stomach, but it was a moment before he understood why. Then the events of the last two weeks came flooding back to him, and he felt like turning over and going back to sleep, so he could blot it from his mind for a little longer. It hurt to think that someone so close to him had committed such wicked crimes, and for such paltry reasons.

'It was not your fault,' came Redmeadow's voice from the other side of the room. He had heard his teacher moving, and knew he was awake. Bartholomew assumed that he had also spent a restless night, reflecting on what Quenhyth had done. 'Or mine. We had no idea what kind of man he was.'

'I should have been alerted by the fact that he was so ready to kill the cat and Bird.'

Redmeadow nodded slowly. 'Perhaps. Shall we return his chest to Julianna this morning? I do not want it in here.'

'I do not think so!' said Bartholomew, heaving himself out of his bed and rubbing his eyes. 'Edward might claim we are trying to kill his wife by giving her a poisoned box. We will burn it.'

Just then, a piercing scream rent the air. They regarded each other in alarm, before dashing into the yard to see what had happened. Deynman was standing near the porter's lodge with something under his arm. Walter was with him, and the surly porter's face was split with a grin of savage delight. Bartholomew saw bright blue-green feathers trailing from the bundle Deynman held.

'Deynman felt sorry for Walter when Quenhyth killed Bird,' whispered Redmeadow. 'And he promised to buy him a replacement. It is not a cockerel, though. I do not know what it is. I have never seen its like before.'

'It is a peacock,' said Bartholomew heavily. 'They are rare in England, although common in the East. They are very expensive.' Another shrill shriek rent the air as the peacock made its presence known. Scholars were beginning to emerge from their rooms in a panic, wondering what was making such an unholy racket. 'And noisy,' he added.

'Walter will like it, then,' said Redmeadow. 'He only loved Bird because the thing caused so much aggravation. Let me help you carry the chest outside, so we can burn it before we go to church.'

A number of scholars followed Bartholomew and Redmeadow as they hauled the unwieldy object into the orchard. Bartholomew insisted the fire should be at the very end of the garden, where no stray sparks could fly into the air and cause trouble in the town. He wrapped the chest with straw from the stables, and set about making a fire. Several students exchanged amused glances when Walter's peacock screeched again, although Bartholomew suspected they would not find it funny for very long.

No one spoke as the kindling caught and flames began to lick up the sides of the chest, hissing and spitting when they reached the deadly grease on the lock. Bartholomew had refused Redmeadow's request to open the box and retrieve what was inside it first. It crossed his mind that Deschalers might have poisoned other parts, too, and he did not want to find out by losing another student.

When the blaze died down most of the scholars wandered away to ready themselves for their devotions, but Bartholomew lingered, waiting for the last flames to die out. He wanted to make sure the chest was totally consumed and the embers raked away, so no trace of Deschalers's inheritance would remain. He felt that the little tongues of gold were purifying something unclean, and the cremation left him in better spirits than when he had awoken. William hovered at his elbow, watching him prod the glowing embers with a stick.

'The Lavenhams have gone,' the friar said quietly. 'But they left you this.'

'No, thank you,' said Bartholomew, eyeing the proffered package suspiciously. He could not imagine why the apothecary should give him a gift, and was certain it would not be anything he would want to own.

'I know what it is inside,' said William. 'And you will like it, I promise.'

Donning a pair of heavy gloves, and ignoring William's indignation that the physician should question his assurances, Bartholomew opened the parcel, making clumsy work of untying the twine that bound it. Inside was a small book. He gazed at it in astonishment.

'It is by Ibn Ibrahim!' he exclaimed. 'My Arab teacher. I knew he had written a tome containing his various theories, but I did not think I would ever see a copy. But why did Lavenham have it? And why did he give it to me?'

'You have good friends to thank for that,' said William. 'Paxtone saw it in their shop, and he knew this Ibrahim was your teacher. He and Wynewyk have been negotiating to purchase it for you for the past month or so. They never succeeded – Lavenham did not want to part with it because it came from his father. But yesterday he decided he needed the money, so I arranged the sale.' He turned and gestured to someone who was standing a short distance away, smiling shyly. It was Wynewyk.

Bartholomew was seized with abject guilt. 'Is that why they have been acting so strangely of late?'

'They did not want you to know what they were doing,' explained William. 'They suspected Lavenham would not sell it, and did not want you to be disappointed when they

513

failed. They met in the orchard, because Wynewyk said no one ever uses it except him. I should have mentioned your penchant for that old apple trunk, I suppose. He said they were discussing Rougham's accusations against you once, and were appalled to imagine the conclusions you must have drawn.'

Bartholomew was surprised to feel the prick of tears behind his eyes, and supposed he must be more tired than he had thought.

'Thank you,' he said as Wynewyk came to stand next to him.

'You almost caught me with it once,' said Wynewyk, smiling at the memory. 'Lavenham lent it to me for a day, and I brought it here to show Paxtone. I fell asleep waiting for him, and the next thing I knew was Michael trying to grab it from my lap.'

'I remember,' said Bartholomew. 'I saw something hidden under Gratian's *Decretia*.'

'Rougham was a wretched nuisance,' Wynewyk went on. 'He somehow guessed what we were trying to do, and went to extraordinary lengths to thwart us. He claimed he did not want your mind sullied further with heathen texts, and did all he could to persuade the Lavenhams not to sell it to us.'

'He foiled you at every turn,' mused Bartholomew, recalling what he had overheard. He was ashamed now of what he had thought.

Wynewyk did not seem to notice his chagrin. 'Then we were afraid it had gone up in smoke, along with Lavenham's house. Paxtone had a good look for it in the rubble – you doubtless wondered why he was covered in soot – but it was nowhere to be found. But then we discovered it in the most unlikely of places.' He gestured for William to continue.

'I was called to give Thomas Mortimer last rites,' said

514

William. 'Property he had looted from the Lavenhams was spilling from his clothes, so Wynewyk and I gathered it up to return it to them. The book was one of the items.'

'It was Quenhyth who tried to steal the Dumbleton from the hall, you know,' said Wynewyk, when Bartholomew seemed unable to speak. 'Not Thorpe, as we assumed. After I repaired the chain, I caught him at it again. The chest made him greedy, because it was somewhere private to store stolen goods. But I must tell Paxtone that all our plotting paid off. He will be delighted.'

'Wait for me by the gate,' Bartholomew called after him. 'I would like to go with you.'

Bartholomew handed the book to William while he raked out the fire, keen now to finish with Quenhyth's business, and spend some time with two men who had been to such lengths on his behalf.

'My God!' breathed William suddenly. 'I hope that is not what I think it is.'

Bartholomew looked to where the friar pointed. His mouth went dry when he saw that some of the charred embers were hand shaped. He poked them with the stick, revealing large blackened finger bones and the remains of a blue-green ring. He exchanged an uneasy glance with the friar.

'So, Quenhyth stole the Hand of Justice,' he said. 'We thought he might have done, and I should have guessed where he had put it. Still, at least we know the thing was not holy, or it would not have been eaten by flames.'

'Oh, dear,' said William nervously. 'This is all rather embarrassing.'

'Only if people find out about it,' said Bartholomew, raking vigorously, so the bones broke up and became indistinguishable among the charred remains of the chest. He scooped up the ashes and wrapped them in the material that had held the book. William followed him out of the garden and watched while he flung the parcel into the river. It sank slowly from sight.

'Find out about what?' asked William.

Later that night, the Fellows of Michaelhouse sat quietly in the conclave. Bartholomew was reading Ibrahim's book, completely absorbed, and Wynewyk watched, smiling at his friend's pleasure. Langelee was telling Suttone how annoyed he was over the loss of Quenhyth's fees, while William wrote a letter to the Chancellor, resigning as Keeper of the University Chest. When he passed the document to Michael, to check for errors in the grammar, the monk tore it up and threw it in the fire. He gave the friar a conspiratorial wink, and William grinned back in startled delight.

'I do not want him reclaiming his post as Junior Proctor,' Michael muttered to Bartholomew, as the Franciscan went to celebrate his unexpected reprieve by fetching wine from the kitchen. 'I know he caused havoc as Keeper, but I think he has learned his lesson. He is safer where he is.'

'What is that?' demanded Langelee, looking out of the window at the reflected light dancing on the College's pale walls. 'And listen!'

He flung open the window shutter and the Fellows exchanged horrified glances when they detected the unmistakable sounds of riot – people shouting, dogs barking, the frightened whinnying of horses and an occasional scream. Feet hammered on the ground as folk ran here and there, and torches sent eerie flickers into the darkness.

'Stay here,' ordered Michael, reaching for his cloak. 'All of you, except Matt, who may be needed professionally. Bar the gate and be ready to douse fires. I do not like the look of this.'

In St Michael's Lane, apprentices were everywhere. Scholars were out too, wearing the uniforms of their hostels and Colleges, and Bartholomew saw students from Gonville nudge each other and edge closer to Stanmore's lads. He did not think they were about to exchange pleasantries about the cloth business, and ordered his brother-in-law's boys home. They grumbled and kicked at the ground in frustration, but did as they were told. Michael did the same with the scholars, threatening them with a night in his cells, if they did not obey.

'Will this town never be still?' demanded Michael, as he turned into the High Street and saw that he and Bartholomew had only scratched the surface of the problem. People were massing, running down the High Street in the direction of the Trumpington Gate. He snatched the arm of someone who darted in the opposite direction. It was Ufford from Gonville Hall.

'This chaos is Rougham's fault,' said Ufford in disgust. 'He went to pray to the Hand of Justice, to ask for absolution for selling rat poison to Deschalers, but Father William would not let him near it. They began to argue, and William ended up confessing that the Hand has been stolen. Unfortunately, they were overheard.'

'By whom?' asked Michael.

'By Mayor Morice. He has been telling everyone – and the townsfolk want it back.'

'Oh,' said Bartholomew guiltily.

'But why is everyone storming around?' asked Michael. 'It *was* stolen, but that is no reason for all this mayhem. Rioting will not reveal what happened to it.'

'Because Morice says Mortimer and Thorpe have it,' said Ufford, glancing around uneasily. No ambitious courtier with good family connections wanted to be caught up in anything as unseemly as a brawl, and he was anxious to be away. 'He says they came to Cambridge with the sole purpose of reclaiming the Hand, and it is in their possession. Thank God we did not let Thorpe bring it to

517

Gonville, or *we* would now be under siege instead of Mortimer's Mill.'

'The mill is being attacked?' asked Michael. But Ufford was gone, making his way to the quiet end of town, where he would secure a room in a respectable tavern and emerge only when the fighting was over.

Bells were sounding the alarm, and soldiers on horses thundered along, all heading for Mortimer's Mill. The roads and lanes were full of shouting, clanging and general alarum. As the noise levels increased, more folk spilled into the streets to join the throng, or to cover their windows with planks of wood to protect them from looters. Furious hammering joined the cacophony.

'Look!' cried Bartholomew, pointing into the night sky. It was stained orange, indicating that a steady blaze was burning somewhere. He and Michael joined the stream of people flooding down the High Street, through the Trumpington Gate and along the side of Peterhouse to the river.

'We do not know who fired Mortimer's Mill,' panted Sergeant Orwelle, who trotted along next to them. 'There are rumours that it was scholars – because Edward Mortimer and Thorpe stole the Hand of Justice from St Mary the Great. Both felons are now hiding in the mill. But there are also rumours that the fire was set by townsmen – because of what happened to Lenne and Isnard.'

By the time they arrived, Mortimer's Mill was well and truly ablaze. Flames danced high in the air, lighting the onlookers with an amber glow. Some folk cheered, but most just stood and watched, uncomfortable with the sight of another building consumed by fire. Because there was so much wood and grease, it was being devoured like kindling, and Bartholomew knew it was as doomed as Lavenham's shop had been. Flames licked over the great waterwheel, painting its shape in the sky.

On a balcony at one end Bartholomew saw two figures standing side by side. One was taller than the other, and they were unmoving, watching the crowd as intently as the crowd watched them. Flames licked all around them, lighting them as dark silhouettes against a dazzling orange curtain.

'Mortimer and Thorpe!' yelled Michael in horror. 'They will die if we do not help them! Fetch water, quickly!'

'It is too late, Brother,' said Bartholomew in a soft voice, barely audible above the snap and pop of burning. 'They are already dead. It is corpses you see there, not living men.'

'I suppose that explains why they are not moving,' said Michael unsteadily. 'I thought it was unnatural. I hate fires, Matt. I hate the smell and the sound. They make me feel helpless.'

'We *are* helpless,' said Bartholomew, watching the still shapes as the mill blazed ever more fiercely. He wondered whether enough of them would be found the next day to give them a burial, and whether he would be able to prise them apart. He had seen enough of such infernos to know the two would be a fused, indistinguishable mass, barely recognisable as human. Sickened, he wandered to the river, where he stared at the flames' reflections dancing in the water. He jumped in alarm and spun around when he became aware that someone was standing close behind him.

'It is done,' said Lenne in a soft voice. Bartholomew could see his white teeth gleaming in the darkness. 'Thomas Mortimer will never kill an innocent man again, and my poor mother and father are avenged. He and his mill are no more than ashes, to be blown away by tomorrow's breeze.'

'You did this?' asked Bartholomew, aghast. 'You set the fire?'

'Why not? The law failed me, so I decided to exact my own justice. But I left no evidence. No one will be able to prove that his death was anything other than an accident. Just like my father's.'

'But Thomas died yesterday,' said Bartholomew, realising that Lenne did not know. 'He was crushed by a beam in the inferno that destroyed Lavenham's shop. I saw his body myself. You have killed his nephew and Thorpe instead.'

'Truly?' asked Lenne uncertainly. 'I only returned tonight, and have not wasted time in gossip. I did not know my mother's curse had already worked.'

'Sergeant Orwelle said you had gone home.'

'I had, but I could not rest easy knowing that the man responsible for the deaths of my parents walked free.' He took a deep, shuddering breath. 'Well, I suppose it does not matter. I have rid the town of two men who are violently hated. Folk will probably thank me for what I have done.'

'That does not make it right,' said Bartholomew.

'Right!' sneered Lenne, and Bartholomew saw for the first time that he held a knife. 'What does this town know about right? It allows drunken sots to trample frail old men, while self-confessed killers enjoy King's Pardons. There is no such thing as "right" here.'

'Thorpe and Edward did not harm you,' argued Bartholomew. 'It is not for you to punish them. Tulyet was right: the law may not be just, but it is all there is between us and mayhem.'

'Except that its very existence is sometimes the cause of that mayhem,' said Lenne. 'Goodbye, Doctor. I have seen enough, and I shall never visit Cambridge again. If you promise to look the other way and watch the sparks until I have gone, I will spare your life. And if you ever repeat this conversation to anyone else, I shall deny that I was here.'

Bartholomew turned around, seeing the dancing cinders that lit the sky in a celebration of orange and yellow, and when he looked behind him some moments later, he was alone.

Bartholomew turned around towards the door, yet
visible in the grey morning light. Michael followed his
glance and noticed a shadowy figure standing near the
door.

EPILOGUE

The following morning, just as dawn was breaking and an
early mist hung over the river like a pale grey veil,
Bartholomew and Michael walked to the blackened spars
and timbers that were all that remained of Mortimer's Mill.
Others were already there – soldiers to prevent anyone
from straying too close to what was a dangerous structure,
and townsfolk waiting for the soldiers to look the other
way, so they could see whether there was anything worth
salvaging. For a while Bartholomew thought the great waterwheel had survived, for it looked charred, but otherwise
unharmed. Then a soldier leaned on it and there was a
tearing groan as the whole thing collapsed. From the direction of Michaelhouse came a screeching echo, as Walter's
peacock answered it.

'Are you sure you have not made a mistake?' asked
Michael of his Corpse Examiner yet again. 'It would be
easily done in all that confusion last night. Look again,
now it is light, so we can be certain.'

'It is not necessary, Brother. I am sure. But I will check
again if it makes you happy.'

Bartholomew crouched by the blanket that covered the
two corpses, which had been recovered from the mill after
the fire was out, and repeated the examination he had
now conducted three times. He assessed the teeth that
were conveniently exposed by the loss of facial tissue, the
bones of the pelves and the shape of the heads.

'Well?' demanded Michael.

'As I said, neither of these is Thorpe or Mortimer. One

522

is a female, and the teeth of both indicate older people, not men in their prime.'

'Damn!' breathed Michael. 'Then they are still at large. They used the confusion created by the fire to let folk believe they are dead, and now they intend to conduct their mischief from afar. This is terrible! At least when they were here, I could watch them.'

'I am fairly sure these are the bodies of Lavenham and Isobel,' said Bartholomew. 'God alone knows how they ended up here, after we thought they had escaped from Cambridge.'

'Thorpe and Mortimer killed them,' came a low voice close behind him that made Bartholomew jump out of his skin. 'They thought we would blame Quenhyth.'

'Dame Pelagia,' said Bartholomew, standing up quickly. He supposed he should not be surprised to see her, now that the murderer was unveiled and all that remained was to work out the answers to one or two loose ends. 'How do you know Thorpe and Edward murdered the Lavenhams?'

'Because I saw them,' replied the old lady. 'Unfortunately, I was too far away to prevent it from happening. They wanted the Lavenhams' gold, and killed them for it near the Small Bridges after dark. They carried the bodies to the mill, where I watched them set the fire. Young Lenne may have *thought* the blaze was his doing, but all he did was give Thorpe and Edward the idea.'

'Lenne did not burn the mill after all?' asked Bartholomew.

'His pathetic little blaze flickered out within moments. Thorpe and Mortimer watched him, and I thought they intended to kill again, but they merely decided to carry out what he had failed to do. They wanted you to believe they were dead.'

'But they did not take my Corpse Examiner into account,' said Michael proudly. 'I have always said it is good to hire a physician who can tell his men from his women.'

Bartholomew was too agitated to be amused. 'Where are they now? What do they intend to do?' He realised that part of his unease was because he did not trust Dame Pelagia, and he had the distinct impression there was something she was not telling them.

She gave one of her enigmatic smiles. 'Who knows?'

Michael was morose again. 'I suppose we shall have to go through all this again in a couple of weeks, when they decide to return.'

'The King would not like that,' said Dame Pelagia. 'He is fond of this town – probably because it is good for imposing extra taxes – and he does not want to see it in flames. A destroyed city is not a good source of revenue.'

'The King is expecting a great deal of revenue from Deschalers's death taxes,' said Michael bitterly. 'The town is obliged to pay them all. God knows how we shall find the money, what with the Great Bridge falling to pieces and fire damage to repair. And what about this compensation – or does the fact that Thorpe and Mortimer murdered the Lavenhams for gold absolve us of that?'

'I shall have a word with a Westminster clerk or two about Deschalers's taxes,' said Dame Pelagia comfortably. 'His heir will be ordered to pay, have no fear. And you can forget about the compensation, too. I doubt Thorpe and Mortimer will press their claim for it.'

'We thought they intended to use the Hand to cause trouble in the town,' said Michael. 'As revenge for being sent into exile. But we were wrong.'

'They were opportunists,' said Pelagia. 'The Hand presented them with an opportunity to stir up strife, and it was easy for them to give it a new name – to increase its importance and put strain on the relationship between University and town concerning its ownership. But that is not why they came.'

'Why, then?' demanded Bartholomew. He held his ground when the bright, intelligent green eyes settled on him. He wanted answers and felt the old lady had them; he would not allow her to intimidate him into not asking the questions that burned in his mind.

Dame Pelagia smiled, showing small yellow teeth, like Michael's. 'You will have to work that out for yourself. I do not see why I should explain everything to you.'

'They wanted revenge on some of the people who brought them to justice for their original crimes,' said Michael, thinking hard to make the evidence fit into a pattern that made sense. He could not bear to leave his grandmother's challenge unanswered. 'We thought they came to bring chaos and tumult, but they were not so ambitious.'

'Then they aimed to leave with as much gold as they could carry,' said Bartholomew. 'Mortimer never intended to run Deschalers's business, which is why he dismissed the apprentices and cared nothing about retaining the good-will of the other merchants.'

Dame Pelagia smiled. 'You are both right. Because they inspired such terror, folk attributed to them a grander plan than they were capable of carrying out. They did nothing to dispel these rumours, which elevated them to a status they should never have been given. They are loutish youths, of average intelligence and mediocre fighting skills. You discovered that, Matthew.'

'You mean when Edward attacked me on the High Street?' asked Bartholomew. He thought back to the struggle, and recalled his pride when he had defeated a man whom everyone held in such fear.

'Exactly. He and Thorpe beat Ufford in a brawl, but there were two of them, and poor Ufford is not the swordsman everyone imagines. He prefers reading to fighting, and even *you* could defeat him in a fair contest. All these things were

525

gossiped about and exaggerated. There was no plan to destroy the town. That was all in your fevered imaginations.'

'But they wanted to kill Michael, the Sheriff and my brother-in-law,' said Bartholomew. 'And possibly me, too. They have tried three times now.'

Dame Pelagia raised her eyebrows. 'I only know of once: in Dick Tulyet's house the night Mortimer tried to set it alight. He has a gash on his leg – inflicted by Dickon's wooden sword.'

'They have been trying to get several of their intended victims under the same roof at the same time,' said Bartholomew. He was gratified to see he had her attention. 'Their first attempt was last Monday, when Dickon had the pea in his ear. Thorpe asked whether Michael was going to join us. Had I said he was, I think they would have done something then. The second attempt was at Michaelhouse a week later.'

'The inexplicable invitations to the midday meal,' said Michael, wanting to show his grandmother that Bartholomew was not the only one who could think. 'They sent messages to Oswald and Dick, asking them to Michaelhouse, but both declined for different reasons. We were fortunate.'

'Yes, there were nettles to eat that day,' said Dame Pelagia disapprovingly. 'I do not allow weeds to pass my lips personally, but there is no accounting for taste.'

'That was the day Thorpe came to hear Matt's lecture,' Michael went on. 'We knew he planned some sort of mischief, but did not know what – not at the time.'

'Their attempts were bumbling at best,' said Dame Pelagia. 'And grossly incompetent at worst. You were never in any real danger. But they would have persisted until they died in the attempt.'

Bartholomew eyed her warily. 'What makes you think they will stop now?'

Her eyes twinkled. 'I have had a word with them. Their killing days are over.'

'Were you ever in Albi?' he asked, when he saw she was going to say no more on the matter. 'Thorpe and Mortimer are supposed to have learned their fighting skills there.'

'I saw Wynewyk in Albi once, with a group of travelling clerics,' said Dame Pelagia. 'But Thorpe and Mortimer strayed no farther than Calais. They were too frightened to go deeper into France.'

'A false connection,' said Michael. 'They must have heard Albi mentioned, and decided it sounded more impressive than Calais.'

'And you have no idea where they might be now?' pressed Bartholomew, regarding Michael's grandmother intently.

She smiled and reached up to pat his cheek with a hand that was surprisingly soft. 'Look after my grandson, Matthew. But I have tarried here too long, and the King needs me in other places.'

She turned and walked away. Langelee waited nearby with a splendid palfrey, and they all watched her spring lightly into the saddle. Then she gave them a jaunty wave and was gone.

'I imagine Thorpe and Mortimer fled for their lives after she spoke to them,' said Michael, answering Bartholomew's question as they turned back to the ruins of the mill. 'They are not stupid, and will not risk making an enemy of her.'

'It is a bit late for that,' said Bartholomew. 'They made an enemy of her two years ago. That is why she came back.'

'Yes, I suppose it was,' said Michael.

In order to reach the bridge that would take them back into the town, Bartholomew and Michael had to pass the King's Mill. As they walked, the physician became aware of an uncomfortable scratching sensation near his neck. He rubbed it impatiently, then stared in surprise at the

527

parchment that fluttered to the ground. He retrieved it and scanned its contents, while Michael watched with raised eyebrows.

'She must have put it there when she touched my face,' said Bartholomew. 'I should have guessed her small demonstration of affection would have another purpose.'

'What does she say?'

'She explains how Quenhyth killed Deschalers and Bottisham, dropped them in the mill engines, and then escaped without being seen by Bernarde.'

'Damn!' muttered Michael. 'I had hoped to discover that for myself, to impress her with my insightful analysis of facts. Did you know she deduced Quenhyth was the killer before you did? She had pieced the mystery together from conversations with Bess and Redmeadow. We made mistakes, Matt. We should not have dismissed Bess as a rambling lunatic, and *I* should not have assumed that Bottisham and Deschalers's deaths were connected to the mill dispute. That led us badly astray. Of course *she* did not make such a basic error of judgement.'

'And what did she plan to do about Quenhyth?' asked Bartholomew. 'Stab him during mass? Poison him at his lessons?'

'She planned to inform me about him,' said Michael sharply. 'And let justice take its course, on the understanding that the King would not be so free with his pardons in the future. But tell me what she fathomed about Quenhyth's escape.'

'Come with me,' said Bartholomew.

Wreckage from Mortimer's Mill was still bobbing and swirling in the river, and it meant the King's Mill could not operate that day. The Millers' Society did not want to make expensive repairs because charred wood was entangled in their waterwheel, so it had been hauled clear of the water that surged below it. Bernarde's slow-witted son had opened the building, ready to accept grain for future grinding, but the apprentices had been given an unexpected day off. The lad nodded a greeting to Bartholomew and Michael as they entered his dead father's domain, but made no move to follow them inside, or even to ask what they were doing.

'She says there is a pit near the waterwheel that allows routine maintenance to be carried out,' said Bartholomew, walking to the far end of the building. 'This allows the wheel to be inspected while it is turning, so you do not have to shut the whole thing down every time it needs a little grease. Dame Pelagia believes Quenhyth hid in it after the murders, and waited until the mill was deserted again before escaping.'

'But that means he was here while we inspected the bodies,' said Michael, aghast.

'That is what she says. No wonder he was so well acquainted with the details of our investigation the day after – he knew Edward Mortimer was on our list of suspects, for example.'

'God's blood!' breathed Michael. 'That is a sobering thought! I should have considered the possibility that Bernarde did not see the killer because the killer was still here. That was another mistake we made: Bernarde forgot to mention this pit, and we took his word that there was nowhere for a killer to hide.'

'It is easy to say that now,' said Bartholomew. 'But you had just discovered the mutilated corpses of two men you knew – one of whom you liked. You should not be too hard on yourself.'

'*She* does not make stupid errors,' said Michael bitterly. 'How can I ever hope to attain her standards when I am so careless?'

Bartholomew peered into the pit, which was exactly where Dame Pelagia had said it would be, then jumped back in alarm. He gazed at Michael in disbelief, then leaned forward to look again, to be sure that what he had seen was really there.

'Do not emulate her too closely, Brother,' he said in a low voice. 'I have just discovered Thorpe and Mortimer, both dead from knife wounds. There can only be one person who killed them, and who chose such an appropriate hiding place for their bodies until she was safely away.'

'No, Matt,' said Michael, manoeuvring himself into a position where he could see the corpses for himself. 'My grandmother had nothing to do with their deaths – they killed each other. They are both holding daggers, and you can see the dust all over their clothes from where they struggled with one another. Look at Thorpe's hand – he is even holding a tuft of Mortimer's hair, ripped out during the fracas.'

Bartholomew saw he was right. 'And part of the floor is broken here, suggesting that it crumbled under them as they fought, and toppled them down into the pit.' He measured the stab wounds against the widths of the blades, and found they matched precisely.

'It was a case of a falling out among thieves,' said Michael. 'Perhaps they quarrelled over the gold they stole from Lavenham. Or perhaps their murderous inclinations simply boiled to the surface and they were obliged to relieve them on each other.'

Bartholomew supposed he was right. There was certainly no evidence to suggest anything else had happened. 'Then where is Lavenham's gold?' he asked. 'It should be here.'

But the box of coins was nowhere to be found, and there was something rather too neat about the pair in their pit and their conveniently simultaneous deaths. Bartholomew glanced at Michael, and saw he was not the only one troubled by the tidy conclusion to the case.

'Do you think . . . ?' began the physician uncertainly.

'I do not think anything,' replied Michael softly. 'And neither should you.'

Two days later, Bartholomew was deeply engrossed in the book Wynewyk and Paxtone had gone to such pains to secure for him, when Michael wandered nonchalantly into his chamber. The physician was in the enviable position of having a room to himself again, because Redmeadow did not want to sleep in a place where his classmate had died, and had gone to share with the Franciscans instead. Bartholomew smiled at the monk and leaned back on his stool, stretching muscles that had grown stiff from too much sitting in one position. The smile faded when Michael waved something at him.

'What do you think?' asked the monk. 'William and I were up most of the night with this.'

'It looks like what it is,' said Bartholomew, taking it disapprovingly. 'An assemblage of chicken bones and parts of those pig feet Agatha served for dinner last night.'

'I see you are not lacking in anatomical expertise,' said Michael, laughing. 'What else would you have me use? Is my Corpse Examiner prepared to procure me a real hand one dark night? No, I did not think so. And anyway, these are not just any old chicken feet. They belonged to Walter's cockerel.'

Bartholomew was unimpressed and a little disgusted. 'But why resurrect the Hand when you know what harm it can do? Why not let it go?'

'We cannot afford a missing relic loose in the town. Who knows where it may appear next? No, Matt. The Hand of Justice must be seen to leave Cambridge for ever, if we are to be completely free of the thing. Chancellor Tynkell and Mayor Morice are taking it to the King this afternoon.'

'You are going to send him that?' asked Bartholomew in horror. 'But he will see in an instant it is not real. Even the most deformed of his subjects is unlikely to have fingers shaped like trotters. And then he will accuse Tynkell and Morice of cheating him – and Tynkell has more than enough to worry about. Deynman is telling everyone he is pregnant.'

'Deynman is doing no such thing,' said Michael. His eyes gleamed with amusement. 'Well, not any more. My grandmother had words with him about spreading those sorts of tales, and he is now more than happy to keep quiet about his diagnosis. She appealed to his sense of loyalty to the University – along with promising a little help with his disputations when the time comes.'

'Lord!' muttered Bartholomew, thinking Dame Pelagia would have a massacre on her conscience – if she had one – if Deynman was ever allowed to qualify. His eyes narrowed as something occurred to him. 'But all this bribery implies that Tynkell does have a secret about his body, and that Dame Pelagia knows what it is.'

'Yes,' said Michael. 'Isobel de Lavenham knew, too, which was why Tynkell was prepared to help her after the fire. Isobel is now dead, so only my grandmother knows the truth.'

'And you,' surmised Bartholomew. 'Come on, Brother. What is it?'

'My lips are sealed,' said Michael smugly. 'You will just have to fathom it out for yourself, as I have done. Suffice to say you will be very surprised. But let us return to the relic. There is something very appealing about sending the King something called the "Hand of Justice", after what his dubious pardons did to our town. Of course, no one seems to know what Quenhyth did with the real Hand. You do not, do you?'

'I have no idea where it is now,' said Bartholomew, not inclined to confide in Michael when the monk would not share Tynkell's secret with him.

'I thought you might say something like that,' said Michael with another grin, which led Bartholomew to wonder whether Dame Pelagia had found out anyway, and had told her grandson. She seemed to know everything else. 'But it does not matter. I have told Tynkell to let Morice do the talking until the King is satisfied the relic is genuine. Only then should he step forward and accept credit on the University's behalf.'

'And what happens if the King is able to tell his chickens from his saints?'

Michael's grin widened. 'Then our corrupt and dishonest Mayor will have some explaining to do.'

HISTORICAL NOTE

In 1353 Cambridge's bailiffs complained to the King that a man named Thomas Mortimer had recently built a mill that diverted water from the King's Mill. On 17 April the King appointed four men to serve on a Commission and investigate the matter. These four men were Robert Thorpe, who was Master of the Hall of Valence Marie, William Warde, William de Lavenham and Gilbert Bernarde. Records go on to tell what the Commission discovered.

Thomas Mortimer had raised himself a mill upstream from the King's Mill, and although Mortimer's structure was originally designed for grinding corn, it had been expanded into a fulling mill the previous Christmas. Because extra water was required for fulling, the loss of power to the King's Mill was considerable. Worse yet, it meant that the rent that should have been paid to the King for use of the King's Mill had been delayed. The King did not like his dues to arrive late, and it comes as no surprise to learn that the Commission found against Mortimer.

The Mortimers were a powerful family in fourteenth-century Cambridge, and one Constantine Mortimer – presumably a relative of Thomas – is mentioned in a number of documents. The Deschalers were also rich and powerful. One Hardwin de Scalers was a principal knight of William the Conqueror, who was rewarded for his loyalty with land in no fewer than forty Cambridgeshire parishes, including an impressive administrative centre at Caxton and later at Whaddon. Branches of the family ventured into Cambridge, where the name Deschalers appears in several documents as men of wealth and influence.

Stephen Morice was another force to be reckoned with. He was Mayor of Cambridge from 1353 to 1355, and again in 1361 and 1363, and he had been a bailiff before that. Richard Tulyet was Mayor in the 1340s, and was accused of instigating riots against the University at various times. William Tynkell was Chancellor of the University 1352–1359, while Ralph de Langelee (Master), Thomas de Kenyngham, Thomas de Suttone, John de Clippesby and Michael (de Causton, who hailed from Norfolk) were all scholars associated with Michaelhouse in the 1350s. Wynewyk came later.

Both Trinity Hall and Gonville Hall were institutions founded by William Bateman, the Bishop of Norwich, although Gonville only fell into his lap when its original founder died. Gonville's first Master was John Colton of Terrington, although records indicate that he spent little, if any, time in Cambridge. He was one of Bateman's chaplains, and was probably at the papal court in Avignon on 6 January 1355 when Bateman died. There were rumours that Bateman was poisoned, although these were never authenticated.

Gonville's second Master was Richard de Pulham, and the third William de Rougham. Rougham and Pulham presided over what was probably a struggling, impoverished institution at first, and there is some evidence that they were obliged to sell their precious books in order to raise funds for their slowly emerging chapel. They obtained a licence to start this in 1353, but it was not finished before the 1390s, indicating that progress was very slow. Rougham was a physician, and records indicate that he was probably a good one. He may have been the personal physician of Bateman's successor – Henry Despenser – in the 1360s. John Ufford (died 1375) and Nicholas Bottisham (a civil and canon lawyer, whose dates are uncertain) were probably also Fellows around this time.

Cambridge has several medieval churches that date from the fourteenth century or earlier, and one of the most glorious of these is Great St Mary's, the University Church. St Michael's Church, which was rebuilt specially for Michaelhouse by its founder Hervey de Stanton in the 1320s, stands a little way down the street, and has recently been renovated as a community centre and café – aptly named Michaelhouse. It welcomes visitors, and is a peaceful and atmospheric place to sit and relax after a tour of Cambridge's wonderful medieval past.